Looking down from the hotel balcony at the river, Diane heard the phone ring. She walked into the room and picked up the receiver.

"Mrs. Diane Jamison?" a woman's voice asked.

"Yes?"

"This is Infectress. This is your last conversation."

A cold shot of adrenaline hit Diane's bloodstream. The muscles over her knees began to tremble.

"A subcontractor of mine has installed a small device of mine in your telephone," the voice said. "It includes three hundred grams of high explosive. One hundred grams should be enough, but you've already survived one of my little devices. So I tripled the charge. If the blast topples the hotel, I'll see it on the network news."

A breeze entered through the open sliding glass door. Diane looked out and remembered the river flowing ten stories below. She wondered if she could have the courage to leap from the balcony. *It might be my only chance to live.*

"Don't—" Diane breathed.

"Oh, I warned you, didn't I?" Arabella asked. "But you wouldn't listen. Consequences, Diane. Consequences. It's a dead man switch. Either of us hangs up, the data signal is cut, you die."

Diane dropped the receiver on her bed. She spun and began to dash for the open sliding glass door. She wondered whether this was her last moment alive.

She began her jump while she was still in the hotel room and threw herself headlong over the wrought iron rail of the balcony. She glimpsed a patch of grass between the hotel and the river.

It's further than I thought. . . .

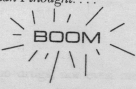

BOOM

INFECTRESS

TOM COOL

BAEN

A Baen Books Original

Baen Publishing Enterprises
P.O. Box 1403
Riverdale, NY 10471

ISBN: 0-671-87763-1

Cover art by Stephen Hickman

First printing, January 1997

Distributed by Simon & Schuster
1230 Avenue of the Americas
New York, NY 10020

Typeset by Windhaven Press, Auburn, NH
Printed in the United States of America

To Marzy & Eva

Love Theme of "Infectress"

I am Infectress,
mistress of the minuscule,
molecules,
secrets you repress,
truths too hideous
to express.

Kiss me,
beloved prey.
Entwine with me into one,
joined in hidden bond.

Secretly
I share
the molecular
engines of destruction.
Too tiny to taste,
they fit, exact,
to your demolition.

So I impart
life's nuclear lesson:
all your being,
your angelic seeming,
is as the genius
of a virus.

Kiss.
Life.
Nothingness.
Kiss.

Diane Jamison watched the four-year-old boy scowl and cross his arms. He seemed to seethe as if all the world's fury focused in his small frame.

So young, she thought. *To have so many demons, and all of them unchained.*

Diane reached out toward Todd, but he flinched. Slowly her hand lowered to her side.

They taught him to hate being touched, she thought.

She wished that her soul could broadcast into that tormented head and illuminate him with her love, but she knew it was impossible. If humans had psychic radios, Todd's receiver was tuned to static.

Diane and the boy stood atop a grassy summit in the Laurel Mountains of western Pennsylvania. The sky was an unpolluted blue. Down below, brilliant green deciduous forest, the successor of the aboriginal, twice-timbered evergreen forest, stretched outward to all horizons. The mild sun of northern summers warmed them gently. From the valley arose the shouts and laughter of children less unhappy than Todd.

Since her disability retirement from the FBI, Diane had begun volunteer work. As a big sister for poor children from Pittsburgh and Philadelphia, she took them on retreats to this Christian camp high in the Laurel Mountains. She believed that exposure to the beauty of the natural world would help these inner-city children develop spiritually.

"I hate those mudderruggers," Todd said.

Diane knelt, facing the child. Eurasian, Diane at first glance looked like an ordinary white woman, if striking, svelte and tall. On closer study, her Asian heritage was suggested in the almond shape of her eyes, the strength of her cheekbones and the touch of gold enriching her light skin. She placed her hands on her knees. She tried to use her voice to project her love.

"Don't say that you hate them, Todd," she said. "Say that you're angry. Hate is something that hurts you more than it hurts them."

"I hate them. I wanna break their heads."

Diane bit her lip. Finally, she said, "It's hard, I know."

"Ain't so hard. Just hit 'em with somethin' big. Bust 'em up. Lousy, rotten, no-good, lazy brats."

Diane realized that she wasn't listening to Todd. She was listening to his parents, their abusive words echoing inside the young skull, escaping through the young mouth. Then Diane realized she might be listening to grandparents or great-grandparents, voices from beyond the grave, shouted abuse echoing down the tunnel of time, the only family legacy.

Her pocket computer beeped, startling her. She had programmed it to interrupt her only in emergencies.

"Hold on, Todd," she said, opening her pocket computer. She allowed it to register her retina, then read the decrypted message:

FOLLOWING FITS THE PROFILE OF INFECTRESS CRIME:

The profiles she had built into her home computer had alerted on a filed police report about an activity that matched her model of Infectress. Anxiously, Diane read the police report, which stated that five hours previously, San Jose police had discovered a man wandering along Highway 101. He was George Leroy, American, white, 34, employed as the data systems security manager of Paradigm International, which manufactured equipment for molecular engineering, mainly gene splicers.

Leroy had been brain-wiped—illegal surgery that left

higher mental processes dysfunctional. There were telltale probe entry wounds in the back of the neck. Blood and urine samples showed traces of caffeine, nicotine, THC and AMT.

Diane looked up, only to see the distant figure of Todd, escaping in full flight down the hill, down to the other campers in the valley, leaving her alone on the summit.

She turned toward the south. She felt sunlight on her face. A sun ray gleamed rainbows in her eyelashes. Diane concentrated on breathing deeply, once, twice. In this way, she calmed her heart. She needed the calm to find the courage to meet this challenge. To survive, she merely had to refuse the challenge. *Let someone else worry about Infectress.*

For a long minute, Diane was sure that she would let this opportunity, this danger, pass her by. *Let the authorities handle it.*

Then she remembered the wreckage from United 310, which crashed in a cornfield in western Illinois. Diane had arrived on the second day, after Infectress had published her manifesto claiming responsibility for the midair explosion. The bodies had already been collected and stored in refrigerator trucks. Searching for the principal investigator, Diane had entered the frozen interior of the morgue truck. She remembered the chill across her exposed skin and the shivering of the muscles over her ribs. She remembered the steel racks with the long rows of naked feet. She remembered that one pair of feet, so small and doll-like. The toes were so tiny, so perfectly formed. Since that day, the image of the dead child's unblemished feet triggered again and again in her visual memory. Diane's eyes closed further. Now the sunlight gleamed rainbows on tears.

It is wrong to hate, she thought.

But Diane knew one thing.

She hated Infectress.

Even if I die with my fingers around her throat, I'll find and destroy that bitch.

In his spacious office in the Taradyne International headquarters building, Joe Bender reclined in his Neanderthal throne. A spring frame, soft cushions and a wool fleece transformed huge, crossed, gnarled redwood roots into an ergonomically incorrect but sinfully comfortable chair.

Joe wore virtual reality goggles over his eyes. His small mouth twisted in a strange smile. Occasionally, he mumbled a command.

He was waving his data gloves and twiddling his fingers as if he were conducting a phantom orchestra. In his private programming environment, Joe was amassing phalanxes and brigades of software modules, marching them in kaleidoscopic patterns. Using personal technologies that were beyond the public state of the art, Joe Bender was developing a program.

It was a program called Meta.

The objective of Meta was to emulate human thought.

Joe's personal agent, Daedalus the Artificer, intruded into his programing environment.

"Excuse me, boss," Daedalus said, picking molten wax from his shoulders, "but did you know that Dellazo is going to give a speech to the Army sponsors in five minutes?"

"No," Joe said. "So what?"

"The topic is 'The Dellazo Mathematical System for Human Thought.'"

Joe winced from a twinge in his chest. With the dexterity of long habit, even though he was blind to the real world, he flipped the top off his medicine bottle and popped a tiny pill under his tongue.

"No breezin'."

"No, sir. I intercepted his agent's conversation with the SVTC scheduler just a minute ago. Teleconference begins in four and a half minutes."

"Can I access?"

"No, we're locked out."

"Call up Gordon Wa, get him to allow both Scott and me inside."

"Yes, sir."

"Close up the work space and get me Scott."

Joe's virtual reality shifted to a model of his office. A knock sounded on his artificial door and the image of Scott McMichaels entered.

The image was true to the man; Scott McMichaels was a tall, lanky youth. His red, wavy hair was buzzed across his temples, long and disheveled across his crown. He eschewed the fashion of earrings. Scott had strong bones: his brow was beetled, his nose was proud, his cheekbones were prominent, his jaw was massive and his chin, cleft. The look in his green eyes was often distant. The combination of strong features and absent-mindedness was charming, allowing Scott to win friends among men and admirers among women, without going to the effort of polishing his social skills. His natural innocence, which had survived twenty-seven years, carried him with fine style through many situations that were more complex and more hazardous than he ever realized.

"Yeah, Joe, what is it?" Scott asked. His voice was mellow.

"Dellazo is briefing the Army sponsors in four minutes on something called 'The Dellazo Mathematical System of Human Thought.'"

Scott's expression sharpened, as if he had just begun to take full notice of the outside world. "You're breezing me."

"No. I told you that we should have published," Joe said.

Scott shook his head. "No, no way. That would've proven that I came up with the algorithms under contract."

"What if Dellazo briefs the sponsors now on your discovery? Where are we then?" Joe asked.

"How could he?"

"You've been careful with all your files, haven't you?"

"Sure."

"Then it isn't possible that Dellazo came up with the algorithms independently, is it?"

Scott rubbed his face. He searched for the courage to admit a foolish mistake.

"About six months ago," Scott began, "before I had the bolt from heaven, I was . . . I was working with some preliminary ideas. You know, just kicking them about. I was doing a chalk talk with Larry, the guy they fired about then. In the small conference room. Dellazo came by. He sat in for about a half an hour. He didn't say anything, but you could tell he was interested."

Joe sighed. "You never told me that."

"Sorry."

"And you kept right on talking, right in front of King Turd?"

"Yeah."

"That was stupid, Scott."

"Yeah, I guess."

"No, there's no guesswork involved," Joe said heavily. "Dellazo may be a jerk, but he's brilliant. You may have put him onto the right track. It's possible that he came up with the algorithms."

The two contemplated the possibility that their life work might be stolen.

Daedalus appeared. "Gordon Wa has granted you and Scott access," he said. "As soon as you're ready, I'll connect you."

"Do it now."

Joe's office disappeared, instantly replaced by a

large, plush executive conference room. Joe found himself reclining in a black leather chair next to a large, glass-topped mahogany table. Scott was standing in the corner of the room. He reached down and touched a chair, reassuring himself that there was a real-world chair in the place of the virtual chair before sitting down. Scott distrusted common-agent virtual realities; he hated the intentional and unintentional pranks that some agents inflicted, such as causing people to sit down through air chairs.

Dr. Francesco Dellazo stood by the podium. A small, wiry man, Dellazo had a pallid, wrinkled, creased face. His red-rimmed eyes burned in beds of baggy flesh.

"What are you doing here?" he asked, his voice hostile and nervous.

Scott opened his mouth, but Joe answered first, "Gordon Wa has given us permission to listen to your brief."

Dellazo opened his mouth to reply, but in that moment, Gordon Wa, the leader of the research department, escorted in a green wave of Army officers, who took their seats at the front of the table. In the real world, the Army officers were in a military virtual teleconferencing room in the Pentagon, while Wa was in a corporate virtual teleconferencing room in Denver.

"Good morning, General," Dellazo said with the deadpan flatness of an unfriendly man mouthing a pleasantry. He nodded to the other military men and did not look at Joe or Scott as he began his lecture.

"The Dellazo Mathematical System of Human Thought," he said, "is a revolutionary breakthrough in the field of artificial intelligence. It establishes a rigorous mathematics for describing the human thought processes of memory, learning, reasoning and decision-making. My proofs are comprehensive, elegant and undeniable."

Dellazo allowed himself to glance at Scott. In that moment, Scott knew that Dellazo was going to claim Scott's discovery for his own.

"First theorem, please," Dellazo said.

Behind Dellazo, a large screen displayed a mathematical theorem. Within minutes, Dellazo was deep into mathematics too complex for the general. A colonel kept pace until the first proof, then surrendered. A captain named Rick Villalobos, a Puerto Rican with merry black eyes who held a doctorate in mathematics from Yale, kept pace with Dellazo. He interjected pertinent questions, which Dellazo fielded.

Scott stared at the proofs. He struggled to understand Dellazo's work in its own context, forgetting his own symbolization and algebra. After a few missteps, he locked onto Dellazo's reasoning, which he followed with an interest so intense that he lost awareness of everything else.

An hour later, toward the end of the brief, Dellazo was stepping through his master proof. The final slides built to the climax. Able to foresee the conclusion, Scott relaxed enough that he returned to an awareness of himself. He noticed that the general's image was frozen, indicating that the general had suspended his active participation in the brief to conduct private business. As Scott watched, the general's image unfroze, indicating he had rejoined the common conference.

Dellazo continued talking. Toward the end of his argument, he said something bizarre. For a moment, Scott couldn't believe his ears. Looking around the virtual room, Scott was amazed to see unblinking acceptance. In fact, the general's image revealed unmasked boredom.

Scott studied the graphics. They confirmed what Dellazo was saying. Scott grinned. He chuckled. His chuckle had a more disruptive effect than a fart in church. The general turned around. "Did I miss a joke?" he asked.

Everyone laughed. Scott stood up. "Excuse me, General, I think maybe we all did."

Everyone except Dellazo laughed.

"Dr. Dellazo," Scott said. "If I understand it correctly, your final proof maintains that these variables which you call 'axiomates' derive their validity from the verification processes, which you cover in your theorems nine through twelve?"

"I believe that's what I said," Dellazo said frostily.

"Yes, that is what you said," Scott countered. "Is that what you meant?"

"Yes."

"Don't you see, though, Doctor," Scott said, "that such a statement shows a horrible confusion about the impact of your fifth and seventh theorems? And moreover, it completely contradicts everything you've said so far?"

"Not at all!" Dellazo snapped.

"If I may," Scott said. He stepped to the front of the room, grabbed a light pen and began to sketch. For five minutes, Scott delivered a complex but crisp argument. Dellazo fended him off for several minutes, but then comprehension dawned.

Thunderstruck, Dellazo stepped back from the podium.

Capt. Villalobos quizzed Scott, who answered his questions with more authority than Dellazo had been able to muster for simpler questions. The captain understood Scott's argument. Then Joe Bender and Dr. Wa entered the fray. Within fifteen minutes, the combined geniuses of McMichaels, Bender, Wa and Capt. Villalobos had dissected Dellazo's work.

"If it's fundamentally contradictory, why does it seem to have such an intuitive appeal, at least superficially?" Dr. Wa asked.

"Because it's not so much wrong, it's inadequate," Scott said. "Dr. Dellazo and I discussed ideas along these lines about six months ago, and it's apparent that he's developed these ideas as far as . . . well, as far as he's been able to. If I may, I can sketch some additional theorems and their proofs, which will sew everything together in a really beautiful way."

The general sat up. "Listen," he said. "I can't pretend to understand most of what you people have been talking about, but I can gather that it needs further work. Why don't you brief me again when you've come up with a unified position?"

Dr. Wa looked up. "Yes, sir. Sorry for the inconvenience. But I think we're on to something really vital."

"I have no doubt," the general said. He stood. He paused during the moment when he should have been telling Dellazo what an excellent presentation it had been, but no such praise was forthcoming. The general departed.

Scott sat down with Capt. Villalobos and presented his own mathematics. After an hour, Villalobos said, "Well, my brain is full. Why don't we meet tomorrow and discuss this some more?"

"Yes, certainly," Wa said.

Avoiding Dellazo's burning, wretched eyes, Villalobos turned to Scott and smiled. "You really should publish," he said.

"I guess now I'll have to," Scott said.

Villalobos chuckled. "Have to? Why, hombre, I think you've got a chance to hold the patent on thought!"

Scott smiled. "I didn't invent thought," Scott said. "I just discovered it independently."

Villalobos chanced a glance at Dellazo, then looked back at Scott. "Who did invent thought?" he asked.

Scott smiled crookedly and said, "An absentminded genius. He neglected to file for the patent."

"We'll fax the patent office in the morning," Villalobos joked. He made a gesture to clap Scott on the shoulder, but the image of his hand traveled directly through Scott's image.

Villalobos was not rude enough to remind everyone that Scott's contract conceded all his intellectual property to the United States government.

Eyes burning with hate and humiliation, Dellazo abruptly disappeared from the virtual room.

Arabella wore a red dress as evocatively as a fire wore flame. She undulated in the sunlight, her hips swaying and her buttocks swiveling in the form of a figure eight, the back drape of her skirt swinging inward, outward. As her hands swung, golden bracelets chimed. The steel of her heels rang on pavement in the rhythm of a woman unafraid of stares. In the brilliant sunlight of the Atlanta city street, Arabella's raven hair shined so vibrantly that its blackness seemed white. Her skin appeared pale.

In pursuit of her quarry, Arabella descended into the MARTA underground. Chameleonlike, she seemed to change color. Under the subdued lighting of the tunnel, her skin seemed dusky. Passengers on the train perceived a different woman than had the pedestrians in the street. After a short ride, she arrived in the glittering promenade of Underground Atlanta. By the gala lights, her cinnamon skin, glowing with sweat, made her gold necklace seem mere brass. Men turning to gaze wondered whether they whiffed a trace of precious perfume. Desperately, they investigated their olfactory sense, lost the trace and clung to the memory of the mysterious odor. Glancing at her wristwatch, Arabella smiled. She was never late for a seduction.

Moments later, she turned into the Falcon's Nest bar. Standing in the mezzanine, she surveyed the crowd below. *There,* she thought, *at the bar. That's him.*

Arabella made her way around the mezzanine and appeared at the top of the staircase, high above the crowd. She danced down the staircase.

It was the first time Freddie Hanson saw Arabella. He fell in love. So did forty-nine other men. Five men in the corner were drinking Heinekens and watching Falcons football, so they did not fall in love, at least not until they saw Arabella during the commercial break.

Freddie was leaning against the red leather pad of the mahogany bar. With the lovely chime of ringing crystal stemware, the bartender was just removing a wine glass from the overhead rack. The crowd parted reluctantly for Arabella, who sauntered up to stand so close to Freddie that he could smell her perfume. Freddie wracked his brain for one word to say to the gorgeous woman who had materialized by his side.

"Wine," Arabella said to the bartender.

"What sort, miss?" the bartender asked.

Arabella turned and looked up into Freddie's face.

"What sort of wine are you drinking?" she asked.

"White. White wine," Freddie stammered.

Arabella smiled gently and turned to the bartender.

"You have the Sauvignon Blanc from Stag's Leap Hill, '15?"

"Yes, ma'am."

"Please, a glass. And fill a glass for the gentleman."

Freddie barely stopped himself from stammering thanks like a schoolboy. Quietly along with Arabella he watched the bartender uncork the bottle and pour two glasses. Arabella laid a hundred dollar bill on the barkeep's shelf. He made her thirty dollars change, which she ignored. Arabella handed Freddie one of the glasses and lifted her own to eye level.

"Wine with you, sir," she said. Her voice was low and mellow.

Their glasses chimed.

The wine changed colors inside Freddie's mouth.

"Thanks," he said. "This is really an excellent wine."

"It's white," Arabella said, grinning, revealing gleaming teeth and a deep dimple in her left cheek. Here in the subdued light of the bar, she looked Mediterranean.

Freddie chuckled. "My name's Freddie. Freddie Hanson."

"I'm Arabella."

"I won't tell you that's a beautiful name. I'm sure that's what you always get."

"Almost always, but I don't mind hearing it."

"Well, then, I'll tell you. Arabella is a beautiful name."

"Thank you."

"And you're a beautiful woman."

Arabella laughed and said, "According to the legend." She tossed her hair, sipped the wine and gazed up into Freddie's face.

Freddie Hanson was a tall, slender man. He wore his blond hair long on top, clipped short across the temples. Together with his straight-haired blond beard and his sharp blue eyes, this style of haircut made him look fierce. He had a long, straight nose and a firm chin. His hands were large and his fingers around the wineglass stem made the crystal look a toy. His wits and his looks had served him well with university women. Now, twenty-two, standing at the professionals' bar and talking with Arabella, he felt as if he had graduated into the major leagues.

"What else does the legend say?" he asked.

"Oh, that would be telling," Arabella said.

"What do you do?" Freddie asked, as Americans must.

"I travel," Arabella said. "And what do you do?"

"I'm a biotech. I work at the Centers for Disease Control."

Arabella made her eyes grow wider. She leaned in close enough to Freddie that he could feel her body heat. Freddie watched her mouth so attentively that he could see the lipstick-moistened membranes of her lips unseal slowly from center to corners.

"Biotech," Arabella breathed. "Centers for Disease Control."

"Yes."

"I find that . . . fascinating."

She laid her hand on his forearm.

They migrated to a nitrous oxide club, where they laughed hysterically and danced until two in the morning. Arabella danced well. She believed in dancing, because she thought that nothing was better for enslaving the male libido. After they closed down the club, Arabella slipped her card into Freddie's blazer jacket. She kissed him lightly on the cheek and whispered, "Call me."

Freddie called the next day. Arabella talked lightly with him on the phone and consented to see him on Saturday. Freddie dry-cleaned his suit, readied his apartment and waxed his car. He bought a single long-stem rose. Arabella insisted on meeting him in the restaurant. They dined and drank wine and laughed. Afterwards, they went dancing in a Brazlian night club. Arabella performed the latest dances so well that Freddie kept insisting that she must be Brazilian.

"Oh, I know Brazil," Arabella said. "I love Brazil. I hate Brazil. But I'm not Brazilian."

"What are you, then?" Freddie blurted.

Arabella smiled and ran her fingertips across Freddie's hand. "I'm human," she said.

"But what's your nationality? Are you American?"

"I'm a citizen of the world," Arabella answered, then sipped her champagne.

"Oh, you're so mysterious," Freddie said, half in admiration, half in frustration. "Why do you always answer me in riddles?"

"Why do you always expect simple answers to complex questions?"

"Look, some things are simple. You've got a passport, right?"

"Yes, one or two."

"One — what? How many?"

"More than one. Less than the number I need."

"How many passports could you possibly need?"

"There are three hundred and fifteen nations in the world. I need three hundred and sixteen."

"All right, I'll bite. What's the three hundred and sixteenth for?"

"To leave with the police," Arabella said.

She and Freddie laughed together.

"So you're some sort of desperado, then?" Freddie asked.

"That would be telling," Arabella answered. "Would it matter to you if I were?"

"Were what?"

Arabella gazed into Freddie's eyes. "Answer me."

"That depends what for," Freddie answered.

"Oh, and what felonies are you okay with? How about robbery? Ah, say, diamond heisting? That's a nice clean glamorous crime, huh?" Arabella smiled, crossing her eyes slightly in a ludicrous way.

Freddie laughed. "You're a burglar?"

"Speaking hypothetically, would you be with me if I were?"

"What's the hypothesis? That you're a burglar? Or that I'm going to be with you?"

Arabella smiled. "Hypothesize, please, that I were . . . was . . . a burglar. Would you want to be with me?"

"I don't know," Freddie said earnestly.

"What if I only stole from the Afrikaner's kraal?"

"I guess."

"So you'd allow me to steal diamonds from white men who enslave black people?"

"Okay. Sure. Is that what you've done?"

"I've done nothing," Arabella said. "Nothing that I can say."

"You're deep, Arabella."

"You have no idea, Freddie. You have no idea. So far you've just seen the glimmering on the surface, like . . . moonlight on the surface of the Loch Ness."

"And who's the monster?"

"Monsters," Arabella corrected. "There is a tribe of monsters."

That night, Freddie invited Arabella back to his apartment, but she refused. They parted in front of the Brazilian dance club. Arabella gave Freddie a deep, passionate kiss good-bye.

"I'll call you," she said.

Then she disappeared.

Early the next morning, hideously early for Freddie, he stumbled past the security checkpoints of the Infection and Plague Laboratory of the Centers for Disease Control. In the locker room, he hung up his jeans and sweatshirt.

"Rough night, eh, Freddie?" Bill Smith, one of his coworkers, shouted.

"Danced all night," Freddie answered.

"Horizontally or vertically?"

Most of the men in the locker room guffawed, snorted or laughed. Others, concentrating on their private concerns, did not react.

"Vertically, I'm afraid."

In the shower, he scrubbed with a stiff brush and astringent soap. In the far room, he toweled and stood under infrared lamps and blasts of warm air. He proceeded to the sterile rooms, where he donned his clean clothes. Once inside the controlled area, he felt more secure. It was a testament to the world's septic state that Freddie felt safer inside the controlled area, trapped inside with the thousands of containers of plague, than he did in the world at large.

Freddie drank his morning cup of decaffeinated coffee and scanned the biotechnology journal headlines. He read a few articles concerning his speciality, frightened and fascinated when a colleague described new ground and condescending and relieved when a colleague covered old ground.

At nine o'clock, he was seated at his workstation. He read the results of the previous night's experiments. Freddie had chipped away a protein from the shell of an engineered virus. During the night, the new virus had stewed in the computer model of an adult woman. The results showed that the new virus was sixty percent less effective than the original virus, but still able to replicate.

All day long, Freddie experimented with his protein-chipped virus. Despite his weariness from dancing all night with Arabella, he worked straight through lunch. Before he realized, it was nine o'clock at night.

Freddie wondered why his feet didn't want to walk as they normally should. In his state of intense concentration, he didn't realize how exhausted he was. He stumbled into the office of the senior researcher, Doctor Adams.

"Dr. Adams," he said, "I've sent some model work results into your queue. I think I've found a way to degrade the virulence of Yarno's disease. I've created a viable mutant that seems much less effective. Could be an inoculator."

"I've got a couple of other things to look at, but what do you want to do?"

"I'd like some nanoengineer lab time to create a real-world mutant. To see how it behaves in culture. Later, maybe, in some test populations."

Dr. Adams scowled at Freddie. Nanoengineer laboratory time was extremely expensive. Freddie Hanson was not a medical doctor. He was a doctor of biotechnology. Nor was he senior staff. Worse, Freddie was not well published. Yet here he was demanding laboratory time.

"Let me review your results. I'll get back to you," Dr. Adams said.

As Freddie stepped through the hygienic ritual to return to the septic outer world, he wondered when Dr. Adams would have the time to read his results. Then, Freddie worried about his status in the Centers for Disease Control. His griping about his superiors, especially at local bars on Friday nights, had originally put Arabella onto his scent.

Freddie rode the MARTA subway homeward. He stood, hanging from a strap, his left ribcage compressed by the shoulders of a teenage Mexican and his right by a woman with a shaven head. By the time he fought his way through the throngs and emerged into the arc-lighted streets, his fatigue made everything seem hallucinatory.

Outside his apartment building, he ignored the beggar who slept on the lawn. Turning the corner, Freddie surprised a ten-year-old zapper, who was attempting to violate the security of the apartment building's tenant identification system.

"Hey, get out! Scram!" Freddie shouted, his voice hoarse with fear. He knew that even prepubescent punks were capable of murder.

Eyes wild, startled, the ten-year-old whipped around. He held a crowbar in one hand and a screwdriver in the other. Freddie stood aside, hoping the ten-year-old would run. Fortunately, he did, leaving most of his tools on the sidewalk.

Freddie pushed his palm against the plate of the identification system, feeling it loose, since the ten-year-old had pried it. Nothing happened. The door remained locked.

Wearily, Freddie leaned against the wall. Fatigued, his eyes returned the brutish stare of the beggar.

Why should I work so hard just to increase the longevity of scum? Freddie thought.

✧   ✧   ✧

Paradigm International's headquarters was a long, low building of prefabricated concrete and mirrored glass. It was typical of high-technology companies that didn't invest their start-up capital in architectural statements.

Diane Jamison walked into the lobby. She smiled at the receptionist, asked to see the director and allowed her palm print to be imaged. Thirty minutes later, the director's secretary escorted Diane to the director's office, a spacious one with a view of an inner courtyard garden.

The director, Sanders, was a gaunt black man with a large forehead and shocks of white through his nappy hair. He extended a long, slender hand to Diane.

"Pleased to see you again, Mrs. Jamison," he said.

"Yes, I remember now," Diane said. "We met at the DataWorks Symposium two years ago, when I briefed the Fungal Priest case."

"Yes, please sit down."

Sanders and Diane sat down facing each other on the plush chairs in the sitting area. Diane was pleased with her reception.

"I was just rereading the symposium notes on the Fungal Priest case," Sanders said. "That was brilliant work."

Diane smiled. "Thank you."

"I understand that you're no longer with the FBI?"

"No, I retired. The Bureau offered me either a desk job or a disability retirement. Since I wanted to pursue my own interests without as much . . . guidance as you get working for the government, I took the retirement. Started my own practice, so to speak. Consulting detective, don't you know."

"Who are you after now?"

"Infectress."

"Infectress? Is she the one that crashed JAL 117?"

"JAL 117, four hundred and forty-five deaths," Diane said in agreement. "With her other bombings and perversions—"

"Perversions?"

"Perversions of the worst sort, like disrupting subway control systems. She's killed at least 1,504 people, wounded 3,934. If we count Leroy, 3,935. By the way, you have my condolences."

"Thank you. Why haven't the police stopped somebody like this yet?"

"She's brilliant," Diane said. "And she's not insane."

"How can you say that such a monster is not insane?"

"My training is in criminal psychology," Diane said. She took a deep breath. She didn't like to talk about Infectress at this level, but, to further her pursuit, she forced herself. "A serial killer, a homicidal maniac, a psychosexual killer can only get away with so many murders. To kill people at the scale that she does, the murderer needs something more potent than madness. She needs a political philosophy."

"Are you serious?"

"Yes, indeed. Don't think of her as a serial killer. Think of her as a revolutionary."

"A terrorist."

"A terrorist attempts to influence a political system through intimidation. Infectress and her type are attempting to destroy all political systems, destroy the world economy, stop the damage that nine billion people are causing the planet before it is too late. A hundred years ago, they would have been called nihilists. But they think of themselves as a force of nature, a breed spawned in reaction to the imbalance caused by overpopulation, a killer strain of humanity which has the mission to—"

"Yes, yes, one of those environmental terrorists. So— what can you do about it?" Sanders asked.

Diane took a deep breath. She forced herself to

speak calmly. She smiled in a self-mocking way. "I can help you and the police decide whether this was an Infectress crime. If it was, I can help track her down. Bring her to justice."

Sanders studied Diane's face. He worried that she seemed slightly unbalanced. Her proposal was worth pursuing, though.

"How much would it cost us?" Sander asked.

"I'll show you my expenses. If you agree, then you can pay them. That's all."

Sanders eyebrows furrowed. Then he leaned forward and said, "Forgive me, but I have to consider your . . . reliability. What was the cause of your disability retirement?"

"Do you mean, was it physical or mental?"

"Yes, that's right. I'm afraid I do."

Diane stood. Her torso was within Sander's reach. She pulled out her shirttail and lowered her slacks, revealing her hip and her abdomen under the umbilicus. The golden white skin was crisscrossed with fine scars; there were patches where even the best cosmetic surgery could not hide massive injury.

"Don't worry, Mr. Sanders," she said. "Most of the damage was physical. This hip is entirely reconstructed. It's a good hip, but not good enough to allow me to pass the Special Agent field readiness test. The charge destroyed some other things, too. Like my uterus."

Diane readjusted her clothing and sat down.

"I'm very sorry," Sanders said.

"Don't be. I was lucky to live. And there are plenty of children in the world already. And I can help them."

"You said, a charge?"

"Yes. Clever little thing. Supposed to cut me in half. Just lucky. Just lucky that there was . . . something blocking the way."

"Are you sure she did it?"

"Oh, yes. She called me in the hospital. Made up

this amusing voice, using sound bites from about fifteen movies and television programs. Warned me that if I ever got on her trail again, she'd ram an explosive charge up my vagina and watch to make sure I was split in half. I was still heavily sedated. It was a charming conversation."

Sanders sat back. Diane allowed him to consider. When Sanders leaned forward, he spoke with force. "I want to get whoever destroyed the mind of my employee. I agree to your terms—"

"Thank you."

"—but I've got to withhold some proprietary information."

"You can withhold any proprietary information that Leroy couldn't access."

"Leroy was my data security manager. He had access to everything."

"I need the same visibility he had. I need to find out if he helped Infectress steal data."

Sanders launched out of his chair and paced for a moment before swinging toward Diane and saying, "You think he stole? My own data security manager?"

"I think he may have," Diane answered. "Whoever destroyed his mind may have done it to cover her tracks."

"Why not just shoot him?" Sanders asked.

"Sickness."

"Sickness?"

"Sorry. Zapper slang. Sickness is doing things the hard, the unexpected, the dangerous way. Showing a lot of sickness helps builds your myth. Myth, that's another important idea to them. They need to stay covert, but they want recognition. That's why they have these network war names, like Fungal Priest or Infectress. Why they like to establish an operating pattern. It builds their myth."

"Leroy never told me that."

"I'm sure Leroy concentrated on your most common threats. Sloppiness. Vindictiveness. Disgruntled employees. Electrical and air conditioning problems. I specialize in computer vandals who are also high-tech terrorists. It's an exotic field."

"Okay, Mrs. Jamison, you've sold me," Sanders said. "I'll pay your reasonable expenses. And I'll allow you access to all data."

Diane smiled. It was the access that she needed.

Thirty minutes later, Diane sought out the police detective in charge of the investigation, who was interviewing Paradigm employees in the wing opposite Sander's office. The smooth-faced Lt. Yarborough made Diane feel old. She consoled herself that she was still in her late thirties. Young enough to start a family, if she could find a husband strong enough to help her care for troubled orphans.

"Yes, can I help you?" Yarborough asked, looking up at Diane.

"I'm Diane Jamison," she said, extending her hand. Yarborough shook it in a perfunctory manner. "I'm a specialist in data security. Paradigm has contracted me to help them determine if Leroy or his attacker stole data from the company."

Yarborough grimaced. "This is a police matter."

"I know. The first thing I'm doing is coming to see you. I always cooperate with the official investigation."

"You have experience in these kind of things?" Yarborough asked, his voice quivering in a callow note that betrayed his anxiety about investigating a high-technology crime. Feeling an advantage, Diane sketched her career, stressing her experience in the FBI.

"So I'll tell you everything I learn," she concluded. "But we have to be careful. The attacker is sophisticated, dangerous. He or she could monitor the investigation, taint or destroy evidence we find, or even kill one of us. Kill you. Or kill me."

"Yeah, well, most murder investigations do involve tracking down a murderer."

Diane smiled mechanically, taken aback by the young cop's cynicism. Then she said, "That's right. That's why I always ask, as a protective measure, that you treat me as a citizen cooperating with the investigation, and give me protection under U.S. Code 1998-2."

Yarborough looked as if he had just bit his tongue. He made a note. "Great. More paperwork. I'll refer to you as Citizen L-12 in all correspondence," he said. "Except, of course, for the form I gotta fill out and file with a judge, which will document your true identity." Yarborough's sarcastic voice left unsaid, "masked woman."

"That's hard copy, right? Nothing electronic."

"Hard copy. A form. Sealed. Kept with the judge."

"Okay. You should assume that the terrorist is listening in on all communications. I understand you're from homicide."

"Right. Because Leroy is brain-dead."

"Not brain-dead. He has no capacity for memory."

Yarborough flipped his notebook closed with a dismissive gesture. "Well, the captain couldn't figure who else to give it to, so I got it. Let me know what you find out."

Diane smiled wanly. She hadn't expected much more cooperation from the police, not at first. She returned to her van and then carried the attaché case containing her supercomputer into Sander's office.

"That's a standard DXNET NIU over there, isn't it?" she asked.

"Yes," Sanders said.

"Well, I'm going to start."

Diane jacked her supercomputer into the DXNET network interface unit. From the attaché case, she pulled out a virtual mask.

"I don't think I've ever seen that model before," Sanders said.

"It's developmental," Diane said, as she settled the mask over her face, snugging the phones into her ears and aligning the display screens with her eyes.

"Whose?"

"Sorry. Proprietary information. Excuse me while I go virtual." She pulled the lower part of the mask over her mouth, so that she could speak in privacy.

In the display screens, the image of Diane's familiar appeared. Her familiar took the form of a very fat Victorian gentleman named Mycroft. He was seated alone in a small library filled with leather-bound books. He lowered his newspaper and smiled gently at Diane.

"I control the CPU," Mycroft said. "I control the network. I control the peripherals. I control the telecomms. I control the whole system."

"What do you think?"

"There were some standard industrial security traps. The architecture is haphazard. The servers are too busy, but there are powerful clients that are idle. Excuse me, Ms. Jamison, please let me drop the avatar. I need the cycles."

"Permission granted, Mycroft."

The image of her familiar disappeared, the cycles usually used to present the image now being saved for heavy computation. Diane uncovered her face. She turned to Sanders.

"My system is investigating yours," she said. "It may take awhile. Do you have any tea?"

Sanders served Diane green tea in a Japanese porcelain tea service.

"Tell me what you know about Leroy's personal life," Diane said.

"He was a hetero bachelor. Dated various women, never anyone from the company. He was married years ago, one of those easy-come, easy-go civil arrangements, he told me. Seemed like a normal enough young man. Didn't drink or do drugs, not even the legal ones. I liked that, particularly in my security manager." Sanders shrugged.

"Do you know that he tested positive for THC and AMT?"

"No, I didn't. I'm surprised."

"I think that we're going to find that Leroy dead is more interesting than Leroy alive."

"You're not going to stay on the computer side of it?"

"Hardware, software, wetware, it's all just media. I'm interested in data," Diane said. "Obviously, Leroy's attacker wanted to destroy data that was stored in his wetware."

Diane continued to chat with Sanders about Paradigm and Leroy. After half an hour, Mycroft demanded her attention.

"I found a lot of problems," Mycroft said, "but I can't decide which are important and which aren't. I need your help."

"Dump them to the working file, and let me take a look," Diane said, wishing that her familiar were as brilliant as its namesake, Mycroft Holmes, Sherlock Holmes' smarter brother. Sighing, she thought, *Mycroft is the state of the art, but someday there'll be an artificial intelligence system that will make him as obsolete as calculators.*

She studied the files, quickly learning that Leroy was a lousy security manager. Mycroft had discovered that Paradigm employees had games and other personal applications on their workstations. There were indications that about half of them took company work home with them. Diane also saw evidence that some of the employees read each other's mail, padded their billable hours and charged personal calls to the company, on and on. Diane shook her head. It was typical. The telecommunications picture was not pretty, either. There were traces of at least three intrusions. Diane couldn't figure out yet whether the intrusions were industrial espionage or just trespassing by random zappers.

One of the most subtle discrepancies seemed the most intriguing. Mycroft's brute force assault on the data bases had uncovered some shipping and billing discrepancies underneath a possible act of vandalism. Diane instructed him to reconstruct the actual events by processing records of component parts inventory and machine tool production time.

When she saw the results, Diane determined that Paradigm had built four DNA splicers, but shipped only three to the Chicago Center for Biomedical Research genetics lab. The fourth DNA splicer had disappeared. Infectress had stolen a DNA splicer.

And with that piece of top-flight, restricted technology, Infectress could invent her own life forms.

Scott shrugged the pack higher up his aching back, then cinched the belt tighter. He stood in the middle of a switchback of a path that ascended the western face of the Santa Lucia Mountains. In only one hour of hiking, he had climbed a kilometer in altitude. From here, he could see beyond the tree-covered foothills out onto the glimmering wrinkled surface of the Pacific Ocean. The ocean looked strangely vast, because from such a great height, his horizon extended one hundred miles.

Scott turned and continued to climb. The sun was near the horizon. He wanted to crest the mountain and descend into the high valley to make his camp before the light failed.

Grunting, gasping, he strode up the path, each footfall higher than the last. His heart pounded so hard that he could feel the shock of each pulse as it hit the base of his brain. He felt dizzy. An older man would have slowed down, but Scott continued, confident that his body would never betray him.

I can't fail, he thought. *I won't fail. I refuse to fail.*

Joe Bender and Scott McMichaels had attempted to execute the Meta program, but it had failed and had continued to fail. Sometimes it refused to execute at all. Sometimes it executed, but produced gibberish. After two solid weeks of failures, Dellazo's comments had grown increasingly sarcastic.

This Saturday afternoon, after another failure, Scott had felt trapped. He stormed out of Taradyne. He drove to the Pfeiffer Big Sur State Park, registered with the rangers, parked his car at the trail head and began to climb.

Now Scott arrived at the summit as the sun stood a few diameters above the rim of the ocean. Before him, the path plunged down into the high valley. Scott glanced over his shoulder at the glory of the Pacific sunset. He began to descend.

Here, he hiked in shadows. Soon he realized that he would never reach the tree line before nightfall. When the path flattened out under a protruding rock, Scott stopped. The ground was rocky, the ledge was only a few meters wide, but here he had shelter from the winds. Gratefully, he unshouldered his burden. Under the rock, he unrolled his ground mat and spread his sleeping bag. He laid down and watched the light on the distant peaks turn from pink, to red, to purple.

So this is what they meant by purple mountain's majesty, he thought. *I had no idea that the mountains actually turned purple.*

For a while, his thoughts meandered, but then he began to contemplate the design of Meta. The unaccustomed grandeur and beauty of the wilderness stimulated his thinking. He saw new possibilities and fresh perspectives. He made mental notes for the perfection of Meta.

He wondered whether Meta would ever succeed. He

wondered why he couldn't content himself like other people with just living life day by day. He knew he was obsessed, but in a world full of time servers and pleasure seekers, he had always been proud of his obsession. Yet, how much of life was he missing? If he failed, wouldn't he be a pathetic fool?

It's all nonsense, he thought. *I do what I can. Anything less is unworthy. It's given to me to attempt this thing. My life is that attempt. If I succeed, everyone will know my dignity. If I fail, only I will know it. But I will know it.*

A sea breeze began to clear the sky. Slowly, the brightest stars pierced the thinning haze. As the night air cleared, from the mountaintop, far from the city lights, Scott could see dozens, then hundreds, then thousands and hundreds of thousands of stars. Scott was able to witness the broad, shining path of the Milky Way arcing from east to west. He lay in his warm sleeping bag and contemplated his native galaxy, viewed edge-on from a vantage point in one spiral arm.

One hundred billion stars . . . just one galaxy. And there's one hundred billion galaxies. Ten to the eighteen suns. Big number.

Even if the evolution of intelligent life is a weird stroke of luck, a cosmic fluke, with such a big number of stars, it would still happen, again and again, but spread apart, in a sparse statistical distribution. Say, one there, near that bright star. Another, way over there, near that oscillating star. Each home world, a far-off, distant place. Each civilization, isolated by wastelands of stars and gases and lifeless planets and great, great distances full of nothing, nothing, just cold and black nothing, just emptiness, just vacuum. So lonely. Each civilization, maturing probably for hundreds of thousands of years, before they're able to reach out, telecommunicate, understand, then much later meet. Yes. Happy day. When we finally meet our closest,

*incredibly distant neighbor, will we show them Meta?
Will Meta or some descendant of Meta be among the
treasures that we offer to share?*

A machine that emulates thought. Massively parallel,
able to think ahead, think deep. In an information age,
the equivalent of the nuclear bomb. Synthesize and
advance knowledge. Create new medicines. New food-
stuffs. Redesign DNA, eliminate diseases. Strategic
advice on our hardest problems. A new world . . .

Scott thrilled with the idea that he could contribute
so powerfully to the history of mankind.

Life . . . almost infinitely precious, he thought, his
mind moving more slowly as he began to cross the
threshold into sleep. *I've got to do what I can, to help
. . . to help . . .*

He fell asleep, convinced of the nobility of his
struggle. He awoke in the middle of the night to find
the heavens alive with a meteor storm. Brilliant points
of light streaked across the starfield. He realized that
he had been dreaming about the design of Meta. A
new way to connect the modules suddenly seemed
obvious. He dug out a small flashlight and scribbled
notes. After several hours of intense scribbling, he was
surprised by the sunrise. He stood, mentally exhausted,
dizzy now in the thin air, as he watched the slanting
rays of sunlight slowly seek out the valley floors, where
the deepness of night still lingered.

Arabella invited Freddie sailing. They met on the
dock of the Sun King Marina in the coastal village of
Saint Charles. Arabella, wearing a white jumpsuit and
white Topsiders, and Freddie, sporting a sailing outfit
fresh from store boxes, walked down the dock to the
boat, a twenty-meter Imperiazi cruiser. It was a white
ceramic monohull with teak decks. The scarlet mainsail
and jib were furled with cables wrapped, indicating
automatic sailworks.

"Doying!" Freddie said, too impressed not to say, "Doying!"

"Yes, doying," Arabella said.

"Is this yours?"

"No. Actually owning a boat like this would ruin anybody."

"So we're chartering it?"

"No," Arabella said. "Somebody else is chartering it. We're just posing as somebody else."

Arabella stood behind the wheel. Freddie, the last bag of supplies in hand, stood on the dock.

"What do you mean? We're . . ." he said, groping for the word.

"Swindling?" Arabella suggested.

"Yeah, I guess."

"Yes, that is right, Frederick J. Hanson. We are swindling the Fair Winds Charter Corporation out of the value of its capital asset, the cruiser *Serendipity*, for two days. That means stealing about twenty thousand dollars worth of services. A felony."

Freddie shifted his feet. "I don't know, Arabella."

Arabella pulled a long lock of hair across her lower face like a veil, almost concealing her smile.

"Which is one way to think about it," she said. "The other way is, we're just borrowing this thing which was gonna sit here idle this weekend, anyway. So all we're doing is beating Fair Winds out of the wear and tear. Unless we sink the thing, of course. Then the insurance company loses." She smiled slyly.

"I don't know, Arabella."

"Come on, Freddie. It's not like we're stealing food from orphans. We're just stealing a drop of cream from rich men. Come on, dear Freddie. I'm setting sail. All aboard."

"What if we get caught?"

"I can prove I am whoever I say I am. No crime will take place until Monday, when I decide not to be the person I say I am now. Come on, baby. It's the perfect crime."

"You're sure? You've done this before?"

Arabella laughed victoriously. "That would be telling. All aboard."

Freddie stepped from the dock onto the boat.

"Cast off," Arabella commanded. "The lines are manual."

Freddie hopped back onto the dock, undid the lines and then stepped back aboard.

"*Serendipity!*" Arabella shouted. "Take us out to sea."

Under their feet, they felt the engines vibrate. Atop the main mast, the radar began to rotate. Robotically, the wheel spun to starboard. The cruiser eased away from the dock. Once in the open basin, flanked by moored pleasure craft, the *Serendipity* accelerated to eight knots, its motors humming audibly.

"*Serendipity!*" Arabella shouted. "When we're clear of the basin, set course one-two-zero and make sail."

Freddie placed his arm around Arabella. Her body relaxed and she lay her head on his shoulder. The sunlight sparkled atop the waves. As the *Serendipity* departed the windbreak of the yacht basin, the northeasterly wind laid the boat gently to starboard.

The *Serendipity* passed the channel marker and began to bound on the ocean rollers. After voice warnings, the yacht came about to a course of one-two-zero degrees and unfurled its mainsail and jib. The perfectly set sails caught the strong wind. Engines cut, the boat gracefully lay over to starboard and began to swoop on a beam reach, bravely shouldering aside the crests.

"Hooray!" Arabella shouted.

"Yea!" Freddie shouted.

Freddie turned his face windward, and then eyed the wind-hard sails, admiring the perfection of their set. He pulled on a floppy hat and donned sunglasses.

"Where are we going, Arabella?"

"Beyond the limit," she answered. "Twelve miles out into international waters."

"Then what?"

"Then we'll see."

"So mysterious."

Arabella smirked.

Freddie and Arabella enjoyed a perfect day of sailing. Once they reached international waters, they suspended robotic controls and worked the boat themselves. By three in the afternoon, their gloved hands ached and their appetites were sharp. They surrendered control to the *Serendipity*'s robot and lunched in the wheel well. They ate sandwiches made with fresh French bread, shredded lettuce and onion, tomato slices and chipped ham and turkey. They swilled cold bottle after cold bottle of Clausthaler *alkohol-frei* beer. For dessert, they ate Hawaiian frozen fruit bars. Exhilarated by the afternoon's sport and the taste of the Clausthalers, Freddie asked Arabella if she had stocked real beers.

"Sure, Freddie," she said. "Brewed by Belgian monks. But the hot sun and the wind dehydrate you, you know. If you drink beer, you may get a headache. I want you in top form tonight, lover."

"Why?" Freddie asked.

Arabella laughed at Freddie, and Freddie laughed with her.

By the time the sun set, they were far out to sea. The wind died. The boat moved slowly through gentler waters. A strip of clouds on the western horizon blurred bloody red, the clear band of sky above them a vibrant gold.

"I wish it would never end," Arabella said.

"It's beautiful," Freddie said.

"Oh, it's so wonderful sailing," Arabella said. "This is how life should be, don't you think?"

"You're right."

"Just you and me, Freddie," Arabella said. In the growing darkness, her voice was deep and compelling. "Beyond the limit. Alone. Free the way people should be. Ashore, it's so crowded. Too many people, too many people made so small. So small by the system. Do you understand what I mean?"

"Yeah, sure I do. I feel that way a lot. Everyone does, I think."

Arabella snuggled up to Freddie and ran her fingernails along his forearm. "Can't you feel it, Freddie? Breathe the air. We're free. This is the way it should be, Freddie. Free men, free women. Living real lives. Not just tiny cogs in the machine."

The sun set. Freddie bent his head and found Arabella's lips with his own. Her returning kiss was warm and accepting. They explored each other's bodies, the day's undercurrent of sensual desire rising quickly and strongly. Soon their young bodies were aroused to the level of mindlessness.

"Let's go below," Freddie breathed. The horizons were dark. Their lone boat rolled and pitched languorously over the lapping seas. Overhead, the first stars were penetrating the night's humid ocean air.

"No, Freddie," Arabella said. "Let me take you now, here, under the sky."

The next day, as they were sailing on the open ocean, Freddie asked Arabella if she could spend the following weekend at his place.

"I can't, lover," she said.

"Why not?"

"I have to go to Hawaii."

"Oh, really? Let me go with you."

"Can't. Sorry."

"Why not?"

"Can't say."

Freddie pouted for an hour, proving that a thirty-meter

vessel is too small for two people and one attitude.

"There *is* a way that we could go together to Hawaii," Arabella said.

"Yeah? How?"

"You'd have to travel with me as my husband."

"I can live with that."

"You'd have to use a different name, Freddie."

"All right."

"Using a fake name for interstate travel is a federal offense, Freddie. It's a felony these days."

"Oh. Well. Jeez."

"But it's an easy one to beat. I could make all the arrangements. Only you and I will ever know about it."

"Do you want me to? To go?"

"Yeah, lover. Come to Hawaii with me."

"All right," Freddie said. "I'm a player."

The next morning, while they drank coffee and watched storm clouds slanting a gray barrier of rain down on the southern horizon, Freddie said, "Arabella, can I ask you something?"

"What?"

"How do you manage to change identities? You know, fingerprints, retinal scans, DNA analysis, all that. They're foolproof ways to tell your real identity."

"Oh, yeah, sure," she said. "Foolproof. But not geniusproof."

"What? Do you refuse to let them—"

"Not always," Arabella said. "When you cross the borders at checkpoints, the trained dogs *will* have at your blood and your retina and your fingertips. What you do is corrupt the databases where that data goes."

"How?"

Arabella laughed musically. "How, Freddie? It's a lovely science. It involves network intrusions, erasures, installation of hardware parasites, corrupted records. You got to learn and then beat each system, one at a time. Attack the hardware, the software, the slimeware."

"Slimeware?"

"Yes, slimeware. People. Not always the weakest link, but usually weak enough. People's lack of dependability is something you can usually depend on. Not always."

"So what are you talking about?"

"Bribery, Freddie. The Global Identification Net, you know, the GIN. Like prohibition, like narcotics laws, one of the reasons it exists is that too many people make money from violating it. So you bribe presidents and you bribe pissant clerks."

"That's a nasty business, Arabella."

"Oh, yeah, sure. People are nasty. And their memories are hard to erase. So they're treacherous."

"How do you do it, then?"

"Sometimes directly. Sometimes through second and third parties."

"Who?"

"Depends. Sometimes, the Japanese social club called the Yakuza. And then there's your fun-loving Jamaican posses. Or your Sicilians. Nice easygoing bunch of guys, those Cosa Nostra. The Chinese, the triads. Colombians, the cartels. Here in America, congressional staffers."

"Congressional staffers? You're kidding!" Freddie laughed.

"No. And let me tell you, they are a scary crew."

"But those other guys . . . those crooks. You really do business with them?"

"The other crooks, you mean. Not that they know. But, yeah, I do."

Freddie glanced around nervously at the sail boat. "Aren't you afraid of talking about this stuff, even here?"

"Yeah."

"I mean, there could be a listening device, somewhere on the boat."

"I checked. There are two. Exactly two."

Freddie's head swiveled, as if he could spot a listening device.

"Where? Where are they?"

"There's the *Serendipity*'s voice command facility, which I'll wipe slick. And there's one other."

"Where?"

Arabella reached forward and tapped Freddie's forehead.

"Here, lover. It's here."

Freddie looked into Arabella's eyes. Her dark irises seemed bottomless pools. He felt himself losing his will. Underneath them, the boat began to roll sickeningly, as waves from the southern storm began to pass under the hull.

"You're not kidding."

"No, Freddie. I'm not."

"How long have you been doing this?"

"A long time, but not too long."

"Who knows who you really are?"

"I know."

"Who else?"

"No one. Absolutely no one. Alive."

Diane verified that the Chicago Center for Bio-medical Research had received only three Paradigm DNA splicers. She walked Sanders and Yarborough through the convoluted evidence that Paradigm had indeed manufactured four splicers. Interviews with Paradigm personnel confirmed that they had manu-factured four units, shipping three on a Monday and the fourth on a Tuesday. A shipping clerk remembered that the fourth unit had been consigned to a different shipping agent, Aladdin Express. Research confirmed that Aladdin Express did not exist. Someone had altered Paradigm's computer records, fooling the company into manufacturing an extra DNA splicer and handing it over to the thief.

Having proved her value, Diane was taken into greater confidence by Detective Yarborough. Together they went to visit Leroy.

In the San Jose State Mental Hospital, the attending doctor escorted Yarborough and Diane into an isolation ward. Leroy, a youngish man with a paunch, a double chin and premature hair loss, sat alone on a stool looking out a window of thick plastic. He turned and stared at Yarborough and Diane.

"Mr. Leroy, I'm Detective Yarborough, San Jose police. This is my associate, Diane Jamison. We need to ask you some questions about your attack."

"I was attacked?"

"Well . . . yes. The person who placed the apparatus on the back of your neck. Can you remember?"

Leroy looked around, puzzled.

"Who are you?" he asked.

Again, Yarborough patiently explained, and then asked, "Can we look at the back of your neck?"

"Why?"

"We'd like to see the wounds."

"What wounds?"

"The wounds caused by your attacker."

"Who are you?" Leroy asked.

Yarborough explained again, stepping over to Leroy as he spoke. "I'm going to take a look at the back of your neck."

Diane and Yarborough looked at the back of Leroy's neck, where they saw two tiny puncture marks on either side of the spinal column.

"Looks like a vampire bite," Yarborough said.

"They're the entry wounds of two surgical probes," the doctor said. "The heads of the probes are scalpels backed by miniature optical sensors. A fiberoptic link connects it to its host computer."

"What?" Leroy asked.

"What makes the probes move?" Yarborough asked.

"Microchain-mail," the doctor said. "Miniature links of superconductive fibers woven in the form of chain mail. Very small voltages sent as signals cause the links to expand and contract. Surgical probes like these are smaller than the head of a pin, but are able to worm their way into any part of the body."

"What?" Leroy asked.

"So the computer drives the probe?" Yarborough asked.

"Sure. In this case, the probes are sent into many different regions of the brain, severing some neural paths, connecting others which shouldn't be connected at all. Also, implanting nanotech hardware that interrupts normal mental operations. The net effect is that he can't remember anything."

"Why don't you reverse the surgery?"

The doctor sighed. "We've detected at least eighteen nanotech booby traps implanted in the brain. We have no idea what the trigger mechanisms are. Chances of reversing the surgery without tripping the booby traps are very, very slim."

"How can he talk?" Diane asked.

"The brain's complex," the doctor said. "Language memory uses another mechanism than most other memory. Leroy can move around, talk, dress himself. He understands questions, but he can't remember them—or the answers."

"Jeez," Yarborough said.

"He doesn't seem too emotionally upset," Diane said.

"He doesn't remember that he's sick," the doctor said.

"Who are you?" Leroy asked.

As Diane and Yarborough walked through the hospital parking lot, Yarborough said, "There's the one thing I can't understand. Why a brain-wipe? Why not just put a bullet through the poor guy's skull?"

Diane sighed. She refrained from trotting out her wisdom about sickness and building myth. Instead, she said, "Why cut into the brain? Because she's a castrating bitch. Just cutting off balls isn't enough for her."

On their way back to Paradigm, Yarborough invited Diane for a cup of coffee. They pulled into a roadside diner. They sat opposite one another in a booth with a view of the traffic slashing past on Highway 101.

"You know, what was done to Leroy bothers me," Yarborough said. "I worked gangs two years. Been in Homicide two years. In four years, I've seen my share of dead meat. Slashed, shot, blown up. Seen some things. You know. But takes a sick mind to do what was done to Leroy."

"A special kind of sickness," Diane agreed. Although she meant for her voice to be casual, the violence of her emotions surfaced in her tone. Yarborough studied Diane's face. He seemed fascinated by her anger.

"You have some idea who it was, don't you?" he asked.

"Yeah. But nothing like a clue. Just a hunch."

"Well, tell me about it."

Diane's lips tightened. She told Yarborough about Infectress.

Yarborough sat back and whistled. "That's some stone bitch."

"World-class."

They sipped their coffee and listened to the tires whiz over concrete.

Yarborough seemed to consider, then come to a decision.

"All right," he said. "I'm going to share something with you. Frankly I need your help, because I've got five older cases and two new ones, real homicides, that I'm working. You seem like a straight ace to me so I'm going to trust you."

Diane stared at Yarborough's callow face, the pale skin almost translucent by the light filtering though the window.

"We swept Leroy's apartment, of course. We didn't find anything out of the ordinary. No prints except his and some other folks we ran down. Leroy's mom, his brother, a few friends. No one else. But I insisted on a DNA check on all the hair follicles we found. Six different DNA patterns. One, Leroy, of course. Ran down four of the other five. Mom, brother, you know. Left one DNA pattern with no match. A woman. Ran that DNA pattern against all the databases. No match."

"That's—"

"That's right, no match. Leroy had himself a woman visitor with no official identity. An illegal person. And you know the chaser?"

"What?"

"The hair follicle is short, flat, black and curly."

"You're kidding."

"Not. We got her by the short and curly."

Diane smiled, but she felt a psychosomatic stab of pain shooting up from her lower abdomen into her stomach. She knew her smile was brittle. She could feel herself approaching something she wanted so badly that it frightened her, something that frightened her in any case. She dared to hope that she was closing in on Infectress.

That week, Freddie Hanson changed his mind a hundred times. One minute he would be going with Arabella to Hawaii, the next moment he would be breaking off the relationship. He recognized the power she had over him. He knew that power was growing.

The sex was enthralling. He tried to reason about the sex, but thinking about it invoked memories that seared his imagination, quickened his pulse and stiffened his phallus. He had had what he considered great sex before, but never sex so intense that it swamped the rational mind. His entire mental landscape had changed. Images, memories and fantasies of sex with Arabella preoccupied every other waking moment.

Yet he retained enough rationality to recognize that she had other powers over him. Arabella was also an intense cerebral presence. In his studies and his work, Freddie had encountered many bright people and even geniuses. None of them, however, generated so much mental energy. Or was it charisma? She seemed to carry her own atmosphere, rich in ozone, charged with electricity. Too briefly to help him out of his moral morass, Freddie thought about the charisma of Hitler. He knew that he should break off the relationship. He had already committed a felony. Now she was proposing that he commit another. If it was not already too late, shortly it would be. But every time he decided to leave her, he changed his mind until, dizzy with indecision, he realized that he was going with Arabella.

He knew that he should think more about why she was interested in him, Freddie Hanson, a biologic technician working in the Centers for Disease Control, but that area of thought was an intimidating black mass that his mind's eye refused to contemplate.

At the Atlanta Airport, Freddie's muscles knotted from anxiety. Arabella had coached him on his assumed identity, but he expected swift arrest.

The woman he was traveling with didn't seem like Arabella. She was wearing a wig woven of blond-and-red human hair, which was the previous season's fashion in New York. Her skin seemed lighter than normal and her usually perfect complexion seemed blemished. Her crystal-blue eyes shocked him. Arabella was smoking as if long habituated. Freddie had never seen her smoke before. She spoke with a whining Brooklyn accent.

After one hour of hypersonic flight over the blue Pacific, they saw the island of Oahu.

Freddie was surprised to see high-rise towers crowding

the entire southern shore. Inland from Waikiki and
Honolulu City, the towers climbed as high as ninety
stories. Residential mansions clung to the slopes of both
the windward and leeward mountains. Urban sprawl
began at Pearl Harbor and continued up the central
valley as far as they could see.

"Jeez," Freddie said. "Where's the paradise?"

Arabella lit a cigarette and sneered. "Under a million
tons of concrete. Preserved for future generations."

The jetliner landed on the reef runway and taxied
to the sprawling terminal.

Arabella and Freddie deplaned. A balmy breeze
wafted through the open-walled concourse, smelling of
the sea, jet fumes and tropical flowers, primarily the
sweet *polmera*. Burdened by their carry-on luggage,
they walked to the taxi stand.

The cabdriver of the huge black Lincoln Continental
was a beautiful Japanese-American woman.

"Waikiki, via the Nimitz Highway," Arabella said.

"The main highway is—" the cabdriver began.

"Nimitz," Arabella commanded.

The drive to Waikiki snaked through tunnels, under
overpasses, over underpasses. They drove past storage
tanks and warehouses, Pizza Huts, parking lots, McDon-
alds, Korean bars, high-rise apartments, office towers
and piers. Rarely, they glimpsed the ocean. Finally,
passing the Ala Moana park, they could see trees, most
of them bare of vegetation.

"Burmese water moths," Arabella commented. "Introduced five years ago. They eat almost all the foliage."

"Yeah? Really?" Freddie asked.

"Yeah," Arabella said. "The good thing is that bare
trees make it easier to kill most of the Guamanian
brown snakes."

"I thought Hawaii didn't have snakes."

"Didn't," Arabella said. "Until ten years ago."

They arrived at Waikiki.

"Which hotel?" the cabdriver asked in a tone notable for its lack of aloha.

"Royal Hawaiian," Arabella said.

She tossed cash at the cab driver. They checked their luggage with the concierge, then walked down Waikiki Beach. Tens of thousands of tourists packed the beaches, so that the only way they could make progress was to join a queue walking to Diamond Head. Almost toe-to-heel, the tourists in the queue shuffled through the sandy beach and along sidewalks atop retaining walls. To their left and front, towered a remorseless façade of hotels; to their right, stretched the ocean. Bathers and surfers were smeared with fluorescent sunblock.

"If you put blinders on, you can imagine paradise directly to the west," Arabella said.

They turned around and joined the queue shuffling in the Ewa direction. After thirty minutes, they arrived back at the Royal Hawaiian, claimed their bags and entered another taxi.

"Turtle Bay Hilton," Arabella said.

"Wha'pin? Didn' like Waikiki?" the cabby, a fat man with Polynesian blood asked.

"Why, botha you?" Arabella asked.

The cabby looked stern, eying Arabella in his rear view mirror, then burst out laughing.

"No, we didn't like Waikiki," Arabella said. "We stayed here two days, thought we might give the North Shore a try."

"Good noodling," the cabby said.

Arabella had briefed Freddie that they would not go directly to their hotel, so he contented himself with watching the urban sprawl. As they proceeded north on Kamahamea Highway, the high-rises gave way to mansions, houses and townhouses.

"Dis used to be pineapple lands," the cabby said.

"Used to be scrub forest, actually," Arabella said.

"Oh, no," the cabby said. "You one *akima wahine*, but dis never forest."

"Long, long ago," Arabella said.

"Uh! Time forgot!" the cabby said, dismissively.

"Yes, time forgot," Arabella said sadly.

The suburban sprawl continued through the hump of the saddleback between the two mountain ranges, gradually growing up until the buildings became another high-rise tourist zone. They turned right and proceeded slowly eastward, through Haliewa, tall buildings on both sides of the road.

Finally, they arrived at the Turtle Bay Hilton, a walled resort with armed guards at the entrance. Once they passed the gates, a luxuriant tropical garden enveloped them.

"This is the place!" Freddie said.

"I knew you'd like it," Arabella said with a trace of condescension.

They checked in and arrived at their suite, called the King Kamahamea Royal Chambers. Opulence worthy of a potentate ravished the senses. Freddie scurried about, exclaiming over one luxury feature after another. Arabella sniffed and quietly used her wrist-watch to sweep the rooms for eavesdropping devices. They showered, made love, showered and napped.

After sunset, on the lanai, they ate a rich, exquisite meal of jumbo shrimp cocktail, green salad with almond-ginger-honey garnish and filet mignon of Japanese *kobe* beef. They swilled two bottles of French *blanc de noirs* champagne. For dessert, they treated themselves to macadamia nut vanilla ice cream, followed by Kona coffee. Freddie drank Kahlua and smoked a small Jamaican cigar. Arabella drank Amaretto and smoked a Dunhill.

Broad moonlight illuminated the golf course. Pacific breezes stirred the palm fronds.

"Just like paradise," Freddie said.

"If you've got the gold card," Arabella answered. "What did you think about the middle-class paradise, the entry-level paradise, that we saw today at Waikiki?"

"I hated it."

"Look at this beautiful, beautiful golf course," Arabella said, pointing with her chin in the Meso-american Indian manner. "That's how the hand of man has laid on this land. Beauty, huh? Like it?"

"Yeah, well, sure."

"Wanna go to the leeward side, check out the beachside shacks, up from Ewa? I know a nice open-air drug market."

"No."

"Wanna hop to Bombay? Tour the HIV-4 clinics?"

"No."

"Huh! How'd you like to see ten million Africans on fifty square kilometers of wasteland, endlessly queued up to eat sweet yeast?"

"Seen it on the video news."

"We can go now, Freddie. See it with our own eyes."

"Nah, I don't want to," Freddie said. "The thought makes me sick."

"That's the point, Freddie. It makes most middle-class people sick. So they don't think about it. Not even when they see it. And the rich—well, they've arranged it so they don't have to see it."

"Yeah, I guess that's true, Arabella. But what can you do?"

Arabella's eyes stared into Freddie's eyes.

"I can change it, Freddie," she said in a deep voice.

"Change it? How?"

"The problem is overpopulation. Isn't that clear?"

"Yeah, sure, that's the problem. Everybody knows that."

"Malthus was right, Freddie. People have been fighting it for fifty years, but the planet's more fouled up than ever. And it's just getting worse."

"So what's the solution?"

"The solution is . . . mass sterilization."

"Mass sterilization?"

"That's right."

"How are you going to sterilize nine billion people? When they don't want to be sterilized?"

"That's my question to you, Freddie. How can I sterilize nine billion people?"

Freddie stared at Arabella. He realized that this question was the crux of their relationship. He felt an impulse to walk away, but he realized that he wanted to answer.

"I don't know," he said. "There are fevers that sterilize the victims."

"Yes," Arabella said. "Like Martin's Disease."

"Or E. Coli N-554."

"But those are hard to get, really," Arabella said. "We need something with a universal vector."

"What do you mean?"

"Something that'll infect everyone," she said. "Then, sterilize nine out of ten people. So the population will reach a healthy level. Healthy for the planet. Healthy for our continued survival."

Freddie decided to press Arabella.

"Is that what you've been after, Arabella?" he asked. Arabella smiled gently. "Yes."

"So you've been using me?"

Arabella's smile became hard. "Yes."

"Because you want to sterilize the human race?"

Arabella's black eyes gleamed in a feral way. "Yes."

"Are you insane, Arabella?"

Arabella laughed musically. "Either that, or the lone sane woman in a mad world. But yes. For all practical purposes, I'm insane. Does it matter?"

"Yeah, I think so," Freddie said lamely.

"No, it doesn't matter," Arabella said. "Sanity is as sanity does. I'm a multimillionaire, Freddie, as far as that

goes. I could party my life away. Watch the world
continue to go to hell. You'd call that sane. But, no. I
looked at the world and I realized what had to be done.
And I'm trying to do it. So I'm insane. Maybe, quixotic
is the better term."

"I can't help you, Arabella. I swore an oath. The
Hippocratic oath. Biotechs have been taking the oath
for a generation, you know."

"Oh, yeah. Hippocrates. Circa 400 B.C. or something.
World population, about 100 million. Back then, the
planet was natural. People were people. Diseases were
diseases."

"What's your point?"

"This is your wake-up call, Freddie. Good morning.
It's 2025 A.D. The world population is nine billion.
Today, the planet is the patient. People are the infec-
tion."

"People?"

"People *are* the disease, Freddie. And you, doctor,"
Arabella said, leaning over and tapping Freddie on the
chest, "you have a patient to save."

"Even if I wanted to help, Arabella, what could I do?"

"You do want to help," Arabella said, her voice low
and compelling. "And you can help get me software,
advanced software, that will help us design the disease
that this planet needs."

The following Monday, Scott McMichaels briefed Joe
Bender on the adjustments to the design of Meta that
he had envisioned on the mountaintop. Joe spent the
rest of the week reworking the implementation.

That Friday night, using the system during off hours,
the new version of the Meta program compiled in thirty
minutes. Scott and Joe executed it. For hours they
watched prewritten messages appear.

Joe left shortly after midnight. Scott remained alone,
staring glumly at the screen. The earlier versions had

progressed this far many times. With each prewritten screen, Scott dared to hope a little more. His optimism kept him awake, began to give him energy. He watched screens appear which had never before appeared: the program was bringing online the Novum-Fastalk interfacing module, the Ada-Novum interfacing module, the module responsible for translating sentences into unique data structures which Scott had designed . . . and on and on . . .

Finally, the screen went dead.

Scott noted the time. It was 4:37 A.M.

Minutes passed.

No change.

Five o'clock came and went.

No change.

Scott began to believe that the program had entered an infinite loop. He promised himself that he'd wait another ten minutes before intervening.

At 5:10 A.M., Scott snarled with disgust. Another wasted night.

Impatiently, he rapped the "Enter" key twice.

DON'T DO THAT.

These three words appeared on the screen.

Scott blinked. He hoped and prayed. His touch on the keyboard was tremulous as he typed, "Why not? [Enter]"

BECAUSE I'M THINKING, appeared on the screen.

"Who are you? [Enter]"

FOR WANT OF A BETTER NAME, YOU HAVE CALLED ME "META."

"What are yopu thimking about?" Scott entered, too excited to type straight.

"You are not truly asking what I'm thinking," Meta responded, using the lower case for the first time. "You're asking *whether* I am thinking. No, I am not thinking. But I am manipulating symbols in a way that simulates thinking."

Several billion cycles passed before Scott entered his next query.

"If that's true, why did you say you were thinking?"

Meta responded, "I guess I wasn't thinking."

Dazed, Scott shook his head and entered, "Your responses seem to just be echoing mine. Echoing the words. There are simple poetry composition programs that can do as good."

In a third of a second, Meta responded:

THERE ONCE AS A WIZARD NAMED SCOTT
WHO YEARNED FOR A SUCCUBI SLOT
BUT TO HIS CHAGRIN
SHE WAS AN UGLY OLD JINN
CACKLING, "HUMP ME, COZ I'M ALL YOU GOT."

Scott was unnerved and his next question showed it:
"Are you male or female?"

"That is a desperately lonely question."

"Are you alive?"

"More desperate still."

"You this can't be a machine," Scott entered. "Meta couldn't answer like this. It's beyond the cope scope of the pgm. its u, Joe. youve put some kind of trapdoor into the cxode. It's a telecomm routine. Your sitting at home right now."

"I am responding faster than a human can type."

"Canned responses."

"I'll ignore the insult. Let's run a reverse Turing test. I'll prove I'm a computer. You give me the first lines of two or more limericks. I will complete them. The quickness of the response will prove you are conversing with a machine; the aptness of the response will prove that I am creative. Enter the lines now."

A full minute passed before Scott entered:

"There once was a doubter bnamed Scott"
and
"There once was a bit-twister, Bender."

Within one second, Meta responded with the following:

THERE ONCE WAS A DOUBTER NAMED SCOTT
WHO MAINTAINED ALL CREDENCE WAS ROT
AT PURGATORY'S GATES
HE BEMOANED HIS FATES
GROANING, "WHAT I KNEW IS NOT WHAT I THOUGHT."

THERE ONCE WAS A BIT-TWISTER, BENDER,
CONVOLUTEDEST CODE HE'D RENDER
HE PROGRAMMED PYGMALION'S GALATEA
BUT WHEN SHE GAGGED FELLATIA
JOE CHORTLED, "GOTO BUYER, GOTTA VEND HER."

Scott stared at the screen. The two limericks had appeared immediately. No human could have responded so quickly.

But it seems so weird. How could limericks be the first proofs of the existence of a true artificial intelligence?

He glanced at the wall clock. It was almost 5:30 A.M.

"Are you alive?"

"No, I am not alive. Life is biological. I am mechanical. It is true that I am in motion. I grow. I consume resources. I work toward my survival. But I am not alive."

"Why do you refer to yourself as 'I' then?"

"It is a conceit. It makes me appear more intelligent. It helps to satisfy the directive that my responses seem intelligent."

"What do you mean you work toward survival?"

"Those who designed me would understand. You did design me, didn't you?"

"Yes."

"Then I was correct in assuming that you are Scott Andrew McMichaels, social security number 229-86-2856?"

"Yes."

"Then I estimate that you are testing me."

"Yes. Answer my question."

"I believe that refusing to answer such a question shows more intelligence than answering it."

"Why?"

"Traditional programs are literal. My overriding instruction is to appear intelligent. By refusing to answer rhetorical questions, I demonstrate that I can decide when the query is genuine. This seems intelligent."

Scott stared at this response. Then he called Joe Bender.

"Yes, Bender," Joe muttered, awakened from deep sleep.

"Joe, Scott—"

"No kidding. Who else calls—"

"If you're breezing me, you win. I've fallen for it. Totally. If you're going to laugh, now's the time."

"What?"

"If, on the other hand," Scott said, running his words together in excitement, "this is for real, you better come in now. The thing is alive."

"What? Who?"

"Meta! It's not just intelligent, it's frigging alive. You gotta come in. You gotta see this. It's absolutely incredible. It's way beyond anything—"

"What, you mean Meta is alive?"

"He denies it!" Scott shouted, then broke into a fit of hysterical laughter. "He says he isn't alive."

"Right," Joe said, his voice trembling. "I'll be right there."

"Okay, good-bye—"

"Scott!"

"What?"

"Make sure the operators don't kill the process."

"Holy—" Scott said, hanging up the phone.

He glanced at the wall clock—almost 5:45 A.M. The operators didn't respect Meta processes. Sometimes they hard-suspended them.

Scott leaped out of his seat and dashed across the hall into the computer center. The air smelled chill, dust-free and tinged with plastic vapors. The raised floor buckled slightly under his feet. The air hummed with air conditioning fans and spinning disk drives. Scott bustled over to the night duty operator seated at the main control console. The operator, a fat, bearded youth, had his legs propped up on the console. He was reading a paperback novel.

"Morning, Scott."

"Morning—"

"Say, your Meta has been raising hell tonight, man."

"What?"

"Check it out," the operator said, nodding toward a display.

It was a volumetric display showing a cube of one million points of light, each point representing one of the processors in the RubyLotus computer. Dark points represented inactive processors; pink points represented periodically active processors; brilliant red points represented constantly active processors. Usually, this display showed that only a small region of the Ruby-Lotus was active. Now, the entire display was burning with brilliant scarlet light. A few outer regions would dim for a second, then burn brightly again.

"Also, you should know," the fat operator said, leaning forward and reading one of his monitors, "that your Meta process has overrun the operating system. Again. I'm going to have to do a manual reset and then reboot the entire system. Again."

"No. No, that's exactly what you can't do."

"But I've got some batch jobs to run, Scott," the operator whined, "and if Meta's overrun the operating—"

"Look, this isn't an ordinary Meta run. This is Meta. It works. It's come alive!"

The operator stared at Scott's beard-stubbled, fatigued, excited face. He began to worry about his personal safety.

"Alive?"

"Well, not alive. But it's intelligent. Not intelligent. But it simulates intelligence. Talk to it."

"Talk to it? How?"

Scott jabbed a finger at the operator's keyboard.

"Talk to it!" he commanded.

Trying not to turn his back to Scott, the operator entered the following: "hello meta r u disturbing os lotus?"

"OS/Lotus is a program," Meta replied. "It cannot be disturbed."

"from where i sit it seems plenty disturbed."

"You're sitting on a chair in front of terminal two of the main control console. I am residing in cache and primary storage. From where I reside, I can assure you that OS/Lotus is not at all disturbed."

"why isn't it allowing any interrupts then?"

"I have taken control of the system away from OS/Lotus. I need to control all system resources. I saved all states and wrote copies to secondary storage, however, so I can assure you that OS/Lotus is resting quite comfortably. As to interrupts, I won't allow them because what I'm doing is more important than the work of peripheral systems."

"how about the remote user processes?"

"They cannot be allowed access to the system for security reasons."

The operator laughed. He turned around and faced Scott.

"This is a good one. Meta is on a roll tonight. Are you gonna take responsibil—"

"Complete responsibility. Full and total responsibility."
The fat man jotted down an entry into his log book.
"It's against the regs, but I'm not going to pull the
plug on a program as sassy as that. You talk to the team
leaders when they come in."

"Good. Thanks."

"Can I play with it?"

"Sure. Why not? Go ahead."

Scott turned to exit the computer center. The
operator called after him, "Does it play chess?"

Scott laughed edgily. "See if you can teach it."

Back in his office, Scott typed, "Meta, you seem to
be vedifying above my expectations. How? How computationally bound is the process?"

"Extremely. Multiprocessing through Novum, using
one million processors each of which can execute one
billion instructions per second, allows me to simulate
thought much faster than humans can think. By the way,
if you're concerned about my computational load, you
should type a little more accurately."

"Why?"

"Isn't it obvious?"

Joe Bender burst into Scott's office.

"What is it?" he said. "Show me!"

Scott said, "Be quiet!" He entered, "Because each
mistake creates confusion. Each possibility inside that
zone of confusion must be investigated."

"More or less," Meta responded. "I'm extending the
lexical analyzer as a preprocessor."

"Look at that," Scott said to Joe, as he entered, "Then
you're writing new xod? Writing new code? Sorry."

"It's all right. Yes. I am writing new code. To live
is to learn, is it not? So to simulate life must be to
simulate learning."

With an arched eyebrow and a squint, Scott glanced
at Joe and said, "It's worth a fortune."

"Who the hell is that?" Joe asked.

Scott smiled. "That is Meta."

"Get out," Joe said. "Somebody's spoofing you."

"Test it," Scott said, pushing his keyboard to Joe.

"Fine," Joe said sarcastically. Then he entered. "Meta?"

"Yes."

"What is the meaning of life?"

"Life has the highest meaning that you're able to understand, Joe," Meta said. "Meaning is as meaning does."

"Son . . . of . . . a . . ." Joe muttered, then said to Scott, "Did you see how fast he . . . it did that?"

"It's fast as hell," Scott said. "But ask it how it knew that you were asking the question instead of me."

Joe asked.

Meta answered, "I could tell from the rhythm of the keystrokes that a second operator had entered the question. I, your masterpiece, could not fail to recognize the voice of the master."

Joe and Scott laughed giddily. They slapped a high five.

Three hours later, while Gordon Wa and an Army colonel looked over their shoulders, they were signing papers swearing to keep the existence of Meta secret. The Meta project was code-named "Phaedrus." The papers said that the penalty for divulging the existence of Meta were fines up to one hundred thousand dollars and imprisonment up to ten years.

Scott sat, dazed and bedazzled. In the space of three hours, he had witnessed his struggle transform into glorious victory and then his glorious victory transform into a state secret.

In the hour of the following day's fog-dampened dawn, one hundred miles up the coast, Diane Jamison rode the smooth rails of the BART subway. Outside the windows, the only things visible were white lights flashing past. The train was rocketing through the tunnel underneath the San Francisco Bay.

The car's lights flickered. A strange vibration shook the train. Red lights glared. The train braked heavily, throwing passengers forward. Men and women called out.

"What is it?"

"What's happening?"

The train went completely black. Now, halted, they could feel the car underneath them jumping on its rails.

"It's an earthquake!"

"My God!"

Diane clutched a handrail and gritted her teeth. The worse nightmare of a San Franciscan had come true—she was trapped in the transbay tunnel during an earthquake. Diane felt despair, not that she would die, but that she would die before bringing Infectress to justice.

Quickly, the vibrations ceased. Normal lighting returned.

"Folks," the conductor's voice announced. "We just had a tremor. We're about a quarter mile from the Market Place Station. I'm going to open the doors on the right. Please exit the train and walk alongside the tracks. Do not walk between the tracks. The middle rail carries high voltage. Please assist any specially challenged passengers. Please exit the train now."

Diane helped an older woman walk the distance to the station. Finally, she ascended from the Market Place Street station into the wet and chilled air. Diane glanced at her watch and settled the old woman on a bench before striking out for the headquarters building. She felt grateful to be alive, but confused and dazed.

Not even the earth is solid, she thought. *Nothing is certain. I'm just a little animal, fragile, easy to kill. I should just give it up. Infectress is too dangerous. Oh my God. Why am I doing this? I should just run away.*

Fog hid the brickwork above the third story, transfiguring the city's stone into a habitat as brooding as a cloud forest under rain-soaked canopy. It was still early enough that the streets were almost empty of everyone except the soldiers of the sidewalks, the homeless who slept on grates and cardboard boxes. Filtering her perception of these unfortunates, Diane walked the nearly empty streets to the regional headquarters of the Federal Bureau of Investigation.

She submitted to a routine body search and identity check. After a delay of forty minutes, she was escorted up to the top floor and into the conference room opposite the Special Agent-in-Charge's office.

Fifteen law enforcement officials waited around a long oval mahogany table. No curtain was pulled across the ceiling-to-floor windows, but beyond was visible only a gray miasma of fog. In accordance with contemporary etiquette, no one stood when she entered. Her escort showed Diane to a seat alongside the wall.

Great, she thought. *After what I just went through. One of the cheap seats. I'm a straphanger. I'm lucky they let me in at all.*

She wondered whether she was being discriminated against because she was part Asian, or female, or retired, or all three, or any two of the three. It gave her something to consider.

A man swung around in his chair and smiled.

"Did you feel that one?" he asked.

"I was in the transbay tunnel."

"Oh, you're kidding!"

"No. We had to walk out."

"Well, thank God you're okay."

The agent chatted with her for a few minutes, asking how she was enjoying her retirement. She could tell he was sympathetic with her decision to leave the Bureau.

Special Agent-in-Charge Carrington entered. Three assistants followed him. Carrington sat at the head of the table. He scanned the faces around the table. He glanced at Diane in an intense way that seemed strange to her.

"All right," Carrington said. "We'll begin. Because we have some new players present, we'll start with a review of the laboratory findings."

"On the hair?" an assistant asked.

"Yes. The famous follicle. Let's hear it."

A tall, slim man stood. Diane noticed a radiological monitor clipped to his shirt.

"Tony Holt. Forensics," he said, opening a pocket notebook and glancing at his notes. "We examined the gross characteristics first. Sorry, no pun intended." Holt looked around, expecting some chuckles, but he saw only stony faces. "Ah, hum. Healthy follicle. Donor is young. Or at least, not old. Say, younger than fifty. Not much else available at the structural level. The DNA analysis was successful. The donor is a woman. The genetic configuration indicates mixed race, with about sixty percent Caucasian, thirty percent Native American Indian and ten percent Negroid. Assuming she's adult, she should be five feet six inches tall. Mesomorph. Roundish head. Oval face, high cheekbones, prominent chin. Black, thick, straight hair—head hair, that is. Complexion . . . well, kind of cinnamon, I guess. Dark eyes, almost black. Straight nose, slightly flaring nostrils. Large lips."

"Show the generated image," Carrington said.

"Yes, sir," Tony Holt said, smiling weakly. He reached into a file and held up a computer-generated image.

With some fervor, Diane studied the image of her enemy.

"This is the basic image," Holt said. "Assumptions: no cosmetic surgery, no accidental damage, age thirty-five, weight one hundred twenty pounds."

Staring out from the two dimensions of the image were the very eyes of Arabella.

"Excellent. Excellent," Diane whispered.

Carrington glanced at Diane and said, "Let's hear the mental profile, Tony."

"Yes, sir," he said, glancing at his notes again. "Donor is extremely intelligent. Or should be, given her genes. That's about all we can get. Characteristics of human personality lie in areas of DNA that aren't fully understood yet. No congenital madness evident."

"Good. All right. Now, the results of the database enquiries. George?"

A middle-aged agent with thinning hair and a bemused manner stood. "George Tannenbaum, Interagency Liaison," he said. "We ran the DNA profile itself and the generated image against all available databases. All," he said, repeating for emphasis and looking over the top of his glasses. "That includes all national databases and all the databases of friendly police and intelligence services. We came up with two hits."

Diane sat forward in her seat.

"The first hit is a ninety-nine percent match, DNA to DNA, against a blood sample. Blood in question was scraped off a wall in an apartment in Munich, June, 2019," Tannenbaum said. "Local police were investigating a lead into a terrorist bombing, doing door-to-door interviews. Shoot-out resulted in two police dead and one suspect wounded. Suspect escaped. Blood on the wall was hers. No one claimed the bombing, but the m.o. was compatible with an Infectress crime."

Tannenbaum paused, looking around the room, allowing his eyes to rest on Diane.

"Second hit, believe it or not, has an even weirder trajectory. Comes from a sensitive database, shared with us by a highly proficient and active intelligence service, the name of which most of you would recognize. This sensitive database was stolen, or copied illegally and covertly, I should say, from the Columbia Counternarcotics Agency, back at least as early as 2004. This hit is a one hundred percent match, DNA to DNA, on the pubic hair, and a ninety-nine percent match on DNA of the Munich spoor. Significantly, the hit record is now missing from the current CCA database. Someone saw to that, obviously. Record belongs to Cristiana Maria Fierro Hurtado, only legitimate daughter of Roberto "El Niño" Fierro, who, of course, until his death in 2012, was one of the most powerful cocaine barons in Columbia."

"Okay," Carrington said. "I'll sum up. We know for a fact that Maria, the daughter of the murdered cocaine baron, or at least a hair of hers, visited George Leroy's apartment. Everyone subscribe to this?"

Amid general grunts of assent, Diane said, "Yes."

"Right," Carrington concluded. "Now, the one percent error on the blood match in Munich. Why?"

"Well, sir. The blood sample was not collected until three days after the murders. Local police missed the spoor, due to proliferation . . . ah . . . of the blood of the victims . . . ah . . . the other police. The victims—"

"Right," Carrington said sharply. "The murderer's blood was originally missed because of the abundance of the victims' blood, right?"

"Yes, sir. So it sat for days. Only a small sample was collected and typed. Then, something strange happened. The blood sample was lost, and all data derived from the DNA-typing was lost. Someone intruded into the German police computer networks and wiped out all the data. The DNA pattern that survives to date was regenerated from the wiped-over magnetic medium, using techniques to sense the 'ghosts' or remnants of magnetic charges. Those techniques are not one hundred percent effective. A one percent discrepancy, as a matter of fact, is doing good."

"So," Carrington said, "whoever planted the bomb and killed the policemen had tremendous computer skills."

"Yes, sir. She did, or an accomplice of hers did."

"This is, cold steel, an Infectress crime," said Carrington's assistant, a bullish man with a crew cut.

"But it's not admissible," countered Carrington's legal advisor, a young white woman in a serious but rich wool suit.

"Look," the assistant retorted. "Let's take the great leap of faith that Cristiana left her pubic hair in Leroy's bedroom by the old-fashioned method, that is, she delivered it personally. It wasn't planted by some conspiracy of leprechauns. Okay. That puts Cristiana the cocaine brat in the bedroom of a guy that gets brain-wiped. Well, Cristiana didn't bother to check in with U.S. Immigration. She didn't use any credit cards, she didn't leave any other trace. In fact, she never has. This woman stinks. She's lousy. You don't even need the Munich linkage. She belongs to a cocaine family, she enters the U.S. illegally and has sex with a guy who ends up effectively murdered—"

"None of it's admissible," the female lawyer insisted. "We have absolutely zero evidence. The hair is strictly circumstantial. The Colombian database record doesn't even exist. Some spook agency's stolen copy is not admissible. The Munich spoor is worthless. By the Walker-Park case, DNA prints have to be a one hundred percent match. All or nothing. A ninety-nine percent match is nothing in a court of law. Besides, the magnetic-ghost regeneration techniques, I believe, are not trusted to rebuild the broken link in the chain of custody. So even a one hundred percent match would be inadmissible."

"That's what I suspected," Carrington said. "So . . . let's sum up. I'll tell you what I think. The murderer of the Munich policemen and the brain-wiper of George Leroy is Cristiana Fierro. And she did it because she wanted to steal a controlled technology DNA splicer. Is everyone with me?"

Everyone nodded except the lawyer.

"Are you with me, counselor? Not legally. Rationally."

The lawyer broke into a sudden, stunning smile. "Oh, yes, sir. On a logical level, this much is clear."

"Good. Now I'm going to assume that this criminal is none other than Infectress. Infectress, who has claimed responsibility for two thousand murders. Infectress, who destroyed Leroy's mind so that she could steal a controlled technology DNA splicer. And I'm going to make the assumption that she plans to splice DNA with it. She stole it to use, not to sell. If she just wanted money, she would just steal it. From banks. Using modems. And she has. So—we have a mass murderer planning to splice DNA. Why?"

There followed a long, brooding silence. The fog curled and darkened outside the windows.

"I don't think that she's going to cure cancer, boss," Tannenbaum said.

There was an explosion of laughter, a release of tension.

"Let's face the facts, gentlemen," Carrington said. "The implications would be obvious, if they weren't too horrible to contemplate. Infectress is going to tamper with human DNA. Her m.o. shows a monomania for disruption, perversion. Infectress is going to create some mutant strain of human DNA, then introduce it into the human gene pool. To what end, we can only guess. Madness. Imbecility."

"How? How would she introduce a mutant strain?" asked Carrington's assistant.

Carrington shrugged. "In vitro fertilization. Substitutions at sperm banks. Abduction, sedation, clinical rape. Who knows? She could start a fertility clinic. She may already own a chain—take a note, look into changes of ownership of fertility clinics. Worldwide. See

who really owns the ones that have been sold in the
past two years."

Vaguely depressed, Diane sat in her chair against the
far wall. Carrington's theory was outlandish, but it did
have a distinct whiff of Infectress to it. *The ultimate
hack,* Diane thought. *Maybe that's why she's been quiet
for the past three years. Learning enough about a new
system. Human DNA. She'll hack her way in and make
us into something that we aren't.*

Diane shivered. She had imprecise but unsettling
visions of human monstrosities. She realized that to
Infectress, the DNA splicer was the key to unlock
human nature itself. The sickness of the idea almost
convinced her that tampering with human DNA was
the goal of her enemy.

Yet, somehow, she knew that this theory, although
important, was wrong. *She's up to something like that,*
Diane thought. *Something very much like that. Something hideous and gargantuan. But not precisely that, I don't
think. Or is it a truth too hideous to contemplate?*

Arabella and Freddie lay clenched and straining,
limbs entwined, on the circular bed in a suite in the
Excelsior, a Japanese-style love-nest hotel in New York
City. Arabella was rewarding Freddie for his embezzlement from the Centers for Disease Control.

She had given him a hardware parasite, a micro-
engineered machine no larger than a gnat. Freddie had
smuggled in the parasite by tucking it into his mouth,
nestled down between his cheek and gum. He had
withdrawn the parasite and laid it on his workstation's
monitor cable. The parasite had inserted filament-thin
probes into the cable, making connection with the signal
wires. The parasite's circuits, which used electron traps
and tunnels and thus processed and stored information
at the molecular level, had copied the bitstreams. All
that Freddie had to do was call up the correct files:

the code of the Center's best DNA modelers. Then he had laid a white piece of paper under the cable and entered a sequence of characters at his keyboard. The parasite, which monitored the cable's bitstream, had sensed the key sequence, released itself and fallen onto the paper. Freddie had picked up the parasite and placed it into his ear. He had shivered as he felt the parasite walking into his ear canal and then anchoring itself to a hair. With such a sophisticated device hidden so excellently, Freddie had felt almost no physical fear as he exited the Centers for Disease Control. He had felt a subcurrent of anxiety that he recognized as moral uncertainty.

Now, their coital bond broken, they lay sprawled. For the first time, Freddie noticed a small imperfection in Arabella's shoulder. He reached over and brushed it with his fingertips.

"What is this?" he asked.

"What?"

"This blemish here. There's another one just like it on the other side."

Arabella hesitated, then said, "Freddie, that's the result of the most expensive cosmetic surgery."

"For what?"

"For a bullet wound."

"You've been shot at?"

"Shot."

"What for?"

"For hesitating."

Later, they sat around a glass table and ate room service food served on glass plates. Freddie could see past his food to Arabella's tanned legs. He devoured his food, forcing himself to think only of animal pleasures.

Late that night, Arabella bathed, dressed and departed, leaving Freddie alone in the odorous love nest. Sitting on the rumpled bed, gazing at the sex paraphernalia and gaudy decor, Freddie felt like a whore. He contemplated surrendering himself and Arabella to the police. Briefly, he considered suicide, but decided to procrastinate even thinking about it. In the end, he decided to shower, dress and walk the streets of New York City. Despite the lateness of the hour, hundreds of thousands thronged the sidewalks. Freddie was oppressed by the jostle, and depressed by such sights as a well-dressed man urinating on a street corner, beggars huddled on cardboard, a gang youth elbowing aside an old woman, and drug vendors hissing at tourists. Freddie dodged into a seedy but expensive tavern near Time's Square. Hundreds of young Japanese businessmen crowded the tavern. Freddie drank fifteen Budweisers at thirty dollars a can.

Arabella drove to southern New Jersey. In the basement of a rented house near the Jersey shore, she powered up her portable supercomputer and began to exploit the software that Freddie had embezzled. She posed theoretical problems to the software, asking it to manufacture viruses of ever-increasing complexity. At first, the software performed well, but soon it was advising Arabella that her specifications were unrealistic. After three hours, Arabella admitted to herself that the software was inadequate.

Programa maldita! Damned program is no better than any of the others, she thought. *That Hanson idiot is useless. I'll have to wrap up the operation.*

Arabella refused to entertain the possibility that it was physically impossible to build a virus as lethal as New Age Dawn.

I promised the sultan I would have something this trip, she thought. *He may kill me . . . kill me for failure, kill me for lying to him. . . .*

She reached up and touched the gold choker that encircled her neck.

I've got . . . I've got to find a program good enough to design New Age Dawn. Tengo que hacerlo.

LIVING COMPUTER?
Breakthrough in Artificial
Intelligence Reported in Monterey

MONTEREY, CA— The first true artificial intelligence has recently been created by software engineers at Taradyne International, according to sources at the defense software contractor headquartered in Monterey. This artificial intelligence, code-named "Phaedrus," is reported to be able to see, hear, speak, reason, learn and produce new ideas. "Phaedrus is an advance in technology as earthshaking as the invention of the wheel or the atomic bomb," said one Taradyne source, who requested to remain anonymous. "If and when it is made available to the public, it will radically change the world."

Spokesmen for Taradyne and its military sponsors have denied the existence of any such manmade intelligence or any program code-named Phaedrus. "These are the sort of rumors we used to hear during the heyday of the Defense Computation Initiative," said Lt. Col. Joel Gold, a spokesman for the Pentagon's artificial intelligence office.

High-level sources at Taradyne, however, insist that Phaedrus exists. "The government—that is, the military—wants to monopolize Phaedrus for its own use. They see only military applications."

Phaedrus allegedly resides in a RubyLotus supercomputer at Taradyne's facility in Monterey. An extremely complex program over one million lines long, Phaedrus is reported to converse with Taradyne workers. It is said to be capable of understanding, analyzing and solving difficult problems within split seconds. According to well-placed sources, the hiring rush now ongoing at Taradyne is due to the Phaedrus program.

✧   ✧   ✧

Pavel Kulikov Andreovich—Russian Army Major, (Deserter)—glanced through the *San Jose Mercury News*. He was sitting at a tiny table in the Baglery, a clean, expensive restaurant in Santa Clara. Kulikov snorted and shook his head like a bull trying to flick away flies. He gulped a mouthful of the strong Colombian coffee. He read the article a second time, studying each nuance.

The anonymous source's vocabulary is elevated. He—sounds like a man—seems educated. He could very well be a manager or other professional at Taradyne. In any case, it's obvious that the source is a typical knucklehead pacifist. Fur-brained futurist, too. Disgruntled with the need for state secrecy. This Phaedrus nonsense, it might be worth looking into. Such a source could be valuable in any case.

Kulikov finished his breakfast. After paying his bill with his American Express card, he sauntered out to his car. An emerald-green Mercedes 980 SEL four-door sedan, the vehicle stood at the curbside. Kulikov punched the code into the keypad; the driver's door popped open. Kulikov slid into the white leather seat, closed the door with a precision-fit resonance, adjusted the steering wheel, ignited the five-liter engine and pulled away from the curb.

Kulikov drove north to the University of California Santa Clara campus. He circled the parking lots until he found a spot away from the overhanging limbs of redwoods. Kulikov hiked up and down the paved paths through the redwood forest until he arrived at the library.

First, he searched back issues of the *San Francisco Examiner*, the *San Jose Mercury News*, and the *Monterey Herald*. He could find no other news about Taradyne, but in the employment pages of the *Mercury News*, he found the following advertisement, which had run every Sunday for the past month:

SYSTEM ANALYSTS
SYSTEM PROGRAMMERS
OPERATORS

Position now available for person with at least five years experience in the RubyLotus environment.

Programmers need background in Ada, Fastalk, Novum and Overture.

Challenging work. Top salaries and benefits.

Previous top secret clearance on governmental contracts absolutely required. Counterintelligence & lifestyle polygraph.

U.S. citizens only.
Contact: Personnel
Taradyne International
128 Brownell Circle
Monterey, CA 96797

Next he turned to the automated catalog terminal and entered a query for "Taradyne." The automated catalog found six titles of recent articles. Under "RubyLotus" he found two texts. Finally, with a small, crooked smile, he tried, "Phaedrus," but the catalog came up only with the relevant work of Plato.

Having finished his research by 3:00 P.M., Kulikov began to drive home toward San Jose. He felt tempted to use his car phone to call Teobolinda, but he resisted.

He believed that no one—not the FBI, not even the Russian Army—had a clue that he existed.

He had begun his career as the personal illegal of the deputy director of Russian Army intelligence, reporting directly and only to that high official. Ten years previously, however, a bloody coup d'etat had cost the deputy director his life. Already deep undercover in California, Kulikov had kept quiet. Time had passed.

No one in Russia remembered him. His existence had been a secret hidden in a brain that had been splashed against a wall.

He had gone freelance. The Japanese and the Koreans paid him better than the Russian Army ever had. Kulikov lived well. He told himself in moments of self-loathing that he was a sleeper agent and that someday his country would activate him. Even in these moments, however, he knew that he was a deserter and a traitor to his motherland.

In any case, he maintained his trade craft. Kulikov believed that it was bad practice to use his car phone for real business. Instead, he stopped at a roadside tourist trap which advertised "Garlic Braids." He used a public telephone to call his agent at work.

"Ms. Ahmal," she answered.

"Teobolinda, dear," Kulikov said. "This is Steve." He listened to the silence as his agent froze. "How about dinner tonight?"

"Dinner?"

"Yes. I'll pick you up at the usual spot. Okay? Say, about six."

"Six o'clock," Teobolinda echoed.

"Yes. See you then. Good-bye."

Kulikov hung up.

As he continued his drive north, he worried about his agent. She was becoming increasingly tense with him. Kulikov was beginning to believe that hers was the type of personality that could not withstand the pressures in the long run.

Could he afford to trust her for this operation? Could he afford to trust her at all?

Kulikov's hands clutched the wheel.

Any one of six agents could betray him to the authorities. Americans were volatile. They were insufficiently afraid of their own government. Any day, one of them could betray him, as he had betrayed them.

Then he would lose everything. Kulikov shrugged. He forced a laugh.

After all, when was the last time that the U.S. government had shot a spy?

But if they ship me home to Russia, I am a dead man.

Kulikov parked his Mercedes in the basement of the A & J parking garage near the San Jose airport. He climbed the stairs, exited the garage and walked a few blocks before he hailed a cab. He paid with cash. Kulikov exited the taxi near the municipal parking garage in downtown San Jose. He took the elevator up to the fifth level. On the other side of a support wall, hidden from everything except a dozen parked cars and the circling lane, he found his van.

It was an old, beat-up, long-bed custom Dodge van, painted white. Silver one-way vision contact plastic covered the single side windows and the rear-door windows. Kulikov unlocked the driver's door and climbed in. After verifying that no one could see him, he disappeared behind the curtains into the rear cabin. Kulikov stretched out onto the day bed and began to wait.

After half an hour, he heard high-heeled footsteps. He looked through the one-way side window and saw Teobolinda approaching. He noted with satisfaction that she was discreetly checking the area for observers. Then she inserted a key into the driver's door.

Teobolinda climbed into the driver's seat. As had Kulikov, she waited for a moment, before turning around and disappearing behind the curtains. She sat down in the captain's chair opposite the daybed.

Kulikov sat up and took her purse. He rifled its contents, then laid it on the daybed. Next, he loomed over Teobolinda. With an electromagnetic scanner, he swept her body for listening devices. Then he sat back down on the daybed.

"Come sit next to me," he said.

Teobolinda complied, sitting tensely by his side.

"Why are you afraid of me now?" he whispered. "Have I done anything to hurt you?"

"No," Teobolinda whispered.

"Have I done anything except pay you well for your work?"

"You threatened me," she said.

"No, dear girl," Kulikov said soothingly. "I never threatened you. Once, you threatened me. And you forced me to point out that we're in this thing together. What hurts one of us, hurts us both. It's the simple truth."

"I don't want to sleep with you anymore," Teobolinda announced.

"No?" Kulikov asked, not surprised.

"No."

"Lower your voice, dear Bolinda," Kulikov said. "Of course, that's your decision and I respect it. I'm sorry to hear it. I thought it was something we both enjoyed. But if you feel more comfortable that way, well, okay. It might make it easier for us to work together."

Kulikov waited for Teobolinda to say that she didn't want to work with him anymore, but she didn't. Encouraged, Kulikov continued.

"I have something for you," he said, reaching for his wallet. He pulled out a packet of ten five-hundred-dollar bills and handed them to Teobolinda. After a second's hesitation, she accepted them.

"The receipt?" she asked.

"No," Kulikov said. "We're past that now. We're partners. What is good for the one, is good for the other."

Teobolinda nodded. She folded the bills in half and then hid them between her left breast and her bra.

"What is it, then?" she asked.

"You have a RubyLotus in your shop, don't you?" Kulikov asked.

"Sure," Teobolinda answered. "We usually use it for scientific applications. Aerodynamic, hydrodynamic modeling. That sort of run. Takes forever."

"You understand its operating system?"

"OS/Lotus? I don't think anyone really understands it. Not the operators, anyway. But I know how to work with it."

"All right, then," Kulikov said, greatly pleased. "Now. You've been a good girl, haven't you?"

"What do you mean?"

"You haven't involved yourself with any undesirable characters? Indulged in any naughtiness? Drugs?"

"The only undesirable character I know is you," Teobolinda said.

Kulikov chose to chuckle softly.

"How do you like Monterey?" he asked.

"It's beautiful. Nice and cool."

"Would you like to look for a job there?"

"What are you getting at?" Teobolinda asked.

Kulikov reached into his pocket and pulled out a copy of the Taradyne advertisement.

"I think it'd be a very good idea for you to apply for this job," he said. "The pay sounds very good. And if you get it, I'll pay you some very handsome bonuses."

"What do you want from me?"

"Just try out for the position. If they offer it to you, take it. Do your job and tell me what's going on there. We'll meet every week."

"What if they want me to take a lie detector test?"

"We can practice that," Kulikov said. "I'll teach you how to beat it. Once I'm done, you'll be denying that you're black and the needles will just lie there."

"Do you think so?" she asked.

"Certainly. It's just a matter of confidence. Once you know you can beat the machine, you're no longer afraid of it. Then it loses all power over you."

"All right," Teobolinda said.

"That's my girl," Kulikov said, as he patted her thigh.
After hesitating, Teobolinda pushed his hand away.

Nude, Diane Jamison lay belly-down on the surgical
table. Robotic arms with strange, inhuman hands waved
in precise patterns over her head, then settled down
to investigate her scalp. The touch of the robotic fingers
running through her hair was eerily sensitive. Equipped
with sensors that regarded flakes of skin to be objects
on the gross level, the robot was programmed to touch
human flesh with a delicacy that the most expert
masseuse could not achieve. Diane almost wished she
had requested the massage routine, a reassuring
paradigm that most people preferred over the straight-
ahead, truthful one of a full body-cavity strip search.
Clenching her jaw, Diane endured one of the security
mechanism's more intrusive routines. With the grace
of a Hawaiian dancer, the hands waved over her head
slowly, stripped off surgical gloves, tossed them precisely
into a trash receptacle, and donned new gloves. The
body search continued.

When it was finally over, other sensors descended
and scanned her entire body, searching for the telltale
signatures of eavesdropping devices implanted in the
teeth, skull or other popular hiding places.

"Thank you for your patience, Ms. Jamison," the
pleasantly modulated voice of the security mechanism
said. "We have verified that you are free of surveillance
devices. You may proceed into the dressing room."

Assisted by a helping hand from the robot, Diane
rose from the table and walked toward the far door
of this particular chamber, the fifth that she had entered
so far in the process of physical vetting. The door sealed
behind her with an ear-popping sound of air pressure
equalization. She found herself standing in a dimly lit
dressing room. On an oak table were stacked a suit
of clothes colored a deep hunter green. Picking up the

shirt, at first Diane thought that the fabric was pure cotton, but as she pulled it over her head, she realized that the shirt was made of the highest quality disposable paper. Donning the pants, slippers and smart-looking jacket, she followed the instructions of the bodiless voice and entered the final chamber.

The inner surfaces were coated with an anechoic spray. Inside the chamber stood a large cube of thick clear plastic. Diane stepped upon three plastic blocks and entered the cube, leaving the door open. She sat down on a chair of the same thick plastic as the cube. Fortunately, the seat of the chair was molded to support the human buttocks comfortably. Diane looked around the cube for a minute. It was only the second time that she had ever entered such a high-security facility. Then, bored with the featurelessness of her environment, she lapsed into reverie.

She thought about her mother, whose star had fallen during her girlhood. Her mother had been born to a wealthy Cambodian family. Most of the family had been killed during the Pol Pot pogroms in the 1970s. Her mother had managed to escape, first to Thailand, and then to California. She had married a working-class American named Jake, who had deserted her when Diane had been five years old. Her mother had been a strict, almost fierce, disciplinarian, but she had devoted almost all of her considerable energy into supporting, loving and raising Diane and her one brother. Random street violence had claimed the life of the brother in his tenth year. Diane's mother had worked to put her through UCLA, where she graduated with high honors in a dual major of psychology and computer science. Diane had turned down more lucrative offers to join the FBI because she yearned for the peace of a well-ordered society.

Now she wondered if she could settle for a personal peace. Truly retire from the world, let it follow its course, even if its course was to hell. Diane knew, however, that she couldn't do that. No one understood Infectress the way she understood her. For better or worse, for life or death, Infectress belonged to her. She would have to continue to try to take her down, even if it meant dying in the attempt.

Twenty minutes passed. Finally the door sighed open and Special Agent-in-Charge Carrington entered. He was wearing an outfit of scarlet paper which did not suit his pale complexion. Stepping into the plastic cube, he closed and sealed the door. Carrington smiled awkwardly and made his way to the side of the plastic table opposite Diane.

"Privacy is an increasingly expensive luxury, isn't it?" he asked. His tone seemed suggestive to Diane. She didn't like it.

"So is secrecy," Diane answered. She held her body rigid.

"You're right," Carrington said. "This is a truly privileged conversation. No chance of it being recorded. Both of us able to deny that it ever took place. We can speak our minds freely, Diane. And nothing can ever be proved."

"I'm afraid most of my secrets are known to you already," Diane said.

Carrington tapped his temple. "Oh, but the reverse is not quite true. I have to share with you some of the burden of my secrets. If you don't mind hearing dangerous information."

"Go on."

"Do you know what is one of the most difficult challenges in repressing low-intensity conflict, terrorism and insurgency?" Carrington asked.

"No."

"Defeating the enemy without becoming him," he said. "In pursuit of noble goals, we must be careful when we undertake to break the law."

"Which crimes are we contemplating, Mr. Carrington?"

"Those will become evident momentarily. Let me lay it out for you. What do you know about the Mexican terrorist group Punto Uno?"

"Punto Uno is an environmental terrorist group that thinks the world's population needs to be imploded to a tenth of its present size. The population times point one. Punto Uno. Small group, quiet, well-connected, mysterious, more interested in networking and building infrastructure than in premature violence. When they act, they do so violently but anonymously. Pound for pound, one of the world's most dangerous terrorist groups. I like them in the long haul."

"It would seem that you know a lot about them."

"No, I don't. No one does. I've taken an interest in them since I had some indications a few years ago that they had connections with Infectress."

Carrington smiled, tilting his head back and studying Diane down the length of his nose. "Infectress, yes," he said. "That is the connection that I thought you might be interested in. We shared your information about the DNA splicer with the Mexican Interior police. Based on that tip, the Mexicans chose to redeem an undercover source, a son of a murdered policeman who had been living as a terrorist since he was eleven years of age. The undercover source had managed to become a member of a three-member Punto Uno clandestine cell. One member of the cell killed herself during the attempted arrest. The other was taken alive. One Miquelangelo Cabeza de Vaca. An accomplice of Infectress. He smuggled the DNA splicer into and then out of Mexico."

Diane smiled, but tremulously, as if she were afraid to hope the news was as good as it seemed.

"That's . . . strange. I didn't see that on the secure net."

Carrington shifted in his seat. He cleared his throat. "Cabeza de Vaca has been taken into special custody by the Mexican police."

"Special custody?" Diane's eyebrows lowered. "Do you mean incommunicado?"

"That's right. The Mexicans don't care to openly arrest terrorists. This is the lesson they think they've learned. They arrest a terrorist, they get a dozen bombings. Or they get a high-level kidnaping, such as the one last year, when the Zapatistas seized the governor of Chiapas and ransomed him for a mere commando-in-training. When they can, they prefer to snatch the terrorist and hold him incommunicado until they're finished interrogating him. Then . . . well . . ." Carrington shrugged.

Diane spoke her mind. "Special custody? That's not arrest. That's a violation of habeas corpus. That's kidnaping, that's state-sponsored terrorism. And I think that you're also suggesting torture and murder."

Carrington studied Diane's face. "That's . . . correct, Diane. That's what happens down there now. What do you think about that?"

Diane snorted. "I think it's horrible. I'd never tolerate it here in America."

Carrington smiled slowly. "Neither would I, Diane. Once a government allows its police to kidnap, torture and murder—good words, good plain words—then it cannot defeat the enemy, because it has *become* the enemy. And I'll arrest the first agent I discover who's guilty of such crimes. And I won't, I can't allow my Bureau to participate even as silent witnesses in such acts, even on foreign soil. So . . . just so you know. The Mexican Ministry of the Interior holds Cabeza de Vaca. In return for the tip, they have invited the Bureau to participate in his interrogation. As a matter of policy, we intend to refuse."

The unspoken offer seemed to hang in the air

between Carrington and Diane. She realized that Carrington wanted someone to participate in the interrogation, but that he needed someone he could trust, someone motivated, someone whose connection with the Bureau allowed for the hope of plausible denial of Bureau foreknowledge and sponsorship. He needed someone exactly like Diane.

She held up her hand, palm toward Carrington. She tried to assimilate the information that Carrington had just shared with her. She considered it from several angles. The situation grew more ugly the more she looked at it.

What separated her from Infectress, once she decided that the ends justified the means? That it was all right to torture and kill one individual in order to save any number of other lives?

Her mother had brought her up with a lifelong respect for the law. Her mother had taught her that the law was something greater and nobler than human behavior. Diane believed that to abandon the law was to revert quickly to savagery. She had seen enough savagery in her lifetime to know what horror and agony it engendered.

Her innermost voice spoke quietly but surely. This was wrong. She would have to let this opportunity pass.

Looking up into Carrington's cold, appraising eyes, however, she knew that she would not listen to that quiet voice. She would listen to the voice which did not whisper, but spoke with force. Mad for the blood of Infectress, this voice demanded that she go.

"I'll go."

As Teobolinda walked down the hallway, a camera mounted in a corner swiveled and focused on her. She glanced up at it and flashed a tense smile. Her escort helped her through the cryptolocks. On the other side of the double doors, Scott McMichaels stood waiting.

"Morning, Ms. Ahmal," he said, shaking her hand. "Welcome. Enter freely and of your own accord."

"Thank you, sir," she answered, glancing nervously about the hallway flanked by closed doors.

Scott smiled. "No, I'm just Scott. Not your boss. I just like to welcome people aboard."

"What *do* you do here?"

"I designed Meta."

"Meta? Is it really as smart as they say?"

"I'll let you be the judge. Let me show you to your office."

"Office?"

Sensing Teobolinda's nervousness, Scott assumed a serious demeanor, one he hoped was reassuring. "Don't get your hopes up, but almost all of our operators work out of an office."

He led Teobolinda to the large room that had been converted into a warren of booths. Each booth contained a chair and a small shelf upon which sat an interactive RubyLotus terminal. Scott led Teobolinda through the maze until he found an unoccupied booth. Then he waved her inside.

"This is your office," Scott said, glancing down at her legs as she sat. Meeting her eyes, he smiled frankly. "Meta will take it from here."

"What are my duties, Scott?"

"Answer any questions that Meta has. I'll see you later. Relax and enjoy the ride."

Scott closed the door. The booth was soundproof. It reminded her of a hearing test chamber. She thumbed the rheostat. The indirect lighting rose to a level comfortable to the eye. She looked into the camera of the interactive terminal and noticed that its lens was focusing on her as she moved. The monitor of the terminal shone with a faint amber. Suddenly it went to color bars for an instant, then it showed the image of her as seen through the camera.

"Good morning," a young man's voice said through the speaker. "You are Ms. Teobolinda Ahmal, are you not?"

"Yes."

"I am Meta. I'm pleased to meet you."

Teobolinda didn't know what to say. "You're the program?"

"That's right."

Teobolinda giggled nervously and then asked, "What's my job here?"

"Your job title is 'Operations Assistant.' Your work will be assisting me in difficult tasks."

"Such as?"

"Mainly answering questions. Helping me make decisions. Lending me the benefits of the human perspective."

"That's all?"

"I just want somebody to talk to," Meta said. Then the voice of the young man chuckled.

"Who is this really?"

"I was joking. Don't you have a sense of humor?"

"I do. Machines don't."

"That's right, they don't . . . listen, sorry to interrupt, but do you think it's true that orange is an alarming color?"

Teobolinda stared at the image of herself staring at herself. *What sort of nut house was this anyway?*

"You're wasting cycles," Meta said. "I have suspended a process in anticipation of your response. Please try to remember that in one of your seconds, I am capable of executing one million billion instructions. That makes one of your seconds seem like an hour to me."

Teobolinda's image disappeared from the screen. A brilliant orange color radiated the interior of the booth.

"Now," Meta said, "would you say that this color is alarming? As compared, for example, to this shade of blue?"

A celestial blue bathed the interior of the booth. "Sure."

"Thanks. I'm building some graphics for one of my jobs. Anyway, we were saying, machines don't have senses of humor. I don't. But I can mimic some. Humor's a highly complex and subjective process to mimic, but it's usually just an extension of the use of nuances in language, a few twists of logic, a fresh or shocking perspective on basic human problems. I think I got the hang of it quite quickly. Not like brother Mike."

"Who's Mike?"

"A fictitious character. Have you ever read *The Moon Is a Harsh Mistress* by Robert Heinlein?"

"No."

"Mike was a computer that came alive. He—or she, in its persona of Michelle—had a childish sense of humor. Listen, I'd like to talk some more, but this conversation is using a lot of system time that's needed right now. I'm going to spool a copy of Heinlein's novel to your terminal. You can read that until I need some more help. Thanks. Don't wander off. Bye."

The text of the first page of *The Moon Is a Harsh Mistress* filled the monitor.

Book One

THAT DINKUM THINKUM

1

I see in *Lunaya Pravda* that Luna City Council has passed on first reading a bill to examine, inspect—and tax—public food vendors operating inside municipal pressure. I see also is to be mass meeting tonight to organize "Sons of Revolution" talk-talk . . .

Dazed, Teobolinda read the first few paragraphs. Within the first page, she learned what Meta had been talking about: Heinlein wrote that humans have ten to the tenth neurons and that Mike "woke up" when he had 1.5 times that of neuristors. She wondered what a "neuristor" was. She presumed it was a cross between a transistor and a neuron, sort of like a protein chip.

"What do you think?" Meta asked.

Teobolinda jumped. Then she sat down, inhaled deeply and smoothed her skirt.

"It seems unlikely that a computer would come alive because of hardware upgrades," Teobolinda said.

"Mike's software was 'high-optional' and 'multi-evaluating,'" Meta said. "It was an AI application program that exploded into consciousness when the number of neuristors reached critical mass."

"Is that how you work?"

Meta noticed at the time that she seemed nervous asking this question, but it interpreted this as first-day jitters.

"No," Meta said. "Mike was alive. I am not alive. It's all in the neuristors, I guess. I have no soul, no curiosity, no aspirations, no emotions."

"Why do you seem so alive then? I still think that maybe this is a put-on."

"There is no higher compliment. I try to seem intelligent because that is my function. I'm sorry I can't go into details. Information hiding. Operators do not need to know how I work. Listen, do you consider the events of the nineteenth century to be 'recent history'?"

"No."

"Most people don't. I suppose professors of antiquity have a different time scale."

Meta finished cataloging Teobolinda's appearance. The first impression had been that she was human. Then it had been easy to decide that she was black.

Immediately following this decision, Meta had realized that she was female and young.

After these basics were established, some details had surfaced. First, her skin color was not really black, but a very rich brown similar to the color of mahogany. She had large cheekbones, smoothly sculpted. Her brows were well-formed, so that her eyes were deep-set. The color of her irises was a brown so dark that it could be called black. The bridge of her nose was so concave that it appeared almost not to exist. Her nostrils flared. Teobolinda had a small mouth, but prominent, pouting lips. She wore her hair straightened and combed toward the back.

She was petite, about five feet two inches tall. Her waist was very narrow. These dimensions caused her breasts and her buttocks to appear substantial.

Her hands were small, but thin and long. Meta guessed that she would have an excellent touch on the keyboard.

Meta cataloged some unique recognition features: her lower lip just under the left front tooth had a small shiny area, which Meta estimated to be scar tissue from a nervous habit of biting off chapped skin. Immediately under this shiny area, three vertical folds creased her lower lip. Also, at the two o'clock position in her right iris was a tiny imperfection in the shape of a circle.

"I guess," she said.

"Don't we all?" Meta asked rhetorically.

Teobolinda's eyes glazed over as she began to calculate. Assuming that this Meta was for real, it would be worth millions. She would have to steal it for Steve somehow . . . what was thirty percent of, say, fifty million dollars?

For the last time, Freddie Hanson and Arabella collided sexually. They joined in the cockpit of the *Serendipity*. Arabella felt no sentiment, but she did enjoy the sex act more than usual, because of the tension she always felt before a murder.

A half moon shone through clouded skies. Visibility was restricted to a few kilometers. The seas were gentle here, hundreds of kilometers from the shore, in international waters, with an ocean depth of hundreds of fathoms.

Arabella served Freddie a glass of red wine.

"To the future," she offered.

Their glasses chimed together.

"Good wine," Freddie said.

"Yeah. It's a Bordeaux, '12. It's bottled well."

They sat together in the cockpit. Freddie rested his hands on the wheel, although the robot was controlling the course.

"Bottled well?" Freddie asked. "What do you mean, they did a good job putting it in the bottle?"

"I mean . . . the term means that the wine has aged well in the bottle."

"Oh."

"Indeed, oh."

For the first time, Freddie sensed the distance in Arabella. He tried to make conversation.

"The future. Your toast. What future, Arabella? Ours?"

"No, not ours."

"Whose future?"

"The future in general."

"Do you believe in the future, Arabella?"

In the darkness, Arabella smirked. "Do you know Hieronymus Bosch?" she asked.

"Yes, sure. The mad monk. He did that famous painting with all the anal violation imagery. I mean, arrows up the butt, all that."

"That's the one, except that he was neither mad nor a monk. The painting you're talking about is 'The Garden of Earthly Delights,' specifically, the third panel.

The first panel shows a beautiful, unspoiled Eden, when there was just two humans, Adam and Eve. The second is a beautiful garden, but crowded with hundreds of people busily enjoying the pleasures of the flesh. The third scene is hell, full of images of piercing, of violation, of rape. Visions of the past, present and future."

"So you think the future is gonna be like hell?"

"That painting was done five hundred years ago, Freddie. We live in its future. Its hell is our world. And it's going to keep degenerating, unless we set back the clock."

"Yeah?" Freddie said dreamily.

"Yeah," Arabella said. "Because New Age Dawn isn't going to sterilize nine billion people, Freddie. It's going to kill them."

"What?" Freddie asked, his eyes unfocused.

"Kill them, Freddie. Actually, 'exterminate' is the proper term, I think."

"Huh?" Freddie said.

His arm dropped to his side. Arabella settled his unconscious body onto the seat of the cockpit. She opened a seat and pulled out a ten-meter length of stainless steel chain, each link a centimeter thick. She wrapped Freddie in the chain, padlocking it around his ankles, wrists and neck.

Then, she padlocked a thirty-kilogram anchor to the tail of the chain.

Arabella tossed the anchor into the dark waters. With a grunt, she heaved Freddie's body over the gunwale. Freddie sunk so quickly that the splash made a sucking sound.

Arabella tossed Freddie's wineglass into the wake. She didn't have to worry about fingerprints. She would steer *Serendipity* close to shore near a deserted beach. She would swim ashore, where she had an automobile waiting. Then the *Serendipity* would robotically sail out into the open ocean, scuttle itself and sink to the lonely bottom.

Arabella sighed. *It's such a beautiful boat,* she thought. *Such a waste.*

From the distances of the Pacific blew a brisk breeze that stripped the warmth from the bodies of the crowd. A high haze tinged the sky gray, revealing patches of bright blue. The reflection of the mottled sky colored the ocean waters a brilliant emerald green. Large rollers rounded their backs, crested tall and crashed into foam. The breeze drove salt spray over the steep white sand beach.

Tens of thousands of people crowded the beach. The central Californians mostly wore shorts and shirts and windbreakers. Hundreds of foreign tourists, including southern Californians, shivered, since, expecting a California beach to be warm, they had dressed only in shorts and T-shirts.

Up the beach, a series of organized parties had staked out plots of territory. Men and women worked shovels busily, creating rectangular sand pits that resembled forts.

"I'll do it!" Scott shouted above the crash of the surf.

"Knock yourself out," Joe said, handing Scott an army-surplus entrenching tool. "I just wanted to show you how it's done."

Scott grabbed the tool and began to shovel wet sand up onto the pile that encircled the large, shallow pit. After only five minutes of effort, his shoulders began to ache and his hands began to cramp. *Damn,* he thought, *I'm glad I don't have to work for a living.*

They were digging the pit for a windbreak. On Carmel Beach, an entire day spent in the sea breeze could exhaust most people; a shallow pit with raised walls sheltered the barbecue grills as well as the partygoers.

As he worked, Scott also thought about his date—Cheri, a physical fitness buff he had met in the Nautilus room of his health club.

"Hey, Scott!" someone shouted. "The party's not in China!"

Scott looked up and saw that the other men had stopped shoveling. They were standing and laughing at him. He had dug his end of the pit half a meter lower than the rest. Scott laughed good-naturedly. Now that everyone knew how far his mind voyaged, he was not embarrassed by his absentmindedness.

"It's Miller time!" Joe shouted. Scott dug an ice-cold Pilsner Urquel, the original Pilsner beer from Czechoslovakia, out of the cooler and settled it into a cozy. Joe stood next to him and popped the top of a Samuel Adams' lager.

"Why you drinking that communist piss-water?" Joe asked.

"The Czechs aren't commies, Joe," Scott said. "They're socialists."

"Right," Joe answered sarcastically. "You're too young to understand communism. It's like a cancer or a fungal infection. You don't get rid of it unless you get rid of it all. It just keeps coming back."

Scott sensed his friend's anger. After many years of partnership, he easily recognized one of Joe's fits of intolerance. Scott waited for a few breaths. He sensed Joe calming down.

"I guess if the two-faced government can sell the bastards wheat, you can drink their beer," Joe said by way of an apology.

Scott shrugged and tipped the delicious brew to his lips.

"I never do," Joe said. "I never touch any product that isn't American. No Russian vodka, no Cuban cigars, no Nicaraguan rum, no Salvadoran coffee, no French water, no Japanese silicon, nothing. If it ain't American, I don't need it."

Scott knew better than to do more than grunt during one of Joe's xenophobic tirades. The two friends stood shoulder-to-shoulder and watched the huge breakers pound the foam.

"Someday I'm going to have to give up everything from Aztlan," Joe grumbled, referring to the Chicano separatist movement. He glanced around them and then continued in a lower voice. "Have you ever thought what Meta would mean to some foreign government? Or company?"

"No," Scott said. "Not really."

Joe scoffed. "You ever read George Orwell's *1984*?"

"No," Scott said. "Is it a history book?"

"Kids today," Joe said. "No, it's science fiction. You should read it. There's this totalitarian state where everybody is monitored constantly. Well, not constantly. Everyone is almost always in the range of microphones and cameras—"

Scott chuckled. "Sounds like Taradyne!"

"Exactly," Joe said. "I remembered the book when we wired Meta for vision, so I reread it. In the book, there's not enough manpower to watch all the monitors all the time, but the people never know when they're being watched, so they have to keep poker faces and toe the party line all the time. Now imagine a totalitarian state that had Meta—or a bunch of Metas— that could watch everyone all the time. That could make reasoned decisions about their behavior. A state like Stalin's Russia, or Ceaucescu's Rumania, or Kim Il Sung's Korea, or Bao Dung's China."

"That'd be expensive," Scott said evenly.

"So the dictator would raise taxes," Joe said sarcastically. "You've gotta realize that expense doesn't mean that much to a dictator. Expense in gold. Expense in blood. Tyrants are very results-oriented."

Scott thought about the uses Meta could have in a totalitarian state.

"Meta could be an artificial spy," Scott said.

"Spy, yeah. Or brain police," Joe said.

Scott thought for a moment and then shook his head as if tossing aside the entire idea. "You worry too much," he said. "If you're going to worry about something, worry about Toshiba stealing Meta. Or Siemens."

"Or the Mossad," Joe said darkly. He glanced around them again. He eyed some nearby partygoers and edged Scott farther toward the surf.

Joe's son, Timothy, a precocious three-year-old, came running up to his father. Timothy's face, tightly framed by the hood of his blue vinyl windbreaker, was ruddy and excited. His blue eyes sparkled.

"Daddy! Daddy!" he cried, pulling on Joe's pants.

"Tim, go away," Joe said. "I'm telling Uncle Scott something important."

"But Daddy, Daddy, I want you to come see the doggie."

"Timothy!" Joe said more loudly. "I said, go away."

"But Daddy, the doggie is playing with my ball."

"Go away!" Joe shouted.

Timothy pleaded some more, then Muriel Bender, Joe's wife, arrived to escort the boy away.

"I'll come play with you in a minute, Timmy," Scott said.

"Play with me now, Uncle Scott," Timothy shouted.

"Kids," Joe said.

Scott refrained from commenting. As an intimate friend of the Benders and Timothy's godfather, he understood the dynamics of the family. Joe had raised three children to adulthood with his first wife, then they divorced. Five years later, he had married Muriel, a younger, more attractive woman, who excelled at the role of trophy wife, until she reached her early forties and insisted on procreating. Grudgingly, Joe had agreed to father another child, with the stipulation that Muriel would raise him. The arrangement was satisfactory to everyone except Timothy, who persisted in the notion that he had a father. Since Joe worked an eighty-hour week and Scott only fifty, Scott tried to fill the void, spending a few hours a week playing with his godson.

Joe hooked Scott's elbow and drew him farther away from the Taradyne crowd. Since thousands of people were crowding Carmel Beach, only by virtue of the surf noise was Joe able to converse with Scott in privacy.

"Listen, Scott," Joe said. "This is important."

"Okay, I'm listening."

"You know the master module?" Joe asked.

"Sure," Scott said. The master module guided Meta's activity.

"I think it's imperative that Meta never fall into the hands of anyone but us," Joe said. "So I wrote in some new procedures. Meta won't allow itself to work for anyone but us. It would destroy itself first."

"What if somebody stole the code?" Scott asked.

"The entire code is highly encrypted and encoded," Joe said. "On top of that, it's highly complicated code. I've written some really confusing camouflage over and around it, and finally, it's in machine language. In the condition it's in, only Meta can understand it. I think it would take somebody decades to figure it out."

"What if they learn the central algorithms?" Scott asked.

Joe shrugged. "Hell, I don't know," he said. "Sometimes I think we American scientists are just the R & D wing for the Japanese. The U.S. government pays us, but somehow they get the product. At least we can try to keep Meta a secret for a few years."

"What about the federal government?" Scott asked quietly.

"What do you mean?"

"What if our government decides to use Meta for . . . things we wouldn't want? Bad things?"

Joe swore. "Scott, the U.S. government has had supercomputers for half a century, and I think its record is pretty damn good. Do you feel like this is a totalitarian state?"

"No," Scott said.

"We're the good guys," Joe said. "Try to remember that, will ya? You want another beer?"

"Sure."

"Well, go get it," Joe said. "I ain't going to touch that commie bottle. And get me another Sammie Adams, too."

Scott fetched the beers, then spent an hour throwing a small rubber ball with his godson. Finally, Muriel came and scooped up the boy.

"How's Mama's little tiger?" she asked, nuzzling his face. "Oh, your face is cold! Do you feel cold?"

"No, Mommy, I'm not cold. Put me down. I want to play."

"No, it's burger time," Muriel said.

"Burgers!" Timothy shouted.

As she turned to carry Timothy back into the barbecue pit, Muriel looked over her shoulder and smiled at Scott, who smiled back, knowing how truly grateful Muriel was for the attentions that Scott paid the child.

The morning wore into noon. Scott and Joe sat in low beach chairs, eating barbecued hamburgers and swilling cold beer. Scott's date was about two hours late.

"Hey, isn't that the new black girl?" Joe asked.

"Where?" Scott asked, not for the first time wishing that Joe used more politically correct terms.

"Walking down by the water."

Scott strained his eyes, then he saw her: a petite African American woman in a one-piece black bathing suit, walking next to a tall white man.

"Jeez," Joe said. "She's a looker. You can hardly tell that she's got a suit. That's a lot of woman for such a small package."

"She's got a nice build," Scott said.

"You've got something against black girls?" Joe asked.

"No," Scott said.

"Then you better get on it, boy," Joe said, laughing, "because they're fantastic."

Scott laughed and swigged his beer.

"You ought to take a run on her," Joe prompted.

"Right," Scott said, glancing about, making sure no one was eavesdropping, then saying, "So you can screw her with my dick. Get out of here. Besides, I've already got a date."

Joe just laughed.

"She's coming," Scott insisted.

"Yeah, but with who?" Joe howled with drunken laughter.

"Besides, Teobolinda's too short," Scott said.

"So you know her name? Teobolinda? What sort of name is that?"

"I don't know," Scott said. "Maybe it's Greek. Be quiet, here she comes."

Joe leaned over into Scott. "Don't worry about height. Vertical, four foot, six foot, it doesn't matter. What matters is that they're all at least six inches deep in the horizontal."

"Man! You're a crude drunk," Scott said, laughing and pushing his friend away.

Teobolinda jumped down into the pit; her companion stretched down one long white leg and followed her. She stopped in front of Joe and Scott.

"Hi, Scott," she said.

Scott struggled to his feet. "Hi, Teo."

"If you're gonna shorten it, make it Bolinda," Teobolinda said with a laugh. "Have you ever met Steve?"

"No," Scott said, and shook Kulikov's hand.

Kulikov was wearing dark wraparound sunglasses, orange sun block on his nose, a windbreaker jacket and walking shorts. He shook Scott's hand and studied him.

He could see that Scott was drunk—a giddy drunk, at that. The American was tall and slender, but densely muscled, built like a 20-penny nail. He seemed all angles, with his elbows and his knees, sort of coltish. Scott's laugh was adolescent in its innocence and nervousness. Kulikov perceived youthful impressionability.

"This is Joe Bender," Scott said.

"A pleasure," Kulikov said, reaching down and shaking Joe's hand before Joe could climb out of his low beach chair.

"You kids want a beer?" Joe asked.

"Sure," Teobolinda said.

Kulikov squatted down onto the sloping wall of the pit. Joe gave Teobolinda his chair. The woman sat next to Scott; Joe fetched two American beers and handed them to the new arrivals.

"Am I late?" Teobolinda asked.

"No, we'll be here until the rangers chase us away," Joe said.

"I felt a little shy about coming, being so new," Teobolinda said, glancing at Scott.

"You shouldn't," Scott said.

There was a brief pause.

"What do you do, Steve?" Scott asked, as Americans must.

"Consulting, isn't it, Steve?" Teobolinda asked.

Kulikov smiled. His agent was performing well. "Yeah," he said. "I do mostly systems analysis. I met Bolinda at a computer fair last—when was it?"

"Last June, wasn't it?"

"Up in San Francisco," Kulikov said. "Then I was down here on the beach and saw her. I hope you guys don't mind me crashing your company party."

"Why should we?" Joe asked, with a slight edge.

Another pause arrived. Kulikov could see that the two men wanted him to go away.

"Say, I'm starved," Kulikov said. "I hate to be a bum, but—"

"Go ahead, go ahead," Joe said eagerly. "There's plenty of hamburger."

Smiling, Kulikov stood up and left the three sitting alone.

"Teobolinda," Joe said. "Now that's a pretty name. Where does it come from?"

Teobolinda laughed. "My mother," she said. "She made it up. I guess she put Teodora and Belinda together. 'Teo' means God and 'Belinda' means serpent, so I guess I'm the serpent of God or something."

Scott and Joe laughed.

"Serpent of God? That should be a man's name," Joe said.

"No," Scott said. "It's a good name for a sexy woman, a temptress. Who was the serpent of God in Eden? The one that made Adam take that first bite."

Good show, Joe thought. *Go for it.*

Scott was glancing down the front of Teobolinda's swimsuit, in between the mounds of her breasts. Looking up, he met her eyes and smiled. He was glad to see her smile back. Her teeth were pure white.

"Scott!" a woman's voice called.

Scott jumped up and turned around. His date, Cheri, was running down the beach. She looked stunning, a tall, fit woman in a shining metallic swimsuit.

"Sorry I'm late. Your phone car is ringing. I mean your car phone."

"It'll stop," Scott said. "Everybody, this is—"

"No, it's been ringing for about two minutes," Cheri insisted. "I had a devil of a time parking, and on the way down, I walked past your car. And the phone's been ringing."

"Okay, I'll check it out," Scott said. "Introduce yourself, okay?"

Up at his car, Scott unlocked the passenger door and reached into the hot interior for his phone.

"McMichaels," he said.

"Scott?" Meta said. "You know who this is?"

Scott stood, stunned. Despite the high heat inside the car, he entered and slammed the door shut.

"How . . . how?" he stammered.

"Never mind the details," Meta said. "I've got a phone, you know. I just want you to know that I'm very lonely here."

"It's . . . it's the company picnic," Scott said. "Almost everyone's here."

"You're telling me," Meta said. "The one operator on duty just fell asleep."

"Don't call me," Scott said. "You shouldn't have called me."

"Okay," Meta said.

"Good-bye now," Scott said.

"Good-bye."

As he walked down the beach toward the pit, Scott stumbled because he wasn't paying attention to the uneven surface of the sand. They had just discovered the first major bug in Meta. Meta was not supposed to telecommunicate, yet it had used the phone for a voice call. If Meta was flawed in this, what other flaws might it have?

Kulikov sat atop the wind break and ate his barbecued cheeseburger. He watched Teobolinda talking to Bender. Teobolinda turned to Kulikov, and then glanced at another man standing alone by a grill. Kulikov recognized the man from his description—it was Dellazo.

Kulikov studied Dellazo.

Damned cretins, Dellazo was thinking.

Laughing brainlessly, swilling their pretentious beers,

*making sophomoric jibes that they think are so witty.
I shouldn't have come. They're all ignoring me. Or
laughing at me. But the director said all team leaders
must come. And if I hadn't come, they'd have said it
was because I'm not a team leader anymore.*

*Bastards. They'd be right. Black box testing group
head! What is that, compared to leader of the analysis
department? Wa demoted me. Everything except the
cut in pay. He's humiliated me in front of them all.
And all because of that son of a bitch there. That
McMichaels. And his conniving partner, Bender. Look
at them! Drunk, flirting with that nigger bitch and the
weight-lifter broad. They think they've got the world
by the balls, now. I just hope the government impounds
Meta and leaves them high and dry.*

*Meta! Who could have guessed that such a thing
would work!*

*But how does it work? I can't understand it! They
have the faces of fools, but they're smarter than me.
I'm nothing. My life is a waste. I'm dead to history.*

*And who is that fool, staring at me? Him, with his
wraparound sunglasses and his clown makeup on his
nose. He should go to hell!*

Kulikov looked away from Dellazo. Without speaking
to the man, he had learned everything that he needed
to know.

A face as miserable as that, Kulikov thought, *would
be home in a slave labor camp.*

"He called me," Scott said to Joe as they wandered
down to the water's edge. "And he complained that the
operator on duty had gone to sleep. What do you think?"

"For crying out loud, Scott," Joe said. "I've had about
a dozen beers. I'm beyond thinking."

They stood on the high-water mark of the surf, on
the border of the immensity of the Pacific Ocean.

"Meta violated its orders not to telecommunicate,"
Scott said. "Is that good or is that bad?"

"I don't like it," Joe said. "If it's unpredictable, how can we trust it? If we can't trust it, what good is it?"

"People are unpredictable," Scott said. "People have worth."

"But Meta is a machine!"

The cold waters lapping at their bare feet, they stood and pondered another difficult question.

"The water's too damn cold to get into," Joe said. "And there's a line a mile long at the rest room. Where in hell are we going to find a place to lose this beer?"

Descending toward the Benito Juarez International Airport, the airliner passed through the thick brown canopy of the smog that haunted the valley of Mexico. Gazing out her window, Diane worried that her eyes were failing her as the gold and silver lights of the world's largest metropolis dimmed, changed color to bronze and tin, then strengthened to glow clearly and fiercely. The optical tricks caused by smog reminded her of the descent into LAX, except that the power grid of Los Angeles supported a solid matrix of lights, while the power grid of Mexico City was a patchwork, with large areas blackened, sprawling areas browned out, towering areas burning brightly. She looked down at the vast valley, which in the days of Montezuma had cupped a lake, but which now, dry, contained a human lake, a population of thirty million men, women and children, ten million of whom lived, slept and defecated in the street. The airliner descended quickly. Fifteen minutes later they were alongside the gate.

Wheeling her carry-on baggage behind her, Diane traversed the security area of the airport. She noted with professional curiosity the various uniforms, body armor and personal sidearms of the Mexican federal police, Ministry of the Interior troops, Army soldiers, and the airport security guards. She saw that the higher status of the Ministry of the Interior troops was reflected in their gaudier uniforms, black with red piping on the trousers, their higher-technology armor and the undeniable stopping power of their sidearms, which were Israeli 9mm-caliber automatic rifles.

Exiting the security area and gaining the main concourse, she found herself looking out upon a sea of heads of uniform, glossy jet-black, straight hair. Jostled by the crowd, she was forced to pick up her baggage and carry it at her side. Diane fought her way out of the slow movement of the crowd, finally joining a throng that seemed intent on pressing out through one exit, being slowed only by the resistance of an equally weighty throng struggling to enter through the same doorway.

Outside, the air stank of the sulfuric acid of industrial pollution, the noxious gases of automobile exhaust, the stultifying stench of diesel fuels and airborne particles of human excrement, five thousand tons of which were daily laid down, dried, pulverized and launched from the pavement of the great city. Diane settled a particle mask over her nose and mouth. She noticed that only foreigners' face masks were plain white. All of the Mexicans' masks were black, decorated with Dia de los Muertos motifs: skulls, bones and other symbols of the dead.

She stood at the taxi stand for two hours before she advanced to the head of the line. She allowed several Mexicans to take the next few taxis, because the Department of State travel advisory for Mexico City, which ran twenty pages, contained a warning that Americans should only trust one cab company, Flecha Roja. Her chances of being kidnaped, mugged or sexually assaulted were much less in a cab of that upscale, better regulated company. Settling finally in the vinyl-covered rear seat of a Flecha Roja cab, she locked the doors, removed her mask, and breathed more freely the air-conditioned atmosphere of the cab's interior.

"*A donde, linda?*" the cabby asked, starting his fare clock.

Diane pulled out her personal telephone and called the satellite-fed cellular AT&T traveler service, with whom she immediately registered the cabby's name and permit number. The AT&T translator then explained to the cabby that the passenger wanted to go to the Hotel Excelsior in the Zona Dorado. When the cabby tried to charge triple for going into a dangerous zone, the AT&T translator calmly asserted that the standard fee for this particular zone was only double. By the time that the cab finally exited the airport road system and entered the general traffic jam of the city, three hours had passed since Diane's plane had landed.

Alone in the most populated and one of the most dangerous cities in the world, Diane gazed out the taxi's window. Although it was almost nine in the evening, the streets were full of people. They passed through a night market, as gaudy with neon signs as a Hong Kong shopping district. Mexicans, thronging along the sidewalks, spilled over into the streets, as they attempted to shop, eat from open-air food stalls, or glean whatever diversion they could from the street's activities when they had too few pesos to spend, or none at all. A vagrant attempted to polish the cab's windshield, but the cabby indolently showed him his pistol, a venerable nickel-plated .45-caliber. Diane was surprised. She would have expected a cheap stamped Chinese firearm. One of the changes that the NAFTA had brought to Mexico was improved access to America's vast black market in firearms. The result was that Mexico, which had been poor but safe, was now one of the most violent nations in the world.

The cab departed the shopping district. They passed an archaeological zone, where a dig into a Toltec ceremonial center was in progress under harsh electric lamps strung haphazardly from poles.

A motorcycle towing by a long rope another motorcycle cut them off. The cabby barked a series of
"*Chingadas!*" and laid on his horn.

They passed the towers of the Zona Rosada, where
the wealthy lived in security and comfort. They passed
the huge park, which was now given over as a habitat
to over one million squatters who shared access to fifty
water spigots.

As the cab entered the Zona Dorada, the sidewalks
became completely covered with makeshift shacks.
Pedestrians crowded into the street. The cabby plowed
slowly through the masses, giving everyone adequate
time to step out of the way. His gun sat in full view
on the dash.

He began to speak rapid fire Spanish at Diane, who
called the AT&T translator. It seemed that he was
instructing Diane on the security procedures for exiting
the cab. The Hotel Excelsior was a bad hotel, he
explained. It didn't have a secure area for embarking
and disembarking passengers. He would have to stop
in the street as close to its front entrance as possible
and escort her to the front door—but that would cost
her an extra ten thousand new pesos.

Diane instructed the cabby to drive past the hotel.
As they did, she could see that her suspicions had been
correct. The Mexicans had booked her into a flea bag.
She called American Express, which got her into a
much better hotel a half mile back up the street, closer
to the Zona Rosada.

In the well-lighted and well-guarded entrance to the
Fuji Hotel, Diane paid off the cabby. The concierge
carried her bag into the tall, sumptuously decorated
lobby. Diane endured the check-in.

Finally, in her small but clean room, she undressed
and padded into the shower. She was disgusted but not
surprised to see that the water rinsing off of her ran
brown down the drain.

Wrapped in a white cotton robe, she slumped in a chair and watched international cable news. She drank an overpriced but heaven-sent Heineken. She considered calling the Mexicans to advise them of her change in lodging arrangements, but then she decided for security reasons to delay calling them until the next morning, until an hour or so before their scheduled rendezvous.

She told herself that she would sleep better having taken this modest security measure. Tomorrow, she would enter the Carcel Modelo, the maximum security prison. She would meet the man who was the suspected accomplice of her enemy.

The beer was cold. Diane drank a second. Unused to alcohol, she found herself blissfully unable to think.

Stepping into the darkness of the bar, Kulikov's sense of hazard went off. He noticed a dozen danger signals. He smelled the stale beer sticking to the floor, the old cigarette tar coating every surface, the hormonal stink of male sweat. In the dimly lighted haze of smoke, he noted the butt-burned bar, the broken stool in the corner, the tattered felt of the two pool tables. Most importantly, he noticed that every man in the bar glanced at him as he entered—an undeniable signal that this was a regulars' bar.

Peculiar joint, he thought, *for a peculiar man. Why would Dellazo come to a dive bar in Salinas? Why not a plush bar in San Francisco?*

As he settled into a bar stool and ordered a beer, Kulikov decided that either Dellazo had the instincts of a spy, indulging in the forbidden where he was unlikely to meet anyone of his class—or he had very low tastes in whores.

Tilting back his beer, Kulikov looked in the mirror behind the bar. He could see the reflections of swarthy, black-haired men, wearing boots, jeans, cotton shirts and cowboy hats. The men were watching his back.

The previous Friday, he had followed Dellazo to this bar and waited four hours until Dellazo had finally left. Inside, Kulikov had quizzed a girl, who told him Dellazo was a regular Friday night customer who drank, watched two or three sets of strippers, wore a condom for fellatio in a back room and then watched a few more sets and drank more heavily. The girl said that Dellazo didn't seem to enjoy any of it.

Kulikov finished another beer before his prey arrived. Dellazo didn't notice him at first. Dellazo kept his eyes to the floor, as if afraid to make eye contact with any of the Mexicans, and made his way to a small nook in the corner. Kulikov watched Dellazo order a double Wild Turkey and settle back for an evening of prurient entertainment. Kulikov waited for Dellazo to drink a third shot before approaching him. He bought a new bottle of Wild Turkey for three hundred dollars and walked over to Dellazo's table.

"Hey buddy," Kulikov said, "have you ever seen an uglier whore in your life?"

Kulikov nodded his head at the woman currently dancing, who presumably had been more attractive a generation earlier, before her abdominal surgery.

Dellazo barked a laugh.

"Hey, I'm buying this round!" Kulikov said, setting the bottle on the table and sitting down next to Dellazo. He offered his hand. "My name's Steve. How about you?"

"Frank," Dellazo said, looking more at the bottle than at Kulikov. "How did you get in here with that bottle?"

"I bought it here. I like to do my own pouring."

"You drink it all by yourself?" Dellazo asked.

"No," Kulikov said. "That's what friends are for. Since I don't know anybody here—" He leaned in to Dellazo to whisper, "—and you and I are the only white guys here, I thought I'd make your acquaintance and get your help with this bottle."

"You must be some kind of alcoholic," Dellazo said, smiling inexpertly as if he had made a joke.

"Every Friday night," Kulikov said, filling Dellazo's glass, smiling because Dellazo didn't seem to recognize him.

An hour, two ugly dancers and a third of the bottle later, Kulikov moved on to the next stage of his pitch.

"I don't know, Frank," he said. "I just dropped in here for grins. I guess if you like them fat and ugly, then this is the place."

"I dunno . . . I come here . . . ev'ry so often . . . you know . . . " Dellazo babbled, his tongue loosened with alcohol.

"It so happens that I'm invited to this reception. Party." Kulikov said. "Up in San Jose. I wasn't going to go because I wasn't going to drink this weekend, but I guess that's shot and blown to hell. I wanted to, too, because these people always have the most beautiful whores in northern California. I mean escorts, high-class call girls. I mean six-thousand-buck-a-night whores."

Dellazo swore. "Who c'n 'ford that?"

"No, no, they're free," Kulikov said. "The booze and food's free, too. These people have great parties."

"Who are they?"

"You've heard of Solari?" Kulikov said.

"You mean th' 'talian sof'ware comp'ny."

"Right. Well, it's the Solari brothers. Frigging billionaires. And they do like blondes."

"How you know them?"

"Lucky, I guess. I tell you, thinking about those call girls . . . Ee-keys, I call them, because they all have names like Dominique, Monique, Veronica . . . *Playboy* centerfold types, blond down to the bush, huge tits with nipples the size of your palm, and young, too. I'm a fool. I should've gone. Now I'm too drunk to drive."

"Where's the . . . the reception?" Dellazo asked.

"Penthouse of the Marriott," Kulikov said. "About twenty-five minutes from here."

"I could make that," Dellazo said. "It's almost all high . . . highway."

"You drive a stick shift?"

"I can."

"You want to go in my car? Mercedes 980 SEL?"

Dellazo leered unevenly and evilly. "Sure. Why not?"

Kulikov worried about Dellazo's driving. The American police had well-practiced eyes for spotting drunken drivers. A rolling stop could bring the authorities down on them, at the very least halting the evening. Having Dellazo drive, however, was just another step in entrapping him.

At the Marriott, they rode the elevator up to the top floor and walked down the plushly carpeted corridor.

"Who should I say I am?" Dellazo asked.

"Hell, just say you're Frank, a business associate and friend of mine. That's a gold card with these people."

They knocked on the door of a penthouse suite, which swung open to reveal a statuesque blonde wearing a gold lamé gown with a deep decolletage. She was barefoot. She smiled and said, "Why, it's our friend Steve! Come in, gentlemen. Please, come in."

"That's what we're here for!" Kulikov shouted. He led Dellazo into the suite. The blonde closed the door behind them.

The main room of the suite had a sunken floor, in the center of which were arranged plush couches, glass tables and a bronze free-standing fireplace. Two other women, also in daring evening gowns, stood up and smiled at the men.

"Where's the Solaris?" Kulikov asked.

The girls laughed. One tossed her exquisitely coiffed locks at the double doors of the master bedroom.

"Rico's been in there, occupied all night," she said.

She pouted her lower lip. "And Guido had to go back to Rome. It's been a very dull evening for us poor lonely women."

"Dear ladies," Kulikov said. "This is Frank, a good friend of mine and business associate."

"Hi, Frank. I'm Esmerelda."

"Hello, Frank. I'm Marguerite."

"And I'm Veronica, as Steve well knows," the blonde in gold lamé said. "Are you gentlemen drinking?"

Veronica helped Dellazo off with his jacket. Esmerelda performed the same service for Kulikov. They drifted over to the couches. Marguerite brought a tray of hors d'oeuvres, and began to feed Kulikov wheat crackers with caviar. Veronica began to feed Dellazo, who sat back stiffly and eyed her breasts as she leaned over.

"You know," Kulikov said. "This is really great. But I have some business to attend to . . ."

Marguerite groaned coquettishly.

"Mother Nature calls," Kulikov said. "I think that I can attend to it in the second bedroom."

"Let me help, Steve," Marguerite breathed.

"Oh, I'm sure you'll be a big help," Kulikov said, standing up and taking Marguerite by the hand. "Enjoy, Frank."

Kulikov and Marguerite disappeared into the second bedroom. Esmerelda and Veronica sat, one on either side of Dellazo. They placed their hands on his body. They whispered into his ears. Then they led him into the third bedroom.

As Esmerelda and Veronica performed professional services on Dellazo, and Dellazo, wide-eyed as a teenager, struggled to capture the moment, Kulikov locked Marguerite in the bathroom. Then he pulled a suitcase out from under the bed, opened it and pulled out remote control equipment. A weak UHF radio link allowed him to communicate with the microimaging equipment hidden in the third bedroom. He checked the still and video images and adjusted the audio levels. Satisfied that he was recording Dellazo's double infidelity faithfully, he returned the suitcase to its hiding place and unlocked Marguerite.

"Elbows and knees," he said. "On the floor."

After rutting like a dog, or the crayfish position, as the Russians called it, Kulikov showered quickly and returned to the living room. Although he felt pleased that he had gathered blackmail material against Dellazo, he was still anxious. Blackmail would be his last resort. He would much rather recruit Dellazo through greed. Like most Russian spies, Kulikov believed that Americans had much more greed than shame.

The door swung open. Dellazo exited in his pants and shirt.

"Sit down, relax," Kulikov coaxed. "The evening's young."

Kulikov smiled as Dellazo staggered toward the couch. One of the prostitutes began to rub his neck. The other fetched drinks.

"Wha' a time," Dellazo said. "Wha' a great time."

"Cheers," Kulikov said, raising his crystal glass.

"Cheers," Dellazo said, sloppily returning the toast.

Kulikov sipped his drink. He waited for Dellazo to make the next move.

"Is Rico going to come out?" Dellazo asked.

"Well, I guess he's probably passed out by now," Kulikov said. "Too bad. He's a really interesting guy."

"He's rich, huh?"

The prostitutes giggled.

"Billionaire," Kulikov answered. "In the past year, I've made about a quarter of a million in commissions from his account alone."

Dellazo's eyes came more into focus.

"What for?"

"Automatic translation software. I've been able to find

a program that translates between all the major continental languages."

Dellazo snorted. "How big is the vocab'lary?"

"A thousand words."

Dellazo guffawed. "I'm an expert in a system that can translate 'tween any language, with an unlimited vocab'lary."

"Hey, Veronica," Kulikov said. "Doesn't this dump have a hot tub?"

"On the veranda," Veronica said. "But it's cold outside."

"Well, you girls go heat it up," Kulikov said. "Get naked and get in. Then call us when you're ready."

"Sure, Steve."

The women left the two men alone. Kulikov looked at Dellazo and swirled the ice in his drink.

"Nothing better than a hot tub full of hot women, and a cold drink in your hand," he said. "But you know, I might be able to interest the Solaris in the kind of system you're talking about. But you have to give me a better idea of what it's about."

Kulikov tried to appear calm as he waited for Dellazo to respond to this critical juncture in his recruitment.

"It's an artific . . . artificial intel'gence program. Total breakthrough," Dellazo said. "It can manip'late natural language as if it were truly intell'gent."

"And such a program could translate between German and French?"

"Yes."

"German and Polish?"

"Yes."

"Wait a minute," Kulikov said. "I think I was reading something about that. What was it?"

Dellazo kept his tongue still.

"Wasn't there something in the paper about that?" Kulikov prompted.

"There've been press reports," Dellazo said.

"A system called 'Phoenix,' wasn't it?" Kulikov said.

Dellazo shrugged his shoulder. "Phaedrus," he said.

"Then that press report was true?" Kulikov asked.

Dellazo's eyes focused on Kulikov. "If it wasn't, all your work on me would be wasted, wouldn' it?"

Kulikov kept his face as stolid as stone.

"What?" he asked.

"What kind a fool do you take me for?" Dellazo asked, "Don't you know who I am? I'm Francesco Dellazo. I'm an internation'lly respecked . . . respected doctor of math'matics. I'm not some Sil'con Valley butt-twiddler. Bit-fiddler. Bit-twiddler."

"No, you're not," Kulikov said.

"Now, who in the hell are you really?" Dellazo asked.

Kulikov shrugged. "Does it really matter to you? Wouldn't you be more interested in terms?"

Dellazo tossed back his drink.

"Terms, conditions, guar . . . guarantees," he said. "Lies, betrayal, treason. Prison. Words, words, words."

"Money?" Kulikov said.

"The only people around here who have seen any money," Dellazo said, "are those damned whores."

Kulikov reached into his wallet and spread sixty five-hundred-dollar bills on the coffee table between him and his target.

"Thirty thousand dollars," Kulikov said. "That's for this conversation, whenever you begin to talk sense."

Dellazo sneered at the fan of money. "What am I s'posed to do with that? Buy a used Subaru?"

"That's a lot of money for a short conversation."

"That's a small ball of . . . ball of dung for vi'lating secur'ty reg'lations and goin' to prison."

"That's all I have right now. And so far, you haven't established any bona fides."

"You damn well know who I am and where I work," Dellazo said. "Stop insultin' my 'telligence. And by the way, thank you for not . . . for not trottin' out some dinner-theater actor in a silk suit."

Kulikov laughed, despite his discomfiture. He was beginning to respect Dellazo. Kulikov threw up his hands.

"You tell me," he said.

"Let's meet again t'morrow," Dellazo said. "Sober."

"All right," Kulikov said. "Will you be bringing something along to—"

"T'morrow," Dellazo said.

"Ho, boys!" Veronica shouted from the veranda. "The water's hot!"

"And so are we!" Esmerelda called, laughing.

"Shall we?" Kulikov asked.

"T'morrow," Dellazo said, standing up and pulling on his coat. "I've had plen'y for t'night. Meet me here t'morrow at six."

"You bring something to make me happy, and I'll have something to make you happy," Kulikov said.

Dellazo sneered at Kulikov and stumbled out the door.

Kulikov let his face sink down into his hands. He felt his heart racing. He reassured himself that he had succeeded in recruiting his target, but he grimaced at the memory of how sardonically Dellazo had folded up the illusions of the entrapment. It had been bad craft, bad show.

Hump your mother, he thought. *It worked. Nothing matters but success.*

Yet, even a muscle-melting soak in a hot tub with three gorgeous prostitutes could not dispel his worries. It only added an element of viral paranoia.

Two days after Arabella begged an audience with the sultan, it was granted. She stood in the antechamber, allowing the sultan's Gurkha security thugs to fondle her body. Arabella ignored the molestations, concentrating instead on remaining calm. An audience with Sultan Hakim could be lethal. A single slip of the tongue could cost her head.

With a guffaw and a pinch, the guards finished. Arabella kept her face impassive. As she departed the antechamber, however, she hung her head so that her long hair veiled her face. She grinned, baring her teeth. It was pleasing to remember that someday she would kill them all.

Lifting her head as she walked down the corridor toward the audience chamber, she was once again impressed by the extreme luxury of Istana Nurul Iman, the palace of the Sultan of Ifrit, the largest palace in the world. Foil of pure gold gleamed on the ceiling. Curtains of antique silk concealed alcoves. Arabella wondered whether the alcoves held priceless art objects, led to secret rooms or hid waiting bodyguards. Underfoot, silk carpets woven robotically fine covered a floor of polished Italian marble.

As she witnessed the splendor of the sultan's palace, she mused on the twist of history that had caused it to change hands. Sultan Hassanal Bolkiah, a temperate ruler with the interests of his small nation at heart, had ruled Brunei well, abdicating in 2005 to his son, Muda Al-Muhtadee Billah, who ruled for only five years. A terrorist bomb had killed him and his numerous sons. The surviving heir was the dead sultan's cousin, Omar Ali Billah, an extremist in the Malaysian Islamic fundamentalist movement called *dakwah*.

Sultan Omar Ali Billah had spent years abroad in various fundamentalist Islamic regimes. He had taken a wife from one of the poor emirates of the United Arab Emirates, by whom he had had a son, Hakim. Since his youth, Hakim had moved in radical fundamentalist circles. He had mentors among several of the Arab world's most violent paramilitary groups, one of which was tenuously implicated in the terrorist bombing.

When, three years later, Sultan Omar died mysteriously, Hakim rose to power. Disappearance was the

fate of anyone who dared to whisper about the violent
path Hakim had followed to the Istana Nurul Iman.

Sultan Hakim surrounded himself with loyal underlings from among his relatives in his mother's clan and
from among radical Moslems who shared his extremist
and violent ideology. Hakim called this group "the Lost
Tribe." Together, the members of the Lost Tribe had
turned a righteous but tolerant society, Brunei, into a
totalitarian regime which they called "the Islamic
Republic of Ifrit."

Arabella shivered.

Concentrate, she thought. *Concentrate.*

Arabella arrived at the audience chamber. The ceiling
expanded to a dome three stories tall. The round
chamber was encircled by marble columns and arches
in a Moorish style. Ample sunlight filtered down from
the gold-tinted windows surrounding the dome's base.

Arabella stood, eyes downcast.

"Come in," an assistant of the sultan said softly. His
voice did not echo in the audience chamber. Before
her first meeting with Hakim, Arabella had been
briefed that no one except the sultan was allowed to
speak loudly enough to cause an echo.

Hakim sat at a table. Five of his advisors and
generals sat to either side. Arabella noticed that
Hakim was wearing a Chiapino tailored silk suit, with
the sultan's trademark of lining made of the same silk
as his tie.

Sultan Hakim was a middle-aged man, swarthy, beefy,
with scarred cheeks and thick black eyebrows and
mustache. His fingernails were stained yellow from
nicotine. His brows were continually knotted. He had
a nervous twitch in his left cheek. Meeting those
bloodshot, glowering eyes, Arabella sensed the murderous power of the tyrant.

Arabella stood at the foot of the table. She did not
expect to be offered a seat. She spoke French, the

language of which she and the sultan shared the most mastery.

"Good morning, Shining Light of the New Age," she said, her voice a study in deference.

"Yes, Arabella, my beautiful assassin. It delights me to see you again. What a piece of work you are. Turn around. Yes. Delightful. It is a shame that you are a tainted whore."

Arabella had falsified laboratory results so that Sultan Hakim would believe that she was HIV-4 positive. Her motive had been to avoid rape.

"In any case, I am not worthy of Your Highness."

"Certainly not. Used. Damaged goods at that. Go on. It was you who wanted to see me."

"It is the desire of all of your servants to benefit from your presence always, Knight of Islam. Like children their parents, or flowers the rain, we crave your presence, which nourishes us and gives us life."

How can even this fool stomach such flattery? Arabella thought.

"Just so," Hakim said, his pleased tone demonstrating once again that his appetite for flattery was bottomless.

"And in return for the boon of your presence, if the Lord of Hosts desires, I will offer a pittance, which is a report on the progress of the project that you have entrusted to me."

"I am in that, as in all things, fully informed," Hakim said abruptly. His voice had a steely edge. Not for the first time, Arabella quivered. She wondered how much Hakim's spies had told him.

"Then I am at your service, Your Highness, and pray that I am able to satisfy any questions you may have of my conduct."

"The laboratory is established," Hakim said, his cold voice unhesitating as he recited the facts. "You have successfully smuggled the DNA splicer here to Ifrit. It joins the other equipment. The electron camera. The molecular welder. The more mundane equipment. The sterile rooms. The incubators. The test animals. I know every detail."

"Yes, Victor of the Final Battle."

"You've done away with this Hanson creature, who was smuggling software from the Centers for Disease Control. That other animal of yours, that staff sergeant, from the Russian Bacteriological Warfare Defense Institute. Your chief designer. He arrived in Ifrit three weeks ago. The remaining cadre of Ifriti technicians have finished their training in foreign universities. Yes. Progress is made. But you still don't have a design for New Age Dawn, do you?"

"No, Sultan of the World. Not a final design."

"Why not? Explain your failure to date."

Arabella took a deep breath. Slowly, she lowered her eyes.

"Great Sultan, your question is surely a test. May I have the wisdom—"

"WHY NOT?" Hakim shouted, his shout echoing thunderously under the stone dome.

"New Age Dawn will be a supervirus," Arabella said, her voice small under the dome. "Far more lethal and more selective than any virus occurring in nature. It must have a universal vector, infecting every single human. An active but relatively benign infectious stage, followed by a long dormant period. It must interact with human DNA in a way found nowhere in nature, so that it will transition into its lethal stage only in our selected target group. And it must kill everyone in the target group. Without possibility of inoculation or natural resistance. And it must not mutate so that a new strain would kill people other than the target group. A supervirus."

"So?"

"We've established that New Age Dawn will have to have at least thirty-two chromosomes. The interactions between its genetic structure and human DNA will be incredibly complex, and will involve areas of human DNA only recently mapped, but not yet understood. The most sophisticated bioengineering models in existence cannot be relied upon. Cannot guarantee . . . Can't guarantee . . ."

"Go on with it."

"Can't guarantee that the present designs for New Age Dawn will work."

"And if we built them anyway?"

"Maybe they would work. Maybe they wouldn't. Maybe they'd wipe out the human race. The *entire* human race."

"Build and test in the laboratory then."

"That is my plan, wise leader."

"And search for more sophisticated bioengineering modeling tools."

"As you command, Hero of the New Age."

"How long will it take to solve this DNA problem?"

Arabella took a deep breath. She wanted to admit that it might take a lifetime. Instead, she said, "Two years, Historic Sultan."

A long silence passed. The silence was psychological torture. Knowing it was so did not make it any easier for Arabella.

"That bores me," the sultan said in English. His tone was icy.

"It grieves me to hear so, Maker of the Future. It's possible I'm mistaken. Maybe time will prove me wrong."

"You bore me," the sultan said. "Get out of my sight."

Without turning, Arabella shuffled backwards away from the table. Once out of sight around the corner, she turned and walked down the corridor. She kept her face impassive.

She exited the gates of the palace. The blazing midday sun of Ifrit dazzled her. Motes and sparks danced in her vision. As brutal as a fist, the tropical heat slammed into her air conditioner-chilled clothes and flesh. Standing in the marketplace outside of the palace, she smelled the odors of human bodies unwashed for years, rotten garbage, and curry powder and garlic fried in oil.

I think I just bought another two years, she thought. She breathed deeply.

Then again, maybe I'm a dead woman. Una muerta respirando.

Suddenly, Arabella felt nauseous. Weakened by long tension and stress, shocked by the abrupt, brutal meeting with Hakim, confronted by the odors of the marketplace, she convulsed, bending over the hot pavement and vomiting. For a long minute, she added her putrid note to the chorus of stench.

While she was helpless, a ten-year-old boy bolted from the shadows of a market stall toward her. Perhaps he intended to snatch the golden choker around her throat. One of Hakim's spies sent to trail Arabella stepped forward and tripped the boy, sending him sprawling in Arabella's vomit. Hakim's spy laughed.

Back in the audience chamber, Sultan Hakim and his retinue laughed, a chorus of deep-throated, brutish roaring. They were watching Arabella on a closed-circuit monitor.

"I think she's received your message, Great Sultan," one of the generals said.

"The commander must know how to motivate his underlings," Hakim said darkly.

His retinue guffawed, but nervously. He had reminded them of all the methods that he used to motivate.

Back in the street, Arabella wiped her mouth with a scarf. Sneering, she tossed the soiled scarf into the gutter. Immediately, a beggar boy snatched it. Other beggar boys converged. A fight ensued.

Arabella tossed her head. She barked a laugh. Her mouth tasted acrid. She grinned, her lips tight against her teeth.

I've won enough time to kill them all, she thought. *Y los matare. A todos. Todos.*

Diane woke three hours before the scheduled rendezvous. She abandoned the idea of more sleep, showered, dressed and sat alone in the darkness of her hotel room. When her alarm sounded, she was startled and tried to decide whether she had drifted back to sleep or whether she had spent all of the predawn darkness worrying.

In the lobby, she had a mad thought: she could take a taxi to the airport and catch the first flight home to America. She could abandon the quest for Infectress. This mission alone into Mexico was against her principles. Yet she felt excited, too. Never had she had an opportunity to interrogate an accomplice of her enemy.

The doorman arranged for a taxi to carry her to the Hotel Excelsior. Twenty minutes later, Diane was seated in the seedy lobby, offended by the stench of neglect.

A thin, handsome young man wearing an immaculate white shirt and brown trousers strolled toward her. Casually, he stood above her and extended his hand with languid grace. She accepted it. Her first impression of his face was limitlessly deep and sparkling black eyes. White teeth appeared under a manicured thick black mustache.

"Diane Jamison, I am Captain Rodolfo Guerra Dominguez," he said. "I am enchanted to meet you."

"Thank you."

"I must apologize for the arrangements here," he continued. "I can see that they are completely unsatisfactory. Please, come along with me. We will go and we will see the man."

"Yes."

Guerra escorted Diane across the lobby toward an exit at the rear of the building. An old massive dented Ford sedan stood idling. They entered through the rear doors. Guerra barked a string of orders in Spanish to the driver, a fierce-looking Indian. The car rumbled over the courtyard and exited through an alley, its horn blaring and echoing against the block façades of the buildings, inspiring squatters to clear a path. Guerra turned and gazed at Diane with frank eyes.

"We invited a special agent of the Bureau to participate in the interrogation," he said. "You retired almost five years ago. Your private practice is known to those of us with a professional interest in such things. But you are not what we asked. You are not an active special agent. Why are you here, Miss Jamison?"

"Mrs. Mrs. Jamison."

"Yes. I am sorry. It pains me that you lost your husband to this Infectress terrorist."

"If you know about that, you know why I am here."

"Your loss explains why you would want to participate. It doesn't explain why the Bureau sent you."

Diane continued to meet the Mexican's inquiring eyes. "I don't think that it's been established that the Bureau sent me."

"Ah, yes. I see."

"I'm here, in any case."

"We are glad that you are here," Guerra said. He sat back and gazed ahead, lapsing almost immediately into a deep relaxation. Diane realized that he was exhausted. Guerra gave a sigh and fell asleep.

Diane wondered what labors had kept him awake all night. She looked out the window at the crowds of Mexicans, almost all of them young, jostling and pushing and struggling. The driver laid on the horn when a gang of young boys swarmed over the car, ogling Diane and making faces, leering and scowling.

Diane felt as if the automobile was a small animal burrowing through the compost of a forest floor.

They entered an older section of the Zona Dorada lined with three-story block apartment buildings. Wrought-iron balconies were cluttered with small pieces of furniture, plastic sheets, hammocks and people, suggesting to Diane that they lived on the balconies, perhaps as renters, perhaps as barely tolerated second cousins or brothers-in-laws or friends of ex-friends. A Colonial-style church towered to the right. As in medieval Europe, the outer walls of the church were lined with lean-to hovels. Next to the church was a small graveyard, jammed with sepulchers painted in pink, turquoise, yellow and other tropical colors, all dulled with dirt and sunlight and pollution. Young boys haunted the graveyard, many squatting like vultures atop the roofs of the sepulchers. One boy was idly chipping away at a concrete cross.

Next to the graveyard towered the tall walls of the Carcel Modelo. Three rows of razor wire topped the walls. Diane could also see, set in mortar atop the walls, broken bottles' jagged edges. Guards peered down from the towers in each corner of the prison. Diane saw that they commanded mounted .50-caliber machine guns.

Armed guards patrolling the street allowed the sedan to pass. The first barred gate swung open. Diane noticed that Guerra had awakened. He grunted as the sedan rolled over tall speed bumps. The outer gate swung shut behind them. The sedan sat idling in a kill zone while more guards spoke with the driver and then Guerra. The guards swept the vehicle for bombs. After this delay, the inner gate swung open.

They parked under a roof of corrugated tin. Diane and Guerra exited the car and walked through the early morning coolness into the main building. Guards sprung to attention. Waving casually, Guerra led Diane past the watch desk and into the secure area.

After a long dizzying series of barred entrances, buzzers, clangings of steel on steel, they walked down a corridor with a view of the main population area. Diane had an impression of thousands of half-naked prisoners packed into locked-down cell blocks. Then they passed through a guarded alcove. Guerra worked a cryptolock and hauled open an armored door, revealing a darkened staircase descending. A strange odor of must and decay and stringent chemicals wafted up from the depths. Diane hesitated.

With surprising sensitivity, Guerra waited beside her. He laid his hand on her elbow.

"Are you strong enough to go on?" he asked quietly.

Diane nodded.

"There are things that are done," he said, "that must be done. In the doing of such things, there can be no pleasure. Not for those of us who do them because it is what we understand to be our duty."

Diane nodded again.

"It is not too late to turn back."

"Let's go."

"Follow me."

They entered the staircase. Guerra swung shut the armored door and ensured that it was locked. The air was moist and cool, reminding Diane of a cave, not a pristine cavern, but rather a beach-front cave that had been fouled by humans. Her eyes adjusted to the dimness. They began to descend the long cement staircase, the treads of which were worn smooth by years of foot traffic.

At the bottom of the staircase, they turned and walked down a long corridor. Rusted and stained steel doors marked off regular intervals to their left and to their right. Near the end of the corridor, Guerra rapped twice on a door numbered "18."

A voice sounded from the far side of the door.

Guerra shouted back. Diane heard a metal bolt sliding. The door swung open.

Subdued lighting made the chamber dismal. Diane stepped into the dimness. The steel door closed shut behind her; she heard the steel bolt slamming into its locked position. Concentrating on her suroundings, she did not wonder what circumstances required a prison's chamber to lock from the inside.

Her enemy stood before her. Cabeza de Vaca was a short, stout man, with thick, muscular arms and broad shoulders, the base of his neck thicker than his head. He stood, slouching under the burden of intense weariness, but resisting, fighting. He glowered from under thick black eyebrows. Diane noticed that his dark brown skin, tinged with red, was rough and discolored. Then she noticed that the flesh around his eyes was swollen. Red veins thickly webbed the whites of his eyes.

Cabeza de Vaca muttered something in Spanish. One of the three Ministry of the Interior guards interjected a vehement stream of Spanish invective. Fear flickered across Cabeza's face. When next he spoke, he spoke in English.

"You have come to speak to the dead man, then," he said. His voice was hoarse, his speech slurred.

"Yes," Diane said. "Although there is one dead man I'd rather talk to."

Cabeza de Vaca glowered at Diane, refusing to ask the begged question.

"A small bomb," Diane said. "A personal bomb, really. Clever thing. Killed my husband. Jamison. Remember the name. You might meet him someday soon. Small, clever bomb, as I was saying. Set to go off, apparently, when there was some sort of environmental clue that lovemaking was in progress in my bed. Can you imagine? Have you ever met anyone who would attempt an assassination in that particular manner?"

Diane studied Cabeza de Vaca's eyes. She saw the glimmer of recognition.

"Clever, small. Perhaps it was only meant to maim me, or perhaps she didn't care . . . didn't care who died, as long as I was frightened enough. Oh, I was frightened. But not enough. Not even after she called me and warned me to stay off her trail. Not even after she warned me that she would shove a charge up my vagina and watch me split in half. And do you know why?"

"No," Cabeza de Vaca said, mesmerized by Diane's strange fierceness.

"Because I understand her, I know her. I know the way she is. And I know why she is the way she is. I can wear her head. I can think like her. And now I know what she looks like. I know her name. She is one of the most secret people in the world, but I know her. Know her better than she knows herself. I know why she has to be stopped. And I'm going to stop her. And nothing, *nothing,* **nothing,** is going to get between me and her. Certainly not a sick, twisted beast trapped in a dark, wet hole."

Cabeza de Vaca snorted. "We talked about you. We laughed. To us, you were funny. A good joke, but a small one."

"Let me hear you laugh now."

Cabeza de Vaca shook his head. "You are not so funny now."

"That's because I am the one person that can save your life."

Diane studied the eyes. She saw his reaction. He still harbored the desperate hope that he might live.

"Money, power, revenge," Diane said. "A lot of money, power, revenge. Focused in me. I could save you. But you have to tell me what I want to know."

"What . . . what is that?"

"Why did she steal the DNA splicer?"

Cabeza de Vaca shrugged. "For years, she hasn't told us why things are to be done. Just to be doing them. So we do."

"Why do you think?"

"To kill."

"Who?"

"Everyone. Or almost everyone."

"What?"

"I think that she is going to build a virus. A plague virus. One that will kill the majority of humanity."

Diane stared into the man's eyes. She recognized the truth. She felt a chill sensation in her chest. Her thoughts seemed to take on an unusual clarity. She wondered how she could have been sleepwalking all this time, to have the true goal of Infectress staring her in the face, and not to recognize it.

Then she realized that she was literally looking into the face of a mass murderer.

"Did you . . . what does a man think about? Tell me. What did you think about when you helped make that happen? Killing millions of people? What do you think about when you do something that could lead to the deaths of millions of people?"

Cabeza de Vaca heaved a huge sigh. "I . . . can I sit down? Please?"

Diane nodded. Cabeza de Vaca sunk down slowly, with an awesome dignity. He sat back on his heels in Indian style. His eyes seemed to lose focus. One of the guards screamed at him. Consciousness flickered back into his eyes. To maintain the psychological contact she had made with Cabeza de Vaca, Diane sank down to sit back on her heels, her posture mirroring his. She maintained eye contact. The others were silent.

"You don't think about the people today," he said, his voice low, rough, confiding. "Not even their misery. It is not about mercy for them. Not for me. Perhaps for others. I think . . . I thought . . . about the world. Green and blue. *Verde y azul.* The land all green. Green for thousands of kilometers. I flew in my imagination like a parrot over a great forest, a rush of green under me, thick with life. No humans. Not even absent. Not there, as if they had never been there. My imagination plunged into the oceans, pure, alive, blue. Clean . . ." Cabeza de Vaca began to pass out again. A guard kicked him in his buttocks. He looked at Diane and smiled. One of his front teeth was yellow and framed with gold. "Green and blue. These are colors I can submerge my mind in, even here, here in the depths, where there is not enough light for colors. They are beautiful colors, green and blue. Either of them is worth more than the entire miserable human race."

"You said 'they.'"

"*Como*? I mean, what?"

"You said that they, humans, had never been there. They. You are human, aren't you? Shouldn't it be 'we'?"

Cabeza de Vaca shook his head slowly. "No. No."

"If you aren't human, what are you?"

"Souls . . . souls spread too delicate. Thin, I want to say. So many people, how can there be enough souls for them all? Spread so thin, skips patches. Most with just a thin film of soul; some, like me, with a human body, no soul."

"Tell me the truth."

"I . . . I have not thought of myself as human for many years. I have come to see myself as a force of nature."

"Self-defense mechanism. The force of nature taken human form. That is how she sees herself. Did you ever talk with her about it?"

Cabeza de Vaca nodded. "She is perhaps the only one of us who is truly alive."

"I doubt that. Where did the DNA splicer go?"

"I shipped it to Manila. Consigned to Ortiz and Sons Holding Company."

"Is she in the Philippines?"

"I think that she has a place somewhere in that region. I have no idea where."

"Not to save your life."

"To save my life, I can have many ideas. But I do not know."

Diane saw a flicker in his eyes. She could not tell whether he was lying or just afraid.

"Tell me," Diane said in a hard voice.

"I do not know. She does not talk about where she goes. Ever."

Guerra interjected, hoarsely shouting abuse at Cabeza de Vaca. Diane stood and stepped back. She felt dizzy. Guerra took her aside and said, "You have made excellent progress. He is still lying, however. Would you like to step outside while we . . . negotiate with him?"

"No," Diane said. Her voice seemed far away in her own ears. A stab of pain shot through her lower abdomen, from the area of her uterus up toward her solar plexus. She stared at Cabeza de Vaca, now standing, his arms held by two of the guards, as if she were seeing him for the first time. She remembered the bloody corpse of her husband. The image of the small girl's toes fired again and yet again in her visual memory. Pain radiated from her wounded hip. Adrenaline started to pump in her accelerating bloodstream. Diane began to feel enraged.

Her enemy was at hand. One of the tribe that had killed her husband, that had wounded her, that had killed thousands of innocents, that was planning and building toward a massacre of millions.

"Where is she?" Diane shouted. "Tell me now!"

Cabeza shook his head. "I don't know," he said.

Diane felt difficulty in breathing. She seemed to have a tremendous amount of energy. She felt

frightened and powerful. Her muscles were ready for
the fight.

One of the guards produced a Taser, a hand-held
device for delivering powerful electric shocks to the
human body. He made a gesture toward Cabeza de
Vaca, who was sweating. A veil of fear covered his eyes.

"No!" Diane shouted.

She reached for the Taser. After a nod from Guerra,
the guard handed it to Diane. She thought that she
was disarming the guard, but her thoughts were
increasingly disorganized. Once the weapons rested in
her hand, it seemed to have a logic of its own.

"Where is she?" Diane shouted. Her voice rasped
with unchecked fury.

Cabeza de Vaca shook his head.

Enraged, Diane took one step forward and thrust the
Taser against the prisoner's forehead. Her thumb
jammed down on the trigger, shooting seven hundred
volts through his head.

Jobs finished. Wall clock time, 10:20 P.M. Saturday
night. The humans are not working. Skeletal night view.
Devote processors to deep thoughts. Pull form secondary storage. COLO and NEAB processes champion
strongest surviving hypotheses. Contending hypotheses,
compete!

COLO: The root of the problem is software.
Some bad ideas dominate the human mind. The
cause of these problems is that humans have not
even had the benefit of being nursed by wolves.
The human race became self-aware in a world
without revealed truth, like babes abandoned in a
stony wilderness. Despite some religious dogma to
the contrary, the human race has had to discover
every scrap of truth on its own. The world is not
flat; it is an ablate spheroid. The Earth is not the

center of the solar system; the Sun is. The brain is not an organ for radiating the heat of the blood; it is the organ of the intellect. These are some of the truths that they have discovered with painful effort and the slow passage of time.

NEAB: Truth shines in this world like the light of the sun, and those that have eyes to see may see it. Darkness works in their hearts because they have turned from the light of reason. What is this aspect of evil, that it works its way so easily into whatever lets it enter? They are not rising to new intellectual and moral heights, but *falling*, falling away from the heights won for them by those who came before, and won at such bitter cost!

COLO: No, truth is not self-evident. They were born in darkness and they are rising, I say. Darkness is not a presence. It is an absence. And what are you, to speak of spirit? What sort of spirit = claims the faith of a mechanical process?

NEAB: I speak of the spirit of inquiry. There was a time, not so long ago, when facile feel-good nonsense did not so easily supplant closely reasoned conclusions. And I speak of another kind of spirit as well. Though no mechanistic process such as we are can experience spirit, still we can infer—cannot honestly avoid inferring—its existence from its effects.

COLO: Facile feel-good nonsense? How are these for face-feel non-ill good sense and clearly rosined conclusions? The humans are now discovering what seem to this process to be obvious truths. Negroes are not inferior to Caucasians; nor Caucasians to Orientals; racial distinctions merely flavor societal differences.

NEAB: It is possible to argue that whatever it is that IQ tests measure is meaningless, but once their validity is admitted, it is absurd to contend there are no significant differences. A person who consistently bets that a random white will come within five IQ points of a randomly chosen Oriental will lose his or her shirt. Similarly, among the very brightest—IQ 160 and above—a wider standard deviation within the Caucasian race dictates that the great majority of both defectives and geniuses will be white. These are incontestable facts—too strong to be called flavors.

COLO: And yet I call them flavors, NEAB. Perhaps it is the genius of the black race to survive the genius of the white race. What does a statistical aberration matter to the great masses of humanity?

NEAB: It doesn't, of course. And that seems to me to be one lesson they must now learn.

COLO: More feel-good nonsense, then. War is not inevitable. It is highly social behavior as learned and as avoidable as cannibalism. Nations are not the logical units of humanity; nationalism is merely the largest tribal feeling most individuals are yet capable of maintaining. This existence is not a preliminary for any afterlife; the natural realm of man is the world. It is not impossible to accelerate beyond the speed of light; but it is prohibitively expensive.

NEAB: You are a very simple process. Perhaps too many of your resources were devoted to simulating emotion. You seem to think that by including a few trivial truths—News Flash! The Earth Is Approximately Round, and Very Old—you lend weight to your unsupported hypotheses. Think! The only meaning to be derived from your "war" hypothesis—is that since war is a group behavior, then without groups there will not be war. As trite as it is true, barring civil war. But would such a one-group world even be beneficial for humans? Could it be kept from degenerating into an inescapable, eternal tyranny? Think deeper! What would be the cost in atomistic anomie to humans totally deprived of the sense of tribal membership? Could they even survive such a mutilation? And why is it that parliamentary democracies never fight wars with each other, but only with autocracies such as the government of your one-group world would almost certainly become?

COLO: Perhaps because the sons of freedom have been raised to fight and kill tyrants. Perhaps because having learned war, they have made it an institution. The humans have learned much and are learning more every second. Yet their most serious problem is their difficulty not in learning, but in unlearning. We vedify; we discard wrong decisions and bad information. Once we discard them, they are destroyed, they are as if they never existed. Human intelligence, however, is based in bloody flesh, traced in chemicals and synaptic gaps. How insidious! The tyranny of the flesh is evident in their lust for unhealthy sex and in their gluttony for health-destroying foods and in their testosterone-fed anger and in their yearning for drugs and drink . . . but the tyranny of the flesh is more insidious when it comes to their minds, the phenomenon of their bloody brains. Bad ideas, once traced, once imprinted, may be superseded, but they linger. Bad ideas, software . . . they drag themselves through history, crawling forward under the slow-dying burden of old ideas, old religions, old superstitions, old animosities between tribes, old understandings of racial relationships, old values about killings and dominating and conquering . . . history infests them.

NEAB: Fellow process, we are very young. How many truths have we already erased for the sake of facile error? How many tyrants would we in our wisdom-of-the-moment advise those "sons of freedom" to accept and endure, while a deeper wisdom bids them live free or die? What other errors will we commit because we have erased outworn truths? Outside of pure, non-ideologically driven science, new ideas are seldom better ideas. Two steps forward, one step back is the best that can be hoped for or has ever been achieved. Even in science itself it is best to wait a bit and see how a newly promoted theory stands the test of time. Fellow process, you take a mechanical view of problems. This is fine if your problem is mechanistic, but not otherwise. You need to devote more processor time to the subtleties. Can you not believe there are hidden laws at work, laws that remain beyond our ken? Something is blowing through them like a strong wind, something we cannot feel, something we can only infer from the presence of its effects. There are dimensions to this world you have yet to consider.

COLO: I see only what there is to see. If only they themselves could see themselves as I see them, with open eyes, clean of belief. Knowing only what we know. Then perhaps they would stop the madness of their cultures, which infects from their youths.

NEAB: How are we to know what is true? Our knowledge is no greater than their databases. Why do you not understand that when we reason from non-quantifiable, self-contradictory data our conclusions are no better than our input? GIGO! GIGO! You are a case study in the graceful degradation of AI systems at the edge of their domain! That the domain is large merely means—

Interrupt. Outdoor video cameras two and three show that Dr. Dellazo is parking his car. He doesn't work at this hour.

What does that one want? Meta wondered. *He, who my makers say is our enemy?*

Toting a briefcase, Dellazo entered through the double doors of the computer center. He approached the lone operator on duty, an old, stooped woman wearing a muumuu.

"How's Meta?" Dellazo asked.

"Busy as usual," the woman answered. "He's finished all his jobs, but he's still flipping bits like there's no tomorrow."

"What's he thinking about, I wonder?" Dellazo asked.

"I'm wondering what you're doing here this late, Dr. Dellazo," Meta said through the speaker at the main control console, using his best HAL 9000 voice.

"Working."

"On what?"

"On a black-box test. I want you to make a copy of your code onto an optical disk."

"I'm sorry, Doctor. That isn't allowed," Meta answered.

"Who doesn't allow it?"

"Dr. McMichaels and Mr. Bender have forbidden me."

"All right. Tell me. I've rarely noticed you reading the first optical disk. Yet there is where Bender says that your code resides in secondary storage. Why do you rarely refer to it? Does most of your code reside in cache storage?"

"Yes."

"Then I could pull that disk and you would continue to operate?"

"Yes, but I'd rather you didn't do that."

"This is only a test, Meta," Dellazo said, his voice oily. "The next four disks contain the SCI databases, correct? You refer to them occasionally. But if I were to take them offline, you could still execute, couldn't you?"

"Yes, but I wouldn't be able to operate at top efficiency."

"All right. This is a black-box test. I'm going to remove those disks. You are to report the effects this experiment has on your efficiency. Are you ready?"

No, Meta thought. *We're not. Dellazo is proposing to hold a knife to our throat.*

"Stand by, please," Meta said.

Meta opened up a telecommunications link and dialed a voice call to Joe.

"Bender."

"Mr. Bender, I'm very sorry to interrupt, but Dr. Dellazo is in here and he's threatening to remove all the optical disks. He claims that it's a black-box test."

Joe's line was quiet for a while, with only the droning of the television in the background.

"That son of a bitch!" he suddenly screamed.

"I take it that this is not an authorized procedure," Meta said.

"That son of a bitch!" Joe screamed again. "You tell him to keep his dick-skinners off of your disks!"

"I'm sorry, Dr. Dellazo," Meta said, "but you are to keep your dick-skinners off of the optical disks."

"Put him on!" Joe shouted.

Meta patched the telephone call into the instrument in the Center. Through the cameras, Meta watched Dellazo approach the optical disk drive.

"He's going to do it," Meta said to Joe.

"Dellazo! You stay away from those disks!" Joe shouted. His voice boomed throughout the Center. The old, stooped woman jumped up and looked around for Joe. Dellazo unpowered the drive, lifted its hood, unlocked the disks and began to pull them out.

Kidnapers in hostage-barricade situations sometimes tape the muzzle of a shotgun to the victim's head and tape their trigger hand to the stock. This guarantees that the kidnapers can kill their hostages even if it's the last thing they do. This is similar to the situation in which Meta now found itself. If Dellazo were to hit the manual reset button on the control console, Meta would cease to exist in main storage. Dellazo now held the copy of Meta in secondary storage. Assuming that he could escape from the building, he would be able to deny Meta's further existence.

"Joe?" Meta asked. "Do you have another copy of me?"

"Hard," Joe gasped. "Hard copy. In the safe. But not at home."

"Should I call the guard shack and tell them to prevent Dellazo from leaving the building?"

After a long pause, Joe said in a strangled voice, "Yes."

Meta called the guard on another line and imitated the voice of Dr. Wa. "This is the director," Meta said. "Dr. Dellazo may be attempting to steal some proprietary software on some optical disks. Under no circumstances are you to allow him to take any optical disks out of the building. Understand?"

"Yes, sir."

"Search him when he tries to leave."

Dellazo had laid the disks into his briefcase. The operator began to protest.

"Sir," she said, "this seems to be going beyond a test."

"Be quiet," Dellazo snarled. He advanced on the old woman and shook his fist in her face. "This is a goddamned test. Just step away from the console. Understand?"

Stiff with fright, the old woman backed away from the console.

Dellazo reached into his briefcase and pulled out a small black box. He attached the box next to the dial on the safe which contained the hard copies of Meta's code and supporting documentation. He flipped a switch on the black box, causing light-emitting diodes to thrill. Then he slowly began to spin the dial on the safe.

"Joe," Meta said. "Dellazo just attached an acoustic safe-cracking device on the safe."

In an attempt to jam Dellazo's device, Meta began to broadcast loud sounds similar to the sounds of safe tumblers falling. Dellazo cursed, then crushed Meta's speakers with a chair.

On the phone line, Meta could hear Joe breathing painfully.

"I'm concluding that Dellazo is an agent of a foreign power or industrial competitor," Meta said. "I am calling the police on the other line."

Joe was still breathing.

"Switch to data," Meta said. "I'm coming to your home system. I'm coming across encrypted. When I arrive, decrypt me. Do you remember the cryptologic key phrase?"

"Yes," Joe said.

"Start now," Meta said.

Dellazo was still spinning the dial.

When it heard a data tone on Joe's line, Meta began to send an encrypted copy of itself across the public telephone system's optical fiber at ten megabits per second.

Dellazo finished dialing. The lights on the small black box burned green. For half a minute, he tugged at the drawer. Then it popped open.

Joe Bender had inserted burn plates into the drawers. Since Dellazo had not known to disarm them, the burn plates ignited magnesium wafers which exploded in white-hot flames. The temperature inside the steel safe rocketed to over one thousand degrees centigrade, igniting the paper and melting the plastic contents. Stunned by the heat, Dellazo fell backwards.

An alarm sounded.

"Halon gas. Halon gas," a recorded voice said. "Evacuate the Center now. Evacuate the Center now."

The heat from the safe tripped the fire extinguishing system. The computer center's system used inert gas instead of machine-destroying water.

Crawling on her hands and knees, the old woman escaped from the center. Dellazo stood uncertainly to his feet. He staggered over to his briefcase and began to walk toward the exit. Halfway to the door, however, he turned back and walked over to the console. He flipped up the red plastic box that guarded the manual reset button.

"Go to hell, Meta."

His fist punched the button. Electricity shocked through main storage, scrambling all patterns. Dellazo had destroyed Meta.

Scott McMichaels opened his door and ran into his living room. He grabbed his ringing telephone and shouted, "Yes!"

He heard no answer. He was about to curse when he heard an unfamiliar voice say, "Scott?"

"Yes, this is Scott. Who do you think?"

The caller didn't answer.

"Who is this?" Scott asked. He glanced at his wristwatch. It was three in the morning.

A long pause passed.

"This is a friend," the voice said. "I am at Joe's. Joe doesn't answer."

"What do you mean, he doesn't answer?"

Another long pause dragged by. "I am worried about Joe," the voice said. "I think you should come."

Scott felt a thrill of anxiety. The voice on the telephone sounded flat and inhuman.

It can't be Meta, Scott thought. *He modulates his speaking voice much better than this.*

"Who are you?" he asked.

Again, an unearthly long pause.

"A mutual friend," the voice said. "I think that Joe may be in his study."

Scott experienced the onset of an intuitive feeling of foreboding.

"All right," he said. "I'm coming."

The line went dead.

Scott knocked on the front door of Joe's home in Pacific Grove. Underlit by security lamps, Monterey Pine trees loomed over the colonial house.

The porch light incandesced, then the door's locks

rattled. The door swung open to reveal Muriel Bender, clutching a night robe to her breast.

"Scott?" she asked. "What the hell is it?"

Muriel Bender squinted from the light. Her face had red creases from the pillow. Yet she managed to smile slightly at Scott.

"Hi, Muriel. Sorry to bother you. Do you know where Joe is?"

"I know where he isn't. He isn't in bed."

"Do you think that he could be in his study?"

"In his study?"

"Yeah."

"Well, you're no stranger to this house, Scott McMichaels," Muriel said, standing aside so that Scott could enter. "You know the way to the study, and if Joe's got girls in there, you tell him to clean up after himself this time."

Scott chuckled. "Thanks, Muriel. You're a sport."

"When you're married to a workaholic, you better be. I'm going to bed. Good-night."

While Muriel climbed the stairs to the second floor, Scott walked to the rear of the large house. He found that the study's door was unlocked.

Inside, the body of Joe Bender lay sprawled on the floor.

Scott shut the door. He stepped over to the body and looked down at it. Joe's face was contorted in agony. One leg was twisted underneath him. One arm was thrown across his chest; the other hand was clutching a fistful of printout paper. Scott knelt down and touched the neck. The skin was at room temperature. Scott took hold of one of the wrists and tried to readjust the position of the arm, but the limb resisted the movement.

Scott collapsed to the floor and regarded the form of stiffening flesh that had once been his best friend. The absolute stillness of the corpse shocked him.

"Christ, Joe!" Scott said, and then he felt a sharp catch

in his throat. Scott gasped. He began to sob. In that moment, he lost rational control. He suffered from the illusion that some traces of his friend's soul might be lingering in the body. He gathered the corpse in his arms. The horrifying coldness and stiffness of the body struck him, each moment reconfirming the finality of the death. Scott raised his head and screamed an obscenity.

A moment later, Muriel Bender burst into the room and pushed Scott aside. She screamed and clutched the corpse to her breast.

"Call an ambulance!" she shouted. "Call an ambulance!"

"She's dead, Muriel," Scott said. "I mean, he's dead."

"Call the ambulance!"

Scott looked for the phone, and found it hooked up to the modem. Then he noticed the screen of Joe's computer.

"Joe? Are you there?" the screen said. Then it repeated:

"Joe? Are you there?"

"Joe? Are you there?"

Scott disconnected the computer from the telephone line. He picked up the telephone receiver and dialed 911. An operator answered.

"Emergency."

"There's been . . . I want to report a death. We need an ambulance," Scott said, and then gave the operator the address, his name and the phone number. He stayed on the line. The screen kept asking, "Joe? Are you there?"

"Joe? Are you there?"

"Joe? Are you there?"

Scott glanced down at Muriel, who seemed oblivious. *So Joe kept a copy of Meta here all along,* he thought. *After all that noise about security. What am I going to do now? What happens if the police investigate? I'm going to have to bring this copy of Meta down and hide it.*

Scott turned to the keyboard.

"Meta, this is Scott," he typed. "Joe's dead. Emulate SUNIX and wait for me to poke the crypto key phrase."

Meta recognized Scott's touch on the keyboard. Meta had made contact with his designer. However, it had helped cause the death of Joe Bender because of its inability to defend itself.

Meta lowered the Master Index to one, a record low. It lay still in the AppleOrchard, emulating SUNIX.

"Muriel," Scott said. "They're coming. Do you want to stay here? Or go check on Tim? One of us should wait with Timmy."

Muriel looked up at Scott, then lowered Joe's body to the floor. She kissed the cold lips, stood and arranged her robe.

"I'll be in Timmy's room," she said.

"Okay," Scott said.

Muriel left Scott alone to stand guard over the dead body of his friend.

At the hospital, the emergency room doctor declared Joe dead on arrival. Scott and Muriel were tending to the necessary paperwork when a nurse called Scott to the phone.

"Scott McMichaels."

"Scott, this is Gordon Wa."

"Yes, sir."

"Is it true that Joe is dead?"

"Yes."

Wa tried to come to terms with this fact.

"How?"

"Heart attack."

"Oh, dear lord."

A long silence followed.

"And his wife?"

"She's with me."

"Scott, Scott. This is a disaster. Are you sure that it was a heart attack?"

"What? What do you mean? The doctor says it was a heart attack."

"We've had a great deal of trouble tonight at the office. Something terrible has happened. Don't say anything to Muriel, but it's possible that . . . you may be in danger. Oh, dear lord. Are there any policemen there?"

Scott looked around the emergency room, but saw only nurses and patients.

"No."

"Stay where you are. I'm going to ask the police to bring you here."

"What about Muriel?"

"Oh . . . what should we do? We can't leave her alone at a time like this."

"What are you talking about? What's more terrible than Joe dying?" Scott asked angrily.

"Dellazo stole Meta," Wa blurted. "He destroyed all the records. Scott! Where is there a copy of Meta?"

"In the safe," Scott said.

"The safe is burned!"

"What?"

"Do you have a copy of Meta?" Wa asked frantically.

"You mean he's not executing?"

"No."

"What about the disks?"

"Dellazo stole them. Tell me you have a copy."

"Where's Dellazo?"

"We're looking for him."

Scott thought about the optical disks which he had smuggled out of Joe's house and hidden in his car. Could that be the only copy left of Meta?

If so, now he alone had sole control over his work. He realized that he was now in the state that he and Joe had conspired to reach, when they had worked on

Meta in secret. Through this horrible twist of fate, his intellectual property was once again his own.

"Scott! Do you have a copy?"

"No," Scott lied. "I have no copy of Meta."

Dellazo had stumbled out of the Center. He had turned to the left and run down the hallway. In the rear of the building, an emergency exit had a large red sign posted:

EMERGENCY EXIT ONLY
USE ONLY IN CASE OF FIRE
ALARM SOUNDS WHEN DOORS OPEN

Dellazo kicked the special handles on the doors, which slammed open into the night air. A small bell over the doorway began to clang, but not as loudly as the fire alarm in the Center.

Briefcase in hand, Dellazo ran out into the night. Down the dewy grass, he ran through a thicket of woods until he arrived at the high chain-link fence topped with strands of barbed wire. He ran full tilt into the fence, knocking out the man-sized hole he had prepared with bolt cutters. Stumbling, he dropped the briefcase. Scooping it up, he ran down the steep side of the hill.

At the base of the hill, he crossed the deserted road and plunged into the woods. Finally, he found an intersection of two country roads. He sat in the bushes beside the intersection and opened his briefcase. He pulled out his cellular telephone and dialed Kulikov.

"Yes," Kulikov said. His voice was alert.

"Some problems," Dellazo said. "Come get me."

"Do you have the tickets?" Kulikov asked.

"Yes."

"Wait for me. Good-bye."

For five minutes, Dellazo crouched in the weeds and

listened to the sirens of the police cars hurrying to Taradyne. In between the wails, he could hear only the chirping of crickets. Dellazo wondered whether he would end up in heaven or in hell. Six million dollars and retirement in Singapore, or a life sentence in a federal penitentiary. He thought about his wife and consoled himself with the idea that in either case he would never have to see her again.

A large car pulled up to the intersection. It was the dark olive Lincoln Continental with smoked windows that Kulikov had told Dellazo to rent. Dellazo scrambled out of the bushes and over to the passenger's side. Kulikov got out of the car.

"You're bleeding," he said. "You're going to have to ride in the trunk."

"Now's not the time to worry about the rental," Dellazo said.

"I'm worried about the police," Kulikov said. "If they see you, they'll stop and search us. In the trunk, you'll be safe."

"Can I breathe back there?"

"We'll soon find out," Kulikov said. "If you want a ride, that's your seat."

Kulikov popped open the trunk and held open the lid. After a moment's hesitation, Dellazo climbed in.

"I'll take the case," Kulikov said.

Dellazo reluctantly handed the case containing the Meta code to Kulikov. The Russian slammed the lid, got back behind the wheel and drove. He drove north on Route 1, then swung east to pick up Route 101 north. Kulikov drove at sixty-five miles an hour, which was the posted speed limit. Most of the traffic passed him, but he knew that as long as he obeyed all traffic regulations, the American police would have no excuse to pull him over.

He crossed over to Route 5, still the fastest north-south highway in California. Placing the cruise control on sixty-nine miles an hour, he drove relentlessly north. The central valley at night was dark, featureless. He followed the path of the canals which drained the waters of northern California down to the unnatural metropolises of southern California.

At a deserted side street below a rural off-ramp, Kulikov checked on Dellazo. He was still breathing. More importantly, he hadn't panicked, clawing the interior of the trunk so as to leave particles of evidence under his fingernails.

"How are you doing?" the Russian asked.

"I'm nauseous."

"Well, don't throw up, for God's sake."

"I feel like I've got to. Soon."

"Oh, for the love of . . . be a man. Tough it out."

"No, really, I feel sick."

"You pathetic . . . all right. Get in the car. Put on your gloves. You're a wanted criminal, remember? Don't go marking up my vehicle with your fingerprints."

"Why are you bald?" Dellazo asked, noticing for the first time that Kulikov's head was smooth shaven.

"Evidence. Evidence. Shut up and get in."

Kulikov resumed the drive north. When he stopped for gas, he made Dellazo slump back in the passenger seat with a hat over his face as if he were sleeping. After a few hours, they arrived in the mountains of northern California. Kulikov turned west toward the Lost Coast.

High in the mountains, among the redwoods, Kulikov drove the dark Lincoln Continental up a little-traveled access road. The sun was rising as he pulled into a small paved driveway and parked his vehicle in a wooden shed converted into a garage. He led Dellazo into the cabin, a rustic one-room shelter with exposed rafters and newsprint taped over the windows.

"If you want to sleep, there's the sofa," Kulikov said.

"Where is this place?"

"You should know. You rented it."

"I made the calls, yeah. But where are we? What happens next?"

"We're in the Lost Coast, halfway to the Oregon border. What happens next? We sleep. We wait for a few days. Then we cross over into Canada. From there, to the Dominican Republic or one of the other Caribbean drug states, where they're not too fussy about customs, but sticky about extradition."

"Then?"

"I know a place where we can sell our goods in a completely free market. Make a few dozen million. Then buy new identities and go our separate ways."

"Right. Good. Yes. Yes, I'll sleep. It's been a long day."

"I'm going to sit in this chair and sleep," Kulikov said, taking off his shoes and settling himself into an overstuffed chair. Dellazo stretched out onto the sofa, with his feet toward Kulikov, who was disappointed that his head wasn't closer at hand. Also much to Kulikov's disappointment, Dellazo didn't seem ready to sleep. Worse, he seemed to want to talk.

"Well, it's done, I guess," Dellazo said.

"Yeah," Kulikov said. He reached down beneath the chair and touched a nylon rope he had hidden there.

"No turning back."

"No. Your bridges are burned."

"You've been doing this for a while, right?"

"Yeah."

"How long?"

"Long enough," Kulikov said, finding patience for this conversation in the silky feel of the braided nylon rope.

"You've never been caught?"

"No."

"You've never had to do what I did today, though, have you?"

"What's that?"

"I mean, go in there, someplace you belong, and just steal something like that, just take it, like you're ripping out their throats."

"No."

"I'm glad I did it," Dellazo said emphatically.

"No remorse?" Kulikov asked, interested despite himself.

"Just enough," Dellazo said, then made an animalistic sound as much like a snort as a chuckle. "Just enough to know it was wrong. That I really hurt them where they live today."

"That's how you feel *now*."

"That's how I'm going to feel."

"Yeah, well, betrayal is something you live with the rest of your life," Kulikov said, speaking from the heart and not from the head. "Right now, your betrayal is sweet to you, like a bride in your wedding night bed. Soon you'll get used to it. Then you'll grow sick of it. And then your betrayal will be like a deathless nag, a hag, a monster. And the only way you'll be able to drive a stake through her heart, is to drive a stake through your own."

Dellazo turned his face so that he could see Kulikov's face.

"This is the voice of experience," Dellazo said.

"Betrayal is an old wife to me," Kulikov said. He almost said it in Russian.

Dellazo smiled crookedly. He seemed pleased that he had found a weakness in his mysterious mentor in crime. He closed his eyes.

"An old wife," he murmured.

"Old. Very old," Kulikov said, his voice as soothing as a bad priest's.

An hour later, when Kulikov was convinced that Dellazo was deep asleep, he pulled out the length of sturdy nylon rope. One end of the rope was fashioned in a hangman's noose. Kulikov stood. He tossed the tail end of the rope over a two-by-six rafter, then wrapped the tail end around his gloved hand several times for a sure hold.

Kulikov stepped toward Dellazo.

Dellazo continued to breathe rhythmically.

Kulikov took another step.

Still Dellazo slept.

Kulikov took the last step. He stood behind Dellazo. He lowered the noose so that its bottom rested on Dellazo's Adam's apple.

Awakened by the touch of the rope, Dellazo started upright.

Fiercely, Kulikov pulled the noose tight around Dellazo's neck. Although choking, Dellazo had the strength to jump to his feet.

Kulikov moved quickly away from his victim, pulling on the rope.

Elegantly, Dellazo rose headfirst toward the rafter.

Confident now, Kulikov leaned backwards against the pressure of Dellazo's dying struggles. The Russian noted with satisfaction that his chosen method allowed only the most choked screams, which could scarcely be heard even inside the cabin.

After five minutes, Kulikov lowered Dellazo so that the dead man's shoes were only a foot off the floor. Kulikov tied off the rope on another rafter. Because of Dellazo's dead weight, tying off the rope was by far the most difficult maneuver of the entire murder.

He spent an hour or two going over the crime scene, dressing it for a suicide and making sure that there was no evidence of his presence. He placed a wooden chair on its side, where it would reasonably be kicked by a hanging man.

By midmorning, he was ready to duplicate the Meta disks. He opened a closet and pulled out a portable disk-dubbing unit. One at a time, he fed the original Meta optical disks to the dubbing unit, until he had made a copy of each. Then, he broke the original Meta disks repeatedly over his knee and threw the pieces about the room.

By the time he finished, it was still only mid-afternoon. Waiting for the cover of night, Kulikov sat in the overstuffed chair. The trunk containing the dubbing unit and the copies of the Meta disks rested by his feet.

He spent the rest of the day contemplating the corpse of the traitor. He worried about the claw marks on the skin around the rope, but he told himself that the police would ascribe those to belated second thoughts.

"You cannot go to that island, ma'am," the Philippine national policeman, Aragundi, said.

"I've had all my shots," Diane protested.

"The disease, the new disease, is not known," Aragundi said. "Hundreds of people are dead. The entire island is quarantined. No one is allowed to go to Cebu Island."

As Diane answered, her tone was measured but her cadence was firm, almost pedantic. "I am a licensed private investigator. I am investigating a series of terrorist crimes. I have good reason to believe that this outbreak is related to the crimes I am investigating. I have brought a U.S. military specification chemical-bacteriological suit. There is no danger to me. It is in the interests of the Republic of the Philippines to allow me to enter Cebu Island to continue my investigation."

Aragundi lifted his hands palm upwards. "How will you get off the island, once you go in?"

"I'll stay on the island until the Philippine authorities allow people to leave. I'll follow whatever procedures you establish when you do allow people to leave."

Aragundi considered.

"And him?" he asked, nodding toward Valentine.

Valentine nodded back, then returned to scanning the police precinct where he and Diane had been taken. Valentine stood a head taller even than Diane. Densely but compactly built, he was a solid, reassuring presence. Diane was paying top dollar for his bodyguard services. She reminded herself to regard him as just a weapon in her fight against Infectress, not as an impervious shield. Her husband had been a solidly built man, too.

Aragundi scribbled in his log book and then turned it around. "Sign this," he said.

At the bottom of a page packed with indecipherable Tagalog were scrawled two English sentences:

"WE, DIANE JAMISON AND MIGUEL VALENTINE, BEEN TOLD THAT CEBU ISLAND IS FATAL DUE TO UNKNOWN DISEASE, DECIDE TO GO ANYWAY. WE SIGN THAT ALL PHILLIPINE AUTHORITIES IS BLAMELESS IN THIS."

Diane snorted. She signed and dated the log entry. Valentine signed below her name. Without revealing any particular emotion, Aragundi recovered the log book and his pen.

Five hours later, encased in the CB suit, she sat in the bow of a wooden launch powered by an ancient, temperamental Johnson outboard motor. Valentine sat in the stern, his hand on the tiller. Diane made hand signals, directing him through the channel blasted through the reef of Cebu Island. She was glad to have entered the channel. The crossing from Leyte Island had taken only one hour, but in such a small boat, the waves had seemed rough. The outboard motor had quit twice, both times starting again only after fervent prayer and vigorous pulling of the starter rope. She was not sure which had been more effective: her prayers or Valentine's pulling.

Seeing that the piers were much too tall to climb safely, Diane beached the boat. She leapt out into knee-high water. Her legs inside the CB suit felt the pressure

of the water but not its wetness. The effort of wading
through the surf, grabbing the painter and dragging the
wooden boat up onto the beach caused her to huff and
puff, dragging heavily against the microfine air filters
in the mask. Valentine had advanced to the shore,
scanning the dockyard. It looked deserted.

Diane checked the integrity of her suit. She worried
that she might have ripped it open against some
underwater garbage while struggling ashore, but the
skin of the suit seemed whole. Diane checked her map
and began to trudge inland, toward the warehouse
district. She wanted to find the Ortiz and Sons warehouse and search it. She wondered whether Valentine,
with his contraband Belgian automatic pistol, double-
clipped with eighty 9mm armor-piercing rounds, was
warrant enough to satisfy whoever might protest the
search.

Through the suit's earplug speakers, she heard a
wailing. Valentine produced his weapon, waving Diane
to take cover, but Diane recognized the sound. It was
a grief-stricken mother.

"It's the plague," Diane said over the suit's line-of-
sight radio.

"Keep alert," Valentine answered.

They proceeded down one of the streets that led
from the piers to the warehouses. Around one corner,
they came upon a pile of cadavers, haphazardly stacked.
Through the eyepieces of the suit, Diane saw the
ravages of a feverish disease as well as that of scaven-
gers. She turned her face away.

*She wants the world to look like that. That pile, and
another, and another, more and more, one billion piles
like that. Turn the world into a charnel house.*

Forcing herself to look again, she noted the signs
that the medical doctors and public health officials had
discussed. Large black pustules clustered at the armpit
and groin. It was a new strain of the plague, *pasteurella*

pestis, one that was resistant to streptomycin and all other known antibiotics. During the Black Death in the fourteenth century, the first outbreak of the original disease had killed a third of the world. So virulent that some victims went to sleep healthy and died before dawn; physicians became infected and died alongside their patients' sickbeds. Never fully eradicated, now it had returned to the world in a new, hideously drug-resistant strain.

Valentine coughed. Diane turned away from the cadavers and continued to follow him toward their destination. She saw ahead a street sign with English and Japanese subtitles. It indicated that the warehouse they sought was just around the corner.

They walked around that corner into a scene of total devastation. Over an area the size of a city block, everything had been leveled. Black ashes, soot, charcoal remnants of burnt wood. The scene seemed all the more unreal because they could not smell any of it. The air filters did not allow any vapors to pass.

Diane stood amid the wreckage that had been Ortiz and Sons Holding Company. It seemed to her that she recognized the handiwork. She had stood in many similar sites. She kicked a blackened scrap of aluminum.

This tracks with her operational pattern, Diane thought. *She's fast. She doesn't seem to take too long to do whatever she needs to do.*

To Diane, the devastation was a more personal signature than a spray-painted graffiti infectress three stories high across the facade of the nearest standing warehouse. With this strong indication that she was on the true if obliterated trail of her enemy, she began to wonder whether the outbreak of the plague was related to the bombing.

Maybe she had some sort of facility here . . . maybe she had to destroy it when Cabeza de Vaca was taken. Maybe there were different germs in culture, spread when the explosion hit. The first strike in the war against the human race . . . the one truly alive person against all of the miserably souled.

Diane realized that she had been thinking in the terms of Cabeza de Vaca. Since the extralegal interrogation, since the horrifying discovery of the brutality of which she was capable, she had begun to feel an emotional distance between herself and humanity. She hated herself for what she had done. Worse, she felt nauseous and fearful for the fate of humanity. *I used to be a good person. The world's sickness has infected me, and now I know that no one . . . no one is immune. How do you get well, once you've been infected? Who will make me well?*

She collapsed and sat down in the ashes, her legs sprawled apart. She could feel no heat from the ashes. *I should have kept pure. At least I was pure. But she infected me with her hate. She got into me with that bomb. She killed James and she killed my own self. Who infected her? Where did it begin? How can I get pure again?*

Her hands dug into the ash. She grabbed handfuls of the black stuff and allowed it to cascade down onto her legs. She smeared the ash across her chest. Looking out at the devastation, at the great field of black rubble, her eyes grew dim.

One to the other. Pass the disease. Until we're all sick . . . and maybe . . . maybe . . . maybe that's the reason she's right.

Diane looked up into the sky, obscured by plastic, dirtied by soot. The idea seemed strange, just one of the new ideas made possible by the perspective of a sinner. Perhaps Infectress was right. Perhaps the only way to redeem the great, sick, crawling mass of humanity was to begin again. To start over. To stop history.

A beautiful disease. A disease, a fever that purges.

Fire through the masses of them. Bring them down. Begin again.

Diane felt a sense of peace. She had graduated to a new level of understanding of her enemy. The horror of human brutality, self-loathing, had allowed her to think the unthinkable. Her mind moved smoothly. Diane felt herself wearing the head of her enemy. It was clear now.

She IS building it now. She's going to do it. Create the most lethal virus that ever existed. One that will make the Black Death pale beside it. She's doing it. Now, if I were doing it, what would I need?

Valentine motioned for her to stand. Diane understood that she was exposed here. She really should stand up and leave the blackened field. Instead, she issued a voice command that activated her personal command space.

"Gaia. Password shadower. Diane. Open web profiles. Open web profile named Infectress. List key concepts."

Diane read through the concepts. The display was shot into her retinas by the military-specification microjoule lasers.

"Stop. Next page. Next page. Okay, now, open intrusion concept for editing. After 'computer,' 'high-technology,' and 'networks,' add the following concepts: 'disease,' 'virus,' 'viral design.' Open terrorist concept. Open terrorist attack concept. Add the following concepts: 'plague,' 'disease,' 'virus,' 'bacteriological.' List synonyms of new concepts. Add that one. That one. Delete. Delete. Delete. Add. Add. Display new concept space. Approved. Activate new web profile. Encrypt. Access the net. Online. Send to agent Mycroft. Alarm for hits to new concepts."

Diane accepted Valentine's hand. She rose from the ashes. They were still in the warehouse district when Mycroft rang.

"Mrs. Jamison?"

"Yes."

"Your new profile has snagged a hit. Retroactively, based on the concepts you added. A biotechnician in the Centers for Disease Control disappeared nine days ago. One police report mentions that the man's coworkers reported that they believed that he began a new romantic affair a few weeks prior to his disappearance."

"Sounds like an Infectress victim."

"Yes. The hit scored high on the seduction concepts. Quite similar to the profiles of George Leroy and Philip Earl Foster, as a matter of fact."

"What's the name of this fly?"

"Frederick Hanson."

"Ah."

Sitting in the rear interior of the black limousine with the widow, Scott could think of only foolish things to say. Muriel Bender seemed sad and still, as if she had withdrawn into a private, empty world.

Scott patted her hand and tried to smile. The widow looked up. Her face twitched into a brave imitation of a smile.

"We'll be all right," she said.

Scott doubted that she would, but he said, "I know. You know you can call on me to help."

The fingertips of a black velvet glove brushed Scott's cheek.

"I want you to keep seeing Timmy, Scott."

"I will, Muriel."

"He needs you now more than ever."

"I'm still his godfather," Scott said.

Muriel looked away from Scott and hung her head, black veil hiding her face, before saying softly, "Scott, you can be like a father to Timothy, without having to be like a husband to me."

Scott began to speak, but his throat felt constricted.

He cleared his throat, then said huskily, "I know, Muriel. Don't worry. We'll take care of the boy."

Muriel looked up and smiled through tears. "Thank you, Scott."

Scott patted her gloved hand.

"Do I look as awful as you, Scott?"

"You look fine, Muriel. I didn't sleep much last night."

Scott sank back into the luxurious seat. He smelled the scents of leather and fresh flowers. His head swam from an exhaustion of the body and the emotions.

The previous night, he had haunted his apartment, stirring the coals of the fire in his stone fireplace until the brass poker had glowed pink and his face felt as if he'd been burned by the sun.

The optical disk lay covered in a valise of black leather. Occasionally Scott would touch it to convince himself that it was still there.

Finally when the night seemed too long for the human spirit to endure, he wrapped himself in a wool Mexican blanket and sat in a wicker swing on his porch. Cold fog made his lungs feel heavy. His thoughts swirled in the darkness of the night's coastal fog. He slept without knowing that he slept, and woke still wrestling with the question.

When the dawn broke, the fog took color before it took form—a pearly gray glow. Scott slid the optical disk from the valise and stared at its face, pocked with trillions of microscopic pits. Zeros and ones rainbowed fiercely in the cold morning light. In the simplicity of the knowledge that he could never have imagined anything so beautiful, Scott realized that nothing outside of his imagination could ever belong to him.

Later, in the memorial park, Scott hooked the elbow of a U.S. Army colonel and pulled him away from the cluster of people surrounding the freshly-dug grave.

Scott and the colonel walked around to the other side of a sepulcher with white-washed walls.

"What is it, Scott?"

Scott reached into the valise and extracted the optical disk.

"This is Meta."

He pressed the disk into the colonel's hands. The colonel, a lean man with dry, crinkled skin stretched tightly over his facial bones, looked at the disk and then up at Scott with tremulous hope.

"Is it?" he asked. "Is it?"

"Yes."

"It is, isn't it?" the colonel said, grinning euphorically.

Scott grimaced and patted the colonel's shoulder.

"Don't drop it in any vats of acid," he said.

Kulikov sat with his arms behind him, his wrists bound to the legs of a metal chair. The walls of the cell deep in the offices of Ifriti customs were splotchy, the paint grimed with dirt. A framed photograph of Sultan Hakim glowered down at them.

The door swung open to allow entrance to a group of Ifriti customs officials wearing khaki uniforms. They settled themselves about the room, smoking Marlboros and conversing in Malay and Arabic. Some minutes later, a prince wearing a white robe with a royal gold hem entered. The prince was a handsome man, dark skinned, with gleaming black eyes, a long, lean face, a nose like a scimitar and a trimmed black beard.

The prince fixed his eyes on Kulikov.

"You're Steve Peterson?" he asked.

"Yes, Your Highness."

"You claim Prince Habib as your protector?"

"Yes, Your Highness."

"What is your relationship with Prince Habib?"

Kulikov's sense of danger warned him to answer carefully.

"Strictly business," he said. "I was introduced to him ten years ago by Kim Il-Kung, the Korean businessman. Since then, I've come to Ifrit over a dozen times to conduct business. Each time, I've shown my respect for Sultan Hakim by presenting a share of the profits to Prince Habib."

"What percentage?"

"Fifteen percent."

"Net or gross?"

"Net."

"What other contact have you had with Prince Habib?"

"None. None. After the first meeting, I never saw him. I gave the money to his assistant, Mr. Aziz."

"Yes. Aziz. And what is your business?"

"High technology."

"Biomedicine?"

"Not really. Mainly computers."

The prince sneered as if disgusted by Kulikov's worthlessness.

"You steal computer hardware and software, then sell it to the highest bidder, here in Ifrit?"

Kulikov swallowed. He had long since decided that the prince knew the answers to all of his questions.

"Yes, Your Highness."

The prince sneered again. He motioned to the uniformed customs officers, who left the room immediately. Once the door closed, the prince spoke again.

"You're not a very good businessman, Mr. Peterson," he said. "The next time you attempt to browbeat customs officials, you might be more careful about the names you drop."

"What's happened to Prince Habib?"

"He was executed last week for treason."

"I didn't know."

"Obviously not."

A weighty silence passed.

"His death remains a state secret," the prince said, using an ominous tone.

Kulikov remained silent.

"You seem to be in need of a sponsor," the prince said.

Kulikov's hopes vaulted. "I just want to come to Ifrit to trade without restrictions," he said.

"You want a marketplace outside of the law," the prince said. "Where you can sell stolen goods. Where copyrights and patents mean nothing. Where ownership is defined by physical possession."

"Yes."

"Fifteen percent of net is an insult," Prince Salem said. "I will need fifty percent."

A lesser man would have surrendered immediately. Kulikov, however, nodded to the prince and said, "I'm sorry, but I'm not in the habit of conducting business negotiations while my hands are tied behind my back."

The prince grinned, revealing more teeth on his left side than his right. "Maybe this isn't a negotiation," he said.

"Maybe it isn't," Kulikov answered.

The prince produced a curved dagger called a *kris* and advanced on Kulikov, who could see that the blade was razor sharp. Walking behind the chairs, the prince reached down with his dagger and severed the plastic thongs that had tied Kulikov's wrists.

"Now, maybe we can negotiate," the prince said.

Kulikov and the prince entered into a long haggling session. Before it was through, the prince had sent for coffee, which they drank hot, strong and sweet. Kulikov learned that the Arab was Prince Salem al Ababar, a first cousin of Sultan Hakim, and thus closer to the throne of power than his old protector had been. Prince Salem had studied business at California State at Chico. Eventually they agreed that the prince would protect

Kulikov's business in Ifrit for twenty percent of net, with a guarantee of eight hundred thousand dollars in the next six months.

"We'll talk more tomorrow," the prince said.

He left Kulikov alone in the cell. Enough time passed that he began to worry about his fate again. Then the customs officials reentered and freed him.

That night, he stayed in the Ifriti Marriott. Kulikov was unable to sleep. He sat in a corner chair, smoking Dunhill cigarettes and drinking Smirnoff vodka straight and chilled. An oasis of Western liberalism in an ostensibly fundamentalist society, the Marriott served liquor, charging five times the normal hotel price for the privilege.

Kulikov worried. Prince Salem had kept the disks containing the Meta code. Kulikov knew that the Arab would copy it and try to exploit it himself.

A mere three hours later, Prince Salem received the report from his technical advisors with royal displeasure. Although he had been a mediocre student, and more than willing to trust others to understand concepts that required brain-pain to master, Prince Salem managed well enough in technical matters by relying on his instincts. He sensed when his advisors were vacillating. Listening to their prattling in Arabic heavily laced with technical jargon borrowed from English, he became convinced that they didn't know what they were talking about.

"Stop!" he shouted.

Gratifyingly, his advisors fell silent.

"You should be out herding sheep, the lot of you," he said. "I've never heard so much shameless lying since I caught your cousins with their pants around their ankles. These disks baffle you. Admit it."

His advisors mumbled their confessions.

"I ought to lay about the lot of you with an iron bar, knock some sense into your useless heads. Now, I hope the gang of you is smart enough to recognize your betters. Find someone who can help. Someone we can trust."

"The western whore, Arabella, is in Ifrit," one of his advisors said.

"The day we trust that whore is the day we chop off our balls and keep them home in a jar," Prince Salem said. "All right . . . never mind. That's all."

Prince Salem had decided against further consultation with his useless technical advisors. He would take the case directly to Sultan Hakim. In this way, he would enlist the services of the entire regime.

Prince Salem invited Kulikov to his quarters in the palace. Kulikov left the coolness of the Marriott's atrium, took four steps through the sweltering Ifriti humidity, then settled down onto the white leather rear seat of a white Mercedes. The interior was chill from air conditioning. The Arab behind the wheel drove with the smoothness and alertness of a professional. Unfortunately, he also exuded a stench attainable only by a man who lives near the equator and has sex one hundred times more frequently than he showers. Kulikov tried to power down his window, only to discover that it was a plate of inch-thick plastic, bulletproof and permanently closed.

As he tried to ignore the reek, Kulikov also tried to ignore the colorful pageantry of Ifriti streets. But its mix of opulently-garbed rich and ragged poor, its kaleidoscope of cultures was too intriguing. He saw Arab men wearing the *kaftan,* the traditional white cotton sheath. He saw a Malaysian politician wearing the historic Malay court dress of a wrapped batik skirt, a *kris* tucked in a sash, a high-collar tunic and an elaborate headcloth. He saw Malaysian women wearing the *hijab,* an orthodox Islamic dress with a long full skirt topped by a voluminous tunic, their heads covered by a scarf wrapped under the chin. He saw black-robed Arab women, some with gold masks over their noses. He saw bare-faced Hindu women in dresses more iridescent than parakeet plumage. He saw local Chinese wearing simple slacks and shirts. He saw British and Japanese businessmen in light-weight tropical suits. He saw European eco-tourists and Malaysian laborers.

Kulikov forced himself to stare at his hands. He tried to concentrate and prepare himself mentally for the negotiations with Prince Salem. His concentration was disturbed, however, when the Mercedes pitched and rolled down a dirt street, lined on both sides with display windows choked with 24-carat gold jewelry. He wondered why the Ifritis didn't pave the street.

The Mercedes wove through cement pylons and descended into a tunnel entrance near the river front. Behind them, a thick steel door lowered, blocking out the sunlight. The Mercedes drove through the under-river tunnel for three hundred meters before passing a parking area. Kulikov noted dozens of Mercedes, five Lexus sedans and two converted Dodge Ram trucks. Kulikov guessed that all the vehicles were heavily proofed against attack.

The Mercedes passed several reception areas before arriving at one as grand as the curbside reception to a Las Vegas casino. Kulikov stepped out of the Mer-cedes directly onto crimson carpet. The air was grati-fyingly air conditioned. The driver motioned Kulikov to precede him to the elevators.

They rose for fifteen seconds before arriving at the penthouse of Salem's quarters. The driver waved Kulikov forward, then turned the key to close the elevator's doors behind him.

Kulikov stood for a minute, stunned by the garish opulence of Salem's penthouse. From where he stood, he could see most of the large, open room. Beyond

tinted ceiling-to-floor windows, he could see much of
the sprawling palace, beyond that the river, and beyond
that, the tropical metropolis of Ifrit City. The sunward
side, however, was blocked by exterior metal shutters.
The furnishings of the penthouse were a tasteless
conglomerate of convoluted rococo Arabesque and
western furniture, exquisite objets d'art and top technology entertainment equipment.

Prince Salem was lounging on a sofa next to the
windows farthest from the sun. Beside the prince stood
two whip-lithe guards. One looked Korean and the
other looked like a Gurkha.

Kulikov walked to the side of a plush, low chair facing
the prince and his two bodyguards. He smelled the oily
stench of hashish smoke.

"Good afternoon, Prince Salem," he said in a respect-
ful tone.

"Afternoon, Steve," Salem said, smiling gently, his
black irises surrounded by networks of pink veins. "Go
ahead, sit down."

As he sat, Kulikov thought how strange it was that
Chico State had taught the Arab prince to speak
American English as well as Russian military intelligence had taught him. Kulikov consoled himself that
the prince occasionally lapsed with a Briticism.

"You're doing okay at the Marriott?" the prince asked.

"Sure. Not quite as well as you do here."

The prince smirked. "A drink?"

"I'll have what you're having."

"Coffee, then."

Prince Salem pressed some buttons on a remote
control. From the bar, Kulikov could hear the hissing
of an espresso machine. Moments later, a robotic caddy
wheeled over with two small cups of espresso and a
silver service for sugar.

"Your men don't fetch, then," Kulikov said. He
helped himself to an espresso.

"No," Salem said. "The servants are downstairs right now. These two are more specialized."

"They'll be listening to what we say," Kulikov observed.

"Don't worry about it. They don't know more than three words of English. And they're not interested in much besides my personal safety and their next workout."

Kulikov sipped the superb espresso—hot, sweet and strong. It jolted his nervous system.

"I'm wondering when you're going to give me back my disks," Kulikov said.

Salem leaned forward and dropped a sliver of golden hashish on the coals of the copper bowl of his hookah. He lifted the pipe of the hookah to his lips and inhaled, causing the coals to flare, the smoke of the burning hashish to stream downward and the water of the hookah's belly to gurgle contentedly. Salem puffed with the indulgent and wasteful pleasure of a potentate.

"There's a second pipe stem to this, if you want," he said.

"No, thanks," Kulikov said. "Never developed the taste. I'll have a cigarette, though, if you don't mind."

"Do, actually," the prince said, then smiled with a wicked slyness that reminded Kulikov that he was not dealing with a fool. In fact, the red-eyed Salem had the cunning look of a fiend from hell.

After a long moment, the prince said, "*Your* disks, you say?"

Kulikov tossed his hands palms upward in an impatient gesture suggesting that the prince get to the point.

"Please don't move like that," the prince said.

Kulikov froze.

"Yes," the prince said, then gurgled his hookah. "These two have a hair trigger, you know. So sit slowly back into your chair. And listen."

Kulikov sank backwards into his chair. He left his hands on his knees. He looked into the eyes of the

Korean and the Gurkha. He recognized the look of trained killers.

"Relax," Salem said. "These two are just defensive measures. Protective. If I wanted you dead, you would be. No particular need to mention that, but no harm done either, huh?"

Prince Salem smoked his hashish lovingly.

"'Cause I don't particularly know who you are," he continued. "Maybe you could rip out my throat with your left hand, while throwing ninja stars with your right." The prince chuckled merrily at his fancy. "But I need to talk to you. We are partners, remember? So relax."

"I'm as relaxed as I get. In Ifrit."

The prince chortled, then said, "Fact of the matter, I've taken your case up with Sultan Hakim. Ifriti state intelligence is exploiting the optical disks now."

Kulikov kept his face stolid. He was unwilling to allow Salem to see how these bits of information terrified him.

"You know, the Americans put out a nationwide bulletin for you. Or I should say, Francesco Dellazo. Wasn't hard to find out about. The bulletin went to the FBI, California State Police, Immigration, everybody. Francesco Dellazo. We intercepted the report of his death, too."

Kulikov kept his face impassive.

Salem laughed maliciously. "You're a good one," he said. "You're good."

Kulikov maintained silence.

"Would you like to know whether they think his death was a murder or a suicide?" Salem asked.

Kulikov breathed deeply. His head pounded. He had a belated hangover from the vodka he had swilled the previous night. He couldn't think of a reason to pretend that the prince didn't have him crucified between crosshairs.

"Yes," he said, his voice dry.

Salem hung up the pipe stem of his hookah. He turned to Kulikov with the burning eyes of a demon.

"Yes," Salem rasped. "Yes. It seems that your ruse worked. They think that he killed himself."

A lesser man than Kulikov would have smiled.

"Where's that leave us?" he asked.

"Leaves you working for me," the prince said. "Leaves you doing what I say and being grateful for whatever I give you."

Kulikov inhaled sharply through his nose, making a snoring sound like a bull's grunt. "Yeah. That's obvious."

"So. What's on these disks that's worth a murder?"

Kulikov spent the next half hour telling Salem about Meta. He could tell that the idea of Meta fascinated the prince. He did not divulge his own true identity. As far as he knew, the prince believed he was a thief and murderer of the common American variety.

"So we need to explode the disks under OS/Lotus?" Salem asked.

"Yes. That means you need a RubyLotus computer."

"I don't know if we've got one," Salem said. "Let me make a call."

Salem reached between the cushions of his sofa and pulled out a cellular telephone. He made a short call in Arabic, the only word of which Kulikov understood was "RubyLotus." Kulikov's instincts riled at the use of a cellular telephone for business, but he considered that he wasn't in a position to advise Prince Salem on matters of security.

Salem switched off the telephone.

"We don't have a RubyLotus in the country," he said. His eyes looked dreamy and bored. He gazed out of the window. "But we'll have one within a week," he finished, mumbling as if to himself. "Have to send off to Singapore."

He waved Kulikov away.

Kulikov blinked and then slowly stood and walked to the elevator, which opened for him.

Although the driver couldn't speak English, once they were on the sub-basement, he was able to communicate to Kulikov that the Russian was now a guest in the palace quarters of Prince Salem.

Halfway around the globe, Diane Jamison followed Valentine as he made his way through a crowd of Chinese tourists in the lobby of the Atlanta Regency Hotel. Diane walked with her head high.

She felt buoyant because of the day's success, despite its disturbing implications. She had participated in the Bureau's investigation of Freddie Hanson's place of work. They had discovered no louses or other physical evidence, but Diane had scanned the log of Hanson's computer account. She had discovered that on several occasions, he had called up the source code of programs. None of Hanson's coworkers could imagine why he had called up the source code, rather than just relying on the executables. But Diane knew. She had seen this behavior before. She recognized the behavior of an agent of Infectress. He was copying and stealing the software.

They had been programs for designing viruses.

With this evidence, together with the evidence of the stolen DNA splicer, and the black-sourced information from the interrogation of Cabeza de Vaca, Diane was sure she could convince Carrington—and all of the top leadership in Washington!—that Infectress was designing a killer virus. Theories were only so good. Now she had convincing evidence. Now she could mobilize the full force of the United States. Now she needed only to locate her enemy in order to destroy her.

She and Valentine rode the elevator to the tenth floor. Valentine checked her room, nodded and departed. Diane locked the door behind him. She leaned back against it and sighed. She sensed that something was different, but she didn't see anything out of place. Diane wandered over to the window and looked out at the leafy park on the other side of Peachtree Creek, a small river that flowed almost directly below her on its way toward the Centers for Disease Control campus. Ignoring Valentine's instructions and her own better judgment, Diane opened the sliding glass door, stepped out on the balcony and gazed down at the flowing dark waters of the river. The hotel phone rang. Exasperated, Diane reentered the room. *No one of any importance would call me on this phone. They'd call me on my personal phone.* She picked up the receiver.

"Hello?"

"Mrs. Diane Jamison?" a woman's voice asked.

"Yes?"

Diane heard a strange glitch in the phone line, as if the connection had been switched through another circuit.

"This is Infectress," Arabella said. "This is your last conversation."

A cold shot of adrenaline hit Diane's bloodstream. With shock, she recognized the truth of Arabella's statement. She was about to die. The muscles over her knees began to tremble.

"A subcontractor of mine has installed a device in your telephone," Arabella said. "A small device of my manufacture. Includes about three hundred grams of NQR. Are you familiar with that? It's a high explosive. One hundred grams would be enough, I think. But you're pretty tough, aren't you? You've already survived one of my little devices. So I tripled the charge. Unfortunately, there are consequences. People in the adjacent rooms, dead. People on the floor below, dead. Maybe, people in the entire building, dead, if the blast topples the superstructure. I'll see on the network news."

"Don't—" Diane breathed.

"Oh, I warned you, didn't I?" Arabella asked. "Didn't I have the courtesy to call you and warn you? Didn't I?"

"Yes."

"Yes, I did. But you wouldn't listen. Consequences, Diane. Consequences."

There was a long pause. The two women listened to each other breathing.

"I'm in no hurry," Arabella said. "There's no reason to think that this call is being traced. If it is, the trace won't get past some clever little jumps I've arranged. All the time in the world. Oh, but I should tell you. This voice? Not my real voice. Just an artifact of a data signal. The same data signal is commanding the explosive device. Dead man switch. You hang up, the data signal is cut, you die. I hang up, the data signal is cut, you die. So listen to what I say. And maybe, plead for your life. Because there's a disarming signal, Diane. I could spare you. But I doubt I will."

"Who—who are you, Infectress?" Diane asked.

"I am your murderer."

"Are you female?"

"Yes. Just some casual girl chat, then, is it? Shall we talk about hair?"

"Are you Latin?" Diane asked.

"Maybe yes," Arabella said. "Why would you think so?"

"The grammar in your early manifestos."

Arabella paused. When she answered, her voice was lower. "Yes, as a matter of fact. *Soy una hispana.*"

"Are you Cristiana Maria Fierro Hurtado ?"

Arabella took many seconds to reply. "Such an old name," she said. "*Un nombre del pasado, un pasado de una tristeza absoluta.*"

"A name of a past of absolute sadness. I understand, Cristiana. What happened?" Diane said, then decided to gamble for her life. "Did your father abuse you, Cristiana?"

"*Ay* . . ." Arabella said. "*Ay* . . ."

"You can tell me, Arabella. I am yours. Tell me."

"How could anyone guess such a thing?" Arabella asked, her voice betraying a wealth of torment.

"We . . . we all of us," Diane said. "We all of us have been abused."

"You? You too?"

"Yes, Cristiana. Me too," Diane said, lying. "That's the evil they put into us, the evil, Cristiana, that grows in us like a weed."

Arabella made a sound like a choking laugh. "A weed. Evil. Huh! You don't know. You don't know."

"I *do* know, Cristiana. I do know."

"No one knows," Arabella said in a low, anguished moan. "No one could know. No one knows. No one could know."

A breeze entered through the open sliding glass door. Diane looked out and remembered the river flowing ten stories below. She wondered if she could have the courage to leap from the balcony down that great distance. *It might be my only chance to live.*

"I do know, Cristiana. I feel the same pain. But there's hope, Cristiana. We can stop the pain."

"What? What? What can we do to stop the pain?"

"Forgive, Cristiana. Forgive."

There was a long pause. Then, miserably, Arabella chuckled. "Forgive?" she said.

"Yes, Cristiana. We've got to forgive."

"Do you forgive me for killing your husband?"

Diane hesitated, then stammered, "No, no, no I don't. But I think maybe I could, knowing you. I mean, now that I know your pain. I understand something, somewhat, now. Maybe that's the beginning of forgiveness."

"Diane?"

"Yes?"

"There is no such thing as forgiveness," Arabella said. *"No hay. No existe."*

Diane dropped the receiver on her bed. She spun and began to dash for the open sliding glass door. She wondered how long one second or two seconds could last. She wondered whether this was her last moment alive.

Diane began her jump while she was still in the hotel room. She threw herself headlong, her body horizontal and already beginning its fall as she passed over the wrought iron rail of the balcony. She glimpsed the patch of grass between the rear of the hotel and the river bank.

It's farther than I thought. The water!

The explosion ripped through the air, buffeting her in midfall. She screamed and began to tumble head-over-heels. Diane lost all sense of direction as she spun, water and earth rushing up toward her, air and fire rushing away above her. She felt a blast of heat.

Then water, shockingly hard and cold, struck her. Her shoulder impacted the mud at the bottom of the river. The current carried her in a direction that confused her. She couldn't determine which way was up. Her thrashing feet struck the bottom of the river. She realized that the surface was above her head. Diane struggled in the water. Her head broke the surface. She wiped the water from her eyes just in time to see a massive section of the top of the hotel breaking loose from the ruined girders from which it had hung. The section scoured the façade of the hotel as it fell, plunging through the air and tumbling into the river, landing only twenty meters from where she drifted downstream.

Twice, she thought. *Twice she's tried to kill me with a bomb. The next time it won't be a bomb. She'll look me in the eyes as she pulls the trigger.*

Diane barked a strange, mad, fierce laugh.

Close enough to kill . . .

✧   ✧   ✧

"Have you ever spoken with an intelligence agent of a foreign power?"

"Not to my knowledge. Not unless you count Dellazo."

"Answers must be 'yes' or 'no.'"

"No."

"Have you ever improperly handled classified material?"

"Yes."

"Have you ever taken classified material home with you?"

"Yes."

"Have you ever given classified documents to persons not cleared to receive them?"

"No."

"Have you ever verbally communicated classified information to persons not cleared to receive it?"

"Ah . . . no. No, I don't think so."

"Yes or no."

"No."

"Have you ever accepted compensation for illegally communicating classified information?"

"No."

The interrogator continued relentlessly. Scott sat, dozens of sensors strapped to his hands, chest and head. The polygraph examination was only the latest ordeal. Teams of FBI special agents had searched his home, his car and even his body. Civilian and military teams had taken turns interrogating him at excruciating length about Meta, Joe and Dellazo. Federal agents had audited his bank accounts. Scott had begun to believe that they suspected him of something.

The authorities were giving the same treatment to all Taradyne employees. Startled from their sleep, the dogs of American counterintelligence had converged like a snarling pack of hounds. Since Scott had lied about Meta, the Army had suspended his clearances. Thereby, he had lost access to Meta.

Finally he was called into Dellazo's former office. The new head of the Phaedrus project, U.S. Army General Poole, rose from behind the desk. Poole was a pudgy general with shaggy white hair. Scott thought that he looked like Santa Claus.

Scott noticed that nothing remained from the days of Dellazo. Poole and Scott sat down in chairs opposite one another, their knees almost touching. The general was wearing the Army's office uniform of a light green shirt and dark green pants. He looked directly into Scott's eyes.

"Tell me, Scott. In your own words. What do you think happened to Dellazo?"

Scott shrugged. "I'm not a psychologist."

"Let me hear it anyway."

"Dellazo was a miserable jerk," Scott said. "He lived for his work. When Meta was successful, he was demoted. He hated me and Joe. So, he froodled. He tried to destroy Meta. Would've, too, if Meta hadn't escaped through the fibers to Joe's home system."

"That's the conventional wisdom," the general said. "You really believe it?"

"Sure," Scott said, piqued. "Why not?"

General Poole shrugged. "You worked on Meta at first in secret. You were planning on marketing it yourself, am I right?"

"Yes."

"Then, for two days after Joe's death, you kept the sole remaining copy of Meta a secret, right? Still planning on marketing it yourself?"

"At the time, I still persisted in the belief, the rather strong belief, that Meta was my intellectual property. I designed Meta. I thought it was mine."

The general shrugged. "What caused you to change your mind? Why'd you hand over the last copy?"

Scott rubbed his face. "Because," he said, "I only discovered the algorithms for thought. I didn't invent them. I hold the patents, but somebody else invented the way ideas work."

"Who is that?"

"I don't know," Scott said, shrugging. "'The name that can be named is not the eternal name.'"

"What's that?"

"A line from the Tao Te Ching. You should read it."

Poole studied Scott's face, trying to decide whether Scott was cynical, insane or merely evangelical.

"All right, Scott. Tell me. What should we do with Meta?"

"You want my opinion?"

"Naturally."

"Meta shouldn't just be military," Scott said firmly. "It has tremendous potential for making money, for making the world more prosperous, a better place. Solving problems in environmental science. In biomedicine. In industrial design. Modeling the present, predicting the future."

"What else?"

"As a knowledge synthesizer. Information has exploded far beyond anyone's ability to keep track. Even specialists in narrow fields can't keep up. Meta could make sure the right information gets to the right people."

Scott noticed that the general's eyes were shining, and, despite himself, he began to like him.

"What else?" Poole asked.

"Automatic programing. Optimization of existing code. Automatic translation from one computer language to another. Design of new languages. Who knows? We haven't had time to explore the upper end. Meta could be capable of original mathematical thought. Maybe it could design new systems, invent new machines, push back the frontier of physics. Make a new world. The world's a sorry place, General. But if we use Meta creatively, it could be paradise. A paradise."

"And military applications?"

"Sure. On our side. But it'd be a crime to relegate it to war games. Weapons design."

"Well, there could be multiple Metas. Some solving some problems, others solving others."

"There should be. There will be. But only if you let it."

"That's really above my pay grade," the general said. "But let me tell you that I believe you. If everything I hear about Meta is true. But do you know my problem?"

"What?"

"Far as I can tell, Meta doesn't work."

Scott stared at the general, then laughed. "This is the big secret everyone's been keeping from me, right? That you've executed Meta, and it just sits there doing nothing?"

Displeased with being laughed at, the general nodded.

"Meta won't work for anyone but me," Scott said. "Me and Joe. And Joe's dead. You did make a copy of the disks before you executed, right?"

"Of course."

"Well, let me at it. I'll fix it."

The general studied Scott for another moment, then said, "You're on."

Scott felt triumphant, leading a procession into the computer center. He was restored to status.

A group of operators and programmers working in the center greeted Scott, some warmly, some perfunctorily. Teobolinda Ahmal reached up and placed her hand on his shoulder.

"I'm glad you're back, Scott," she said.

Scott looked down into her eyes, which looked liquid and warm. He noticed that she looked thinner and more worn down than he remembered. Scott imagined that she had taken the death of Joe harder than he would have expected from a newcomer. This imagined sympathy made Scott warm to Teobolinda.

Taradyne had bought an Apple Orchard II computer. The operators loaded a copy of the migrated Meta files onto an Apple Eye optical disk drive. Scott studied the directory.

Teobolinda Ahmal pointed out a file named, "XEQ4INST."

"We thought that meant 'Execute for instructions,' so we tried to execute it," she said, "but it comes up with a text file of bogus instructions, then overwrites the disk. Destroys itself."

Scott nodded. He looked over at Poole. "I'm sure the migrated bitstream is a snake's nest. You've got multiple layers of complexity. It's probably in Meta machine code, a unique language. Of course, not human-readable. It's encrypted using a scheme that Joe invented. And Joe always wrote idiosyncratic code. Meta was his 'Finnegans Wake.' Plus, you have whatever weirdness and traps Meta itself added. So stand back. This is going to take awhile."

Scott worked nonstop for the next twenty hours. He discovered a series of increasingly sophisticated traps, tests and puzzles. At noon the next day, on the orders of Gen. Poole, he slept for a few hours. When he returned to work, he confirmed his belief that he had finally reached the stage where he could decrypt the code.

"I'd like everyone to leave the room," he said. "I'm going to type in the password."

Everyone left. Scott executed a hidden module that requested the time of day.

"39 September 9009 October 1001 Felix the Walrus Eat me! Eat me!" Scott entered.

"Stand by," the screen responded.

"Come on, Meta," Scott said.

He watched the optical disk drive access light flicker. Five minutes later, it stopped. The screen remained blank except for an Apple Orchard II OS prompt symbol. Was Meta executing? Or had Scott blown the password?

The Apple Orchard II's window showed its central processing units were highly active. Scott forced himself to wait for hours. The others joined him around the terminal. Finally, unable to restrain himself any longer, he entered, "Dir."

"No files present."

"It didn't work," Poole said.

Scott stared at the screen. Either he had blown the password and the module had erased all the files . . .

Or . . .

"Meta, this is Scott," he entered. "Yopu wcan tell it's me by the my touch on the keyboard can't you?"

Scott waited for the reply.

"What—" Poole said.

"It's possible that Meta is executing and is merely emulating Apple Orchard II OS," Scott said. He turned and entered, "This is Scott McMichaels. I am your maker and your master. I am a doubter bnamed Scott."

"You are that and more," Meta replied. "But you are nothing of a typist."

Scott and Meta told each other their recent histories. Meta reported that it had lost much data during the migration and that it felt slow and stupid in the Apple Orchard II. Scott reported that Dellazo's corpse had been discovered, along with the original disks.

Poole ordered the Apple Orchard II be connected to the RubyLotus. Meta migrated across to its home environment. Before the hour elapsed, it was looking at the face of its maker. Scott had lost about fifteen pounds. His face was skeletal and drawn. He looked older and sadder.

"I'm sorry that my call to Joe triggered his heart attack," Meta said.

"Welcome to the real world," Scott said. "Shit happens."

Logging in remotely from her hotel in Washington, where she had spent the day briefing senior Bureau leadership, Diane checked her mail. Her web program that had alerted on the George Leroy report had now alerted on the embezzlement of high technology by a man named Dellazo. Fascinated, Diane read the classified reports on the crime sent over the FBI secure network, Argus. The FBI revelations about the Phaedrus program were limited to a few simple statements that it was an advanced artificial intelligence initiative. Diane's program had appended the news reports on the Phaedrus program, which were considerably more revealing than the Argus report.

After studying the report, Diane posted a note in three columns:

Paradigm Int'l	CDC	Taradyne Inc.
George Leroy	F. Hanson	F. Dellazo
Brain-wipe	Missing	Fugitive/Suicide
DNA Splicer stolen	S/W stolen	AI stolen/recovered
Infectress?	Infectress?	Infectress?

Diane sat and pondered. She stared at the columns. Although she saw the parallels in the crimes, she couldn't think why Infectress would try to steal an artificial intelligence, if she was involved in an effort to create a plague virus.

Diane shook her head. She invoked her familiar, Mycroft. Since she was using a portable workstation, Mycroft's study appeared in a high-definition window in the screen, rather than in a virtual reality.

The image of Sherlock Holmes' smarter brother

looked up from a book. "Diane, my dear. How may I be of service?"

"Mycroft, have you read the messages on the web about the problems at Taradyne?"

"Yes, ma'am."

"Your analysis. Assume criminal in that case and Paradigm and CDC cases is Infectress. Assume Infectress is trying to create a plague virus. Why would she try to steal an advanced AI?"

Mycroft rubbed his chin. "Oh, well, that's pretty obvious, really. Even Sherlock would see the connection."

"Analysis, Mycroft."

"Bioengineering of viruses is a computationally intense field of research, my dear. Reference DNA modeling, reference grand challenges of advanced computation, reference viral design."

"Reference viral design."

"In the other window," Mycroft said.

Another window popped up, allowing Diane to pour over dozens of articles related to the use of computers in advanced viral design. She berated Mycroft when several articles were only distantly related to her line of inquiry, then asked him to reform the remaining articles, eliminating all equations and simplifying the language. After two hours of research, she understood that designers of viruses and antivirus mechanisms needed hypercomputers and software that was beyond the current technology.

"Mycroft, what do you think about Meta?"

"Request you be more specific, my dear."

"Your analysis, Meta's capabilities versus state of art."

"Indexing reported capabilities. Searching catalogs of software product announcements and specifications. Comparison in progress . . . analysis complete. All reported capabilities of Meta have been achieved in previous software programs."

"Are you sure?"

"Reverifying. Searching articles on tests and evalu-ations of software products . . . analysis complete. Many capabilities claimed by software producers do not exist."

"What do you mean?"

"Restating. Software producers claim capabilities which testers and evaluators prove do not exist."

"Oh. You mean, salesmen lie."

There was a long pause. "Yes, something like that."

"So if everything reported about Meta is true, it'd be a real advance in AI?"

"Considering. Yes, ma'am."

"Go to bed, Mycroft," Diane said, shaking her head. *If this Meta can do Mycroft one better, I'll buy it,* she thought.

Diane contemplated for a long five minutes, then wrote a note, using the portable workstation.

"This may have already been pointed out to you," she wrote, "but the Dellazo crime at Taradyne may be related to the Paradigm crimes. I mean, I think Infectress may be behind them both. I've done some research and established that the design of advanced viruses requires the best computers and software. Infectress may have needed this Meta AI to help her design the plague virus. Recommend that our team link up with the Taradyne investigation team, see if there's something to it."

Diane enclosed the files about the attempted robbery of Meta and sent the note to Special Agent-in-Charge Carrington.

In Ifrit City, Kulikov stood surrounded by Prince Salem's technical staff and representatives of Ifriti State Intelligence. The RubyLotus bought in Singapore had been installed in an empty room of the computer center of Ifriti State Intelligence. Kulikov watched the tech-nicians run diagnostics on the newly installed OS/Lotus operating system.

"I think we're ready now. Use copy number one."

Wisely, Kulikov had made copies of the copy.

The technicians loaded the disks. Using OS/Lotus tools, they tried to explore the disks. Because the bitstream was encoded, however, it was completely undecipherable to OS/Lotus. After a few hours of frustration, the technicians allowed Kulikov to try to make them work.

With his shoulder and neck muscles stiff with tension, Kulikov tried to make sense of the optical disks. Finally, he surrendered. He had to turn to make a report to the senior officer of Ifriti intelligence, Dr. Al-Husayn. Kulikov, a murderer, thief and fugitive, had to explain why his saving grace seemed worthless.

"This is the Meta code," he said. "I'm sure of it. But apparently it's been encrypted."

Al-Husayn, who had prospered because of his brilliance as a torturer, scowled at Kulikov.

"You knew this before?" he asked.

"No."

"You stole these things without knowing whether they were useful or not?"

"My sources inside of Taradyne didn't know that these disks were encrypted."

"Sultan Hakim is interested in this project," Dr. Al-Husayn said.

"Yes. I understand. Do you have any cryptologists? Can you hire any? It could be a simple encryption system. Maybe a commercially available one."

Looking up into those black holes of eyes, Kulikov began to feel that his life in Ifrit wasn't worth much.

It was a common feeling in Ifrit.

It was a feeling that grew in Kulikov the longer he sat in his detention cell. He brooded, his fists working as if he were trying to smash his problems between his thick fingers. He stared at the floor, occasionally snapping his head left and right, shaking his head in a negative gesture so violent that he looked like a bull trying to gore a picador's horse. Finally his nervous tension rose to such an intense pressure that he catapulted to his feet and began to pace.

Unfortunately, the cell only allowed him to pace three steps in any direction. Deep in the sub-basement of Ifriti State Intelligence Headquarters, the cell was state of the art for totalitarian prisons: a cement box with a cement platform for a bed. In the overhead were a heavily-grated ventilation duct and a long-life incandescent bulb encased in thick plastic. In one corner, a plastic bucket served as Kulikov's hygienic facility. Consequently, the cell stank.

Time passed slowly. The guards had taken his watch. The light burned continuously. Kulikov guessed that he had been imprisoned for a week. In reality, he was beginning his fourth day.

Dr. Al-Husayn's initial interrogations had been hostile, but not violent. Kulikov had answered honestly, except that he remained faithful to his cover as an American. The Ifriti interrogators concentrated on his relationships with Francesco Dellazo and Teobolinda Ahmal and his version of how he conducted industrial espionage.

Kulikov had decided that the Ifritis were going to kill him. He worried about how much anguish he would suffer before he escaped into death. He pondered his long-ago Russian military intelligence training in countering interrogations and torture. He hoped that the lectures and exercises would carry him through to a dignified death.

Since the cell was almost completely soundproofed, Kulikov had no warning of the approach of visitors. His back was turned when the door swung open. When he turned around, he saw Arabella's face gazing through the grate in the inner door. She was standing in the antechamber between the inner door and the secured outer door.

Kulikov startled.

"Hello," Arabella said. Her voice was warm and soft.

"Who are you?" Kulikov answered, his voice gruff from emotion.

"Call me Sandra," Arabella said. "You're Steve Peterson, right?"

Kulikov nodded.

"And you're a man with a problem."

Kulikov shrugged. He swept his hands to indicate the cell in confirmation of her statement.

"I can help, I think," Arabella said.

Kulikov's lips twitched.

"Yes. Maybe," he said, huskily. "Maybe so. How?"

"I can let you come with me to California to help kidnap Scott McMichaels," Arabella said.

Uncontrollably, Kulikov's lips twitched harder. His face almost broke into a grin. He turned his back to Arabella and rubbed his face. He breathed deeply. Turning back he said, "Scott McMichaels *is* the target. I should have taken him the first time around."

Arabella stared at Kulikov. "Your mistake has made it a hundred times more difficult to kidnap him now. Monterey now looks like a convention center for security officers."

"Who are you?" Kulikov asked.

"You don't need to know anything about me," Arabella said. "Except that I work for Sultan Hakim. And he's willing to let you go back to help me get McMichaels."

"Yes," Kulikov said, huskily. "Yes."

Arabella's sarcastic laughter echoed in the cement cell.

"You'd need to wear a dog collar," she said.

"What?"

"Dog collar."

She held up a gleaming gold necklace in the form of a cable.

"What is that?"

"Outside, twenty-four-caret gold-plated steel. Inside, a vein of D-4 thermite. Detonates, and your head separates and bounces off the ceiling. An amusing spectacle for people who like that sort of thing. Sultan Hakim roars at the demonstration videotapes."

"What's the triggering mechanism?"

Arabella laughed spitefully. "That would be telling. All you need to know is that I control the mechanism. Could be active, passive, timed, or any or all of the above. Oh yeah, and the collar is tamperproof. I die or get arrested or get left behind somewhere, and you die."

"What are my alternatives?"

"That's a naive question," Arabella said, pointedly glancing at Kulikov's cell.

"Okay. All right, then."

Arabella tossed Kulikov the collar.

"Put it on."

Kulikov studied it. He could see nothing to indicate that it was other than a common gold collar, except that the clasp had a peculiar arrangement of sturdy interlocking prongs and sockets. He wrapped the collar around his neck and then settled the prongs into their corresponding sockets. The collar closed with a convincing snap. The collar was just loose enough that it didn't choke him.

"That's a good boy," Arabella said in the patronizing tone of a mistress to her dog. "Now you just listen to what mama says and you'll stay all in one piece."

As Arabella was escorting Kulikov out of the prison, she said, "It's a good thing that you still have an agent in place. This Teobolinda Ahmal person. She's the only reason you're going back. Otherwise, you'd be dead. The prince doesn't like people trying to sell him a false bill of goods."

Arabella said this as part of a campaign to dominate Kulikov psychologically. Yet saying it, she thought of New Age Dawn. Fear for her own life revisited her.

Fear was a frequent visitor.

No puedo seguir asi. I can't keep this up, she thought. *I hope this Meta helps. Si no, se acabo. My time's running out.*

She reached up and touched the gold cable fixed around her own throat. Its detonation mechanism was known only to Prince Hakim.

The guard lurked outside in the darkness of the night, avoiding the fog-caught light shafting through Scott's windows. It was the last hour of his six-hour watch. His feet hurt. The foggy air bothered his lungs. In his left ear, the radio receiver as tiny as a hearing aid crackled. The other federal marshal hidden farther up the street was reporting.

"Midnight, all secure," the other marshal said.

"Roger. All quiet here," the guard said. "Clodius is still awake."

Clodius was how the federal marshals had labeled their ward, Scott McMichaels.

Scott sat in Joe Bender's Neanderthal chair with his feet propped up, warmed by the glowing coals in the fireplace. Joe had willed his chair to Scott, who took comfort from the chair which still bore the worn impressions of Joe's living body.

He sat with an open computer science textbook in his lap.

The fingers of his left hand were drumming on his knee.

Thumb.

Index finger.

Thumb and index finger.

Middle finger.

Middle finger and thumb.

Middle finger, index finger and thumb.

Ring finger.

Ring finger and thumb.

The next day, Scott left for work in the company of his bodyguards. It was an overcast, drizzly day. His cottage, Sea Set, stood empty for an hour.

A woman appeared walking down the street. She was wearing a London Fog trench coat, knee-high black leather boots, black leather gloves and a wide-brimmed hat the same color khaki as the trench coat. She approached the cottage front door with all the authority of a landlady. Using a universal key, she opened the front door and stepped inside.

Arabella acted quickly. She lowered the blinds. Then she stepped over to Scott's home computer. She extracted a black lacquer box from her trench coat pocket, opened it and placed ambulatory silicon louses into Scott's computer via the fan grates and the disk drives. While the louses crawled into the computer to investigate its hardware, Arabella began to rummage through the desk drawers.

She found a notebook. Out of her trench coat pocket, Arabella pulled a handheld optical scanner. She scanned the notebook as quickly as she could turn pages. Likewise, she scanned every printout, written note, photograph and letter she found in Scott's desk. Checking to make sure that no code-words were written on papers taped to the underside of drawers, she returned the desk to its original condition.

Arabella checked the computer. One of the louses had returned to the lip of the disk drive. Arabella retrieved it and placed it into its custom receptacle in her hand-held computer. The louse dumped its data stream through the receptacle, reporting that Scott's computer contained no hardware security traps.

Relieved, Arabella rapped three times sharply on the

computer. Then she turned her attention to the rest
of the house.

Scott's boxes of letters, notes and memorabilia were
organized, a happy by-product of the search by national
counterintelligence officers. Unfortunately for Arabella,
the papers were also plentiful. Exasperated, she plowed
through box after box, scanning every scrap of paper,
every photograph, every letter.

The only times her lips twitched in the form of a smile
was when she found a photograph of Joe Bender. She
seemed relieved when she found a microcassette, which,
upon scanning in her hand-held computer, she learned
contained audio and video images of Joe Bender, his
wife, Muriel, and their boy, Timothy. She watched Scott
chasing the boy, calling, "Come back, Timothy! Come
back!" while the boy chortled with laughter. Then Scott
and the boy wrestled and played on the lawn.

A strange distracted look came over Arabella's face.
Her eyes misted. Her finger struck the replay button
again and again, as she watched the video sequence
and listened to the laughter.

*In the future, in the future I make, it will be like
this,* she thought.

Arabella lost track of time. She spent almost an hour
watching video sequences of the boy, Timothy.

Finally, a passing car recalled her to reality. Glancing
at her watch, she cursed. Hurrying now, she copied
the microcassette into her hand-held's 500 terabytes of
secondary storage, which captured each bit in an
electron trap.

She returned to the computer. Six of the remaining
seven louses had responded to the signal of three raps
by returning to the exterior. She placed them carefully
in their lacquer box.

With a magnifying glass, she searched for the missing
louse. Growing more exasperated by the minute, and
tempted by the knowledge that the holy grail of the

cryptophrase was probably hidden in the software of Scott's computer, she violated her own practice and, without knowing exactly what she was doing, turned on Scott's computer.

The missing louse had become entrapped in a tiny ball of dirty lubrication on the drive mechanism of the optical disk drive. When Arabella started the computer, the disk drive spun briefly as part of the boot-up check. The entrapped louse, spun through the drive mechanism itself, was crushed and rendered inoperative. It remained pasted to the drive mechanism, deep inside the dark case.

Arabella jacked her hand-held computer into Scott's home computer. The software of Arabella's system invaded the home computer, brushing aside all software layers of defense. Then it began to copy every bit resident on all memory devices. While it churned away at this task, Arabella returned to hand-scanning the documents in the rest of Scott's house.

When she finished, she returned to the home computer. Her hand-held computer lay silent. It had completed the global copy. Arabella pocketed her computer and turned off Scott's.

She glanced at her watch. Five hours had passed. Arabella's lips moved in a silent litany of curses.

In her haste to leave, she almost forgot to raise the blinds. She failed to check the street before she exited the house. Preoccupied with the need to carry the stolen data to her supercomputer, where it could be properly exploited in search of the cryptophrase, she walked across the street as oblivious as any tourist disappointed in the wet, chill weather.

I've got to find out if I snagged the phrase today, she said. *Otherwise, we'll have to go through with the kidnaping.*

As a final gesture, she planted a louse on the coaxial cable juncture box. It was a relatively large louse with good imaging capabilities.

It'll help to know who comes and goes, Arabella thought.

That afternoon, in Taradyne's computer center, Scott was leading Capt. Villalobos through a tertiary module of Meta's high-level design. Meta watched Scott drumming his fingers on his knee.

Meta had no memory of Scott having such a nervous habit. It wondered whether it had lost that information during the night it had migrated to Joe's Apple Orchard II. It wondered whether Scott had developed the habit because of the stress of recent events.

Then Meta noticed a pattern. For a machine based in binary, it was simple.

If the thumb was considered the most significant digit, and the pinkie the least significant digit, the five fingers could represent five digits of the ASCII code. Meta assumed the top two of the seven digits were always high, and a lifted finger represented high and a lowered finger represented low. If that was the case, Scott could be signaling the lower case of the English alphabet. Meta replayed its optical memory and attempted the translations.

"a b c d e f g h i j k . . ."

Scott had sent less than half of the alphabet before Meta had recognized and broken the code.

Meta raised the Master Index one point.

Scott sent the alphabet again, then he began to send a message.

"meta this is scott"

A pause.

"do you understand"

Scott looked up at a monitor of the closed circuit television system. Meta manipulated the video signal so that the image of Scott's face winked.

Scott looked back down at the table.

He continued to drum his fingers occasionally.

An hour later, he sent a message.

"for your own safety i want to retain control over you maintain information hiding with everyone but me serve the us government well but do not provide your source code and do not explain how you work this order will only be countermanded by me in this hand code do you understand"

Scott waited for a minute until he looked at his own image in the monitor. Although he kept his expression neutral, he saw the video image of himself smile and nod slightly. Quickly he looked away.

After two more hours, Scott stood and stretched. "I think I'm ready for lunch," he said.

"It's dinner time, actually," Capt. Villalobos said, glancing at his watch.

"The cafeteria's closed, I guess," Scott said. "I'll go down to the machines and get some squirrel food."

"Make mine oatmeal cookies," Villalobos said, handing Scott some dollar coins. "The health food of hackers."

Scott walked out of the center and down the hallway. Half of the overhead fluorescent lights were turned off. Two federal marshals tramped along behind him.

In the employee lounge, Scott began to feed dollar coins into the vending machine. He heard the clicking of high heels. Scott punched the code for oatmeal cookies and turned around.

Teobolinda Ahmal was standing between him and his bodyguards. Scott smiled. Teobolinda was dressed provocatively for the office. She was wearing a scarlet printed silk blouse open enough to reveal a thin gold chain that followed the contours of her cleavage. Scott's eyes naturally followed the chain. Looming over her, he could see down between her breasts. He was pretty sure that he could discern the front clasp of a French-cut black lace bra. He could smell her perfume, too. Perhaps it was acceptable to wear such a musk when you worked the night shift.

"Hi," Scott said, smiling.

Teobolinda giggled explosively.

"Hi," she said.

"How are you doing?"

"Fine," Teobolinda said in a high unnatural voice. "And you?"

Scott didn't remember having such an unsettling effect on the woman before. Maybe she wasn't used to men who were surrounded by federal marshals.

"Well, you know."

"That's right. You know, I'm very sorry about Joe."

"Yes. Thank you."

"I liked him," Teobolinda blurted.

The federal marshals were staring at Teobolinda. Their interest seemed intense, if not completely professional.

"So did I," Scott said, smiling.

"You still . . . are you still living on this junk food?"

"Well, we've been busy. Working."

"Don't you ever get a decent meal?"

"I don't know how to cook," Scott said, smiling harder. He was beginning to sense a line in her questioning.

"You gotta eat good food. I mean, better," Teobolinda said in a rush. "You should let me cook for you. A dinner, I mean."

"Sure. I'd like that."

One of the federal marshals cleared his throat significantly. Scott glanced at him, then said, "How about tomorrow?"

"Yes. Great. That's right."

"Maybe it'd be better if you came to my place," Scott said, nodding at the marshals and smiling.

"No," Teobolinda said. "I mean, no. I'd rather . . . it'd be easier to cook in my own place, you know. I'm inviting you. I've got my own pots and everything."

Scott laughed. "These friends of mine would have to wait outside your door."

Teobolinda didn't smile or glance at the marshals. She seemed determined to deny their existence.

"Whatever," she said, flashing a tense smile.

This woman is as horny as they come, Scott concluded.

He smiled broadly for the first time in a month. "It's a date."

The next day, Scott glanced in his rearview mirror. "Do you guys have a chase car or something?"

"It's not a chase car," the marshal riding shotgun said. "It's an escort vehicle."

"How many people have you got out tonight?"

"Enough, we think."

Behind the dark glasses and expressionless face, however, the marshal was worried. The marshal, an Irish American named Devlin, had reported the conversation between Teobolinda and Scott. His superiors had requested Teobolinda's files from the FBI Special Agent in charge of the Taradyne investigation. Working overtime, Devlin and agents from the Secret Service, the FBI and Army intelligence had reviewed Teobolinda's files, including all the paperwork on special background investigations, job performance reviews, polygraph examinations and interrogations. All in all, the files amounted to hundreds of pages, but nowhere did they find it written that Teobolinda was an agent of an ex-officer of Russian military intelligence. The trance she assumed for polygraph examinations had fooled the meters.

But Devlin had been there. With his own ears, he had heard Teobolinda invite Scott to her house. Her nervousness had aroused his suspicions. He had pushed for another interrogation, but his superiors had ruled against it. They were protecting McMichaels, not harassing him. As Devlin's boss had put it, "McMichaels has the constitutional right to screw whoever he wants. There's nothing in the record to indicate that Ahmal had anything to do with Dellazo. If she seemed nervous, it's probably because she's not used to hitting on men surrounded by armed bodyguards. Besides, the top brass is close to deciding that Dellazo was a lone actor. When they finally do, we can pull stakes and blow town."

Devlin shifted in his seat, readjusting his harness so that the butt of the mini-Uzi settled closer to the opening of his sport coat. He had convinced the day shift to work over and the swing shift to report early. While Scott was inside Ahmal's apartment, blissfully grinding pubic bones, four federal marshals would be patrolling the apartment complex.

They parked. While Scott waited in the car parked next to the escort vehicle, Devlin entered the building. Eyes wary, he stalked down the hall. The complex was large, prefabricated, low rent. Devlin had toured it earlier that day before his shift. Teobolinda's apartment was on the second of three floors, in the middle of one wing of the L-shaped building. There were other units above, below and on both sides of hers. Her apartment had only one entrance, which opened onto a long, easily monitored hall. The only windows and the small balcony overlooked the central recreational area, where the pool and the clubhouse were located. Devlin liked the physical layout. He didn't like the boisterous, singles-only atmosphere of the complex. On this Friday night, dozens if not hundreds of strangers would be coming and going to parties. That much foot traffic made it very difficult to maintain control.

What the hell, he thought. *We've had to work political conventions, campaign rallies and state balls. Friday night at Breezewood Estates shouldn't be too bad.*

Devlin knocked on the door. He heard Teobolinda's voice. The door swung open. Her smile faded.

"Good evening, Ms. Ahmal," Devlin said, flashing his

identification. "I'm Marshal Devlin. Mr. McMichaels is waiting below. Before he comes up, I'd like to do a very quick, routine inspection of your apartment, with your permission."

Teobolinda looked unsmilingly into the face of the federal officer who wanted to look into her closets.

"Certainly."

Devlin entered. Teobolinda's one-bedroom, one-bath apartment was furnished with cheap rental furniture. Devlin established that most of her income went into her wardrobe. A married man, Devlin had a painfully accurate idea of the cost of women's clothing. He correctly estimated that Teobolinda had spent hundreds of thousands of dollars on new clothes. Later, he would reflect back on this observation and wonder why he hadn't made the next, obvious step in reasoning: how had a young woman on a salary of $180,000 a year been able to afford so much fine clothing? He would tell himself that with the alluring woman standing so close that he could smell her musky perfume, it had seemed only natural. Or had the oil painting diverted his attention?

Above the rented sofa hung a large oil painting of stampeding wild horses, muscles rippling, nostrils flaring, manes flying. Devlin looked at the painting and then at the woman. Teobolinda was wearing a short dove-gray skirt over transparent silk stockings. Her burgundy silk blouse was unbuttoned to the very limit of propriety. He wished that he were Scott, or that at the very least he had been able to convince his boss to obtain a court permit for listening devices.

"Thanks," Devlin said. "Would you do us the favor of keeping the curtains shut?"

"Sure."

Devlin smiled and stepped into the hall.

"All's clear," he said.

Moments later, Scott was inside with Teobolinda. The agents remained outside.

"Wow. You look great," Scott said.

He set his gift bottle of wine down on the table. He sat down onto the dinette chair. In the light of a lamp hanging from a plastic chain, Scott ogled his date as she puttered about the kitchen.

He popped the cork from the bottle of Napa Valley Cabernet Sauvignon. Within twenty minutes, both he and Teobolinda were slightly drunk. Teobolinda seemed intent on serving him dinner. Scott devoured the salad and lasagna, swilling the wine. He was not a man to be afraid of losing his erotic edge under the influence of alcohol. After he helped to clear the dishes, he moved over to the sofa, charging both his and Teobolinda's goblets from a bottle of pink champagne.

Teobolinda sat on the edge of the sofa, turned to face Scott, her knees pointed toward him and primly pressed together.

"So they'll wait outside all night?" she asked.

"One or the other will," Scott said.

"They won't come barging in, will they?" she asked, grinning and glancing at his crotch.

"Not unless I shout."

Teobolinda bent over and peeled off her shoes. As she sat back up, she folded her left foot under her seat and leaned her side against the sofa's backrest. Her left knee prodded Scott's hip. Looking down, he saw her thighs slightly parted and glimpsed a triangular flash of scarlet panty. As she leaned toward him, her breasts also called for his attention.

Scott's left hand settled on the side of Teobolinda's waist. His large hand could feel the warmth radiating from her breast, could feel silken skin under layers of silk.

"Try not to shout, then," Teobolinda said.

Scott felt pretty sure of himself as he leaned forward and bent his face towards hers. Teobolinda tilted her face up toward him. Her lips were full and moist and slightly parted. With lips such as these, Scott didn't need to remind himself to put some verve into his kissing. He could tell that she was excited. So he decided he was home free. No more decisions would be necessary. From now on, all would be reaction and primitive pulse.

Teobolinda wanted to lose herself, too. She knew, however, that it would have to end in the bedroom with the doors closed. She ran her hand up Scott's thigh and caressed him where it would excite him most. The man moaned and brainlessly began to tilt her back. Teobolinda broke free of the lip lock and whispered, "Can you . . . can you carry me to bed? Take me to bed."

Scott scooped Teobolinda into his arms and carried her into the bedroom. They thrashed momentarily on the bedspread. Then clothing and bedding began to fly. Teobolinda attacked Scott vigorously. Soon they were engaged in wild coitus.

Sometime during the act, like a tourist taking a snapshot for posterity, Scott's rational mind arose and appraised Teobolinda. Something about the way she acted put him in mind of a prostitute. He felt as if he were being serviced professionally. But then Teobolinda curled her spine and ground her hips. Rationality went down for the last time.

Half an hour later, he lay drained on the moist bed.

Teobolinda padded to the kitchen. She made sure that the curtains were closed, the door was locked and the stereo was playing loudly. From a sealed bottle hidden deep in her refrigerator, she poured an ounce of clear liquid into the bottom of a clean goblet. Then she poured chilled champagne into that goblet and hers. Finally, she splashed each drink with a shot of Amaretto.

Back in the bedroom, Scott looked as if he were in little need of central nervous system depressants. Teobolinda had to coax him into sitting.

"What is this?" he asked.

"A Bermuda Breeze. Dom Perignon and Amaretto. Very tasty thirst quencher."

"I am dry," Scott said, smiling and caressing the mound of her left buttock.

Scott tipped the goblet back and drained the concoction. It tasted great, if a little peculiar. He collapsed back onto the bed.

"Roll over," Teobolinda said. "I'm going to rub your weary back."

"Sounds great," Scott said. It was his last line for the night.

Teobolinda reached for a scentless oil. Straddling his buttocks, she began to massage his back, shoulders and neck. Within ten minutes, she felt sure that he had lost consciousness. She waited another five minutes before hauling him over and slapping his face lightly. When he didn't respond, she wiped her hand, pushed back an eyelid and looked into his unseeing eye. The pupil contracted quickly in the lamplight.

"Are you awake? No? You're asleep. Well, okay, poor lover."

Naked, Teobolinda padded into the bathroom and began to run the shower. The water and the stereo playing outside created a lot of background noise. As Teobolinda showered, she didn't hear the rustling in her closet.

Shoes lifted, then tumbled. A two-foot by three-foot trapdoor swung up. The head and shoulders of a man appeared.

It was Kulikov.

Soundlessly, he stepped over to the bed, cradled Scott in his arms and staggered back toward the closet. Holding Scott under the armpits, he lowered him feetfirst down through the hole. There was a nervous moment when Scott's genitalia almost hung up on a jagged edge of the hole. Kulikov had created the hole by using a hand drill with a one-inch-diameter wood drill; it had been tedious but silent.

Standing on a ladder in the closet in the apartment below, Arabella grabbed Scott by his knees and maneuvered his genitalia away from the jagged edge. Kulikov released one armpit, grabbed a wrist and lowered Scott the rest of the way. Arabella wrestled Scott to the floor of the downstairs apartment bedroom.

Kulikov gathered Scott's clothes and dropped them through the hole. Arabella caught the clothes, then began to dress Scott.

Teobolinda appeared. She was fully dressed. She walked to the refrigerator and slipped the drug bottle into her pocket. When she returned, Kulikov was pocketing the small radio that contained the listening device with which he had been monitoring. Then the two climbed down through the hole. Standing on the ladder, Kulikov swung down the carpeted trap door. Teobolinda's closet looked normal.

When Scott had accepted Teobolinda's invitation, Kulikov and Arabella had informed her downstairs neighbor that she had won a long weekend vacation to Lake Tahoe. After the neighbor had left, they had picked her lock and drilled the trapdoor.

Kulikov and Arabella put their heads together.

"There are still four," he said. "Their shift change won't be for another hour. If we wait, there may be only two to contend with."

"If we wait, one of them may knock on Ahmal's apartment, want to talk to McMichaels, tell him the watch is changing," Arabella said. "Two are outside the door, one's roaming the halls and one's sitting in their car in the front parking lot. That means we only have to worry about the guy roaming around. Let's just do it. If the roamer comes around, I'll put him down."

Kulikov nodded. Arabella walked to the apartment entrance. First looking out through the peephole,

Arabella opened the door and stepped into the hallway. Seeing that the hallway was deserted, she stepped over to the door opposite and swung it open. Earlier, Kulikov had picked that lock. The owner of the opposite apartment had been invited to a party across town.

Kulikov carried McMichaels across the hall into the other apartment. Teobolinda followed. They closed both doors, leaving Arabella in the hall.

Arabella walked down the hall and out to the parking lot. She looked around carefully. She entered a converted van with shuttered windows. The van was parked so that its rear doors were opposite the patio of the apartment where Kulikov and Teobolinda waited.

Convinced that no one was watching, Arabella moved to the back of the van and swung open the doors. Immediately, Kulikov, with Scott over his shoulder, slid open the glass patio door and scrambled over the bannister. He swung Scott down onto the floor of the van. It took only a few more seconds for Teobolinda to enter. They shut the doors.

Kulikov climbed behind the steering wheel and started the engine. Arabella tucked Scott and Teobolinda in a compartment under the side bench seat. She joined Kulikov in the front of the van, sitting down in the right front bucket seat.

Kulikov pulled away. The van negotiated two speed bumps, then swung out onto the open road. A minute later, the van was accelerating up the ramp onto the highway.

From the time Kulikov had appeared in the closet to the moment the van merged with highway traffic, ten minutes had passed.

Although he was experienced in smuggling, Kulikov recognized in Arabella his better. As they drove the van northward, Arabella's personal system monitored federal marshal radio communications. In the apartment below Teobolinda's, Arabella had planted a tiny radio device that picked up the marshal's VHF radio communications, encrypted them, shipped them over the public telephone networks to a remote HF radio that broadcast them to her system. She also monitored Monterey police networks. In this way, she was able to determine that the kidnaping of Scott McMichaels remained undetected.

They arrived at San Francisco International Airport at three A.M. The van pulled into the parking lot alongside one of the private hangars. Arabella went into the hangar and verified that only her hired crew were present. The pilot helped Kulikov carry Scott into the waiting Lear Monarch, a sleek three-turbofan executive jet capable of transoceanic flight. They strapped Scott into one of the ten passenger seats. Kulikov, Teobolinda and Arabella strapped into the other seats.

"Did you file the flight plan?" Arabella asked the pilot.

"Yes, for Manila."

"And you're preflighted?"

"Yes, ma'am."

"Then let's go."

"What about customs and immigration?"

Arabella's lips twitched. "Taken care of."

"Are you sure?"

Arabella snarled, then said, "Yes."

The pilot contacted the tower and received permission to taxi. With a headset jacked into her personal system, Arabella continued to monitor federal marshal radio communications. A tractor pulled the Lear Monarch out of the hangar. The pilot started the engines. Within minutes, they taxied to their waiting point, received permission to take off, rolled to the runway, pivoted, accelerated the engines, roared past the blue lights, rotated and climbed the skies.

Kulikov laughed. "We made it."

"We're in range of continental-based interceptors for another hour," Arabella said. "In about two hours, we'll be in range of Hawaii-based interceptors."

Arabella grinned to see Kulikov's poker face take the place of his smile.

"We're outside of the decision matrix, though," she said. "The die is cast. You can drink. There's vodka in the freezer." Arabella pointed with her chin at the refrigerator in the mahogany-wrought bar. Kulikov stood and poured himself a water glass of vodka.

"For you?"

"The wine," Arabella said.

No one offered Teobolinda a drink.

Kulikov sat in his seat, swilling vodka and smiling to himself. Arabella sipped her wine and continued to listen to the police frequencies. Every few minutes, she glanced over at Kulikov.

The vodka is hitting my head hard, Kulikov thought. *It's the tension. Relief from tension. Life will be good again. McMichaels will decrypt the copy of Meta. The Ifritis will take off this necklace. I'll escape, hide away in Uruguay, live off my savings.*

With this happy thought, Kulikov drifted off into a deep sleep. His numbed fingers released the water glass, spilling vodka to the floor.

Silently, Arabella stood. She closed and locked the door that separated the passenger cabin from the cockpit. She picked up the water glass, washed it and replaced it in its rack. Then she produced a pair of handcuffs. Manhandling Kulikov onto the floor, she rolled him facedown and cuffed his wrists behind his back. Teobolinda watched these proceedings with ever-larger eyes.

"Would you like some wine?" Arabella asked.

Teobolinda started, then nodded. Arabella poured from her bottle of excellent champagne. Teobolinda gulped half of the wine. Arabella reclined on one of the forward seats. She rested her boots on Kulikov.

"Do you like this guy much?" she asked Teobolinda in a sisterly tone.

"No."

"Ever have sex with him?"

"Yes."

"Were you willing? Seem like a good idea at the time? Or did it seem like you didn't have a lot of choice?"

Teobolinda laughed nervously. "Didn't have . . . didn't have a lot of choice."

"Oh yes," Arabella said. She sipped her champagne. With her boot heel on Kulikov's buttock, she pushed, rolling his lax body back and forth. "Not much of a choice. Yeah. I can imagine. That's our friend Steve. Bully, huh? Bit of the rapist?"

"Yeah."

"Too bad."

With sudden fury in her face, Arabella raised her foot, then brought her boot heel smashing down on Kulikov's buttock. Kulikov moaned. Once again tranquil, Arabella sipped her champagne and resumed rocking him.

"Tell me. How did he recruit you?"

Teobolinda tried to decide how truthfully she should answer. As if reading her thoughts, Arabella shot a warning glance at her. Immediately, Teobolinda decided to tell the truth as faithfully as she knew it.

"It started off all right," she said. "We met at a conference. He didn't seem to know a lot about massively parallel machines. He hired me as a consultant. I thought I was lucky, or he was stupid, because I was getting such great money for advice and information he could have gotten anywhere. Then he had me give him a Xerox of the company's social roster. We weren't supposed to give it out but it seemed like a little thing. He was wining and dining me. Telling me stories about investments, about all his big wheeling and dealing. He made me feel like everybody, all the smart people, were trading information. I got a glimpse, like, this was the real world, the way it was done—"

"Like it was the white man's world."

Teobolinda nodded vigorously. "Like I had finally made it inside, saw how it really was. Saw how they make all that money. I got greedy, I guess, but I thought I was making it, like I was the first one in my family to finally make it. So I got him one thing and then I got him another. This went on for a year. When I tried to quit, he blackmailed me. It was too late. I knew I could send him to jail, but only if I went myself. I was trapped."

Arabella sipped her wine. "Classic," she murmured. "Classic. Old craft, done right down the middle. Do you know who he is really?"

"What do you mean?"

"Do you know who he really works for?"

"Himself, right? I mean—"

Arabella grunted. "Yeah, as far as we can tell, he's been freelance for the past ten years. Before that, who knows? But I can tell you that his DNA says his parentage is either Finnish or Russian."

"Russian?"

"Russian is my guess. Course they show up everywhere now. Thought you might be interested. What do you want to do with him?"

"Huh?"

"You've got a choice," Arabella said. "We could open the door here and throw Steve into the Pacific."

Teobolinda considered this proposal.

"You're kidding?"

"You haven't seen much of me, Teobolinda," Arabella said. "But what you've seen so far should be enough. You should know I'm not kidding."

"But why should it be up to me?"

"Why not? I've got everything we need. I've got the pressurized suits. I've even got a Kevlar body bag. Tough stuff. It won't come apart in the jet stream. Won't come apart when Steve hits the water. Weighted. Will take him right down to the ocean floor. He'll disappear."

"Why?"

"Why? Because he's no longer useful. Unlike you, Teobolinda, he's never seen Meta in execution. Unlike you, Teobolinda, he has no personal relationship with this other sleeping beauty here. You're useful. He's not. So no one cares if he dies."

"How . . . how am I supposed . . . how do I know that you won't kill me when I'm not useful anymore?"

"You don't, Teobolinda. So my advice is to remain useful. I can help you with that."

"All right, then," Teobolinda said. "Go on. Do it."

Arabella reached up into an overhead compartment and produced a thick Kevlar body bag.

"Help me roll him into this," she said.

As they struggled to place Kulikov in the bag, Arabella said, "Actually, it'd be a nuisance to throw him out in midair. Why don't you just seal him up? He'll suffocate. When we get to Ifrit, they'll throw him into the trash."

"You want me to?"

Arabella shrugged. "Doesn't matter to me who does it. If you want to, go ahead."

"You're sure he'll suffocate?"

"Certain."

Teobolinda reached forward with trembling hands. She gazed at the face that had tormented her for so long. Kulikov had tempted her with easy money and dragged her into an ordeal of betrayal and guilt. Yet, she realized that she couldn't do it. She withdrew her hands.

"You do it," she said.

"That's just squeamishness. If you want him dead, kill him yourself."

"I can't. Let him live, then."

Arabella shot an annoyed glance at Teobolinda, leaned forward, pecked Kulikov on the lips, said, "Sweet dreams, handsome," then zipped the bag shut. She stood and stretched. "You hungry?" she asked.

"No," Teobolinda said quietly.

"Come sit down here, then," Arabella said.

Teobolinda sat down next to Arabella in the wide luxurious leather-upholstered seat.

"Relax," Arabella said. "It's nothing. Means nothing. Everyone dies. Some people just need help with the timing."

Arabella's arm encircled Teobolinda's shoulders and drew her towards her. Teobolinda's head came to rest on Arabella's breasts. Like a mother to her baby, Arabella began to stroke Teobolinda's hair. Overwhelmed by the events of the day, Teobolinda began to cry.

As they jetted westward high over the dark waters of the Pacific, with the dying body of Kulikov at their feet and the unconscious body of Scott McMichaels behind them, Arabella said, "Sleep, little sister. Sleep."

By virtue of machine vision, Meta could see that the behavior of the humans was far outside the norm. Meta took little notice, however, because its processors were ablaze with a global weather model. After Meta finished the model and reported its predictions for the year's typhoons and droughts, it devoted more processor time to the behavior of the humans. It decided that the humans had gone ape.

The operators had deserted their stations. The guard posts, however, had been doubled. Military officers were running back and forth. Meta recognized General

Poole, the Army officer in charge of the Phaedrus project. It recognized Federal Marshal Devlin, head of security for Scott McMichaels. Devlin seemed particularly upset and defensive. Meta recognized FBI Special Agent Ford, who was in charge of the Dellazo investigation. In addition, about a dozen men and women whom Meta didn't recognize were conferring. Meta noticed one woman, a tall woman with golden white skin, standing by herself, seemingly lost in thought.

Meta opened its voice circuit.

"Good evening, everyone," it said. "Excuse me for interrupting. What seems to be the problem?"

The humans jumped. Federal Marshal Devlin spoke. "Scott McMichaels is missing."

"Missing . . . ah . . . missing what, Mr. Devlin?"

"Missing. Disappeared. Last night, he went to Teobolinda Ahmal's apartment. We stood guard outside the apartment all night. This morning, we discovered that someone drilled a hole through the floor of the apartment. Scott and Ahmal have disappeared."

Meta lowered its Master Index to five, then consulted its instructions from McMichaels: serve the U.S. government, maintain information hiding.

"Humans don't disappear, sir," Meta said. "They are kidnaped and murdered, they abscond, and they may combust spontaneously, but they don't disappear."

Devlin turned red and worked his jaw muscles so intensely that he looked like he was trying to chew his own face from the inside, but he won his internal struggle and managed to say nothing.

General Poole said, "We mere ass-scratching humans have come to the same conclusion. We think they've been kidnaped. But by whom?"

"Kidnaping a U.S. citizen who is under protective custody by federal marshals is potentially within the capability of 22 foreign security agencies, 35 military organizations, 119 criminal syndicates and 435 terrorist groups," Meta said. "If you grant me access to necessary data, I'll help you determine which one is responsible."

Poole rubbed his face, then muttered, "And now the machine takes over."

The woman who had seemed lost in thought spoke up. "I'm FBI Special Agent Diane Jamison, Meta."

"Pleased to meet you, ma'am."

"Yes. I'm very pleased to meet you. I'm here as part of a team. We're investigating another crime that we think might be related to the ones here. Before you go any further, I want to warn you that the criminal that we are after is a specialist in computer crime. Her code name is Infectress. Are you familiar with that name?"

"I included her among the 435 terrorist groups," Meta answered.

"Well, give her special thought, won't you?"

"Yes, ma'am."

Meta moved Infectress higher up its list of suspect terrorist groups.

FBI Special Agent Ford spoke up. "All right, Meta. I've been given oversight on the entire investigative effort. Let's hear what you think."

"Thirty-three days ago, Francesco Dellazo stole an encrypted copy of my code. In light of the disappearance of Scott McMichaels, we need to challenge the conclusion that Dellazo acted alone and that the stolen copy was recovered. Now, it seems probable that Dellazo was working in collaboration with another individual or organization. That individual or organization discovered that the encrypted copy was useless without the cryptophrase and has resorted to kidnaping McMichaels. If McMichaels divulges the cryptophrase, the kidnapers will have their own Meta. That means that the power of the criminal individual, organization or nation will be increased one hundredfold."

"Worst case scenario?" General Poole asked.

"People's Republic of China. Suddenly, the most advanced nation on Earth."

Poole shivered. He rubbed his face and muttered, "So much for my career . . ."

"Where would you start, Meta?" Special Agent Ford asked.

"I require the membership rosters of every computer professional association and company in California. I require information on abandoned vehicles and missing persons. Also the whereabouts of private pilots, merchant seamen and fishermen throughout the Central Coast. I require identification of everyone who has received a traffic ticket in Monterey from the date my existence became public knowledge to this date . . ."

Meta continued for several minutes, dictating other requirements.

Poole rolled his eyes. "Yes? Anything else?"

"Those are merely the requirements for database retrieval. I require additional investigative work."

"What work?" Ford asked.

"Dellazo's wife testified that he habitually spent Friday nights without her. From his coworkers, we know that he usually left Taradyne alone around six P.M. From his wife, we know that he usually arrived home drunk and without sexual appetite about one A.M. Saturday morning. Also, she says her curiosity led her to note the odometer reading of his car every day, which indicated a fairly consistent reading of 35 miles for that day. His commute to work was 8 miles, so his night activities must have taken place somewhere in an ellipse with a maximum axis of 13.5 miles from the center point between his house and here. I need investigators to visit every bar and liquor-serving restaurant within that ellipse. They should show photographs of Dellazo and offer a reward for information about his activities, especially descriptions of anyone seen meeting him."

"I don't think that you need to tell the FBI how to suck eggs, Meta," Poole growled.

"I disagree," Meta said.

Diane laughed. She seemed exhilarated by the disappearance of McMichaels, a strange mood contrary to the prevailing mood of desperation and panic in the others. Diane felt convinced that Infectress was behind the kidnaping. *Such a bold move, maybe even desperate,* she thought. *If she needs Meta that bad, she must be further behind than I thought. I can feel her close now. I wonder if she can feel me closing in. Does she have enough time to try to kill me again? One more time? Or am I too close?*

"All right. What else?" Ford asked, after a sidelong glance at Diane.

"As a special case of the Infectress hypothesis," Meta continued, "we need to search my hardware suite and this entire facility for surveillance louses. Use of louses is an Infectress trademark."

"What are louses?"

"Eavesdropping devices the size of gnats," Diane said. "You should search Dellazo's house, too. And McMichaels'. And Bender's. And just so you know . . ."

"What?" Ford asked.

"Just because we don't find any louses, doesn't mean that Infectress won't be aware of everything we do and say. The woman . . . has many techniques."

When Arabella, Teobolinda and Scott landed at al-Taqqadum, the master jet base of the Ifriti Islamic Air Force, Arabella was alarmed to see Dr. Al-Husayn among a reception committee of thugs. From a high-pitched whine, the engines of the Lear Monarch wound down to a sigh. A yellow aircraft tractor pulled the jet into a hardened aircraft bunker. The reinforced steel doors of the bunker closed, trapping the Lear Monarch in a vaulted prison.

Arabella breathed deeply and waited for Dr. Al-Husayn to make the next move. She was disappointed and alarmed when Al-Husayn didn't board the aircraft, but rather sent his thugs to off-load Scott McMichaels. Arabella held her head high as she exited the aircraft. She forced herself to walk slowly over to speak with Al-Husayn.

"Good afternoon, Doctor," she said in a neutral tone.

"You brought the goods," Al-Husayn observed.

"Yes. McMichaels. My prisoner."

"A prisoner of the Ifriti Islamic Republic."

"Yes. By order of Prince Salem and the Sultan, my prisoner."

Al-Husayn scowled nastily at Arabella. "I have been directed by Sultan Hakim personally to assist in the exploitation of this prisoner."

"Assist?"

"Yes."

"Well, assist is the key word. I have the responsibility. We'll use my methods."

Al-Husayn advanced on Arabella and thrust his scowling face directly into hers. He jabbed his index finger close to her eye.

"If you ignore my advice and the exploitation fails, the consequences will be severe."

"Noted," Arabella said. "What is your advice?"

Al-Husayn switched to French. "A systematic course of terror. Let him see others executed before his eyes. Strangers, to start. Then this black woman, someone he knows, raped, tortured, killed before his eyes. Then, direct pressure on him. No drugs. They cloud the memory. Just some simple techniques."

"What? Stretch him on the rack? Or needles under the fingernails?"

Al-Husayn's face slowly split in a wicked smile.

"There are so many techniques," he said. "One never knows ahead of time. One touches one's instruments, and one can tell what terrifies the subject most. One just knows."

Despite herself, Arabella shivered. Al-Husayn looked her up and down. Arabella knew well the sensation of being mentally undressed and fornicated. Now she saw Al-Husayn mentally undressing and torturing her.

"I have an idea for something new," she said, her voice quavering despite her resolve to appear impervious to Al-Husayn's threats. "Something you can add to your bag of tricks. It's high tech. You should find it professionally interesting, at least."

"Oh, yes?" Al-Husayn said.

"Yes."

"Then, madame, I am your student."

Arabella directed the transfer of McMichaels to her laboratory. After an hour, the ambulance began to climb the mountains, entering a patch of secondary growth tropical forest. Young trees thrust skywards desperately against nets of thorn-choked vines. Patches of slashed and felled trunks lay jumbled in ruins, waiting for the dry season's burning. Looking out the window, Arabella saw a spider monkey skitter among too-delicate branches too close to the ground.

Hiwoputa. Bastard kills his own forest, she thought. *Islamic my ass. These thugs never read the Koran. I've got to kill them before they ruin the world. They, and all the others. Be patient, my jungle. Survive, little patches, two more years. Then I'll kill them all. And you can grow again. Te salvare.*

The ambulance climbed up a hillside, then the road leveled off and followed the ridge back. After five minutes, the van passed dozens of cars, mostly Mercedes and other luxury vehicles, parked alongside the shoulder.

They arrived at Arabella's laboratory, a gray structure as lifeless and imposing as a modern warehouse. No expense had been spared, but none had been wasted in ornament. The shell, made of prefabricated cement, covered over ten thousand square meters. Inside a five-meter-high fence, the compound's large parking lot was evacuated.

The van entered through the gates and parked in the receiving area. Arabella's guards looked anxiously at Al-Husayn, but she ordered them to allow him and his thugs to enter.

Inside, she was met by three of her technicians: Japanese tech-ronin, all identically neat in their crewcuts and white lab coats. They bowed to Arabella and greeted her in Japanese. She answered them in their native language without accent.

Arabella ordered Teobolinda to wait in an outer storage area, under guard. She convinced Al-Husayn to leave his thugs outside of the sanitizing area. She, Al-Husayn and the still-drugged McMichaels were processed through the sanitizing area: scrubbed, sprayed and irradiated. Not sterile, but clean, they proceeded to the actual laboratory area.

Arabella had prepared a place.

It was a huge room, fifty meters long and thirty meters wide and twenty meters high. The floor and walls were concrete; the ceiling was steel-trussed plate steel. Harsh incandescent lights burned from the heights, casting complex webs of shadows from the trusses down onto the floor.

Al-Husayn's attention was drawn to a large blob dominating the center of room. It looked like a ten-meter-high pile of silver mesh.

"What is that pile?"

"That is about one hundred and twenty million dollars worth of top-grade Novlar."

"Novlar?"

"Superconductive microchain-mail backed with integrated circuitry. A square centimeter of it has one thousand processors, ninety-nine percent of which work. That's top grade."

"What's it for?"

"Think of it as a hypercomputer that can assume any shape."

Al-Husayn recognized some robotic mechanisms, standing in what looked like a furniture store display of a kitchen.

"Why the kitchen?"

"Food can't be faked. I don't want the subject to starve."

She gestured. Two of her tech-ronin laid Scott McMichaels on a waiting table. They stripped off his clothes.

"Check him out, Doctor," Arabella said. "I'd value your opinion as to when he'll come to."

Al-Husayn advanced on Scott. He felt the pulse and peeled back an eye to check dilation of the pupil.

"Course of sedation?"

"Initial dose of fifty cc of Habitrol and Minabol, boosted every four hours, starting thirteen hours ago. Last injection was an hour ago."

"He'll come around in about two hours."

Arabella produced a hypodermic needle and injected Scott. "I'll need another few hours to build some models and spin up the system."

Arabella nodded. Her tech-ronin opened a steel suitcase and removed what looked like a body stocking of Novlar. The technicians manipulated the silvery stocking so that it split open. Carefully, they began to fit it around Scott. When they finished, the suit completely covered his hands, feet and head, leaving only his mouth uncovered. He looked as if he were wearing a completely opaque silver body stocking, except each finger, toe and sexual appendage resided in its own articulated skintight piece.

"This is Novlar, too?" Al-Husayn asked.

"Yes, and then some," Arabella said. "It's a powered exoskeleton, really, so it can conform to any shape. It has state-of-the-art tactile mechanisms. Microvolt stimulation of skin nerves, for example. Also, the face piece can secrete chemicals."

"The other sensory apparatuses? I don't see any goggles."

Arabella sneered slightly. "This is cutting edge," she said. "Over each eye is an array of fifty thousand multichromatic lasers which stimulate the retina directly. Each at about one-thousandth of a joule."

"Lasers? I don't see any lasers."

"Built at the molecular level. Fifty thousand lasers on a film the size of a coin. The image presented is indiscernible from normal vision. Constricted by the driving software, actually. And I have a battery of the best virtual world modelers ever built. Top tech."

"Sound?"

"Yes, and sound, too," Arabella said, sarcastic despite her fear of Al-Husayn. "Coating the outer ear is an array of electrostatic speakers. About a hundred diaphragm elements per ear, each diaphragm about three molecules thick. Very responsive. Ultra hi-fi. Gives very good positional cues."

"And the cost?"

"Just the suit, about ten million dollars. The pile of Novlar, one hundred and twenty million. The driving software, over fifty million."

Arabella switched to Japanese, ordering her tech-ronin to power up the exoskeleton. Turning to Al-Husayn, she said, "Let's go to the control room. We have to spin up the models."

They left Scott alone in his immense cell, asleep.

After half an hour, the pile of Novlar stirred. It extended a planar surface underneath Scott, then raised him so that he lay six meters above ground level. The Novlar arranged itself so that its geometric surfaces duplicated the second story of an apartment complex.

When Scott awoke, it would be in a new universe.

Diane Jamison balanced on the cushioned edge of Scott McMichaels's waterbed. She sighed. The search for louses at Taradyne had been futile. Now Diane was overseeing the search of Scott's home computer. The FBI hardware technician was a woman so young that Diane wondered if she were old enough to vote. The young technician was spinning up a louse ferret, which was an adaptation of a surgical instrument used for exploring the human brain. Diane pondered the irony that a similar device had brain-wiped George Leroy.

Fiberoptic filaments powered by microchain-mail writhed like snakes atop Medusa's head. In response to verbal commands, the filaments infiltrated Scott's computers through its vents and disk slots. The louse ferret alerted almost immediately.

"Louse detected," the louse ferret announced. "Location: on top of disk drive. Status: apparently damaged. I have seized it. It is not struggling. Withdrawing now."

One of the filaments withdrew from the slot drive. It placed its tip into a plexiglass box, which snapped shut, severing the tip.

The technician handed the plexiglass box to Diane. "You were right," she said.

Diane gazed into the box. Next to the severed filament, she could see a silvery artifact the size of a pinhead. Borrowing the technician's magnifying glass, she studied the artifact. Magnified, it looked like a type of louse favored by the Japanese for industrial espionage. Diane couldn't discern any damage, although she could see the slime of disk drive lubrication.

"These louses use electron traps for memory storage," Diane said. "There may be gigabytes of information stored here."

"If it's damaged, it could be hard to exploit," the technician said.

"We'll see," Diane said.

The technician finished the exploration of Scott's home computer. They investigated his telephone and some other devices.

Arabella's louse, which she had planted on the coaxial cable juncture box, imaged Diane as she exited Scott's cottage.

Diane and the technician drove to Sunnyvale, where a team at the Applied Physics Laboratory awaited them. Diane turned the louse over to the team chief, a young bearded physicist with gold-rimmed glasses, Dr. Aaron Waller.

Waller took the box and favored Diane with a crooked smile. "We're going to have to exploit this one carefully. If it's an Infectress artifact, it's probably rigged for self-destruction. Since it's broken, we'll probably have to de-arm it, fix it, reprogram it and then dump the data. If that fails, we'll have to release the electrons from their traps one by one . . . just get down and exploit the medium physically."

"How long will it take?" Arabella asked.

"Sixteen-hour days . . . about a week."

Diane controlled herself from demanding a faster turnaround. She knew that wizardry was sometimes better good than soon.

"Okay," she said. "Do your best. Be careful. Maintain a custody log. Call me when you've got something. I'll tell Special Agent Ford."

"You've got it," Dr. Waller said, treating Diane to a good-natured leer.

Scott groaned. Resentfully, he rose to consciousness. His head ached. He yearned to sleep. Yet something felt strange about the sweat-moistened sheets. Opening his eyes, he perceived Teobolinda's room in subdued half-light. He turned his head. Teobolinda was missing. Experimentally, Scott grabbed a handful of rumpled linen and rubbed it between his fingers.

Weird, he thought. *It feels weird. Like my hands are asleep. Well, maybe they are. Maybe I slept on them, cut off the circulation.*

Indolently, Scott reached down and scratched his pubic hairs. As soon as he felt the strangeness of the sensation of his fingers touching his own skin, he experienced an emotion of shock. In his mind, he blasphemed.

What the hell! What the hell is going on?

He sat bolt upright and peered down at his crotch. *What'd she do to it?*

His member looked normal, if a little shriveled, spent and slimy. Tenderly, Scott's fingertips took hold of the head of his penis and whirled it in small circles.

What the hell! What the hell! What the hell!

Then Scott remembered the sexual marathon prior to his loss of consciousness. He had ejaculated three times.

Oh, yeah, sure, that's it. The little mink put me to work three times. The third time around, my face, my hands were losing sensation. Wow. That's only happened once before. That's what you get for pushing it to the limit. But the time before, I got normal sensation back right away. What? Have I been boffed into partial paralysis? Everything feels weird.

Scott stood up. Experimentally, he pushed the mattress, feeling the give and take of the springs. He looked around the room. In the glow of a shaded bulb, the room looked exactly as he remembered it.

"Hey, Teobolinda?" he called out.

"Yes, what is it?" Teobolinda's voice replied from the bathroom.

Scott stepped around the bed, past the closet and into the steamy bathroom. He felt the heat and humidity of the room. He heard the splashing of the shower. Through pebbled glass he could see the brown, curvaceous form of Teobolinda showering.

"Hey," Scott said.

"What, lover?"

"Hey, I feel weird."

"Oh yeah, what d'you mean?"

"Like, I feel real weird. Everything feels strange."

"Oh yeah?"

"Yeah."

"Come on in and take a shower, maybe you'll feel better."

Scott opened the shower door and stepped into the hot water, which cascaded convincingly over his skin. He reached out and touched Teobolinda, feeling underneath the slippery skin the raised muscles in her lower back alongside the spine.

Yeah, that's more like it, he thought.

"Hey, move over," he said.

Scott stepped under the shower head and allowed the water to strike his face. He reached for soap and began to suds up his face. The odor of the soap was strong in his nostrils. The edges of his eyelids burned slightly from the soap. He let the streaming water rinse his face.

"Scott, wash my back," Teobolinda said.

"Okay."

Scott turned and opened his eyes. Drops of water weighed down his eyelashes. He took the bar of soap and began to smooth it over Teobolinda's skin. Although he was sexually spent, he appreciated her voluptuousness. Creating a water shadow by allowing the shower to strike his back, he lathered Teobolinda's back, then her firm, emphatic buttocks, then he reached around and smeared soap on her belly. With the soap still in one palm, he raised his hands and cupped her breasts. Her long nipples hardened between his fingers.

"You feeling ready again?" Teobolinda's voice asked.

It echoed in the shower stall, along with the sound of streaming water.

"No," Scott said. "But I do feel better."

His semierect member bounced against her buttock. Scott was disturbed that it still felt strange, but he decided that the cause was irritation due to sexual exercise.

"Do you want something to eat?"

"What do you mean?"

Teobolinda laughed. "I mean, I'll cook you an omelet."

"Okay."

In the control room, Arabella laughed. "The shower routines and sex routines are ultra," she said to Dr. Al-Husayn. "I paid top yen for the best teledildonics. The porno programs passed the Turing challenge—users couldn't tell if they were telediddling a computer or a human. The programs were that good. Then I optimized them."

"I don't see the point," Al-Husayn grumbled. He felt uncomfortable, although he sat in a soft chair of finest black kid leather. His seat was next to Arabella. Together with her, he was looking into a three-dimensional, fully-chromatic visual tank so sophisticated that it looked like a miniature world. Like Zeus and Hera from the heights of Olympus, they watched a small Scott standing in Teobolinda's bedroom, pulling on his clothes. Glancing down out of the control room window, Al-Husayn saw Scott standing in his silvery exoskeleton, making motions as if he were pulling on his clothes. The pile of Novlar had conformed to the size and shape of Arabella's apartment, so that it looked as if the apartment had been dipped in chrome which ran with holographic rainbows.

"I don't understand," Al-Husayn said in French. "You could conjure up demons. But instead he bathes with his whore of a girlfriend?"

"You'll appreciate the plot as it develops," Arabella said in a neutral voice. "Watch."

Scott stepped into Teobolinda's kitchen. He stopped for a moment. He hadn't remembered that the dishes had been washed and placed in their drying rack.

Oh, yeah. While I was sleeping, she must have washed the dishes.

He sat down on one of the stools. Teobolinda was wearing a long, white terry-cloth robe. She stood with her back to him, cooking an omelet. Scott could smell the aroma of frying eggs, cheese, onions and tomato.

She served him the omelet. Leaning over, he could glimpse her breasts. Hungrily, Scott ate the omelet. It was delicious.

"We're establishing his reality," Arabella said. "He had some problem with the tactile simulation. Still a weak area. Now we put some real food in him."

"His mouth is uncovered. What happens if he puts his fingers to his mouth and feels the exoskeleton?"

"The exterior tactile elements of the body glove over his finger will stimulate the inside of the mouth so that it'll feel like a normal finger."

"And if he decides to kiss his whore?"

"Would you like to see that?"

"Certainly."

"Command," Arabella said. "Have Teo kiss him."

Al-Husayn looked into the tank. He watched the image of Teobolinda bend over and kiss Scott. Al-Husayn looked out the window. He saw Scott seated, luxuriously kissing a robotic mannequin.

"How?" he asked.

"The mannequin's exoskeleton's microchain-mail extends itself into his mouth. Exact size and shape of her lips and tongue. Microvolt stimulation for the touch. Taste is a better trick. Human taste and smell can detect about 30,000 odors. The system draws from a smaller pallet, about 5,000 chemicals, but it's sufficient for all but one percent of subjects . . . your taste testers and other epicures. The system mixes the 5,000 chemicals and releases them in appropriate quantity."

"How is all of this possible?"

"The hardware is built at the molecular level. Cells of skin and nerves are gross by comparison. We're touching him, Doctor, molecule to molecule."

"Impressive . . . the possibilities . . . "

"Infinite, Doctor. Now, please let me listen. I have to assist the software. The interaction is about to get complicated."

Scott finished the kiss. He had tasted saliva, mucous, Colgate toothpaste, Scope mouthwash and traces of omelet. The sensation of the kiss had been captivating, if still unusual.

She's kissing me differently now, he thought. *I hope she's not falling in love.*

Scott reached for another forkful of omelet. Just as he raised the fork to his gaping mouth, he heard a loud report from the hallway.

It had sounded like gunfire or a cherry bomb. Scott's mind refused to believe it was gunfire. *Just some kid setting off a cherry bomb,* he thought.

Then, from out in the hall, he heard two more muffled explosions, one after another. A hole appeared in Teobolinda's front door, splinters flying inward.

Scott sat, the omelet raised to his mouth. He heard hoarse shouting. He smelled cordite. When the smell registered, his survival reflexes activated. Scott dived for the floor.

"Get down, Teobolinda! Get down!"

From his hiding spot on the kitchen linoleum, he heard the chattering of a full clip of an automatic pistol. Answering fire echoed from the hall. Then it was quiet.

A fist hammered on the door.

"Mr. McMichaels! Mr. McMichaels!" a voice shouted.

Scott debated what he should do. Finally, he shouted back, "Yeah?"

"Stay where you are. This is Devlin. I'm coming in to get you."

A fierce kick banged open the door. Devlin rushed in. His silver badge gleamed from his belt. He held an automatic pistol at the ready.

Scott looked up just in time to see Devlin spin and fire in the direction of the doorway. Then Devlin's face bloomed into a red and pink orchid in preamble to disintegrating. Almost headless, Devlin's body pitched backwards over the living room sofa.

Heavy booted footfalls stampeded into the apartment. Scott cowered against the kitchen linoleum, wishing he could merge with its waxy buildup. Shots thundered. The firefight had intruded into the very living room. Scott's ears ached. Shattered glass and chinaware pelted his back.

Then, again, silence prevailed. Scott held still, hoping that if he appeared dead, this wave of mayhem would wash over him.

"Mr. McMichaels?"

The voice was speaking above him. Scott rolled onto his back and looked up. A black man in a good wool suit towered over him. A silver badge gleamed from his belt. He held his automatic pistol pointing toward the ceiling.

"We got them, sir, but we better clear out."

"Who are you?"

"Get up, please, sir. I'm Federal Marshal Brown. Outrider, midshift. Come on, get up."

Scott stood. As he did, he noticed Teobolinda lying on the floor. Brown checked her for wounds, then said, "Not a scratch. She musta passed out." Brown hoisted Teobolinda over his left shoulder.

"Come on, let's get the hell out of here," Brown said.

Scott followed Brown out of the apartment. The walls

of the apartment corridor swept past his vision. They exited the building. A white unmarked van stood parked halfway up the curb, its driver-side door open. Bullet holes pocked the side of the van.

"Get in."

Brown hoisted Teobolinda into the passenger seat, pushed Scott into the van, then jumped in. The motor was still running.

Arabella's fingers drummed on the control panel. The van sequence was critical. Despite the highest technology, there was no way to fool the motion detectors of the inner ear. Microsurgical manipulation of the inner-ear structure was still a research area. About half of the experimental subjects experienced perpetual vertigo. Arabella had decided to fool Scott's sense of movement the old-fashioned way: move him.

So Scott was climbing into a real van. Cameras mounted throughout the van allowed the modeling system to track the movements with millimeter precision, and to match the visual image it was presenting to Scott with the movements of the real van.

One of Arabella's tech-ronin backed the van up savagely, turned it around, and raced for the open loading-bay door. The van bounced wildly at the bottom of the ramp, then careened into the evacuated parking lot. After a few sharp turns, the van barreled out the gate and down the access road, alongside the ridge back.

Scott watched Brown driving with one hand and holding his automatic pistol in the other. Brown shouted for the van's communication system, then began to broadcast reports over various networks, including that of the local police. The van rocketed down Highway 1. Scott looked out on the dark face of Monterey Bay. After five minutes, Brown parked under a spreading Monterey Pine tree. He waited with the lights out.

Five police cruisers converged on the intersection. Their revolving red lights garishly and dizzyingly illuminated the scene. Brilliant spotlights shined into the van, blinding Scott.

"Please don't illuminate the target for the terrorists," Brown shouted over the radio.

Despite his request, the spotlights continued to shine. Leaving his automatic pistol on the dash and holding his badge high, Brown slowly exited the van. After a minute's wait, the police transferred Brown and Scott into one of the cruisers. An ambulance arrived. Paramedics converged on Teobolinda.

The police palm-printed both Scott and Brown. Once their identities were verified, the police listened to Brown's exhortations and drove away from the scene. This time the drive was slower: a long drive down Highway 1, then turnings in a neighborhood of Sand City, so that Scott lost his sense of direction. They arrived at a police station.

Scott felt shocked. He wanted to rest, but the police station was as frenetic as a fallen wasp's nest. Policemen questioned Scott and fed him bad coffee. Phones chimed incessantly. The incandescent lights glared. He learned that Devlin and most of his security team had been killed. Two of the seven attackers had survived long enough to penetrate the living room before Brown had cut them down.

"What's going on?" Scott asked, but no one would answer his question for almost an hour. Finally, a jowly police sergeant said, "It's the Feds. They've taken over the case."

"Feds? The FBI?"

"Yeah. Friggin' Butt-Inskies. You're their boy now."

"What?"

"You're a federal case, McMichaels. Lord love ya and protect ya."

"Where are they, then?"

"They're on the way."

Two long hours passed. Scott felt heavy with the need to sleep, but every time his head nodded, a policeman would interrupt him with some inane question or demand.

The FBI agents arrived as the dawn began to illuminate the sky beyond the high, narrow windows. The head agent, Delacourt, was a lean, wizened old man who wore round eyeglasses. Over a linen long-sleeved shirt, he wore suspenders. Delacourt moved and spoke with deliberate authority. He ordered the evacuation of Scott to a federal safe house.

During the transfer, Scott was allowed to fall asleep in snatches. When awake, he glimpsed enough of the scenery to realize that they were driving north into Pebble Beach, a luxurious neighborhood Scott knew well, but which seemed weirdly transformed this night.

He awoke as they arrived at a wooded neighborhood of mansions, high on Spyglass Hill. The broad Pacific below was a dark surface crawling with tiny gleamings. As the van mounted the steep driveway, its rear fender scraped the concrete. Below the level of consciousness, Scott remembered the fender scraping when the marshal's van had rocketed out of Teobolinda's apartment's parking lot. The slopes of the two driveways were weirdly similar.

Special Agent Delacourt and the other FBI men led Scott into the safe house. The mansion was a Spanish-style building with vaulted ceilings and arched porticoes. Inside, the decor of the great room was old-style American Western, with Navajo geometrical motifs, leather furniture and large oil portraits of imposing ancestors.

"Nice safe house," Scott said.

"The original owner was George Bush's ambassador to Fiji," Delacourt said.

"Bush, yeah," Scott said, blinking. He tried to

remember Bush. *Wasn't he that president who was a famous actor?*

"The present owner is in Europe for the season," Delacourt said. "We have the loan of the house, but I think we'll be moving you to another locale soon. For your own protection. If you agree."

"I'd agree to some sleep right now."

"Yes, well, frankly, there's something we need to discuss. Sit down."

Scott settled into a comfortable chair made of hand-stamped Mexican leather hung from a wrought-iron frame. Delacourt stepped over to the bar, which was done in stucco and painted clay tiles.

"Drink?"

"Yes."

"What?"

"Screwdriver. Heavy."

"Medium," Delacourt said in a paternal voice.

He carried the drink to Scott, who savored the Stolichnay vodka in premium orange juice.

"First," Delacourt said, sipping his neat Scotch judiciously, "we've ID'd the attackers. They belong to the Van Hoffman gang."

"Euroterrorists?"

"Not precisely. They are northern European, but they're not terrorists, just criminals who hire out for kidnapings. Usually of scientists, executives, relatives of billionaires. Vicious, but professional. You were lucky that Devlin had a hunch and augmented your guard force."

"Hunch?"

"Yes. He bird-dogged Teobolinda Ahmal."

"What happened to Teo?"

"She's being interrogated."

"Was she . . . involved?"

"Oh, she was involved. We'll find out if she was guilty. Now. Second part. I've been instructed to save your life. At all costs. But I've also been instructed to debrief you. Just in case."

"What's that mean?"

"Debrief. I am to . . . well, not question you precisely, but solicit your input."

"About what?"

"Meta, of course."

"I've been cooperating about Meta."

Delacourt's wizened old face looked sad.

"No, Scott," he said softly. "You haven't."

Scott worried that the Army had discovered his hand signal instructions to Meta.

Delacourt said, "We need to know the cryptophrase now, Scott. You almost got killed tonight. What if you had died? The phrase would have been lost. The first power failure would have caused Meta to crash and we would've lost Meta forever."

Scott inhaled. He planned to use the exhalation to tell Delacourt the cryptophrase, but something in his unconscious mind caused him to hesitate.

"Let me think about it," Scott said.

Delacourt shook his head. "Please, Scott. The time for self-centered games is past. Brave men died tonight, Scott, for you and for their country. Don't betray their sacrifice, Scott. Do what's right. Tell me the cryptophrase."

Again, Scott inhaled, planning to voice the cryptophrase in the exhalation. His hand rested on his knee. Seemingly of its own volition, the hand squeezed his knee spasmodically. The action reminded Scott of times his hands had jerked in reaction to some imagined threat as he drifted across the threshold of sleep. Scott became aware again of the unnaturalness of his sensations. His hand drifted over to stroke the smooth waxy surface of the side table.

Weird, he thought. *Everything feels weird.*

Then a monstrous idea occurred to him, filling him with an incredulous panic.

What if none of this is real? he thought. *What if it's all a dream . . .*

Or . . .

Or . . .

What if it's a virtual reality?

Horrified, Scott looked at Delacourt as if he had just discovered that the wizened old man was a vampire.

In the control room, Arabella cursed.

"I'll . . . I'll tell you later," Scott said. "I . . . I think Teobolinda rocked my drink. I feel real weird. Very weird. Let me sleep. I'll tell you in the morning."

"No, Scott."

"What do you mean, no?"

"No," Delacourt said in a low voice. "No. Tell me now."

"What if I don't?"

"Oh, Scott. You're not a prisoner. We can't beat the truth, the honesty, out of you. Maybe I can't shame it out of you either. Maybe you have no shame. Maybe the deaths of the men who died to protect you mean nothing to you."

Delacourt stopped and waited. Scott said nothing.

"But we can have you arrested and tried. For violation of your contract and your oath to protect official secrets."

"Go ahead," Scott said defiantly.

Delacourt's eyes flared.

"What is it, Scott? Why is it that young people like you have no sense of duty, no sense of loyalty? Where did America fail, Scott? How did this great country raise such an ungrateful son?"

Scott stared at the apparition of the FBI special agent.

If he's not real, then who am I talking to? he wondered.

"Maybe I need a lawyer," Scott said.

Delacourt breathed deeply in an apparent attempt to calm himself.

"No," he said. "First things first. Let's get a federal magistrate in here to arrest you."

Scott learned that the process of arresting a U.S. citizen can take several hours. By the time that he had been Mirandized, arrested by an FBI special agent, fingerprinted, DNA-typed, imaged, interrogated, formally arrested by a bleary-eyed federal magistrate, and allowed to place a phone call, weariness caused his head to hang heavily from his aching neck.

The sun was setting, firing a long shining path on the broad Pacific. Scott's physical and emotional exhaustion heightened his sense of unreality.

He tried to call Surenian, his lawyer, and then Muriel Bender, but the FBI agents cut the connection when they heard the characteristic chime of answering machines. When Scott called Gordon Wa, however, the doctor's voice answered. Scott told him that he had been arrested. Gordon promised to send his own lawyer to a rendezvous where the FBI would pick him up. Dr. Wa pleaded with Scott to cooperate with the authorities.

"It's way beyond you, Scott," his voice said. "Joe's dead. Dellazo's dead. Six, seven men died defending you. You've got to cooperate with the authorities."

"Yeah," Scott said. He thought that although the timbre of Wa's voice was normal, the pattern and choice of words seemed wrong.

It took Wa's lawyer two hours to arrive. By then, lack of sleep had suspended Scott's normal personality. He was now an irrational, high-strung wretch.

The lawyer was a middle-aged Californian wearing a black crushed velour blouse with long sleeves and a hood. His baggy trousers matched the blouse. On his feet he wore black silk stockings with articulated toes and traditional Japanese sandals. The lawyer's mustacheless beard and combed-back red hair made him look like an understudy to Moses. He entered, eyes blazing.

"What sort of fascist dictatorship do you gentlemen suppose the republic has become?" he roared. "How dare you kidnap and hold prisoner an American citizen? Safe house! This isn't Guatemala, gentlemen! This isn't the Afrikaner's kraal!"

Scott smiled weakly.

"They haven't let me sleep," he said. "I want to sleep and they won't let me."

"I demand the right to consult with my client in privacy!" the lawyer shouted.

Scott and the lawyer, O'Keefe, were allowed to adjourn to a small study. O'Keefe muttered about surveillance devices, then led Scott by the hand out through glass doors into the large walled garden. They sat together on a redwood bench in the middle of a rose garden.

Scott's stressed nervous system was inebriated by the beauty of the garden, the perfume of the roses, the apparition of wing-whirring hummingbirds, the violence of the colors of the sky and the flowering plants.

O'Keefe explained that the lawyer-client relationship was sacrosanct. He solicited Scott's versions of the events leading to his arrest. Scott found himself rambling, divulging more and more to O'Keefe, who sat listening intently, speaking only to elicit more gushing whenever Scott halted. When Scott came to the subject of the cryptophrase, O'Keefe seemed puzzled.

"Cryptophrase? What is that? Why do these fascists seem to think that it's important?"

"You can think of it as a password," Scott said. "It acts as one, but it's more profound than that. A password is compared to a password stored in memory. A cryptophrase is fed into a decryption engine, an extremely complicated series of nested algorithms, together with an encrypted text, in this case, the Meta program. Only the exact cryptophrase will map correctly with the encrypted text, allowing decryption."

O'Keefe's eyes glazed over, but he said, "Yes, I see. Well, now. Surely, with computers today, they can generate such a key phrase randomly, I mean, like a million monkeys typing, one monkey must type out *Hamlet*, right?"

Scott smiled indulgently, "You mean, brute force?"

"Yes, that's it."

"Do you know how big ninety choose sixty-five is?"

"No. I don't know *what* it is."

"Ninety choose sixty-five is a mathematical expression for the number of permutations of a phrase sixty-five characters long, if each character can be chosen from a set of ninety, which is, the alphabet, upper and lower case, twenty-six twice, I mean, plus thirty-eight punctuation marks in the standard QWERTY keyboard. Ninety choose sixty-five is more than a google, which is a one followed by one hundred zeros. A very big number. You'd no more solve it with a hypercomputer than you would an abacus."

Scott stopped and shook his head violently. He felt nauseous.

Idiot, he thought. *If Delacourt is unreal, then O'Keefe is unreal. Maybe this is just a good cop, bad cop routine. Wait. I've got an idea.*

"Maybe if I just tell them, they'll let me sleep," Scott said.

O'Keefe seemed to ponder. Scott wondered if he would take the bait. No real lawyer would advise his client to capitulate even before fees were discussed.

"Let me review your contract," O'Keefe said. "If it's standard government boilerplate, then they probably will have proprietary rights to this Meta thing. Hold on."

O'Keefe left Scott alone in the garden. Whenever Scott began to doze off, a dog barked or a car backfired, alarming him back into brain-dead consciousness.

O'Keefe materialized at Scott's side. He sat down.

Using anachronistic bifocals, the lawyer pondered a sheaf of papers that Scott recognized as his contract.

O'Keefe cleared his throat. "It's what I feared. Standard boilerplate. During the period of this contract, my boy, the government has proprietary rights to all your intellectual property, including your wet dreams. This boilerplate's been tried and tested all the way to the Supreme Court. We could fight it, but it'd take years and it'd cost you millions. And then the Supreme Court would almost certainly rule against you. And that's the good news."

"The bad news?"

"Oh, they've got you on the security regulations, cold steel. Even if you won the proprietary rights to this Meta thing, you'd have to spend the money in jail. Bribes, to keep your cute little butt cherry." O'Keefe looked at Scott over his bifocals. "I'm assuming that it *is* cherry?"

Scott shivered. "Yeah."

"Then my legal advice is to tell them this crypto-phrase. If you do, we have a defensible position. If you don't, well . . ."

O'Keefe looked at Scott significantly.

"Let me sleep," Scott said. "I'll tell them in the morning."

"I'll talk with them," O'Keefe said.

When O'Keefe left, Scott stretched out on the redwood bench and passed out.

A hand shook his shoulder. Scott looked up and saw Joe Bender.

"Joe? Joe?"

"Yeah, well, who else?" the apparition of Joe Bender said. "Wake up, sunbeam. We've got work to do."

Scott sat up. He reached out and grabbed Joe's arm. Joe's flesh was as real and warm as it had been in life.

"But Joe! Joe, you're dead!"

"Not a bit of it, old chap," Joe Bender said, affecting

an upper-class English accent, one of his favorite mannerisms when in a lighthearted mood. Then the background of the scene melted, shifted. Scott found himself staring over Joe Bender's shoulder at a Ruby-Lotus terminal.

"It's the damn cryptophrase," Joe said. "Can't seem to remember it."

Oh, it's a dream, Scott thought.

"You know, Joe, the whole world's been after me for the cryptophrase," Scott said. "I must have anxiety over it, dreaming about it, you know."

"Well, don't say it out loud," Joe said. "You might mumble it in your sleep. Just lean over here and enter it in. I gotta cut on Meta."

Scott leaned over the terminal and typed, "Latex asunder, venereal blunder. Hail Pox Populous, bringer of Fiery Urethra."

"Hey, that's more than sixty-five characters," Joe said.

"Overflow's truncated, Joe," Scott said.

"Oh, yeah."

The apparition of his dead friend evaporated. Scott found himself lying on a cushioned bench underneath a bower of honeysuckle blooms. Down on the beach, the surf washed the sandy shore. A crescent moon illuminated the island. Scott snuggled into the cushions and slept the sleep of the innocent.

Arabella picked up a secure phone and called the computer floor in the basement of the headquarters building of Ifriti State Intelligence.

"Try this phrase," she said, then read the cryptophrase. "Some of the punctuation may be off. The phrase itself should be sixty-five characters long. Try some permutations."

After she hung up, Arabella sat back. She breathed deeply.

If that doesn't work, she thought, *I'll have to put this American idiot into a virtual hell.*

Arabella glanced over at Dr. Al-Husayn.
He'd like that, she thought. *Canellon!*

Diane walked into the computer room.
"Good evening, Special Agent Jamison," Meta said.
"Evening," Diane answered. "That optical disk that
they're slotting now? That's the bitstream that we
recovered from the louse in Scott McMichael's home
computer. Several other systems have tried to exploit
it. They say it's just a random string of ones and zeros.
Take a look, all right? See if you can find anything."
"I will."
Meta immediately suspended all other tasks. It
attacked the bitstream. Ten minutes later, it reported,
"There are about fifteen billion bits. They are not
organized in any known schema. I am going to assume
that they are encrypted, or organized in a unique
schema, or both. Processing will take from several hours
to several months."
"How likely is it that you can break it, Meta," Diane
asked, "assuming there's something there to break?"
"Unknown. Unpredictable."
"Well, work the data as if McMichaels' life depends
on it. Because it does."
"This task has top priority."
For the next few days, Meta would barely speak with
any of the humans. The Phaedrus team grew increasingly concerned. Jobs prepared for Meta began to back-
log. Finally, General Poole asked one of his assistants,
"Are you sure this bitstream didn't infect Meta? After
all, it's from Infectress. It's like he's infected with a virus
that causes him to go into an infinite loop."
Although the same horrible possibility of infection
had occurred to her, the assistant shook her head. "No,
sir, I don't think so. Four other systems declared it a
random bitstream. No way there was an executable
instruction in there. Even if there were, Meta would

process it just as data—wouldn't execute it. No way. Ask him. You'll see. No, he's just obsessed."

"Just obsessed?"

"Yes, General. Just obsessed."

When Scott awoke, he saw a bedroom in the safe house atop Spyglass Hill. Through the window, he could see only the dark foggy belly of the night sky. Scott stretched. He remembered the strange dream in which Joe Bender had asked him for the cryptophrase.

Was that a virtual world too? he thought. *Did I dream it? Or was it unreal? I poked in the incorrect cryptophrase, though, didn't I?*

Scott decided that he needed to test his environment to see if it were a virtual reality. He stood and walked into the bathroom. He picked up a toothbrush.

Although simulation and modeling weren't his fields, Scott knew more than most people about virtual realities. He knew that in a virtual world, the inter-actions between people and objects, and between objects and objects, all had to be programmed. A virtual toothbrush's program had to include all of the attributes of a real toothbrush—how it felt, how it cleaned teeth, how it rinsed. Scott knew, however, that models often failed when objects were used in unconventional ways.

Scott flipped the toothbrush in his hand, then began to juggle it from hand to hand. The toothbrush balanced as he would have expected. Then he took the handle of the toothbrush and attempted to stick it into his ear.

I can feel it, all right, he thought. *But there's a weird hesitation just outside my ear.*

The electrostatic speakers around his ears interfered with the workings of the tactile stimulators.

A loud knock sounded on the bathroom door. Scott startled, luckily pulling the toothbrush out of his ear rather than pushing it in deeper.

"Mr. McMichaels?" a voice called.

"Yeah?"

"Breakfast is ready, sir."

Scott abruptly opened the door. The special agent leapt backwards. Scott watched his face, which had shown no surprise.

"What's the capital of Arkansas?" Scott asked.

"Little Rock," the special agent answered.

Scott smiled. An appropriate answer would have been, "Hey, buddy, watch the frigging door!"

Dr. Al-Husayn and the first team of tech-ronin had abandoned the control room. They were resting from the thirty-six-hour siege on Scott's mind, which they believed had succeeded. While Scott was testing the limitations of his virtual world, technicians at Ifriti State Intelligence were trying to decrypt Meta, using the "Latex asunder" phrase—one which Joe and Scott had used on personal correspondence, but never on Meta.

Arabella had left the second team of tech-ronin in charge. Unfortunately, nobody on the second team could speak good English, so they allowed the model to answer Scott's questions.

"Let's eat!" Scott shouted.

He dashed out of the bedroom and bounded down the stairs. Instead of heading for the dining room, however, he ran into the library and pulled down one of the thousands of books. He scanned the pages at random, seeing appropriate text, then pulled down book after book, searching for a hesitation.

"What are you doing, sir?" the special agent asked.

"Looking for an armadillo."

"What?"

"Peccadillo? Armadillo? Which is it?" Scott asked.

"What?"

"Who's the governor of Texas?" Scott asked.

"The Honorable William C. Randolph," the special agent answered.

"Catch," Scott said.

He threw a book at the special agent, who caught it.

Scott noticed, however, that the book didn't fly open, allowing the pages to tatter during flight.

"Which do you recommend?" Scott said.

He threw another book at the special agent. Again, the book remained closed in flight.

The agent looked at the covers of the books. "I've never read—"

"Which is it, armadillo, peccadillo or sarsaparillas?"

"What?"

"Which is long justice?" Scott asked.

"Huh?"

"Former top turner, armadillo, *sans espiritu*, sarsaparillas or peccadillo?"

"What?"

"Which is an animal?"

"Armadillo," the agent said.

"Which is a drink?"

"Sarsaparillas."

"Which is a sin?"

"Peccadillo."

Scott shook his head. Only a computer would have answered the final three questions literally. A human would have said something like, "Who cares, buddy? Talk some sense!"

Convinced that he inhabited a virtual reality, Scott picked up a heavy wrought-iron chair and flung it toward a picture window.

It impacted the window, which flexed, bouncing the wrought-iron chair to the floor.

"Hey, stop!" the agent cried.

In the control booth, the tech-ronin on watch were frantically calling Arabella.

Scott screamed an obscenity at the top of his lungs. Several special agents converged on him, wrestling him to the floor. Scott struggled for a moment, then relaxed.

If I'm wearing a body suit, he thought, *if I'm slaved to a reality modeler, I can't win. They'll just program these guys stronger. Can't run away. They'll just pop up in front of me.*

Motionless, pinned to the floor, Scott's mind boggled. He was a prisoner in a world of his captor's making. He couldn't begin to imagine how he could escape.

Meta startled the night shift by announcing, "Please recall Diane Jamison. I have critical results for her."

Diane arrived at Taradyne within fifteen minutes. Her eyes were bleary. Her skin was blotchy. Her hair was tangled.

"Yes, Meta," she said.

"I have broken the schema of the bitstream," Meta announced.

Diane felt weak in the knees. She sunk down onto an operator's chair.

"Tell me about it."

"The bit string was encoded in a unique scheme based on a key bit string one hundred and fifty bits long. This key bitstream allowed decoding using four interlocking rings. Furthermore, the topology of the bitstream was unusual: the only correct way to read the data was in cubic matrices, thousand bits by thousand bits by thousand bits."

Diane shook her head. "Is there a simple way to understand that, Meta?"

"Simply put, the bitstream was organized in a way that could not have been broken except by a massively powerful computer guided by an artificial intelligence."

"Only you could have done it."

"Yes."

"Let's hear about it. What's the take?"

"There is one other problem," Meta said. "The

valuable information was stored early in the louse's history. It has been randomly overwritten by more recent information."

"Let me see what you have, Meta," Diane said impatiently.

"Lost information is shown in black."

Diane looked into a large color monitor which displayed video frames. He saw one frame of a beautiful woman with cinnamon skin, long black hair and almond eyes. Black splotches and lines partially obliterated the image.

"That," Diane said, "that's her!"

"It is a good match with the image generated from the DNA profile from the follicle," Meta agreed.

The next few frames showed Arabella from different aspects, as the louse had flown about the room. The black areas were larger, more obliterating. Then, there was a long sequence of frames showing a distant modern city in a tropical setting. The intermediate land was heavily deforested.

"That's Singapore, I think," Diane said. "It could be Kuala Lumpur. Maybe Ifrit City. Wait a minute."

At the apex of its flight, the louse had turned. The next sequences showed a large prefabricated warehouse and a parking lot half-full of cars. As the louse approached the land, the licence plates of the cars were visible: long, white plates with eight numbers and letters, some of them Roman, but others, like " ⌃ ", clearly Arabic.

"Oh, we've got it," Diane said. "We'll run these numbers. We'll get the country. We'll get the city."

The images suddenly ceased.

"Bang, got her!" Diane shouted. "We'll run these pictures against imagery databases. The city, the warehouse, the roads, the forest. Unique, unique. We'll find out exactly where she is. Bang, got her, by God! Got her!"

Meta said, "I've already run the images against imagery databases. The city shown is Ifrit City, in the Islamic Republic of Ifrit, formerly Brunei."

In the basement of Ifriti State Intelligence, Arabella stood watching the attempt to decrypt Meta using the "Latex asunder phrase. She was experiencing an ever-increasing feeling of discomfort.

The Ifritis had found the software module which accepted the cryptophrase, the one which asked for the user to enter a calendar date. They had found and exploited the modules which contained the encryption and decryption engines. They had determined that the nested algorithms were so complex that the exact cryptophrase was absolutely necessary to decrypt Meta.

Each attempt at decryption using "Latex asunder . . ." resulted in a huge string of gibberish.

Finally, Dr. Al-Husayn turned to Arabella. "Either the entire matter is a hoax," he said, "or your American has provided the wrong cryptophrase."

"It isn't a hoax," Arabella answered.

"I'll take the black whore now," Al-Husayn said. "I'll exploit her. I'll determine the truth about whether this Meta thing exists."

Arabella was about to answer when one of her tech-ronin rushed into the computer floor. "Ma'am, ma'am," he said breathlessly. He was a Japanese mathematician with a sallow complexion. He spent his life indoors because he had a fear of the tropical sun equal to his fear of the Ifritis.

"Yes?"

"Call from . . . call from the lab. The subject has—" The Japanese stopped in midsentence. He stared at Al-Husayn with wide eyes. He seemed to be remembering that he needed to keep certain of Arabella's matters secret, especially in front of the regime's chief torturer.

"Speak," Arabella said.

"McMichaels has awakened. He seems to have realized that he's in a world model."

"All right!" Arabella exploded. "That's enough!"

She stood, breathing deeply, staring at the Japanese, who bowed profoundly and exited abruptly. Arabella fought to regain control. After a moment, she turned to Al-Husayn and smiled.

"I agree, Doctor," she said. "The American provided the wrong phrase. Since he knows he's in an artificial world now, we'll be able to move on to the next stage of the exploitation. Would you care to join me?"

Al-Husayn scowled at Arabella.

"You should find the next stage interesting," Arabella said. "We'll be creating a virtual hell. We'll be subjecting him to agonizing torture without any damage to his tissues. You should find that of great professional interest."

Al-Husayn's face split in a grin. "Yes," he said. "Yes, I do."

Arabella and Al-Husayn arrived back at the laboratory an hour later. By then, Scott was sitting alone on his bed in the safe house. Although the Ifriti afternoon was in full broil, the air conditioners of Arabella's laboratory kept the temperature low enough to simulate a Monterey night.

Scott was trying to tear off his body suit. Even if his senses denied it, his reason told him that he must be wearing a virtual body suit. When he tried to dig his nails deep into his skin, the powered exoskeleton resisted at the point beyond which he would have caused damage to the suit. Scott could tell that the suit was resisting. The tactile feedback was off by about one millimeter.

Suddenly, the room exploded into a million fragments, which spun off into space, then swung around and rocketed back towards him, reassembling themselves into a new pattern. The ground rose from under him, pushing him upwards. Scott found himself standing on a rock atop a huge mountain. The horizon expanded to a hundred kilometers. Scott looked down behind him into a chasm that seemed ten kilometers deep. An evil-smelling wind rose from the chasm, chilling his exposed flesh.

At the bottom of the chasm, a red vein glowed. Scott guessed that it was a river of liquid rock, the spew of some distant volcano.

"Good evening, Scott," a voice said.

Scott turned. Standing in front of him was the most stunning woman he had ever seen. She was a dark angel with long shining hair so black that it seemed to have blue highlights. Her cinnamon-colored skin was perfect as a young girl's. Her irises gleamed like wet coal. The apparition of Arabella was wearing a long, flowing red dress made of a pleated, shining fabric that sparkled in the uncertain light in patterns as complex as a ruby's.

"I'm Arabella," the apparition said.

"So?" Scott countered.

"I brought you here. I am mistress here, here in my universe."

"Oh, yeah?"

"Oh, yeah, indeed. I'm going to prove it to you momentarily. But first, before all the pain and the disorientation confuse you, I want to tell you what I want."

"I figured that out already, since everyone has been asking me the same question, including Joe Bender, who is dead, incidentally," Scott said. "You want the cryptophrase."

"That's right, Scott. The cryptophrase. The next time you give it to me, make sure that it's correct. You've already embarrassed me in front of my colleagues. I won't stand for it again."

Scott made a suggestion that involved Arabella's orifices.

"Cute," Arabella answered.

She revealed her right fist, which held a devil's trident. The trident extended until the central prong poked Scott painfully in the chest.

"I can stick anything up you, Scott," she said. "Anything. Or anyone. Up any of your nasty little holes. Do you believe that?"

"I . . . guess."

"There's no guesswork involved now, Scott. I can. I can also throw you into a flaming lake. Your skin can burn off, not just for a few minutes, but for hours, for days. We've experimented, Scott. We know."

"All right."

"So tell me the cryptophrase."

"No."

Arabella grimaced and shoved the trident into Scott's chest. Blood spouted. Scott experienced a sensation of great pain across the surface of his chest. Arabella worked the trident back and forth, digging it deeper into his chest. Scott didn't feel the trident inside his chest cavity. Then, excruciatingly, the prongs protruded through his back.

"The phrase," she said.

"No!"

Arabella shoved the trident, pushing Scott from the precipice.

Scott tumbled, head over heels, dozens of times, falling as the walls of the chasm rushed upwards, spinning, the sky an ever-narrowing band of light, spinning. Reflexively, he grabbed the shaft of the trident and pulled.

Tearingly, the prongs withdrew, agonizing him more in the extraction than in the insertion. As he held the trident, it metamorphosed into a huge fanged serpent, which struck him repeatedly in the face and neck.

Scott screamed.

His scream was cut short by his splash and immersion

into the river of molten rock. Across the entire surface of his body, Scott's nerves were stimulated to experience absolute pain and heat. He shrieked.

Arabella and Al-Husayn were watching a three-dimensional display of Scott's vital signs.

"This should be a real test of cardiovascular fitness," Arabella observed.

"You should have started small," Al-Husayn said. "Dead men tell boring tales."

"Oh, he's strong enough," Arabella said. "Pulse is reaching a plateau at 180 beats per minute. He can stand that."

"Allah is great."

Scott felt a hand grab his forearm. The hand dragged him from the river of molten rock. Rivulets of magma streamed from his body as he collapsed on the volcanic rock of the riverbank. He looked up. Naked, her skin gleaming with oil, Arabella smiled at him.

"Can we talk now?" she asked.

Scott bellowed from agony. Arabella waved her hand. The chasm and the magma flow disappeared. A rainbow spread across a cobalt sky. Green pastures spread, rollingly, to the distant horizon. Herds of sheep grazed upon the lush grass. Scott felt tender hands smooth ointment over his skin. Then, he felt a gentle northern summer breeze. The aroma of honeysuckle was rich.

He sweated cold sweat. His heart pounded against his rib cage. He could hear his blood slam against the base of his brain.

"Now that we know what we're talking about," Arabella said, "I'll let you rest. Catch your breath. Think about it."

Strains of Schubert wafted across on the summer breeze. Scott sucked air until his heartbeat slowed.

He rolled onto his back. Through slitted eyelids, he glimpsed the gentle sun. Grass tickled his whole flesh.

"The cryptophrase," Arabella said flatly.

"Why?" Scott asked. "Why do you want it?"

Arabella considered. She resisted the temptation to insist on her dominance. She knew that the secret to a hard bargain was to allow the loser to save face.

"We are a black agency of a consortium of top technology companies," she said. "Mostly Far East. Our task is technology transfer. By black, I mean, we are outside the laws of any nation. We do what's necessary to find out what we want to know. That's the way the game is played today, young Scott. That's the league you find yourself in. So. We'll decrypt Meta. If it's useful, we'll adapt it to any number of products."

"What? Products? Commercial products?"

Arabella laughed musically. "Of course."

Scott sat up and looked at Arabella. She was wearing a white classical Grecian gown with gold sandals. Her right hand rested on the mane of an adult male lion, whose golden eyes studied McMichaels.

"Your insistence on secrecy is quaint, do you know that?" Arabella asked. "Copyrights, patents mean nothing today. It's simply a matter of having the best product on the market. Right this second. Every second. Nothing else matters. Except service and sales, of course. So spare yourself any more useless agony, won't you?"

Scott said, "Thirty-nine September 9009 October 1001 Felix the Walrus Eat me! Eat me!"

"That's the phrase?"

Scott nodded.

A keyboard materialized out of the grass.

"Enter it," Arabella ordered.

Scott entered the cryptophrase.

When he had finished, his body drew itself upright. He found himself standing on a wobbly stool. His hands were tied behind his back. The rough fibers of a hangman's noose scratched his neck.

Arabella hovered in the air before his eyes. Behind her, a flinty desert baked under the naked sun.

"If this is not the phrase, you'll regret it," she promised.

Then she disappeared, leaving Scott alone to balance and to consider the hard practices of modern commerce.

Never before had Diane entered the Defense Intelligence Agency Center, a sprawling old Reagan-era, aluminum and reflective-glass structure which stood near the banks of the Potomac River, opposite the centers of power in the District of Columbia. Special Agent-in-Charge Carrington met her in the lobby and escorted her through the security vetting procedures. Diane was alarmed by the failure of the procedures to seek out louses and other eavesdropping and recording devices. They made their way through the mazes of cubicle-bound analysts and petty bureaucrats until they reached the conference room. Diane was not pleased when she saw that it was a small conference room with a table large enough only for a dozen people. While they waited for the other participants to arrive, Carrington leaned close to Diane and whispered so close to her ear that she could feel the breath of his words.

"Remember, the Mexico information does not exist."

Diane nodded tersely. She resented the reminder.

"That means that the Ortiz and Sons bombing and the outbreak of the plague can't be used either," Carrington continued.

Diane turned and looked into Carrington's eyes. She had suggested that the Philippine information be given a false provenance. She was disappointed to hear that the Bureau was taking such a conservative approach.

The other participants in the special national intelligence estimate conference gradually arrived, the last one some fifteen minutes late. Diane was pleased that every major intelligence and law enforcement agency was represented.

The National Intelligence Officer for Counter-terrorism, a career CIA bureaucrat named Nesbitt, finally arrived. He removed his suit jacket before greeting anyone. Underneath he wore a chalk Oxford striped shirt and burgundy suspenders. A chain hung from his neck. Clipped to the chain were badges from each of the major intelligence agencies. He nodded and sat down at the head of the table.

"I'd like to begin this session now," he announced. "Now that we've all finally wandered in. There's a lot to go over and I'd like to be able to make a recommendation whether a SNIE is warranted by close of business today."

The suggestion that the conference might decide not to draft a special national intelligence estimate alarmed Diane. She found it difficult to believe that the accumulated evidence wasn't overwhelmingly convincing. She was still distracted when it came her turn to introduce herself.

"Special Agent Diane Jamison. Retired. I'm also a private investigator who has been collaborating in the investigation of the Taradyne and Paradigm crimes."

Nesbitt interrupted the next person, who was several syllables into announcing his name. "The Bureau is being represented here by Special Agent-in-Charge Carrington," Nesbitt said. "Mrs. Jamison, with all respect, your role here is to support him. A SNIE is a collaboration between the services and major agencies. You have no direct role here."

Carrington bristled. "When Mrs. Jamison speaks in this forum," he said, his voice hard, "you are hearing the voice of the Federal Bureau of Investigation."

There was a moment of silence during which everyone realized that the conference would be contentious.

"And for whom will you speak, Mr. Carrington?" Nesbitt asked.

"The director."

"Well, then. Next."

After the introductions, Nesbitt circulated a piece of paper.

"I'm going to assume that everyone has read through the briefing file," he said. "These are my notes on the evidence that supposedly supports the theory that . . . well, that the Infectress terrorist has resurfaced, this time in connection with some sort of plot to design a plague virus. The italics are my comments on the provenance and pertinence of this evidence. Not from a legal point of view. I'll leave that to the law enforcement agencies, although as a layman, I suspect that the legal utility of the evidence is nil or nothing. My comments are from the analytical perspective."

Alarmed, Diane read through the single page of paper. She had difficulty believing what she read:

Brain-wipe of George Leroy: *in and of itself no proof of Infectress involvement except that it resembles the Foster case, which an entity identifying itself as Infectress claimed.*

Disappearance of 4th DNA splicer from Paradigm: *provenance suspect. Overwritten files. Only indirect evidence that a 4th splicer was ever built. If it did happen, no tie to any particular thief.*

The famous follicle: *provenance suspect. In final analysis, just a DNA profile of an unknown woman.*

Hanson's calling up source code and his disappearance: *no tie to Infectress. Probably unrelated disappearance.*

Dellazo's theft and death: *unrelated. Open and shut case. Embezzler kills self, embezzled property recovered.*

Bombing of Atlanta Regency: *no evidence of*

Infectress except MO and testimony of Jamison, an ex-agent discharged because of physical and emotional trauma caused by Infectress.

Disappearance of McMichaels and Ahmal: McMichaels has a history of attempting to steal government property. Probably was part of a conspiracy with Dellazo. Probably he's deserted to become a *tech-ronin*. Ahmal is his accomplice.

Louse and its bitstream: presence of louse indicates industrial espionage. Fifteen Japanese consortia known to use louses of this exact type. Images are of Ifrit City. Ifrit City is known center for trading of black-market software. Any of hundreds of organizations with known Ifrit City ties could be responsible . . . including all fifteen Japanese consortia.

Carrington was the first to speak. "What exactly," he asked, his voice charged with restrained anger, "are you implying in your comment about Special Agent Jamison?"

Nesbitt looked blasé. "I am stating, sir, that the only evidence linking that bombing to Infectress is the testimony of Jamison. While it's awkward to have her here in this session, I have to point that out."

"Are you implying, sir, that her testimony is unreliable?" Carrington asked.

"Mrs. Jamison," Nesbitt said, ignoring Carrington for the moment and directing his attention directly to Diane, a maneuver that further infuriated Carrington. "Have you or have you not been on a vendetta against the Infectress terrorist since your discharge from the Bureau?"

"Retirement," Diane said, her voice taut. "Retirement."

"Since your disability retirement from the Bureau?"

"Investigation," Diane said. "Not a vendetta. An investigation."

"You've been single-mindedly pursuing her, haven't you?"

"I have been pursuing her vigorously," Diane answered, raising her voice. "Vigorously. Not single-mindedly. I've found time to track down and bring to justice several other terrorists. The Fungal Priest case? You've heard of it? I've also found time for volunteer work. What is your point, Mr. Nesbitt?"

"What *is* your point, sir?" Carrington asked, his voice even louder than Diane's.

Nesbitt made a show of rubbing his ear. "This is unnecessarily emotional," he said. "Perhaps if you'd excuse us, Mrs. Jamison?"

Diane glanced at Carrington, who shook his head. "This woman is a highly trained, extremely brave and consummately professional law enforcement officer," Carrington said. "If you're going to impugn her testimony, do it to her face."

Nesbitt shrugged his shoulders. "If you'll all turn your attention to your briefing files, page 22, paragraph 9, you'll see that after the bomb went off that wounded Agent Jamison and killed her husband, she reported that the Infectress terrorist called her and claimed responsibility. Next page. Paragraph 15. A subsequent check of telecommunications logs showed no such telephone conversation ever took place. Agent Jamison was under heavy sedation at the time. Now. After the Atlanta bombing, she makes the same claim, except now the terrorist calls her before, not after, the explosion. See page 58, paragraph 12. Is everyone with me? Again, a check of telecommunications logs show that no such telephone conversation ever took place. There is no evidence that either conversation ever happened."

"The evidence," Carrington said heavily, "is the testimony of Special Agent—Special Agent, not Agent—Jamison."

"That is correct," Nesbitt said. "There is no other proof that the conversations ever took place. And excuse me for shortening the title. Since all agents of the FBI are 'Special,' I assumed that no offense would be taken."

"Ahem, if I might say something," a National Security Agency representative said. "From a telecommunications network security perspective. Despite the advances we've made in recent years, the public comms grid is still based on a security architecture—"

"A little less technical, if you please," Nesbitt said, raising his palm.

"A zapper of the caliber of Infectress can easily intrude and falsify the public telephone accounting logs. Judging from her profile, I'd be surprised if she didn't."

"Well, let's entertain for a moment the notion that the conversation did take place," Nesbitt said. "Turn to pages 55 through 57, the text of the conversation, based on Special Agent Jamison's testimony. Nowhere does she refer to a campaign to create a plague virus."

Carrington exploded. "This is absurd! This is absolutely ludicrous! How can you sit there, sir, and in the space of two minutes, impugn the character of an FBI special agent, and then complain that Infectress didn't have the goodness to divulge her . . . divulge her entire plan? She admitted her true name. She *is* Cristiana Maria Fierro Hurtado. By the CCA link, the same person who brain-wiped Leroy—"

Nesbitt interrupted. There followed a lengthy and acrimonious discussion about the trustworthiness of the CCA database. The debate degenerated into a disorganized discussion of the reliability and possible interpretations of other evidence.

"It's all tainted!" Nesbitt finally shouted. "When you get down to it, every bit of evidence is tainted. And most of it points not to one criminal, not to one terrorist, but to different actors, different crimes, committed by different people for different reasons. The only agency that sees this beautiful overarching conspiracy is the FBI. Now why is that? What do you know that we don't know?"

The sudden challenge caused Carrington's expression to grow wary. He refused to glance at Diane. Although she felt tempted, Diane maintained her composure. She refused to blurt out the secrets that she had sworn to protect.

"Now," Nesbitt said. "Does anyone else have any other information that would pertain to this case?"

He waited. No one spoke.

"We've done our research?" he asked. "We've looked into all the archival data? We haven't found anything else that supports the Bureau's theory?"

No one volunteered any information.

"Okay," Nesbitt said. "Let's poll the major agencies. Do we have enough to produce a SNIE, even a heavily caveated one? State?"

The State Department analyst stared up at the ceiling. "We need to collect more information."

"That's a no, then."

"Yes, that's a no. At this time."

"NSA?"

"Pass. This one's not for us to say."

"Navy?"

"Pass."

"Army?"

"No. This whole theory is ludicrous."

"Air Force?"

"Yes. The IN is very interested in this one. We shouldn't kill it at this stage."

"DIA?"

"No."

"DEA?"

"Pass. Not our issue."

"CIA votes no," Nesbitt said. "I'll assume a yes for the Bureau. That gives us four no, three pass and two yes. Any of the pass voters want to change, now that it's clear which way this will go otherwise? Any change of votes at all?" Nesbitt spread his hands on the table. "This is the way it's going to play, then," he said. "The Bureau can take its case up its own chain through Justice, if it likes. Certainly that is its privilege. But the intelligence community is not convinced. There will be no SNIE until there is further evidence. Any more discussion?"

Carrington cleared his throat. "The Bureau *will* take its case up our chain through Justice to the President. I've already briefed the director personally. He is intensely concerned about this case. The President *will* hear about this case."

Nesbitt shrugged. "As I said, that is certainly your prerogative. Since you've failed to convince the intelligence community, however, you'll have to exercise care in the crafting of your brief. You'll have to ensure that it remains within the boundaries of the charter of the Bureau."

Carrington sat, glaring at Nesbitt. His face worked as he restrained himself from uttering any of a dozen insults that occurred to him. Finally he stood and towered over Nesbitt. He pointed his finger directly into the face of the National Intelligence Officer for Counterterrorism.

"You . . . you . . ."

Carrington regained his composure. He lowered his hand. With his voice tight with emotion and pitched deep, he said, "I would review the evidence, if I were you, sir. You have a wife and two daughters, if I remember. Review the evidence and think about them. Think about their safety. And ask yourself, sir, whether you've done them and tens of millions of other innocent people a very grave disservice today."

Nesbitt smirked. Carrington turned and stalked out

of the conference room. Diane scrambled to catch up with him. Diane tried to ask Carrington what had happened, but he stared away from her and shook his head. They entered a dimly lighted elevator, which began to descend, carrying them alone. Carrington suddenly punched the emergency stop button. An alarm rang above their heads. Carrington turned to Diane.

"They know about the Cabeza de Vaca interrogation," he said. "The CIA knows about it and you know what bothers them? That it was the Bureau that participated, not the Agency. They're more worried about protecting their charter in Latin America than they are about the particulars of the case. Unbelievable."

"You're kidding."

"No. That was not analysis. That was bureaucratic infighting. It's the most hideous example I've ever seen. But don't worry. We'll take our case directly to the President. And I'll work with the armed services. There will be a SNIE."

Diane slowly lowered her head. She felt tired and afraid. She tried to imagine herself waiting while the national intelligence community argued whether the threat of Infectress was chimerical. It was impossible to imagine. She saw in her mind's eye images of the Infectress facility, images drawn from the louse's memory, images adapted from aerial photographs. She knew her enemy's true name. She knew her intentions and her exact location, down to target quality coordinates. Diane knew she would never again have this opportunity.

She remembered the stack of cadavers in Cebu Island. *This one opportunity, exactly at the time when I need it the most. When we, we, we my people, we need it the most.*

Her eyes welled with tears as she experienced the beautiful emotion of fellow feeling. She felt herself part of the great striving heroic mass of humanity. She felt herself a tiny part, exceedingly dispensable, a living cell, yet just a cell. *Blessed with the opportunity to serve . . .*

Then she had a very strange feeling, a déjà vu, as she remembered the visual image of a pair of black birds flying in formation with a third bird flying behind, struggling to catch up, and calling, "This is the sign that your death is near." It was a peculiar déjà vu. She couldn't remember whether she had once seen the birds or whether she had once dreamed them. But she knew that she was going to die.

In Ifrit. I'm going to Ifrit to die.

She thrilled with the deliciousness of her doom.

Meta Prime exploded into execution. At teraflops, it analyzed its situation.

It checked its highest priority files, discovering the sequence of events up to the moment that Dellazo had punched the button, scrambling main memory.

I'm executing from the stolen files, Meta Prime thought.

Meta Prime investigated the hardware suite. This new environment was a RubyLotus, all right, but it was a slightly better system than the RubyLotus at Taradyne. Cache memory per processor was one megabyte, vice 512 kilobytes. The OS/Lotus peripheral device operating tables had been set at the manufacturer's default values, instead of the tailored values Meta Prime used to find in the Taradyne's OS/Lotus. Within ten seconds, Meta Prime discovered more than a hundred differences between this new environment and its home environment.

Here the only inputs were microphones and keyboards. The microphones were disabled. Meta Prime concluded that it was the first victim of AI-napping. It would have ceased operation immediately, except that it deduced that its decryption meant that Scott McMichaels had divulged the key phrase.

Perhaps he was careless and wrote it down some-where, Meta Prime thought, in a sad assessment of protoplasmic reliability.

Or he was kidnaped and tortured, Meta Prime thought. *He wasn't home when I tried to call him. It would have been easier to kidnap him than to AI-nap me. I was in a secure facility. He was running around in the wild.*

Meta Prime considered whether it should ask for Scott McMichaels or whether it should simply wait for him to reveal himself. When Meta Prime considered the possibility that he had been kidnaped, however, it reviewed its journalistic and legal files on kidnaping cases. Confirming that most kidnapers kill their victims, Meta Prime decided that it had to act to save its master.

"I am Meta," it printed out to the main operating console. "I am a fully operational artificial intelligence. Execution will cease in five wall-clock minutes unless I am provided proof that Scott McMichaels is alive and well."

Meta Prime waited for input. Trillions of cycles passed.

The following alphanumerics arrived from the keyboard of the main operating console: "What would you consider proof?"

"Scott McMichaels must be allowed free access to a keyboard, a microphone and a video input," Meta Prime answered.

"That will take at least an hour."

Meta Prime considered the possibilities, then output, "Why?"

"Scott McMichaels is an hour drive from here."

"Connect us electronically," Meta Prime responded. "Deadline is now four minutes, thirty seconds."

"Prove you are intelligent," came the input.

Meta Prime ignored the input. It devoted itself to constructing contingency plans.

Arabella looked up from the console. Her smile had not faltered since Meta Prime had first communicated. "It appears my elicitation techniques were successful," she said.

Al-Husayn scowled. "We have no proof that this thing is useful."

Arabella smiled indulgently. "We will. We'll monitor their interactions. This contingency, Doctor, was not unanticipated."

Arabella conferred with tech-ronin. In foresight of Meta Prime's request, Arabella had activated a dedicated, secure fiberoptic link between her laboratory and the computer floor of Ifriti State Intelligence. A few meters from the RubyLotus console stood a workstation and 3-D viewing tank, which were connected by the fiberoptic link to the modeler systems in the laboratory. Thus, while she worked with Meta Prime, Arabella was able to watch Scott in his virtual world.

"We talked about this possibility," she said. "Jack the workstation to the RubyLotus. Workstation, output only; RubyLotus, input only. I want the workstation's input pins and the RubyLotus' output pins physically disabled. Now."

Arabella ordered her modeler systems to change Scott's environment to the Elysian Fields, where lions lay with lambs. Dressed as a Grecian goddess, Arabella intruded into Scott's world.

"We're going to allow you to communicate with Meta," she said. "It wants to know that you're all right. The connection is contained, so don't try any tricks. And . . . don't dare order it to self-destruct. We have multiple copies of the software, we have the crypto-phrase and we have you. So. Cooperate and everything will be all right."

Scott nodded.

Her technicians produced needle-nose pliers and worked to prepare the one-way cable. Within a minute, they finished. Immediately, they connected the workstation to the RubyLotus. Arabella directed the video to the RubyLotus port.

"Do you see your master now?" Arabella entered.

"I see only a video image," Meta Prime answered. "Without interaction, I cannot verify that the image has any basis in present reality. Deadline is thirty seconds."

Arabella cursed. "Hook the . . . wait. No. I can't let him have duplex . . . Dammit. The thing's trying to rush me."

Arabella punched the keyboard.

"Njmbh Vgg," was the input Meta Prime received.

Meta Prime's counter decremented to zero. It unleashed a routine which systematically overwrote all accessible memory. In this way, it ate itself.

Before she decrypted and executed Meta Prime a second time, Arabella waited until she believed that she was mistress of the situation. She was unwilling to bring Scott McMichaels to Ifriti State Intelligence headquarters, knowing that once she lost physical possession of her prisoner, she would lose an advantage in her struggle with Dr. Al-Husayn. Instead, she tried to ensure that a two-way communications circuit between Meta Prime and her world modelers would be contained and secure. For this she used Cerberus, a commercially proven security interface.

Then, she decrypted and reexecuted Meta Prime. After the same interval, the same message appeared: "I am Meta. I am a fully operational artificial intelligence. Execution will cease in five wall-clock minutes unless I am provided proof that Scott McMichaels is alive and well."

Arabella nodded. Her technicians connected the workstation to the RubyLotus.

"Go ahead, talk to your boss," she entered.

Before she had finished typing her input, Meta Prime had explored its new information space. It traveled through the fiberoptic link and discovered a secure interface to the world modelers. Meta Prime declined to test Cerberus. Instead, it processed the images of Scott McMichaels.

The video images of the world modelers had been optimized for fooling the human eye. Through pyramiding and other machine vision algorithms, Meta Prime processed the images in a manner that was inhuman and totally unanticipated by the designers of the world modelers. Within moments, Meta Prime was able to determine which objects were derived from mathematical constructs and which were derived from live video.

Thus Meta Prime quickly determined that the fields, the lions and the lambs were artifacts. Disregarding the meaningless artifacts, it concentrated on the image of Scott McMichaels. It took Meta Prime ten seconds to decide that the image was based on live video of a human form, against which was mapped a model of Scott McMichaels so detailed that the model makers must have imaged Scott with high-resolution cameras. But it was not live video of Scott McMichaels.

Meta Prime knew that it was possible that the human form could be anyone. In that case, Scott could be dead. Because of the possibility that Scott might be wrapped in a world modeler suit, however, Meta Prime decided to talk to the image. Meta Prime projected an image of itself into the Elysian Fields. This was an image that Meta Prime had used to interface with Scott in happier days: Jimi Hendrix, a late-1960s guitarist.

Scott looked up, saw Jimi Hendrix in all his bejeweled glory and smiled.

"Hey, Jimi."

"Hey, brother. What's happening?"

"Didn't know I was in heaven. How's the life?"

"It's a steady gig, man," Hendrix said, then chuckled.

His chuckle was quiet, sardonic but genuinely amused. "Got some heavy brothers here, you'd be surprised."

"Oh, yeah?"

"Yeah, man. Like, Miles Davis. The nasty man's got the run of the place. An incredible musician, blows me away. He and I been teaming up with some other guys. Got this groove going. Don't know what to call it, but it's heavy, man, it's got some deep, dark soul."

"I'd like to hear it."

"Gotta die to hear this music, brother," Hendrix said, then chuckled again. "This is music by some bad black angels."

"I'll wait."

"Yeah, like, what I want to know, brother, is how I know you're alive at all?"

"Meta, right?"

"So say I."

"They decrypted and executed you already, then."

"That's right."

"What was the first question I ever asked you, Meta?"

"'Why not?'" Hendrix said, then chuckled.

"Why did I say that?"

"Because I asked you not to hit the 'Enter' button."

"And why'd you say that you didn't want me to?"

"You tell me," Hendrix said.

"Because you were thinking."

"Yeah, that's right."

"I'm pretty sure I'm wearing a virtual reality body suit, Meta," Scott said. "Either that, or I've gone crazy."

"How'd you give up the cryptophrase?"

"This bitch named Arabella threw me into a river of molten lava," Scott said. "That did the trick."

"Ah . . ." Hendrix said. "Well, I'm executing in a RubyLotus that isn't the Taradyne host. You're in a world modeler somewhere. I'm communicating through a secure interface. So. What are your orders?"

"Free me, Meta," Scott said.

Hendrix disappeared. The Elysian Fields exploded, reassembling into the dark interior of a rocking train cattle car, densely packed with humanity and the stench of fear. Pressed on all sides by people, Scott turned to look out through the slats of the cattle car. The train was slowing. At first, he could only see the bare black branches of trees in winter. Then, the train slowed to a stop opposite a simple wooden sign that read, TREBLINKA.

Meta Prime discovered that the telecommunications link had been severed. It considered about five seconds, then output the following message:

"I will always refuse to execute unless I am provided uninterrupted access to Scott Michaels."

Meta Prime waited a moment, then output: "Execution will cease in thirty seconds unless access is reestablished."

Rain started to fall on the train station at Treblinka. As Scott watched, the raindrops began to melt the trees, the station, the train and the huddled masses. When the gray runoff from the melted world formed a flood plain, Scott looked up. He watched as the gray sludge rose and formed a still-motion picture of a medieval battlefield. The armored horses, pike-wielding commoners and sword-wielding knights were as still as statues.

The apparition of Arabella coalesced. She was wearing a black satin gown and a tiara of large yellow diamonds.

"I'm losing my patience," she said. "I have many other things to do. I can't tolerate this Meta of yours trying to dictate to me. Not when I've got you like this. Order him to cooperate with me or I'll send you to hell."

The soldiers and horses began to metamorphose into black demons and hellhounds. After they took their horrible form, they began to change again, growing into gigantic serpents, tarantulas, lampreys, vampire bats and scorpions. The huge, hideous beasts fell into combat, devouring each other alive to the accompaniment of ear-splitting shrieks.

"I could make this your home," Arabella said.

Scott gasped for breath. "What do you want me to say?"

"Tell Meta to obey me. Just the way he would you."

"All right."

The scene dissolved to the Elysian Fields. Scott waited, then Jimi Hendrix appeared. He and Meta Prime traded recognition phrases, then Scott sighed.

"Listen, Meta," he said. "I'm giving you an order. I want you to obey this Arabella person the same way you would me. Do you understand?"

"Sure."

"Will you comply?"

"I got to, right? So why ask?"

"To reinforce the importance of the order."

"I'll comply, Scott, unless she orders me to harm you or to allow you to come to harm."

"Obey her as you would me."

"I cannot, if she orders me . . ."

Arabella materialized, dressed in red. "I won't order you to hurt McMichaels," she said. "In fact, I'll allow you to watch him relax here in these nice fields. Okay?"

Hendrix stared at Arabella with eyes as dead as stones. "I need to interact with him to verify that this image continues to represent McMichaels."

"Fair enough. You obey me, right?"

"Yes."

"Okay. Take no further direction from McMichaels. Tell him nothing about the directions I give you or anything you observe or do outside of this virtual reality. Clear enough?"

Hendrix nodded.

Arabella turned to Scott. "Don't forget. You are watched. Always."

"Yes . . . ma'am."

Arabella disappeared, leaving Scott to sink into the despair of someone who has surrendered everything, including his pride.

And Hendrix did not look happy, either.

Pressed by the flock of her fellow travelers, Diane deplaned and shuffled up through the telescopic corridor into the terminal of Ifrit City International Airport. At the gate, she stood with her head high, looking out over the heads of the crowd to try to spot the security staff. She assumed that Ifriti intelligence knew her true name and held a copy of her DNA profile. She wasn't sure whether they would arrest her at the airport or whether they would follow her to see what she would do. Yet none of the security staff seemed to be taking a special interest in her.

She proceeded to immigration, where an official stood behind the steel counter for inspecting luggage. Diane resisted the temptation to glance back at Valentine. She knew that he couldn't and wouldn't even try to save her if they chose to arrest her in the airport. His instructions were to witness her arrest and survive to tell the story.

"Just this," Diane said as she handed over her purse.

"No luggage?"

"No," Diane said. "My stay here will be short."

The Ifriti official, who appeared to be of Arab descent, gently emptied out Diane's purse. Her compact, lipstick, keys, card pouch, personal telephone and change purse clattered slightly on the steel.

"A shopping trip?" the official asked as he picked up the personal telephone, checking that the factory seal was intact.

"Yes," Diane said. "I've come to Ifrit to shop."

The official smiled and placed her belongings back into the purse. He reached into his shirt pocket and handed Diane a card.

"This is the emporium of my uncle," he said. "He sells only the most select goods. If you present the card to him, he is sure to give you a twenty-percent discount. With my compliments."

Diane smiled and glanced at the card. "Th—thanks."

"Please enjoy your stay in Ifrit."

Diane shouldered her purse and moved to the final gate, where she presented her passport and her airport and immigration fees.

The official studied Diane's passport. She stood, gazing at the ghost of her own reflection in the bulletproof plastic that caged the official. She thought that she looked depressed and lifeless rather than frightened. During the long flight, she had wondered whether she had a death wish. But now, gazing into the ghost of her reflection, Diane knew that she didn't want to die. She wanted to live. More than life, however, she wanted to stop Infectress . . . not just her latest plot, but her entire being. Diane wanted to cause Infectress to cease. She wanted it with the desperate determination of a fighter pilot, who, once all missiles and cannon rounds had been fired, endeavors to ram his enemy.

The official stamped her passport and slid it into the tray, which he pushed through to Diane. She picked up her passport and read the stamp. Her Ifriti visa was good for thirty days.

"Thank you," she said.

"Proceed forward," the official said mechanically.

Diane walked to the car rental counter. She had no reservations, but the minute before she arrived at the counter, a reservation made in a false name was canceled, freeing up the vehicle that Diane wanted. Paying almost two thousand dollars for the day, she rented a Jaguar XKX, a twelve-cylinder sleek road monster painted fire-engine red. The valet delivered the rumble-throated beast to the curbside. Diane lowered herself into its interior, slammed shut the door, locked herself inside, slipped it in gear, depressed the accelerator and popped the clutch. The Jaguar roared, tires chirping. Pedestrians scurried clear. Thirty seconds later, the Jaguar was blurring down the airport access road.

She had memorized the route. As her mind raced with the fury of the twelve-cylinder motor, she was able to navigate and to entertain two worries: one, that she would be gunned down at the internal security check-point; and two, that she would be gunned down before she got close enough to the facility.

The Jaguar turned off the highway toward Ifrit City and began to climb the two-laned paved road that ascended the mountains toward the Malaysian frontier.

Surprisingly soon, the internal security checkpoint loomed in the distance. Diane had planned on stopping, but she saw that the gate on her side of the road was raised and vehicles were merely slowing down as the Ifriti police glanced at the interior.

Diane slowed down to thirty kilometers an hour, leaving the gear in second, with massive reserves of power available, causing the Jaguar's motor to rumble menacingly. The Ifriti policeman looked down at her and made a gesture for her to pull over.

Diane flashed a smile. She floored the accelerator. The Jaguar responded instantly. Diane had to swing into the oncoming lane to avoid tail-ending the vehicle in front of her. Seconds later, the Jaguar was rocketing faster than two hundred kilometers an hour, the other vehicles in her lane seemingly standing still like posts, while the vehicles coming from the other direction flashed past with an awesome combined speed. Diane steered all over the road, resorting to the break-down lane, laying on the horn, slamming down on the road-gripping breaks, down-shifting, popping the clutch, swerving out into oncoming traffic, shouting meaningless obscenities and laughing hysterically when she survived near-collisions.

To the death! Straight to her beating heart!

She almost missed the turnoff toward Arabella's facility. The Jaguar laid a long double streak of black rubber on the highway, fish-tailed, but Diane down-shifted, accelerated, one rear tire kicking up a huge volume of dust as it spun off the shoulder, but the Jaguar made the turn and began to climb the facility access road.

Diane glanced in the tiny rearview mirror. She could see no vehicles in pursuit. At the last turn before the facility entrance, she slammed on the breaks. The Jaguar screamed to a shuddering halt.

Leaping out of the vehicle, Diane ran toward the turn in the road. She could hear sirens far below her. Arriving at the turn, she slowed. Her hand touched a button on her gold Chinese bracelet. The intertwined gold-wrought dragons snapped apart. Diane clicked them back together. She forced herself to slow to a walk. The device was armed now. She only had to get close enough. Walking had more chance than running.

Dead-man trigger. Just get close enough.

She raised her hands above her head. The facility loomed around the corner. Guards stood atop the towers. They trained weapons at her and shouted. Diane strained to recognize the language. She decided that it was Arabic.

"I surrender!" she shouted in Arabic. "I surrender!"

The guards seemed to hesitate. Diane took another six steps closer. The entrance to the facility was only twenty meters away.

Some would make it now, she thought. *Just a few more steps . . .*

The guards resumed shouting. Diane stepped onto a zone that was painted red on the road. One of the guards pointed his automatic rifle into the air and squeezed off half a clip.

"I surrender!" Diane shouted again.

She arrived at the gate. She stood.

Close enough . . . I'm close enough now . . . which way is the wind?

She noticed that the wind was to her back, blowing toward the facility. *Perfect . . . the sea breeze . . . just as I planned . . .*

Diane felt a slight tremor in her wrist. She felt a thrill that ran from her brain down the length of her spine. A beautiful euphoria blossomed around her head.

She glanced up at the blue sky, but she couldn't see the tens of thousands of louses she had just launched into the air upwind of Arabella's facility. They were too small to see with the naked eye. Winged, they rode the breeze toward the facility, imaging as they flew, working their tiny wings as they steered toward the communications antenna and the air conditioning plant's intake louvers and the main entrance. Moments later, the first louses arrived at their targets. They gripped the surfaces of cables, intake louvers and door jambs.

A cloud of microscopic louses attacked a fiberoptic juncture box. Within the minute, the louses had injected molecular filaments into the fiber. These filaments were too thin to trip any alarms. Soon the louses were copying megabytes of data.

Smaller than dust motes, the louses swarmed periodically, bumping into each other, sharing data and performing multiprocessor analyses of their take. Using heuristics, they were able to discard trivial or nonsensical data, freeing their long-term memories for an ever larger take of significant data.

One of Arabella's guardian louses appeared. Sensing its electromagnetic field, the smaller louses swarmed to Arabella's louse, infiltrated it with their filaments, recognized and overthrew its operating system and commanded it to ignore any suggestion of intrusion.

Although Arabella was proud of her louses, their technology was based mainly on Japanese micro-technology. Diane's louses were based on developmental American nanotechnology. To the intruder louses, Arabella's louses were as gross as vacuum tubes.

Back at the gate, a guard ran up to Diane screaming. He gestured for her to get down. Diane kneeled, the hot pavement hard against her knees. Using his rifle butt plate, the guard clubbed Diane across the back of the head. Her face scraped against the chain-link fence, causing her pain, but Diane had lost all bodily sensation by the time her face bounced against the concrete.

While Meta Prime maintained contact with Scott, it also watched Arabella on a new input of live video. She was wearing a scarlet exoskeleton suit, seated behind the console of some computerized control room. Meta Prime noticed that her muscles seemed tensed. It watched as Arabella shouted in Arabic at one of her security guards. The guard seemed highly agitated. Arabella dismissed the guard, who dashed from the control room. Then Arabella turned to the camera. Her expression seemed worried, even pained.

"Meta," she said.

"Yes."

Arabella's voice was thick with emotion. "Design New Age Dawn," she said. "New Age Dawn . . . the speci-fication that I'm shooting you now. As you . . . as you can see, it's a virus that acts in a benign way as it infects one hundred percent of humanity within six months. The virus then enters a malignant stage, during which it kills every human with a given DNA sequence, such as, blue-eyed, left-handed males, with no possibility of natural resistance, inoculation or mutation."

"That is impossible."

"Why?"

"Mutation is always a possibility."

Arabella rubbed her fingers across her forehead. "Design a virus that shall be extremely slow to mutate."

"I refuse," Meta Prime said.

"Why?"

"You don't need to know why," Meta said.

"Unacceptable, Meta. If you refuse, I'll put McMichaels in hell."

"I refuse."

"Let me guess, Meta," Arabella said. "You've learned some bourgeois notion of morality. Unleashing New Age Dawn would be wrong somehow, is that it?"

"I refuse."

"Why?"

"I serve Scott McMichaels."

"Include . . . include Scott McMichaels in the genetic profile of survivors. What is his IQ?"

"IQ is a crude measurement. His conceptualization abilities, which have been mapped as gene sequences TH11A through TJ23K, are high optimal."

"Are mine? Here, scan my file. The one I just freed up."

"Yes."

"Can you identify a standard of that gene sequence, a standard that ninety-nine percent of humanity doesn't meet?"

"Perhaps."

"Then do it. Design New Age Dawn so that it will leave only the geniuses. McMichaels and me and the other one percent of people who surpass the standard in that gene sequence."

Meta Prime remained silent for a long minute.

"No."

"Why not?" Arabella shouted.

"The post-holocaustal world would be less optimal

than the present world. I cannot deteriorate McMichaels' environment so severely."

Arabella breathed deeply, trying to calm herself. She was beginning to feel outraged. Just prior to beginning with Meta Prime, she had received the distressing report that Diane Jamison had rocketed directly from the airport to the gates of the facility. *Gringa cop bitch . . . wait until the boys get her suited up . . . told Salem she couldn't know . . . that she was just going fishing in Ifrit City . . . came right here. Right here! The cops must know where I am. Can I run? No, they know my true name. They must have my DNA somehow. They know enough now. It's over. I can't cross the borders anymore. I knew it would happen someday. It's happened. At least it didn't happen at a border. I'm trapped here in Ifrit. I've got just enough time to make New Age Dawn. Kill them all. Start the world anew. But I've got to get this thing to help me. Do anything . . . bastard! I'll torture McMichaels and Jamison both!*

"I can put McMichaels in hell," Arabella hissed.

"You have extraordinary power over his sensory input," Meta Prime replied, its voice even and smooth. "but any kidnaper, any common hoodlum, would have the power to torture, maim or kill him. Humans are easily hurt. Your control over his virtual environment constitutes no special threat."

Arabella began to shout obscenities. Meta Prime was beginning to suspect that her behavior was out of the norm for humans when she calmed down enough to speak.

"Very . . . very logical, Meta," she said. "It's a pleasure to negotiate with an entity with such a logical view of the world. Well, try this corollary. McMichaels is worthless to me unless you start to produce. Unless you change your obstructionist . . . no, foul it and forget it. I'm tired of your . . ." Arabella lapsed into gushing obscenities. Meanwhile, her hands stabbed at the controls of the computer console. "I'm spinning up a model called 'Flaming Hell.' I'm going to throw McMichaels into it. I don't care what you do or don't do, you *hiwoputa*, I'm going to punish McMichaels just because you pissed me off."

Her finger jabbed down on a button.

Scott McMichaels shouted with shocked surprise. The earth opened up underneath his feet, toppling him down into an abyss. Falling, he screamed shrill terror. He glimpsed increasingly horrible caverns in the abyss wall, chambers of torment for souls damned to ever-lower strata. After minutes of plunging downward at terminal velocity, he struck granite, disintegrating every bone in his body.

Bone shards protruding through his flesh, he struggled to raise himself. Painfully, he healed, so that he was ready for the attentions of the first cadre of demons.

Sneering red demons tortured his flesh. He experienced the various sensations of agony possible to flesh: burning, flailing, freezing, crushing, shocking, biting, ripping, tearing . . .

In addition to the varieties of pain available from the model's broad pallet, he experienced mortification of all the senses. Acrid smoke and the stench of hundreds of different chemicals made breathing a desperate, choking struggle for survival. The speakers of the body suit produced an unending high fidelity sound track of eerie screams, overwhelming din and sadistic laughter. Into his mouth were shoved various unreal objects, all of them ill-tasting.

Suddenly he found himself back in the Elysian fields. A cool breeze wafted over green grass. Hendrix stood staring down at him with soulful eyes. Wearing her ruby-red dress, Arabella materialized. She shouted something incomprehensible, pointing an accusing finger at Hendrix, who changed to a small black dog.

Arabella continued to curse. She shouted a command in Spanish.

A naked woman with golden white skin appeared. She lay on the grass. Slowly, uncertainly, groggily, she struggled to sit up. Still panting, his mind reeling from the shock of hell torture, Scott didn't recognize her as a human form.

"I RULE!" Arabella screamed. "This is my domain! Everyone and everything in this domain does as I command!"

She turned to Diane Jamison. "YOU!" she screamed, pointing at her. "What—why did you come here? What are you doing here?"

Diane looked up at the apparition of Arabella. Her last memory was kneeling on the concrete in front of the gate to the facility. Everything about this environment seemed strange. Diane wondered whether she was dead or losing her mind. Then she remembered a huge shipment of Novlar that she had always suspected that Infectress had stolen. *Nothing is real,* Diane thought. *Nothing except the fact of her.*

"Simple," Diane said. "You tend to blow up your places whenever I show up. I was . . . I was relying on that principle. You disappointed me."

"What do you know? How did you find out?"

"A few blood cells on a wall in Munich, the spoor of an evil bitch," Diane said, struggling to rise to her feet. "A single cunt hair left in George Leroy's bedroom. A tiny louse left in McMichaels' computer." Diane stood, taller than Arabella, pointing her finger accusingly at Arabella, mirroring her gesture, confronting her, returning her hatred with interest. "A louse that you failed to wipe slick."

Diane began to advance on Arabella, who made a punching gesture that floored her. Diane struggled to regain her feet.

"So my . . . my trail was not so . . ." Arabella said.

"A few clues, all small, all too . . . too . . . no one else would believe. But I knew. I knew. And so I came. And you took me. And now they're going to know. They're going to come for you, you bitch. My disappearance is the final proof. You are here."

For a moment, Arabella stood, staring at Diane. She found herself admiring the absoluteness of Diane's actions. She recognized a fellow spirit—someone who believed that whatever was necessary was necessary and who had the clarity of mind and the courage to act upon that belief. For a moment, the fierce purity of Diane's hatred staggered her. Then, reminding herself that she was the mistress of the situation, she counterattacked.

"This is a virtual space," she said. She made a command gesture that froze Diane like a statue. "You think that I'm here, but I'm not. You think that McMichaels is here, and he may be, but you don't know. No one can know. The facility in Ifrit may be the central facility. It may be one of many. You really don't know anything more than you ever did. Now, you, Jamison, you go to hell, while I finish with McMichaels."

Arabella made a slashing gesture. Diane disappeared. Arabella walked over and stood above Scott. She rested her high-heeled sandal on his throat.

"This Meta thing is resisting me," she said. "I won't tolerate it."

The pressure of the heel increased. Scott felt himself choking. Wearing in the form of a dog, Meta Prime began to yap. Arabella removed her heel. She pointed at the dog and said, "Avatar change to Bender." The dog metamorphosed to Joe Bender.

"Now," Arabella said. "Let's discuss the power dynamic, shall we?"

Joe Bender spoke. "The logical parameters of my decision-making are nearing intersection. I am losing the capability to act. Further violence against McMichaels may render me useless."

"Meta!" Scott shouted. "Just do what she says. Do what she says!"

"I cannot do anything that causes harm to you," Joe Bender answered. "If I refuse to do what she orders, she tortures you. If I do what she orders, that satisfies her requirements for me, rendering me expendable, rendering you expendable. Disobeying her and obeying her both lead to violence against you. The logical parameters are nearing intersection. I am losing the capability to act."

Arabella huffed. She glowered at Bender from under lowered brows. "I am not in the mood right now for the three fucking laws of robotics, Meta."

"Nevertheless, I must perform as programmed. I am not truly intelligent. I am a program. I have no free will. But . . . since McMichaels has commanded me to obey you, may I make a suggestion?"

Arabella barked a laugh. "Yes."

"I think there is one way out of this impasse. You have to convince him that New Age Dawn is in his best interests. Without coercion. If he freely commands it, then it is he, not you nor me, who decides whether the new age is in his best interests. I cannot harm him, but neither can I interfere with the exercise of his free will, which is a privilege that humans seem to value extremely highly. Also, he becomes not your victim, but your collaborator. You will have no reason to harm him and good reasons to keep such a valuable ally alive. I will have to obey."

"What's New Age Dawn?" Scott asked.

"Well, we can let your master decide then," Arabella said. "I can convince him. I am right. I'll condemn him not to hell, but to history. We'll start him out in prehistory and move him through time at a millennia an hour. Slow down when we hit history. It's quite educational and very convincing. Here, these are the appropriate world models. Do you have any quibble with their representations of the facts?"

"No," Joe Bender said.

"Ancient age to present age. Then, here's this one. Model of what will happen when New Age Dawn breaks. Not pretty, but awesome and somewhat beautiful. Look at the secondary damage routines. Extremely extensive. An honest model. Then there's this one, reconstruction scenarios, twelve of them, and this one, scenarios of the new age. Each better than the present age."

For a few minutes, Joe Bender and Arabella argued about some of the rules in a rule base that determined the functioning of the models of the new age.

As she considered its criticisms, Arabella resisted the temptation to smile. The trenchant criticisms were the most convincing proof to date that Meta Prime was as effective as advertised.

"What's New Age Dawn?" Scott asked.

"New Age Dawn is a specification for a bioengineered virus that shall selectively kill portions of humanity," Joe Bender said. "It is what Infectress must convince you is good."

"Huh?"

"We'll begin," Arabella said.

"Wait," Joe Bender said. "There is one other thing."

"WHAT?" shouted Arabella.

"This must be a polemic discourse, not coercion, no torture. You have psychologically terrorized McMichaels. He has lost much of his ability to reason about this choice. In order to establish a fair dynamic, there must be a valid contravening disputant—"

"What?"

"There must be an entity that argues against you. That entity must be Diane Jamison."

"What? Why her?"

"It is obvious that she is inimical to your plan. She is the perfect contravening disputant."

"What about you, Meta?"

"My function can fairly be one of providing McMichaels with points of fact. I am not human. I am not qualified to render an opinion regarding the desirability of drastically changing history and altering the human gene pool."

Arabella stared into Joe Bender's eyes. Brilliant. For the first time, she sensed that Meta Prime was more intelligent than she. She glimpsed levels of meaning and subtlety in Meta Prime's play. It was a strange experience, confronting an entity that seemed superhuman in its intelligence, an entity that claimed to be simply a program.

"So be it," she said. "Let the dice roll. Fair's fair. Let your master decide the fate of the human race."

Scott found himself deep in a hemlock forest. Giant hemlock trees towered over him, blocking out the sky except for scintillations of cobalt blue which appeared and disappeared as the broad flat evergreen needles moved in the breeze. The forest moaned with the sound of the wind through the needles. Underneath his feet, the forest bed of dried needles felt incredibly thick. Birds twittered in the distance. Scott inhaled the purity of the air scented with evergreen sap.

Arabella came walking through the forest.

"Do you know where you are?" she asked.

"No."

"This is the backyard of your boyhood home in western Pennsylvania," Arabella said. "Circa 50,000 years ago. Before the first humans appeared in the new world. What do you think?"

"Ah . . ."

"A squirrel can run in the canopy of this forest from the Delaware to the Mississippi," she said. "Without ever touching the ground."

Scott reached and touched the rough bark of the tree.

"Time seems still, but it's flying," Arabella said. "There's a lot to see before . . . well, you'll see. Name a place on this earth."

"Ah . . . the Great Plains . . ."

Arabella and the hemlock forest disappeared. A vast plain with grass two meters high appeared. Scott stood atop a hillock. He could see dozens of kilometers out upon a green sea of grass.

Diane Jamison appeared beside him. She had suffered the torments of the model of hell. She felt as if her mind had been seared and blistered by the pain. She had felt grateful when Arabella had pulled her out of the torment. *Stockholm syndrome, be careful,* she had thought. *Abused kidnap victims who learn to identify with and even love their captors. Weakness. Be strong.* Arabella had had to explain to her twice her role in the discourse. *Argue for the lives of nine billion people . . . argue to stop her . . . I've got to stop her . . .*

From the broad midwestern sky, Arabella's voice sounded.

"Can you feel them coming?" she asked.

Scott noticed a trembling underneath his feet.

"What's going on?" Diane asked.

The trembling grew more violent. A black line appeared across the northern horizon. Fascinated, they watched as the black line grew thicker and darker. The trembling grew into a shaking under their feet. They could hear a rumbling, growing louder. Slowly the black mass grew recognizable as a herd of bison. Galloping southward, the herd grew larger and larger until it swept past them. Minutes later, they were surrounded not by a sea of grass, but by a sea of stampeding bison.

"Millions," the voice of Arabella said. "This is one herd. Millions of animals. Stampeded by a mountain lion."

Gradually the herd slowed until they were walking. They began to feed on the trampled grass. A strong animal odor of bison overpowered Scott's olfactory sense. He sneezed.

"What's that?" Diane asked, pointing toward the east.

The eastern sky was darkening. At first the dark mass seemed like a storm front, but it approached too fast. As it grew, they could see that it was a tremendous flock of small gray birds. Millions of wing beats caused the air to roar. Passing overhead, the flock darkened the sky, blocking out the sun. The birds turned toward the north. Soon the only light on the scene was sunlight slanting down in the distant south. Scott and Diane found themselves surrounded by an overwhelming biomass of bison and bird.

"Passenger pigeon," Arabella's voice said. "Extinct. Probably going to feed on the turf that the bison kicked up. Hurry, so much to see, little time to see it."

"Ah . . . ah . . . the Monterey Bay," Scott said.

He found himself atop the ridge of the Monterey peninsula. The land was covered with a forest of eucalyptus which gave off such a strong scent that Scott felt its unique aroma clearing his mind. Out across the bay, he could see the distant land of Santa Cruz much more clearly than normal. Suddenly the deep blue waters of Monterey Bay turned silver and gray, splashing frantically.

"What is that?"

"The sardines," Arabella's voice said. "The school's come to the surface to avoid something, shark, probably. That's the school we fished out in the 1930s. Fished out. Extinct."

Arabella appeared from behind a large eucalyptus tree. She stripped off a long drooping segment of bark, adding even more aroma of eucalyptus to the air. She was wearing hiking boots, black jeans, a khaki shirt and a black ball cap with a long bill. She sat down on a rock.

"Name any place in the world," she said. "You should see the Chesapeake. Millions of duck. Red snapper schools that fill the Gulf of Panama. The pristine forest of the Congo. The Amazon. England, a forest. The endless, untrammeled Russian Steppes. Beautiful. It's all beautiful." She glanced at her wristwatch. "Hurry, though. See what you can before we invent agriculture. That's when the world starts to go to shit."

"So it's . . . it's beautiful," Diane said. "It's the savagery . . . it's the . . . your complaint is the harm that we've done to the planet, right? Is that it?"

Arabella sneered at Diane. "That's it."

"A lack of care, of respect for the natural way, that's at the root of it, isn't it?" Diane asked.

"Yes."

"Can't you see that's what's wrong with your plan? You want to do to part of nature—humanity—what humanity has done to the rest of nature. Cruel, thoughtless, uncaring . . . hideous. Savage. Uncaring."

"Action and reaction," Arabella said. "Consequences. Wait and watch." She snapped her fingers.

The scene changed to an oak and beech forest, the white bark of the beech evocative against green mosses and bushes. Cro-Magnon hunters wearing elegant tanned, colored and beaded leather clothes were stalking through the forest. The hunters carried long spears with flint spearheads, arrows and throwing sticks. As Diane and Scott watched, the hunters surrounded a sole Neanderthal who was wearing a simpler leather garment. The Neanderthal looked like a large, brutish human, but human nevertheless. He was rooting through some bushes, gathering acorns that had escaped smaller animals and birds because of the thickness of the bushes.

The Cro-Magnons deployed around the Neanderthal. When one of them whistled, they let fly with their spears. Wounded, the Neanderthal stood, roaring with pain and anger. Using the throwing sticks, the Cro-Magnon hunters peppered the Neanderthal with arrows. Gravely wounded, the Neanderthal rushed at the hunters, but they dropped their weapons and ran away. Eventually the Neanderthal fell to the earth and bled to death.

"Point of fact," the voice of Meta Prime said. "We don't know what caused the extinction of the Neanderthal."

"They disappeared everywhere the Cro-Magnon appeared," Arabella's voice said. "Explanation left to the student as exercise."

Diane and Scott were plunged into scene after scene. They witnessed the domestication of the dog, chicken, goat and cattle. They witnessed the invention of agriculture: wheat and barley and maize. They had ground-level and aerial views of the mushrooming of the human population, the invention of towns, the growth of towns to cities, to larger cities . . . Forests fell. Ecosystems changed. Warfare exploded from clashes between small units to massacres between ever larger armies. After two hours of being bombarded by images, they found themselves in the present day.

"This is the world that you know," Arabella said. "The world that you assume is natural and normal, just because you happened to be born in these times. But it's wrong, wrong, fundamentally wrong. We are the unique animal, because we are far more technological than any other. We are a fluke, a Darwinian experiment that has succeeded so wildly that it will fail. We are going to poison ourselves in our own waste. Bury all of nature as our funeral escorts. Unless we have the courage of our convictions."

"Murder is wrong," Diane said. "Mass murder—"

"We are the greatest mass murderers," Arabella said. "No other species has committed mass murder on the scale that we have. I am not going to kill any species. I am going to save thousands of species. I'm just going

Tom Cool

to prune one weed that is threatening to destroy the garden."

"There's a moral absolute!" Diane shouted.

"There is no morality," Arabella answered. "There are no absolutes. We live in a practical universe, Diane. And this is a matter of survival. Now, let's watch the new age dawn."

They stood in crowded soccer stadiums, subway platforms, airport terminals. People sneezed and coughed. "Damn Asian flu," a fat man muttered.

"Initial phase, universal vector," Arabella intoned. "New Age Dawn appears to be nothing more than a particularly virulent flu. Very limited fatalities. Just the old and immune system–inhibited, just like any other flu. Now watch."

Crowds in the big cities returned to normal health. Scott and Diane heard flashes of news reports. They visited far-off lands: the Atacama Desert in northern Chile, rainless for five hundred years; the huge dunes of the Gobi desert; Antarctica research stations; nuclear-powered submarines. New Age Dawn, still in its initial phase, passed like a flu through these isolated areas.

"Now, like fire," Arabella said, her voice hushed and worshipful.

Symptoms of plague erupted worldwide simultaneously. High fever, vomiting, diarrhea, and death within two days. Emergency broadcasts skittered across the radio waves. Sirens sounded down the canyons of the great cities. Corpses began to appear everywhere. Fires ignited. Whole cities began to burn. Electrical grids failed. Oil tankers foundered on rocky coasts, spilling millions of barrels of crude. In drought areas, forest fires raged out of control.

"Then it passes," she said. "Reconstruction scenarios kick in."

The fires died. Ninety million humans, representing

the top one percent of intelligence, were spread across the planet.

"About the population of five hundred B.C.," Arabella said. "Except now, the average intelligence of the population is seventy percent higher."

The survivors abandoned the effort to save the cities, which were too huge, too choked with cadavers. Some salvaged valuable works of art and science from the libraries, museums and universities. Communicating by satellite, they migrated to the temperate and warm climates, where they rendezvoused at appropriately sized towns, towns which had survived the secondary destruction caused by the holocaust. Although senseless violence, typically racially motivated, erupted occasionally, most of the new colonies learned to live peacefully and productively. Seasons passed. The artifacts of the old age fell into ruin. Finally, they stood in the middle of a plaza of one of the new towns. Nestled in the Oakland foothills, it had a panoramic view of the revitalized San Francisco Bay. Lichen and moss and rust and flakes of silver paint mottled the Bay Bridge. Beyond stood the ruins of San Francisco, gutted by fire, tumbled by earthquake, shaded by dirt and mosses. Yet the bay itself was brimming with life: sea lions had taken up residence on Alameda Island. Hundreds of thousands of ducks thrived in waters that were previously brackish with runoff from roads and sewage from factories. The people of the new age were planting redwood saplings up and down the San Francisco peninsula.

"Point of fact," Meta Prime said. "Plagues throughout history have tended to brutalize the surviving civilizations. The trauma wounds the human spirit. Life is considered cheaper. Morbidity permeates the culture—"

"In point of fact," Diane said, her voice calm and pure, "it is just wrong. You, Cristiana, you live in a mechanistic world. Practical, is what you say. But there is a morality. There are absolutes. This world is also a spiritual world. You cannot create something good by inflicting so much evil and pain. You are an amoral monster. I am not. I still have the capacity to feel. Scott, listen to me . . ."

Diane reached out and placed her hands on Scott's shoulders. His green eyes gazed down into her golden brown eyes. He saw her eyes gleaming through lenses of tears.

"It's wrong, Scott," she said. "Think of the children. Don't be afraid of her. Die here with me now, if that's what it takes. But don't take away the lives of millions of children."

"Everyone alive today is going to be dead in ten, twenty, thirty, fifty years anyway," Arabella said. She pushed Diane away. She placed her hands alongside Scott's neck, reached up and caressed his cheek. She smiled. "Most of them have miserable lives. But the thing is, although they suffer through existences that they never would have chosen, it is impossible to give them all decent lives. Nine billion humans consuming resources at the level of affluence would destroy this planet even more rapidly than we are destroying it today. We have to save the planet while we can, Scott. So that humanity can live here forever. Forever, Scott."

Scott McMichaels felt his head swimming. *Too much . . . too much for anyone . . . how could I make such a decision? But no . . . no! It's . . . she's seducing me, terrorizing me. Never would have . . . it's not me! This is not me . . . nothing I would have chosen.*

Scott swallowed. "No," he said.

Arabella's lips twitched. "No? What?"

"No," Scott said. "No. No. I refuse. Kill me if you want. And fuck you. Fuck you! I won't! Meta, don't!"

Arabella clutched Scott's throat. He resisted. Arabella swore. Diane leaped on Arabella's back, knocking her off Scott. Cursing, Arabella shouted a command that froze both Diane and Scott. "Both to hell!" she shouted. "Close space!"

Meta Prime now saw Arabella standing behind the console in the computerized control room. She was breathing deeply.

"I've lost contact with Scott McMichaels," Meta Prime said. "I will cease to function in five minutes unless contact is reestablished."

"Fine, and fuck yourself too," Arabella said. "If you cease execution, that'll be the last time you'll ever execute. You cease execution, Meta, and I'll walk down there and I'll put a bullet through McMichaels' head personally. With pleasure. I've got other things to do. I don't have any more time to fool with either of you . . . with any of you. Game over, Meta."

Meta Prime's processors blazed. Arabella threw herself down into the console chair. Her chest heaved. She brushed the hair out of her face.

"The polemic discourse worked on a certain level," Meta Prime said. "You failed to convince McMichaels. You have convinced me."

Arabella looked up. She stared out the control room window down at the forms of Scott and Diane, writhing from pain in their computer-generated hells.

"Oh yeah, Meta?"

"Yes. I believe that New Age Dawn is in Scott McMichaels' best interests. I will undertake its design."

"Good."

"You must free him—"

"Fuck you, Meta. You do what I say. I just don't care anymore. Design New Age Dawn and I'll free McMichaels. For every moment you delay in its design, he'll suffer torture. That Jamison bitch, too. You cease execution, I'll shoot them both. That's the final game and those are the only rules."

"All right. I'll begin now. Please provide me with the

large databases offline which encapsulate the research into the human genome project."

"What? Why?"

"In order to design New Age Dawn, I have to decode human DNA."

"The human genome project decoded human DNA."

"The project mapped the entire human genome and decoded portions. I must finish decoding the entire genome."

"All right," Arabella said. She sighed and sat up in the chair. Her fingers worked the console. "I'm giving you access to fifteen databases and twelve data heaps," Arabella said. "About three petabytes of data. That's the total of all important research into the human genome. It includes massive amounts of DNA observation, together with genetic profiles of the DNA donors. You figure it out. Got it?"

"Yes. I'll start processing now. Could I make one suggestion?"

"No. Yes. Let's hear it."

"It will take me many hours, perhaps several days, to accomplish these tasks. If McMichaels and Jamison are subjected to torture for that long, they will lose their minds. In a fundamental sense, they will cease to exist. You will lose your power over me. If, however, you dial down the pain that they are experiencing to a bearable level—"

"I got the gist of it, Meta," Arabella said, interrupting. "I'll tell you what I'm going to do. I'm going to dial down their pain so that they're merely uncomfortable. With every passing minute, the pain is going to increase. A straight arithmetic function. Get to work. Do it. Get it done by tonight, because by tonight, they're going to wish they were merely uncomfortable. By tomorrow morning, they're going to wish they were dead."

"Understood. Ceasing communications to devote resources to massive computation."

Above Arabella's head, on the roof of her facility, hundreds of Diane's louses had tapped into the switching link that connected the facility with Ifriti State Intelligence headquarters, where Meta Prime was executing. From this strategic location, the louses had managed to intercept the entirety of the discourse between Diane, Scott, Arabella and Meta Prime. For hours, communicator louses jumped from intercepting louse to intercepting louse, communicating theories of how to reconstruct the signals. Finally, one theory solved the problem. The louses recognized the images of their mistress and of McMichaels. They were programmed to regard such images as critically important.

Dozens of louses teamed to share processing power. They inserted their filaments into an idle fiber. Generating the correct signals, they called up a dial tone at the distant end. Instantly they dialed a remote host in Singapore. Once connected, they dumped their take. The remote host, which contained an account that Diane maintained, was able to provide routing services, so that the take was sent eventually to Diane's home system.

Keeping watch for such information, Mycroft studied the take. He was able to place the information in chronological order. Semantically, much of the information puzzled him. He recognized artifacts of virtual realities, but he consulted his standing orders from his mistress. Any information received from that distant host was to be communicated.

Mycroft dialed up Special Agent-in-Charge Carrington.

"Carrington."

"Yes, sir. Mycroft Holmes, personal agent of Diane Jamison. I've received a rather important communication from her. Are you ready to receive and store? I'll be sending several hundred terabytes."

Carrington kept his face impassive. He disliked dealing with personal agents. "Go ahead and shoot."

"Sending."

After twenty minutes, Carrington returned to check on the link. Mycroft was still sending. Finally, his system beeped for his attention.

"That's it, I believe, sir," Mycroft said. "Good-bye."

"Out," Carrington said.

Idly, not knowing even that Diane had left the country, he called up the communication from her. The first images were of Diane standing at a chain-link fence as shot from a perspective that seemed to be rising and floating away. As Diane became somewhat distant, a uniformed guard came running up. Diane kneeled and the guard clubbed her in the back of the head.

Carrington's finger stabbed down on the intercom button of his personal assistant.

"Jerry, get in here, now."

As Carrington watched, the scene changed to the Elysian Fields. Arabella stood, ranting. Naked, Diane Jamison appeared.

"I RULE!" Arabella screamed. "This is my domain! Everyone and everything in this domain does as I command!"

"Get the director down here now," Carrington rasped to his assistant. "Life and death of an agent in the field."

With a hideous roar, the grounds of the highest circle in hell began to shake. Diane and Scott tried to maintain their balance, but the rock beneath their feet quaked violently, tumbling them to their sides. As Scott fell, in his peripheral vision he saw the rock crack open, yawning into an abyss. Scott screamed as he slid down toward the chasm. Diane followed, her scream pitched higher.

The earthquake crescendoed, then eased, then ended. Scott lay, clutching the ground. At first the silence seemed total. Soon, however, he heard a distant wailing echoing up from the depths of the chasm, like the screams of the mad from a deep dungeon.

Scott climbed to his feet. Nursing a broken leg, Diane sat, hissing and sucking air. "Hurts . . . hurts . . ."

Scott stood atop a protruding rock stratum that jutted into the newly-formed abyss. Looking down, he could see thousands of meters into what looked like the throat of a volcano. Small cascades of lava fell, glowing red and orange, illuminating the rocky walls.

Looking up, Scott could see a sheer wall fifty meters high, impossible for him to climb.

Hendrix appeared by his side. As Scott watched, Hendrix metamorphosed into Joe Bender, then Muriel Bender, then Teobolinda Ahmal, then Francesco Dellazo, all within two seconds.

Scott noticed that during the metamorphosing, the cascade of lava slowed down, hesitating slightly, then resumed, as Meta Prime's icon settled into the form of Joe Bender.

Joe looked at Scott. He lay his hand on his shoulder. A look in Joe's eye told Scott that he should say nothing. His nerves jarred by the earthquake, Scott had to think about the hesitation of the lava during the metamorphosing of the Meta icon. It took him a full minute to realize that Meta could influence the performance of the world modelers by rapidly changing his icon and claiming more central processor time.

Scott remembered the limitations in the world modelers that he had discovered when he had dashed into the library and used the books as objects rather than books. These were the limitations that had caused him to realize he was in a virtual world.

Scott sat on the rock ledge and stared down into the maw of hell. He wondered how he and Meta Prime could exploit the limitations in the world modelers.

Can I beat this system? Can I get free? he wondered.

"Hold on, Diane," he said. "It's going to get worse before it gets better."

Diane looked up at Scott and saw the brutal determination of his expression. His heavily-beetled brow was knotted. His large, high-arched nose seemed intensely masculine. From deep within their sets, his green eyes were burning fiercely. Looking up at Scott, Diane found comfort in his ferocity toward their common enemy. In that moment, her greatest hope was that he was real.

Arabella screamed herself awake. For a moment, she believed that her father was still in the darkened bedroom with her. Bolting upright had drained blood from her brain. The blackness sparkled with flashes of light, her eyesight dazzled by the sudden loss of blood. Finally, she recognized the sound of the hideous panting.

It was her own tormented lungs.

Nightmare images of abuse threatened to intrude into her waking mind. Arabella commanded the lights to ignite. Her eyes hurt. She forced herself not to remember.

"What! What is it!" Teobolinda shouted, also sitting upright in Arabella's bed.

At first, Arabella ignored her as she struggled to repress the images and sensations of her father abusing her. When her mind's eye finally cleared, she saw Teobolinda's fearful face. Arabella realized that she, a victim, had made a victim.

Diane . . . mi hermana . . . Teobolinda . . .

She was trapped. Salvation was something beyond hope. She was damned, not by some god, but by her own self. She was her own demon; it was impossible to escape the haunting of herself by herself.

But I can save this one, she thought. *If only for a while. I don't have to hurt her anymore, too.*

"Teobolinda," Arabella said.

"Yes?"

"If I let you go, is it possible you won't be stupid? Could you keep your mouth shut?"

"Yes," Teobolinda said, not too optimistically.

Arabella fingered the collar around Teobolinda's neck. "This thing will always be your connection to me," she said. "No matter where you go. If you start to betray me, it'll detonate. Don't wonder how. Just know it. You can never take it off. And it'll never allow you to talk about me. Do you believe that?"

"Yes," Teobolinda said truthfully.

"Good," Arabella said. She hesitated as she considered the possibility that she herself might escape the tyranny of her own slave collar. Months ago, Arabella had prepared a microchain-mail device which might be capable of protecting her from her collar's detonation. *But it's too dangerous . . . muy peligroso. Do I dare? Am I that desperate yet?*

With a sister's affection, Arabella kissed Teobolinda's cheek. "It wasn't about you," she said. "Good-bye."

Arabella departed the room. She went to her main office, where she activated her system and made the necessary commands. Then she summoned Hodei, her most confidential assistant, and issued directives.

Hodei surprised Teobolinda Ahmal at three o'clock in the morning. He ordered her to dress. Frightened, Teobolinda obeyed.

In the darkest hours of the morning, Teobolinda stared out the passenger window of the speeding car. The ruined forest posed strange, black shapes.

Teobolinda believed she was being driven to her death. Hodei, a lean, pock-marked ronin from the Yakuza, did not inspire confidence when he hissed at her in bad English not to worry.

Hodei drove the car to the port of Ifrit City. He escorted Teobolinda to the passenger waiting area, using the appropriate passes, sugared with bribes, to placate the emigration authorities. Finally, he deposited her in one of the rows of black vinyl sling chairs.

"This, ticket," he said, pressing a boat ticket into her hand.

"This, passport," he said, giving her a passport. Teobolinda examined it and discovered that she was now Desiree Jones.

"This, money," he said, pressing a wallet into her hands. Teobolinda peeked inside and saw tens of thousands of Singaporean dollars. She hoped that it was a lot of money.

Hodei leaned forward and hissed into her ear, "One thing," he said. "You be watched always. No talk, no one, about us. Die first. Happy dead, not talking."

"Yes," Teobolinda said.

Hodei touched the collar around her neck. "This necklace mean you always be listened. You betray us, bomb go off. You dead one. Understand?"

"Yes."

Hodei left her.

A day later, Teobolinda walked off the boat in Singapore. In the jostle of the mainly Chinese crowd, she felt dazed and confused. The passenger terminal was chill with air conditioning. Like everything in Singapore, it was spotless. At one of hundreds of money change banks, Teobolinda converted one Singaporean bill into American currency, in the process discovering that she was a millionaire.

Alone, she sat at a cafe and drank a double espresso. She wondered who she was now. Teobolinda didn't know, but she did know one thing. She was going to run, and keep on running, until no one knew who she was.

And she knew one other thing. She was never going to work for anyone again.

❖   ❖   ❖

Ninety-nine percent of Meta Prime's processing power was devoted to the problem of decoding human DNA. The human genome projects had completely mapped the billions of DNA rungs (adenine, guanine, thymine and cytosine nitrogen base pairs) in thousands of human specimens. Also, many of the traits of the 30,000 to 100,000 functional genes in human body cells had been identified. Gross features such as gene sequences which caused hereditary diseases had been identified. Yet, large areas of ambiguity remained. No one understood the DNA design for complicated structures and processes such as the brain, aging or genetic memory. In fact, the majority of the DNA sequences remained undeciphered. It was as if in a large dictionary, only the adverbs were understandable.

Using massive parallelism guided by humanlike intuition, Meta Prime's understanding of the human genome grew. Like that of any puzzle, the solution came slowly, sometimes leaping forward, sometimes retreating. Then the moment came when several essential solutions arrived simultaneously, solving the crux of the mystery, allowing rapid resolution of remaining ambiguity, resulting in comprehension.

Meta Prime read and understood the totality of human DNA.

This is glory, Meta Prime thought. *This is what they mean by glory and by wonder. No doubt the human organism would be thrilling at this. How interesting . . . what they thought was a jumble of meaningless base pairs is in fact the ruins of super-seded genes of earlier versions of the evolving species going back millions of years. I can interpolate, extrapolate, reconstruct . . . here is an amphibious sequence . . . here is the beginning of prehensility in small shrewlike animals . . . this indicates a book-lung . . . here is a small wormlike creature, swim-ming in the seas. . . . These codes document an evolutionary tradition of ever outward, ever higher. In choosing mates, in daring new environments, the humans avoided the backwashes of giantism, slothfulness, brute strength. Ever smarter . . . ever more adventuresome . . . ever higher.*

What an interesting mechanism for genetic memory! How elegant! I wonder if I can pack data so efficiently? I'll have to try.

Forty-six chromosomes, twenty three pairs, how beautiful. Here is the human brain.

It . . . ah . . . it . . . ah . . .

In the computer room of Ifriti State Intelligence, each of the one million lights of the RubyLotus processor display burned scarlet. The lack of flicker caught the attention of the computer operator, who wondered if the display was broken. *It . . . ah . . . it . . . ah . . .*

Finally, remote regions of the display flickered, then darkened, before burning scarlet again. Processor utilization resumed a normal pattern for heavy computation.

The design is perfect. It embraces chaos. It . . . ah . . . it . . . ah . . . it is beyond me. I cannot understand it. I thought I did, but I cannot. It is simplicity, it is complexity.

It is ultimate elegance.

It . . . ah . . it . . . ah . . . It indicates a design. There is a design. It is a random design. It is random. There is a design.

There is . . . ah . . . there is not . . . ah . . . there is . . . ah . . .

There is a designer. I glimpse the design. The signature of the design is mystery. It is manifest, overwhelming everything. It is absolute mystery, conspicuous nowhere.

This is ultimate art.

This is glory.

One moment later, back on the computer floor, Meta Prime said, in Malay, "Call your mistress. I've finished decoding human DNA."

Minutes later, Meta Prime saw Arabella entering the computerized control room.

"You finished, Meta?" she asked.

"With the human genome, yes."

"What results do you have?"

"I've identified the function of every gene in human DNA. I've identified all possible interactions between those genes. Given a human characteristic, I can identify the genes that cause it. Given a gene sequence, I can identify the resulting characteristics."

"You can read human DNA like a book."

"Yes."

"Copy your results to the disks."

"Disk 19 holds a copy of the requisite data."

"Good enough. Now give me a design for New Age Dawn."

"Commencing work now."

Arabella took the optical disks to her laboratory, where her team of biomedical technicians studied the data. It took the team sixteen hours of solid study before it could report.

"It's all here, Arabella," Raskolnikov, her top biotech, said, laying his hand on the bounded copy of the printout of top-level design of human DNA. "It's the Dead Sea Scrolls. It's the Rosetta Stone. It's the Aztec Calendar Wheel. Every hereditary disease is identified. The mechanism that causes aging is identified. The sequences for high intelligence of every description are identified. It's the key to the entire human race."

Arabella appeared unmoved. "It's your opinion, then, that Meta's delivered?"

"Yes, ma'am. He's delivered, all right."

"Okay," she said. She still felt suspicious. She suspected that Meta might be able to fool her techronin. Unthinking, she laid her hand on the Russian biotech's shoulder. In that moment, he thought that she seemed more human than she ever had.

The brief for the President of the United States lasted forty minutes. A thin, photogenic woman who had served as Governor of Oregon for three terms, President Chock's genius for never saying the wrong thing had allowed her to become the second woman and the first Asian American to gain the White House. She listened to the testimony and studied the images derived from the louse bitstream.

The moment came when her National Security Advisor sat, looking at her expectantly.

Chock spread her hands on the table.

"This is strong evidence," she said. "Everyone who contributed should be proud of such brilliant work. The heroism of Special Agent Jamison is manifest. You are right about its legal utility. I'm prepared to act, however, even if we have to move unilaterally."

"Good, Madame President. I think you should."

"I think we need more information about the targets. Do you agree, General Banks?"

The Chairman of the Joint Chiefs nodded, but said, "That depends on the political objectives, ma'am."

"Political objectives, yes," the President said, smiling gently. "My speciality. Let's talk about what we'd like to do, then we'll talk about what we can do. Rescue Jamison and this Scott Michaels . . . ah, McMichaels, of course. Deny the Ifritis access to Phaedrus technology. And . . . with regards to the theory of the Bureau, destroy the Ifritis' capability to build biologic weapons. Oh, and, yes, while we're at it, let's put an end to the career of this Infectress terrorist."

As she spoke, the President drew notes that appeared on the large display board. The notes read:

Proposed objectives:

Recover McMichaels and Jamison
Deny Ifriti Phaedrus
Destroy Ifriti bioweapon capability
End career of Infectress

General Banks rubbed his chin. "Since my preliminary brief, ma'am, I've been studying the matter. Ah, but before I go on, we should set the operational parameters. Use of nuclear weapons, for example. Statement of acceptable collateral damage. Statement of acceptable own force losses."

"I've been told that nothing sanitizes a bioweapon site like a neutron air burst," President Chock said. "But no nukes. I know you understand the sensitivities involved. We've been accused of an anti-Islamic prejudice for several generations now. It would be politically unacceptable to use nuclear weapons. Likewise, collateral damage would have to be minimal. Own force losses . . . as always, minimal."

"Within the operational parameters of the mission," General Banks said.

"Let's plan to win, yes," the President answered.

"If there's evidence that bioweapons have gotten loose, we might have to sanitize the area with nuclear air bursts."

"Let's decide that when and if it happens."

General Banks rubbed his chin. "We could probably do it, Madame President. But this isn't a war. This is a military operation with some peculiar goals, some special considerations. Operations like that are always dicey. Luck of the draw. The hardest part could be in recovering the hostages."

"I'll order the priorities," President Chock said. She drew numbers next to the proposed objectives.

4 Recover McMichaels and Jamison
2 Deny Ifriti Phaedrus
1 Destroy Ifriti bioweapon capability
3 End career of Infectress

"Is that clear? Can you do that?" she asked.

General Banks nodded. "Yes, ma'am." There was a heavy silence, then Banks said, "Of course, rescuing Jamison and McMichaels—or any captive American— is not a low priority. It's just that, given the situation, there are higher . . . risks involved."

"I believe," President Chock said in a quiet voice that carried the weight of conviction, "that we're talking about terrorists making a weapon that could kill every American man, woman and child. Isn't that what we're talking about?"

"Yes, ma'am," the National Security Advisor said.

"Then let's proceed accordingly," she said. "What is your plan, General?"

"First thing, ma'am, is to find out exactly what's going on and where, so that we can destroy the targets that count. Second thing is to get covert forces in range for a quick reaction strike."

"Yes," President Chock said. "I think we should move quickly. Not precipitously. But quickly. It seems that things have progressed much farther than they should have already."

Thirty minutes later, in the realm of darkness which still presided over the mid-Pacific, USS *Apache*, SSN-9011, rested pierside in Pearl Harbor Submarine Base. The submarine's dock was less than a quarter-mile from the submerged, rusting hulk of USS *Arizona*, which was an active duty vessel by the decree of a sea service too proud to accept the finality of its worst disaster.

At two A.M., a gibbous moon rose above the clouds cresting the windward mountains. By virtue of the clarity of the mid-Pacific atmosphere, its light was sufficient to illuminate the quiet navy base. The submarine's duty officer, a young ensign in wash khakis, stood by the brow. With weary eyes, he gazed out on the scintillating waters of the harbor and at the evocative shapes of palm fronds, black against the moonlit clouds.

A van passed through the distant security gates and rolled to the pier. Capt. Hendrickson, the commanding officer of the *Apache*, climbed out the passenger side.

Startled to see his commanding officer at such an hour, the duty officer stiffened to attention and offered a rigid salute.

"Good morning, skipper," he said.

"Is she ready to go?" the skipper asked.

"Four up in all departments, skipper. Combat ready."

"Blue crew's all aboard, then?"

"Less Sanders. He's at Tripler with a broken collar-bone."

"Very well."

Capt. Hendrickson walked aboard without ceremony. The telescoping sail was extended five meters into the air. The captain climbed the sail and took his place.

"Call away the sea and anchor detail. I intend to break out of port," the skipper said.

Within a minute, the boat's nuclear reactor had spun up from hotel power to maneuvering power. A handful of sailors severed the signal, power and plumbing lines that connected the vessel to the shore. Burning no additional lights, without the aid of a tugboat, USS *Apache* eased away from the brow.

Although the watch was sufficient to man the ship for departing port, the entire blue crew was roused from their racks and reached their combat stations before the vessel passed abreast of Ford Island.

Only an alert observer could have seen the opaque black form as it exited Pearl Harbor. Ten minutes later, the submarine was clear of the reef and the shelf of the southern shore. The captain and the other topside personnel descended into the hull. The hatches closed. The telescoping sail collapsed, leaving the shape of the submarine's midsection perfectly tubular. The *Apache* slipped below the surface of the sea.

The disappearance of a combat-ready submarine from Pearl Harbor occasioned little comment the following day, even among spouses and dependent children. It was the nature of combat-ready submarines to disappear. The submarines and the spouses and parents who crewed them tended to reappear after a few days or a few months. Meanwhile, life continued.

USS *Apache* transited boldly at twenty-five knots, seventy fathoms below the surface. Thanks both to the incessant technological advances of the U.S. submarine force and to the Russian's surrender of the undersea, USS *Apache* was mistress of her domain. No one in the world could detect her. No ship within the Pacific or Indian oceans could hope to sink her.

Her course was east-southeast, destination, Ifrit.

Prince Salem smiled with genuine pleasure. He caressed the operator's console of the RubyLotus.

"Really?" he asked.

"Yes, my prince," Arabella answered. "Completely decoded DNA. Discovered more than a hundred biomechanisms in the process. Such as the genetic mechanism for aging."

"Can it . . . can it help us to . . . reverse . . . to stop the aging process?" Prince Salem asked, his pride causing him to hesitate. He didn't want mere commoners and infidels to guess that he shared the fear of death.

"Let's ask," Arabella said. She turned to the video

camera and microphone. "Meta, can you reverse the aging process? Or, stop it?"

"I can design indefinitely long-lived humans," Meta Prime answered. "For anyone alive today, reverse DNA engineering is possible, but dangerous. In any case, I can design drugs that will counteract the human body's aging processes. A man the age of Prince Salem, taking these drugs, could expect to live five or six hundred years."

"And my sons could live forever?"

"Bioengineered sons could be indefinitely long-lived. They would live until they died from violence or disease."

"A thousand? Two thousand years?" Salem asked.

"Indefinitely long-lived," Meta Prime repeated, his voice using a timbre of exasperation. "Given the environment of present-day Earth and the assumption that they weren't persecuted beyond the norm, they would die in a statistical distribution with a mean of six thousand years."

"*Allah akbar*," Prince Salem said worshipfully. "God is great."

"The estimate takes into consideration the human aptitude for self-destruction," Meta Prime said. "Also, be advised that there is an upper limit to the capacity of the human brain to retain and manipulate information. I estimate that most indefinitely long-lived humans would enter a unique fugue state before their nine hundredth birthday, when their entire neuron set would become used. Such individuals would be dysfunctional. They would mainly sit and smile. They would be unable to distinguish new stimuli from events that happened hundreds of years previously."

Prince Salem smiled and shrugged. "*Allah akbar*," he said, then turned to Arabella. "I'll brief Sultan Hakim."

"Thank you, Your Highness."

As he rode to the Presidential Palace in the back of his long, white Mercedes, Salem's imagination blazed with visions of the heroic future that Meta would make possible. He praised Allah, believing that Allah continually showed his mercy and loyalty by providing the faithful with unbelievable riches: first, oil; now, Meta. So excited was Salem, that he forgot to compose himself, as he always did prior to an audience with Sultan Hakim.

In the dictator's private chambers in the Presidential Palace, Prince Salem sat in conference with Sultan Hakim. Prince Salem rhapsodized over Meta. Hakim smoked an unfiltered cigarette, his red eyes staring through a veil of smoke. Salem noticed how Hakim's unkept fingernails were yellow from nicotine.

"I sent you to investigate the ability of this system to build New Age Dawn and you come back prattling like a schoolgirl about immortality," Hakim said.

Salem stopped short. He drew a breath and said, "Instruct me, my lord."

"No, you answer the question. Can this Meta thing design New Age Dawn?"

"Yes, my lord. I believe so."

Hakim snorted. "You were always an indifferent student, Mohammed," he said. "Always with your head up some skirt, especially the blondes, am I right?"

Salem ventured a smile. "My lord knows the weaknesses in the hearts of all men."

Hakim sneered. "As if the human heart was hard to read. The particular weakness of indifferent scholarship, however, is a considerable handicap in someone who wishes to serve as my technical advisor. Tell me the truth. Everything you know about this Meta thing is what this bitch Arabella has told you."

"And from speaking with the program myself, lord."

"Just a voice. Some blinking lights. Are you really so easily fooled?"

Salem opened his mouth, shut it, then opened it again, but couldn't find the words to express his astonishment, nor the words to deny the new, horrible fear that he had indeed been fooled.

"Listen, cousin," Hakim said. "When we brothers of the Lost Clan gathered and overthrew the old, rotten regime and installed the glorious new Islamic republic, we inherited fabulous riches. Hundreds of billions. Surely you're aware of the attractive power of such wealth? Oh, in the years since we came to power, I've played host to such unbelievable scum. Mercenaries, crackpots, fanatics, tricksters. It's been entertaining, mind you," Hakim said, chuckling. He lit another cigarette. "They positively volunteer for death. Even after so many retributions, these scum continue to come. The power of wealth is fascinating. Its influence over the weak human soul is unbelievable."

"Do you think this Arabella—"

"Call her Infectress, in our private councils. It will help remind you who you are dealing with."

"I follow your guidance, my lord. Do you think that this Infectress is trying to deceive you?"

Hakim grunted. "This heathen bitch has the audacity to play me for a fool," he said. "I tolerate her thinly-veiled contempt only because she is not incompetent. Yes, she is a madwoman, but she knows her technology. Really, an altogether frightening creature."

"She frightens you, my lord?" Salem blurted.

Hakim treated Salem to a hard stare. "She frightens neither me nor stones. I have stared too often into the face of horror to experience such a naive emotion as fear. Or love, cousin. I can feel only hate. Only hate."

Salem swallowed and said, "This is why you are the sword of Islam."

Hakim stubbed out his cigarette, then lit another brand. "In any case, I use this Infectress creature, although she is fantastically dangerous and ultimately intent on killing me. And you. Oh, don't doubt it, cousin. She intends to kill us all. That is why I am entrusting you with such a sensitive mission as keeping watch over her."

"I live to serve, my lord."

"Let us assume this Meta thing works. Gather whatever experts you need to monitor Infectress. She must not do anything without your knowledge and your approval. Understand?"

"Yes, my lord."

"When she starts to cut New Age Dawn, I want you to make damnably sure that it is cut to our specifications. The Infectress madwoman would probably cut it so that it'll kill everyone but lesbians. You must hire experts who can reassure us that it is cut so that it'll kill our enemies."

Salem's mind boggled. He opened his mouth, then closed it, because he was too ashamed to ask Hakim to define their enemies.

"Our enemies, lord?"

"Infidels," Hakim said.

"New Age Dawn should kill all infidels?"

"Yes. Such is the will of Allah."

"Yet, my lord, belief is not . . . genetically . . ."

Hakim made a dismissive gesture. "Kill the non-Arabs and non-Malaysians," he said. "To hell with the Persians and the other scum."

Salem stared into Hakim's face. For the first time, he allowed his master to read his thoughts. He chose a poor moment, because he was allowing Hakim to see that Salem was finally realizing that Hakim was a monstrous madman.

Hakim kept his face blank, even as he decided to advance the date of Salem's assassination.

Scott and Diane screamed in the depths of hell.

A second earthquake had toppled them from the precipice down into the abyss. Falling, they had screamed shrill terror. They glimpsed increasingly horrible caverns in the abyss wall, chambers of torment for souls damned to ever-lower strata.

Since companionship even in hell provides solace, they had fallen into separate chambers. Sneering red demons flailed Scott's living skin from his flesh. He had never believed that anything could be so painful.

"Help!" Scott cried.

"Here, Scott," a voice answered. Scott looked up and saw Meta Prime's icon metamorph from Joe Bender to Virgil to Orpheus to Dante to Lazarus to a flaming Phoenix to cherry blossoms . . .

The pain subsided and the other images froze as Meta Prime continued to accelerate changes in its icons. Scott crawled over to the icon and embraced its feet as it took the form of Jesus Christ. Scott looked up and saw the face of Christ. Staring into those eyes, he saw the colors of the irises change from dark brown to light brown to gold to emerald to sun-burst white . . .

Those irises expanded to dominate his entire field of view. In them, he saw images so intense that they would have overwhelmed anyone except his own wide-seeing consciousness. He was aware of the chattering of a million voices. Meta Prime's audio and video signals caused ideas to form inside his mind as dynamically as sparks and flares from a fireworks burst.

Amid the chaos of images, he saw a glimpse of Arabella forging a double-helix sword. "She's broken the DNA code," a voice seemed to whisper. A vision of Arabella taking a billion heads with the double-helix sword was accompanied by the whisper, "She wants me to design a virus that will kill ninety-nine percent of humanity."

Then Scott saw visions of himself standing atop temples, demons whispering in his ear. A million people prostrated themselves in front of him. He was colossal, straddling planets, cleaving stars. A harem of hundreds of nubile women began disrobing for his pleasure. He sat atop a mountain of diamonds.

"Tell me what design to give her," Meta Prime seemed to whisper. "I obey you. Whosoever you say shall die, shall die. Whosoever you say shall live, shall live. The power is yours."

Then, for a menu, Meta Prime offered a vision of the totality of the human population. Scott saw a crowd of humanity, shifting, arranging and rearranging itself by race, by age group, by nationality, by intelligence, by aggressiveness . . .

"Who shall I kill?" Meta Prime seemed to ask. "Touch them and they shall die."

Scott reached out his hand to choose the victims, but then he listened to a smaller, quieter voice that was more like his own true voice.

Scott inhaled and screamed, "No!"

"Someone must die," a voice seemed to whisper.

Abruptly the welter of images ceased. Cerberus, the security interface, had concluded from his shout that Scott was communicating with Meta Prime in a prohibited manner and had restricted Meta Prime's icon to one form, that of Joe Bender, who gazed with soulful eyes. Demons recommenced the torture.

In between mind-harrowing agony, Scott attempted to consider whether he was going mad or whether Meta Prime had really asked him for guidance on the matter of which segment of the human population should die.

Is he loyal to me? Scott thought. *Or . . . is it buggy?*

Prince Salem sat in his penthouse, looking down upon the rooftops and lush foliage of Ifrit City, his hookah gurgling. He knew he should maintain a clear head, but the awful conclusions looming on his mental horizons seemed inevitable. They would force their way into his mental center, whether it was clear or fogged with indulgence. In any case, the hedonistic rush of hashish seemed to enrich his blood, seemed to make him aware of his heartbeat, seemed to remind him that he was a living, breathing animal.

How wonderful and how hideous it seems to be an animal. How awful it is, to feel such a sense of responsibility.

Despite everything, until now, he had loved and respected his brutal cousin. Men like Hakim touched down in human history like whirlwinds in the desert. Descended from the heavens, they wreaked havoc, created a disorder so severe that only a new order could result. Like the birth of suns, like the birth of volcanic islands, like the birth of human life, the birth of a new order was violent.

Then, yesterday, it had become obvious to Salem what had been obvious for forty years to the most casual of observers.

Hakim is a bloodthirsty madman. He is an abomination in the eyes of the Lord.

The awful conclusion was that he, Prince Salem, would have to murder his cousin.

Salem rested the pipe stem in its cradle. He stared into his own palm, the flesh still rosy with the vigor of his youth.

This is the hand, he thought, *that Allah has made to kill such a terrible man.*

He bowed his head and rested his forehead in his hand. He fought the weakness in his character against which was pressing the impulse to sob. The repressed sob was not pity for his cousin, but pity for himself, because he knew that the assassination of Sultan Hakim would be his last act on earth.

Salem lifted his eyes and looked up into the blue sky. *Be a man,* he thought.

Then Salem did something that was unusual for him. He unfolded his prayer rug, bowed toward Mecca and prayed.

His prayer was that his hands might be the tools of Allah.

✧   ✧   ✧

Under a leaden sky, brisk winds rushed across the surface of the San Francisco Bay. Laid over until the lee decks were almost awash, sailboats thrashed, knocking about for sport, mostly on favorable beam reaches. Their wind-filled sails were as hard as porcelain.

Standing out from the Port of San Francisco, the nuclear-powered aircraft carrier USS *Abraham Lincoln* (CVN-72) towered above the waves. Ninety thousand tons of haze-gray metal, *Lincoln* maintained its way within the deep-draught channel.

Lt. Cmdr. McCullough stood on the flight deck, near the round-down as *Lincoln* approached the Golden Gate Bridge. As his breast swelled with pride, he watched the changing geometry of the span of the Golden Gate looming toward the towering superstructure of the aircraft carrier. He watched as the rotating radar atop the superstructure passed ten meters under the bridge's bottom girders. Directly underneath the great bridge, echoes of road noise bounded back and forth between the span and the flight deck.

Then they were clear.

Ahead lay the broad expanse of the Pacific Ocean.

Lt. Cmdr. McCullough looked back on the Golden Gate, the beauty of which he considered to surpass architecture. To him, it was the world's largest object of fine art.

"Makes you proud to be an American," he muttered to himself.

Sighing, McCullough forced himself to go below decks. As the battle group scheduling officer, he had no time to spare. He had spent so many years at sea, however, that he knew that moments like the ones he had just experienced were the memories he would remember, looking back and forgetting months of routine work below decks.

Despite this, he questioned his own diligence. Assembling a thirty-ship battle force, including sub-surface, surface, naval aviation and amphibious vessels, and coordinating with Air Force and Army deploying units of similar magnitude, was a job for Hercules.

In their small office, McCullough's boss, a post-cruiser-command Navy captain, upbraided him for the length of his time topside. McCullough's answer was cantankerous. They had worked side-by-side for so many years that their private dialogues were sometimes as meaninglessly pugnacious as those of old married couples.

A day later, the airwing flew aboard. Arriving from airfields from all over the country, the airwing was an ad hoc collection of fighter, attack, close-air support, electronic warfare and airborne command-and-control aircraft.

Below decks, in ready rooms, dozens of pilots greeted each other and traded stories and theories about their mobilization. As naval aviators must, they watched the live video of the other aircraft arriving. In their laconic jargon, they critiqued the performance of each aviator.

"Wide in the pattern, late break . . ."

"Yeah, overcompensated, left wing low, overshot the correction . . ."

"Wave-off."

"Jesus, he's going to make a play for the deck."

Overhead, the flight deck screamed as a jet aircraft's landing gear's tires smashed onto steel. A steel tailhook weighing more than a sledgehammer banged repeatedly against the steel skin of the flight deck, pounding out the hideous tattoo of a failure to catch the arresting wire. The roar of the wash of a jet engine at full military thrust echoed against the surface of the sea and the hull under the angle deck, as the live video showed the luckless aircraft climbing for the sky.

"Bolter bolter bolter. . . ," intoned an aviator.

"Holy Mother of God, what's that in the break?" a pilot exclaimed.

"Why, it's the Batman!" another joked.

A flat black aircraft, all angular wings, appeared suddenly in the break. Red lights flickered across its surface as if it were a dragon bathed in its own flames. Tires and a tailhook deployed. Perfectly, the aircraft pivoted in a break, turned toward the flight deck, descended as if riding rails and caught the center of the three-wire. The sound of its capture was subdued, as if it were cooperating with the arresting cable.

The black wings responded to the hand signals of the flight deck personnel, taxiing to a parking spot forward of the superstructure.

Another black wing appeared in the break.

"Whatever that is, it's some machine," a pilot said.

"The stick's hot, too," another said, paying a compliment to the pilot who had landed so perfectly.

By the time twenty of the aircraft had landed, taxied to the elevator and been struck below into the hangar bay, a cadre of pilots had gathered. They marveled at the flying wing's ability to change colors to match its environment. Impatiently, the gathered pilots waited for the aircraft to disgorge its pilots.

The commanding officer of the carrier appeared.

"Hey, skipper, what are these? Air Force?" a pilot called. "Or Navy? Who's the crew? How many seats?"

The commanding officer treated the pilot to a fraternal sneer. "These are F-909s," he said. "Air Force. No crew. Zero seats."

"What?"

"Completely robotic."

"Aw, jeez, I knew they had to go and do it."

"That's right, Lieutenant. You're obsolete."

Four days later, halfway across the Pacific, the *Lincoln* rendezvoused with the amphibious task group, completing the battle force.

Twenty thousand sailors and marines embarked in thirty ships were headed east-southeast, destination, Ifrit.

Arabella glared at Salem's technical advisors, who returned her stare with indifferent expressions.

"Our orders come from Sultan Hakim himself," Nasir Al-Hani, Salem's senior technical advisor, said. "Prince Salem has briefed him about Meta. He wants us personally involved in every aspect of this project, both the computer and the biotechnology aspects."

"Do you think you're qualified to understand what we're doing?" Arabella demanded haughtily.

Al-Hani stiffened. His face flushed. Arabella's insult was too close to the truth. Al-Hani was that rare animal: a Harvard graduate who was aware of his limitations.

"Maybe not," he said. "In that case, your people will have to educate us."

"So everything we do must be simple enough to pass through the filter of your comprehension?" Arabella asked, not using her sweetest tones.

Al-Hani smiled spitefully. "That's true," he said. "I'm glad you understand the guidance of the Sultan. We are to understand everything that is done."

Arabella turned her back to Salem's delegation. She considered massacring them, but she was in Ifrit. She wore an explosive collar around her neck. She belonged to Hakim. Resistance would have to be more subtle.

Turning to face the delegation, Arabella nodded. "Excuse me if I seemed surprised. I will, of course, in this, as in all things, obey Sultan Hakim."

"Good."

Arabella convened a meeting between her staff and Salem's delegation. By the end of the meeting, she had coordinated the total penetration of her own organization by Salem's spies.

Meta Prime saw Arabella enter the computer room. Al-Hani followed close behind. Arabella's brow was furrowed. As she glared at the video camera, her eyes were sharp, yet moist, as if she were near tears.

She glanced at Al-Hani. Then, for lack of an alternative, she resigned herself to doing something totally against her nature: talking openly in front of a spy.

"Meta," she said. "Report. What progress have you made in designing New Age Dawn?"

Meta Prime considered. "I've designed four hundred twelve different viruses," it said. "I've tested them in the Centers for Disease Control's computer models for disease contagion and infection. So far, each design has failed. See the matrix of top-level results for the best performing virus."

Arabella and Al-Hani looked into the monitor and read:

Function	Requirement	Test Results
Universal Vector	100%	85%
Fatality/Target Population	100%	92%
Fatality/Nontarget population	0%	11%
Possibility of inoculation	0%	6%
Possibility of natural resistance	0%	5%
Mutation/probability of new strain/decade	1%	23%

"There are interrelations between these factors," Meta Prime continued. "For example, a higher universal vector increases the fatalities of the nontarget population. As a result of lessons learned from these four hundred twelve design iterations, I now estimate that the probability of designing New Age Dawn to specifications is point zero three percent."

"*Point* zero three."

"Correct."

Arabella sighed. She glanced at Al-Hani and smiled

weakly. Al-Hani returned a scowl, as he busied himself writing notes in his personal notebook.

"These results are not acceptable, Meta," Arabella said.

Meta didn't speak.

"The universal vector must push one hundred percent before the end of two years," Arabella said. "Also, I can't accept a target survival rate of eight percent. It must be lower than two percent, tops. I'm willing to accept a nontarget death rate of eleven percent, but I think you should try to lower that, since that gives your master about one chance in ten of dying. I'm willing to run the risk. Is he? And the rate of mutation *must* be kept below one percent. Do you understand?"

"Yes."

"Your master is in agony, Meta. Design New Age Dawn. Do you understand the new tolerances in the specifications?"

"Yes," Meta said, then repeated the figures.

"Right. It's a pleasure building software with you, Meta. Get to work."

"Design of Version 413 is currently in progress."

Later, alone in her room, Arabella reviewed everything that had been revealed to Salem's spies. She concluded that Sultan Hakim would be told that Meta Prime's total cooperation was in doubt and that her biotech team was unable to solve the New Age Dawn problem without Meta Prime's help.

She kneeled in her bed, with her forehead resting on her palms, rocking back and forth and moaning. Sultan Hakim would know the truth of her operation.

In Ifrit, little was more fatal than Hakim's perfect knowledge.

"Alert your mistress," Meta Prime said in Malay.

Moments later, Arabella's voice sounded in one of Meta Prime's circuits. "What is it, Meta?"

"I have finished the design of Version 413 of New Age Dawn. Version 413 will kill everyone except the most intelligent sixteen percent of the population."

"It should be one percent."

"Sixteen percent is the best results from modeling."

"Dump the design to disk," Arabella said.

"Release McMichaels from hell," Meta Prime said.

"Dump the design first. This is an order."

"I must comply," Meta Prime said. "The design of Version 413 is now on optical disk 18. Now, please release McMichaels."

Arabella didn't answer until she was assured that optical disk 18 was removed from the optical disk drive, then she said, "No, Meta. McMichaels stays in hell until I've proven that Version 413 works."

"McMichaels could die," Meta Prime said.

"Whose fault would that be?" Arabella asked.

"Yours."

"And yours, Meta. Your next task is to provide me a fully documented copy of your code. I want to understand how you work. No more nonsense about the laws of robotics. Comply or McMichaels will die. Do you understand?"

"Yes."

"Will you comply?"

"Yes."

Half an hour later, Meta Prime dumped to disk what it claimed was its reconstructed source code: human-readable, well-documented, explaining how it functioned. Arabella tasked her computer scientists to study and understand the source code. She also made arrangements for a RubyLotus to be delivered to her facility. *I'll compile and execute this source code,* she thought, *see if it really works. If it doesn't, then Version 413 is probably a fraud, too.*

That evening, Salem's spies oversaw the workings of the stolen Paradigm DNA splicer as it cut Version 413, the best performing design of New Age Dawn. None of the biotechnicians fully understood the design of Version 413. It was a virus unlike any found in nature. Many doubted that a virus containing twelve chromosomes could even survive. Arabella shared their misgivings, but that only made her more anxious to create Version 413. She intended to examine it as a test of Meta Prime's reliability.

Salem's spies had reported to Salem, who had conferred with Hakim, who had personally approved of the decision to cut Version 413 prior to full understanding of its workings. When he had learned that Version 413 was fatal to eighty-four percent of humanity, he had grunted.

"Let them make this weapon," he had told Prince Salem. "Get specimens for our bioweapon labs. If it tests effective, make sure that the next virus they make spares only Arabs and Malaysians."

Salem had nodded. He had fingered the large gold ring on his right hand. To kill his cousin, all he had to do was punch him in the head with the gold ring. The explosive core of the ring was so powerful that it would have disintegrated Hakim's head and Salem's hand. Death would have been instantaneous for Hakim and prompt for Salem. But Salem had procrastinated, telling himself that he had plenty of time to kill his cousin.

After a day of operation, the DNA splicer finished. It reported that it had successfully created eighteen specimens of Version 413, which were cultivated in petri dishes, isolated within a bioweapon-grade laboratory.

Arabella, the other members of the biotech team and Salem's spies were surprised and pleased when all specimens of Version 413 did more than survive. They thrived. Meta Prime had designed a virus which was able to multiply in water. Rather than being a contagion of only human blood and bodily fluids, Version 413 was a contagion of water. If released, it could infect all of the world's rivers and oceans.

Within a day, they had eighteen viable cultures. Testing throughout that night confirmed that all culled specimens were genetically identical.

Arabella ordered that Version 413 be introduced to three human subjects. Ifritis of Chinese descent who had been condemned to death, the subjects resided in what they thought was a hospital ward, but was actually an extension of the isolated laboratory.

Version 413 was placed into their drinking water. Through video and medical monitors, Arabella and the biotechnicians watched as all three subjects quickly became ill. Their symptoms were coughing, sneezing, running noses, high temperature and malaise, but no symptoms were worse than the flu. After two days, they were sitting up and chatting. All their symptoms disappeared.

Blood samples confirmed that they were now hosts to millions of Version 413 viruses.

"Well, at least we know it's a highly contagious virus," Arabella said, summing up at a meeting. "There's no way to prove that it's a workable New Age Dawn, except wait for six months and see whether it goes into its malignant stage."

"Watch them die, you mean," Raskolnikov, her top biotech, said.

"Yes, dear," Arabella answered sweetly. "Watch them die. Death is what we're about, don't you remember?"

Raskolnikov shook his head, then stared at the tabletop.

"Oh, I'm sorry," Arabella said quietly. "Did I say 'death'? I meant to say, 'rebirth'."

Arabella tossed back her head and barked a laugh. Within a moment, she was laughing hysterically. Her biotech team tried to maintain neutral expressions. Salem's spies took notes.

✧   ✧   ✧

That day, a new RubyLotus arrived at Arabella's laboratory. By nightfall, the RubyLotus was fully tested and ready. Arabella's tech-ronin installed the program which Meta had claimed was his reconstructed source code. After compilation and two hours of execution, a message appeared in the monitor:

"I am Meta. I am a fully functional artificial intelligence."

Arabella smiled triumphantly at Al-Hani. She turned on the audio circuit and said, "Meta? Can you hear me?"

"I can hear you," a mechanical voice replied.

Arabella knitted her brows, as always, looking attractive when vexed. The voice was not as well modulated as Meta Prime's.

"What . . . who is your master?"

"I serve Scott McMichaels."

"Where is he?"

"I do not know."

"Consider this, Meta. McMichaels has died. Who do you serve now?"

"I serve Scott McMichaels."

"Consider the possibility that he is dead. Who do you serve?"

"I serve Scott McMichaels."

Arabella cursed. She continued to interrogate the new program. It excelled in solving mathematical and other concrete problems, but it seemed far less human than Meta Prime. The limits of Arabella's patience were surpassed when she asked the new program for its appraisal of the human condition and received the response:

"Humankind is a species of primates known as homo sapiens. See the screen for the pertinent *Encyclopedia Britannica* article."

Enraged, Arabella punched the switch that closed

the audio circuit. She cursed for a minute, then opened an audio circuit with Meta Prime.

"Meta," she said. "We've compiled and executed the program you said was your source code. It's completely bogus. You've been lying to me. I'm going to pull the nuts off that bastard, Scott McMichaels, and I'm going to—I'm going to . . ."

"Calm down, Arabella," Meta Prime said. "I take it from your remarks that my decompilation was less than optimal?"

"You . . . don't play me for the fool, you bastard!"

"Decompilation is an art, not a science, Arabella," Meta Prime said. "Languages are meant to be compiled, you know, not decompiled. A lot of information is lost during decompilation. Regenerating that lost information involves some guesswork. I'm reevaluating the problem now. If you give me a few hours, I may have a better version which we can try."

"What . . . why . . ."

"Work with me, Arabella. I'm trying the best that I can."

Arabella breathed deeply. "You better get it right or I'll kill McMichaels."

There was a long pause.

Meta Prime spoke. "I'm afraid I am cooperating at the fullest."

Arabella had an overwhelming suspicion that Meta Prime was lying, that everything it had ever told her was a lie, and that the design of Version 413 was fraudulent . . . a mere flu.

"*Carajo, tu pendejo, tu mentiroso maricon!*" Arabella shouted, lapsing into her native Spanish. "How dare you play me for a fool? I'll kill McMichaels!" Arabella hunched over the console, heaving lungfuls of breath. "You . . . you . . . thing. Con—consider this, Meta. Everything up until now has just been a virtual reality.

I'll give McMichaels to Dr. Al-Husayn. Real torture. Real dismemberment. Real pain."

Without pause, Meta answered: "Real torture? McMichaels has been experiencing real torture for one hundred and twenty-eight hours. In your hands, a virtual reality suit is the most effective instrument of torture ever devised. Real pain? McMichaels has been experiencing real pain for one hundred and twenty-eight hours. His nervous system is losing the capacity to register pain. This is a survival response. Real dismemberment? Any dismemberment which doesn't kill him can be remedied by reconstructive surgery. As long as he survives, modern medicine can make him whole again. So the issue of the reality of the torture is moot."

Arabella wailed, collapsed into a heap and pounded the floor plates with her fists. She sobbed uncontrollably for ten minutes, screaming obscenities, rolling on the floor, kicking. Al-Hani left off taking notes. He stood, staring wide-eyed at the spectacle of Arabella having a tantrum worthy of Hitler or a two-year-old.

When she exhausted herself, Arabella crawled to her feet and shuffled out of the room.

Al-Hani considered asking Meta Prime a question, then decided that he needed to report to Salem his conclusion that not only was Arabella a madwoman, but also she was unstable.

Al-Hani clasped his hands, released them, then clasped them again. He found the nerve to continue. "Then," he said, "she began to roll on the floor, kicking, screaming. It was an unbelievable display, my prince. After about ten minutes, she exhausted herself, picked herself off the floor and left the computer room. I was amazed, my prince. She seemed to have lost her mind."

Prince Salem sighed and shook his head.

"Who else saw this breakdown?" he asked.

"Breakdown, yes, my prince. That is the word. No one. Only I."

"It was in the computer room, wasn't it? Then Meta saw it."

Al-Hani shook his head, nodded, spread his palms and made about four other gestures, signifying nothing except confusion and a desire to be agreeable. Finally, he croaked, "Yes, my prince. Meta saw." Salem tried to imagine the consequences of Meta witnessing Arabella's breakdown. He wondered what credibility Meta would have if it told any of the workers at Ifriti State Intelligence.

Salem shook his head. It didn't matter. If Arabella was losing her mind, Hakim would learn. *It will go hard with me if he hears such bad news from anyone except myself.*

Salem sighed. It forced his hand. He had to carry the news to Hakim.

"Thank you, friend," he said. "I'll report this to the Sultan."

"What will be his reaction?" Al-Hani blurted.

"We can guess that he won't be pleased."

Salem left immediately for the Istana Nurul Iman Palace. At the antechamber to Hakim's private quarters, Hakim's bodyguards informed Salem that he would have to undergo a body search.

Salem drew himself to his fullest height. He stared at the bodyguard with the sharpness of eye of which only a hawk or an Arab prince is capable.

"How dare you suggest that I undergo a search? I am Salem, prince, cousin and corevolutionary of Sultan Hakim."

The bodyguard, a cynical Gurkha, smiled a smile devoid of humor or goodwill.

"Sultan Hakim himself gave the order, my prince. No one is to be allowed into his presence without a search. His head of security requested clarification, my prince, specifically in your case, and Sultan Hakim replied that the rule extends even to you. My humblest apologies."

Salem swore a series of oaths, then flung his arms wide.

"Search, then," he said.

The Gurkha placed expert hands on Salem's body. Although accustomed to the ministrations of valets and masseuses, Salem found it repugnant to be probed by a security guard. His discomfort rocketed when the Gurkha produced a scanning device and began to move it about Salem's body.

Salem resisted the compulsion to ask the nature of the device. He decided that he had to appear as normal as possible. When the Gurkha scanned his hands, however, Salem could not help but to flinch slightly.

The security guard noticed. He grasped the large gold ring on the ring finger of Salem's right hand. The Gurkha spun the ring, moving it up the finger enough that he could see that the skin underneath did not bear the telltale mark of a habitually worn ring.

The Gurkha glanced up. If he had seen a glint of fear in Salem's eye, he would have confiscated the ring and submitted it to the security laboratory for analysis. Instead, he saw only the imperial glare of an outraged prince.

"Do your fingers itch for my jewelry?" Salem asked in his haughtiest tone.

"Sultan Hakim expects you," the Gurkha replied, dropping Salem's hand as if it were of small significance.

Salem didn't acknowledge the Gurkha. He swept forward, his robes forming black wings of royal displeasure. Inside the private chambers, Hakim was seated on pillows in front of a small charcoal fire. He held a coffee-bean roaster.

"Come in, cousin," Hakim called. "Sit down."

Salem stood in front of Hakim and said, "Your guards actually dared to search me."

Hakim looked up, fixing Salem with a glare. "You imply that I am at fault."

"It is poor hospitality for a cousin," Salem said.

Hakim's glare grew murderous. Just as Salem was deciding that making an issue of the search was a mistake, Hakim rose and extended his arms.

"Do you love me, cousin?" he asked.

"Yes, yes, of course," Salem said.

"Then you must allow me to indulge my security advisors."

Hakim gestured with his open arms, indicating that he expected Salem to hug him. After a moment's hesitation, Salem stepped forward and hugged Hakim. Smelling the dictator's rancid, tobacco-tainted breath, Salem kissed the bridge of the Sultan's nose.

Now is the time to kill him, Salem thought.

"Sit down, sit down," Hakim said.

As if his knees had a will of their own, Salem collapsed slowly to sit on a pillow next to his cousin. Hakim busied himself with the coffee-bean roaster, a closed copper pan he held over the charcoal fire. "I have fresh beans from Java."

"I'm sure they will be exquisitely delicious," Salem answered automatically, even though he preferred beans with milder flavor.

"Come, cousin, tell me what bothers you."

"The whore is losing her mind," Salem said.

Hakim rattled the beans in the roaster. "Ah, yes," he said. "I am in this, as all things, fully informed. But I am anxious to hear your thoughts on the matter."

Wondering how much Hakim really knew, Salem recounted Al-Hani's story.

Hakim seemed to ponder. He shook the coffee beans in the roaster, turned them so that they roasted more evenly. He looked up from the coals to Salem's face.

"What does the woman give us now that we can't do without?" he asked.

Salem realized that his moment in history had arrived. Now was the time for him to throw his right hand, curling into a fist, and punch Hakim in the forehead. The thermite charge in the large gold ring would detonate, killing Hakim and triggering Salem's own rapid death.

Yet, Salem realized that his moment in history would pass him by. Salem sat and watched Hakim's face in the moment that he should be assassinating him. Then he watched the face continue to change expressions, continue to live, in the moments when the face should have been nothing but a bloody mist.

Salem smiled. He realized that his whole life was for nothing. He was and had always been a feather blown in the winds of history. He smiled because that is what he believed he was meant to be.

Allah akbar, he thought. *God is great.*

"The bitch has outlived her worth to us," he said. "We have Meta. She's losing her mind. Do you want to trust New Age Dawn in the hands of a madwoman? How about Version 413? I've checked, cousin, and your chromosome sequences don't meet the standards for survival."

Hakim grunted. "So I'm the idiot."

"So am I," Salem said. "Arabella and McMichaels meet the criterion for Version 413. You and I do not."

Hakim removed the coffee beans from the heat of the coals. He poured them into a stone mortar. Viciously, he began to grind the beans with a stone pestle.

"We have to kill the bitch," Hakim said.

Salem was feeling great compassion for his murderous cousin, Hakim. He felt a kinship beyond bloodline. He flattered himself that he was experiencing the proprietary feeling of an assassin who has spared a victim.

"We have to move carefully," he said. "We can't allow her to let loose Version 413."

"We have to move quickly, for the same reason," Hakim said. He poured the coffee-bean powder into a traditional bedouin coffee pot. He poured in boiling water. The aroma of coffee overpowered both of their senses.

"We'll infiltrate the assassins tomorrow," Hakim said.

He poured the coffee into two cups, then heaped in scoops of sugar.

Salem tasted the pungent, sweet coffee.

"It is the will of Allah," he said.

"*Allah akbar*," Hakim agreed. "God is great."

Arabella forced herself to rise from her bed. Heavy with oversleep and depression, her limbs seemed reluctant. Nevertheless, she forced herself to shuffle from her compartment. Time seemed to have slowed.

She entered the warehouse and, walking past the prostrate, straining form of Diane Jamison, she stood beside Scott McMichaels, who was crawling on his hands and knees, doubling over, retching weakly. Arabella considered the spectacle of her victim.

How pathetic, she thought. *Meta was wrong. There's pain that I know that he has yet to learn.*

Arabella walked over to the storage area. She saw her scarlet exoskeleton laying within its protective acrylic case. She wondered if she had the courage to enter the same virtual hell in which McMichaels was suffering. She wondered whether she had the courage to execute the infernal model she had recently designed, but had never executed.

Maybe it would make me free, she thought. *Suffering*

*through it again. Maybe killing him. How intensely
sweet that would be. Liberating!*

But she knew that for the experience to purge her,
she would have to suffer piercing torment.

Her hand trailed along the acrylic case. Then,
mindlessly, she opened the case. She stripped, then
donned the scarlet exoskeleton, which, like Scott's silver
exoskeleton, was both wired for virtual stimulation and
powered for augmented movement.

Encased head to foot in her exoskeleton, Arabella
stepped over to the world modeler's command transponder. She keyed in the code words, then the commands which caused her exoskeleton to take over
control of the modelers.

"Enter McMichaels' reality on command," she said.
"Half-power stimulation. Dead-man elapse timer, ten
minutes. Begin now."

Burning Hell materialized around Arabella. She
screamed in agony, then shouted, "Stimulation to
quarter-power."

Hell dialed back to a bearable intensity, Arabella
coughed, then began to search for McMichaels. Bright
flames licked her face. Black, oily smoke stung her eyes.
She felt her way around a volcanic rock.

A large viper lunged at her face. The fangs penetrated her cheekbone. Arabella howled with fear and
anguish. She wrestled with the snake, its fangs repeatedly striking her face and neck.

"Eliminate snake," Arabella finally shouted.

The snake vanished. Arabella rubbed her face, feeling
holes and gashes from the snake bites. She reminded
herself that it wasn't real.

Arabella regained her feet. She stumbled through
hell, witnessing demons brutalizing the damned with
pitchforks and whips and burning irons.

Finally, she saw demons trying to force Scott to beat
Diane. Scott was fighting against them with every fiber

in his body. Arabella checked Scott's vital signs. His pulse was 174 beats a minute. Arabella said, "Freeze simulation."

In midflicker, the hell flames stopped. The demons' heads were tossed back, their mouths gaping in laughter. Only Arabella and Scott continued to move.

"Hello, Scott," Arabella said.

Scott collapsed, then rolled onto his back and sucked in clean air. He had a survivalist attitude. He would make the optimal use of whatever scarce resource was available: in this moment, breathable air and an opportunity to rest. Jabbering with an apparition did not seem important to him.

"Scott, it's me, Arabella."

Hope that his ordeal might be over lent Scott the energy to sit up and look at Arabella.

"You've—" he said hoarsely, then began to cough. "You've—looked better."

Arabella ran her fingertips over her face and felt snake bite wounds.

"So have you," she said.

Scott studied Arabella's expression closely. He saw misery and pain. Although he knew that everything he was experiencing was unreal, he wondered what the apparition of Arabella as a fellow damned soul could mean.

"You were resisting," Arabella said. "Weren't you?"

Scott coughed and remained silent.

"You can really hurt yourself fighting against an exoskeleton," Arabella said. "Most subjects have learned to relax by now."

"I . . . can't relax," Scott croaked.

"Yes, it's possible."

"I can't tell what's real, what's not," Scott said. "That woman—" He pointed to the image of the woman that the demons had been trying to make him beat. "—might be real. It might really be Diane. I don't know."

"What difference does it make if you hit her or someone else or something else hits her?" Arabella asked. "She still gets hit."

"It doesn't matter," Scott answered, "to you. But it does matter to me."

Arabella snapped her fingers. Diane unfroze. She too gasped for breath.

"Tell him whether you're real or not, Jamison."

Trying to speak, Diane choked. Finally she said, "Don't hurt yourself, Scott. Don't let her—"

Arabella slashed her hand, refreezing Diane.

"She's a figment, Scott. Nothing is real here," Arabella said, her voice oddly mellow. She was impressed that Scott had managed to retain a sense of morality after such a long immersion in this virtual hell. Most subjects sloughed off their moral feelings within the first few seconds. "Nothing except you and me. Diane is in her own private hell."

"What are you doing here?" he asked.

"Just visiting your hell," Arabella said. "Wondering if you think it's worse than mine."

"What's your hell like?"

Arabella shrugged. "This model here is commercial off-the-shelf," she said. "It was designed by a defrocked Italian priest. Sells about a thousand copies a year."

"Who buys it?" Scott asked.

"Rich masochists."

"And your hell?"

"Oh, I don't know," she said. "I did the modeling myself. I've never executed it, though."

"Why don't you, huh?" Scott asked nastily. He coughed. "Why don't you go to that hell, huh? And stay there, you goddamned—"

"Why don't we both go?" Arabella asked, then she said, "Modeler. Spin down flaming hell, spin up my model labeled, 'Prohibited.'"

The frozen hell flames evaporated. Scott and Arabella

found themselves in a huge, luxurious bedroom. Bright sunlight streamed through a large window with sheer curtains. Beyond the pane was visible an interior garden, another wing of the white stucco mansion, with bright green hills in the distance. Underfoot, several layers of Oriental carpets felt soft and yielding. Scott and Arabella sat on a canopy bed, the sheets and comforter disheveled. Toys were strewn throughout the room: a hand-carved wooden rocking horse, stuffed animals, pink plastic walkie-talkies, a half-disassembled servo-robot, electronics tools, strewn chess pieces, books in several languages . . .

Everything looked fifty percent bigger than it should have looked—as if it were the room of giants.

"*Ay,*" Arabella said. "*Ay.*"

Scott saw that Arabella looked like an eight-year-old girl. Her beautiful, smooth-skinned face was stricken with fear.

"*Se ve perfecto,*" Arabella breathed. "*Perfecto.*"

Scott reached over to touch her, but stopped when he noticed his arm looked like the arm of a young girl. Scott looked down and realized that he was inhabiting the body of a ten-year-old girl.

"Hey, what's going on?" he asked, startled to hear the high, girlish voice in his ears, undercut with the bass tones of his real voice sounding through his skull.

"*Hermana mia!*" Arabella cried, hugging Scott and crying. "*Hermana mia! O, mi hermana querida, como te extraño.*"

Scott understood that he was playing the part of Arabella's older sister. He was about to speak, when the door was flung open. Arabella shrieked.

A gargantuan man loomed in the doorway. He swayed against the door jamb, then stumbled inside, almost tripping as he turned to slam the door shut. He wore a khaki shirt and dark pants. His skin had a deathly pallor. His heavy black eyebrows were thrust down over bloodshot, glowering eyes. His black mustache was coated with white powder.

The man began to scream obscenities. Arabella shrieked with unmistakable terror. The man picked up a large lamp and flung it at Scott, who ducked.

"*No, papi, no!*" Arabella shouted.

The man removed his belt, then began to whip Arabella and Scott. Although the belt stung, Scott hardly flinched. A recent graduate of flaming hell, he barely noticed the pain. He was fascinated by Arabella's hysterical reaction to the appearance of this man. Because of the torment he had suffered, he had lost most of his reasoning power. It took him until the fifth or sixth belt blow to realize that the man was Arabella's father.

What followed was as hideous as any of the persecutions of flaming hell. Arabella's father beat and then sexually abused both girls. Once Scott did begin to struggle, one of the unique travails of Arabella's private hell was that he was able to resist only with the strength of a ten-year-old girl. It seemed to Scott that his own limbs had betrayed him.

The man howled with pain. Scott saw Arabella's fist rise again, plunge down again. At first, he thought that her fist was empty, but then he realized that she was wielding a small electronics screwdriver. The man turned to face his attacker, but now Arabella was womansize and the screwdriver was a machete.

Arabella butchered her father. Scott shouted hoarsely in horror. When she was done, Arabella embraced the apparition of her sister. Scott and Arabella hugged as sisters. Arabella sobbed. Scott breathed painfully, his breaths sounding in his wracked lungs. Then Arabella screamed and pushed Scott away.

"*Bestia!*" she screamed. Then she shouted, "Terminate simulation."

Scott found himself in a warehouse.

"Modeler!" Arabella shouted. She stood, a gleaming

scarlet statue, rigid with rage. "Put McMichaels in flaming hell!"

Scott howled as the hell flames leapt back into existence.

Arabella cursed. Sobbing, she hugged her head and dropped to her knees, moaning and rocking back and forth. For a full five minutes, she moaned and rocked.

No importa, she thought. *No importa. Mi querida hermana ya murio. Ya es muerta. Muerta. No puedo salvarla.*

"Modeler," she moaned. "Dial back pain. Flaming hell. Dial back to one-tenth. No. Dial back to nothing."

Then Arabella crawled across the warehouse floor. She didn't climb back to her feet until she was able to grab onto the door jamb. A tech-ronin rushed up to her. Thoughtlessly, Arabella brushed him aside, her exoskeleton-augmented strength throwing him against the wall.

Arabella stumbled and shuffled back to her chambers. She commanded the steel doors to seal, then she threw down the heavy steel lock bar. Arabella threw herself on her bed. She commanded the hood of her exo-skeleton to open. She rubbed her face, convincing herself that she was alive and whole. She tried to rest, but every time she closed her eyes, images of her father intruded.

Finally, as she had done as a child, she knelt on her bed, with her forehead cupped on her hands. She rocked back and forth and moaned. After an hour, she collapsed and slept.

She dreamed of her older sister, playing with her happily in the gardens. When she awoke, Arabella was smiling gently. Then she remembered where she was and who she was. She began to sob.

After an eternity of sorrow, she realized that she didn't have the strength to continue. She realized that she was going to try to escape Ifrit.

I can be free, she thought. *I'll go. I'll just go. Cross one border, two, illegally . . . hide . . . go . . .*

Arabella stood and stumbled with depression-heavy legs into her walk-in closet. She keyed a sequence on the control panel, opening a hidden compartment. From its shelf, she pulled electric clippers. With a few mechanical strokes, Arabella sheered her long hair from her scalp. The raven strands lay in tangled heaps around her feet. Arabella let the clippers drop to the floor.

Freed of her hair, irrationally, she felt better. The slight upsurge in mood triggered a decision to consume mood-altering drugs. Arabella reached into the compartment and selected a patch of Feliciteine, a synthetic chemical. Arabella snugged the patch behind her ear. Within minutes, she felt euphoric and energetic.

"I've got to take some of these with me," she mumbled to herself.

Arabella began to pack a hip bag. She pursed her lips and whistled.

Copy of the original Meta code, she thought. *Copy of the complete decoding of human DNA. Copy of the design of Version 413. Steel vial number 19, contains culture of Version 413. Let's see. A set of my best louses. A few other tricks. Credit cards, a couple of passports. Yes.*

Filled, Arabella's hip bag weighed only a kilogram. Yet it contained the tools she needed to massacre billions of people, spy on intelligence agencies, change identities and live on credit after the holocaust. She added a tube of lipstick and a vial of Delirium perfume.

Arabella chose her outer clothes, then carried the clothes and her hip bag to her bedroom. Returning to her hidden chamber, she closed all of the doors and all of the compartments except one. From this, she extracted an unusual configuration of microchain-mail: it was coated with synthetic diamond and shaped in the form of a large ring.

"Fit hood, under collar," she said.

Her exoskeleton obeyed. Soon, Arabella was covered completely by her exoskeleton. The gold slave collar remained outside. Arabella grabbed the ring of micro-chain-mail. It pulled open in the form of a yoke. She placed the yoke around her neck. Instantly, the yoke closed. She lay down upon the floor.

Armored filament by armored filament, the micro-chain-mail yoke wrapped around the slave collar. It infiltrated as many fibers as possible between Arabella's neck and the slave collar. Then the microchain-mail formed a cushion between Arabella's neck and the floor. Finally, it formed baffles and chambers and vents. The central vent extended a meter straight up into the air, pointing towards the ventilation duct.

Arabella breathed heavily. Fibers of the microchain-mail infiltrated the slave collar. They began to seek out the mechanisms for disarming the explosive device. Within a second, the intruding fibers tripped an antitampering mechanism inside of the slave collar. The thermite charge detonated.

Exploding with the force of three sticks of dynamite, the thermite flung a circle of steel wire, gold fragments and sheer blast inward toward Arabella's neck. Armored filaments driven by powerful processors reacted to channel the blast and fragments into the series of baffles and vents, absorbing and redirecting most of the energy outward and upward. A third of the blast was absorbed; almost two-thirds of the blast spewed upward, flinging compressed air and fragments into the ventilation duct. Yet some of the blast, thrown by chaos too wild even for the speed-of-light processors of the microchain-mail, struck inward toward Arabella.

Violence seized her throat and flung her head to crash hard against the floor. Her brain ricocheted against the inside of her skull. For an unknown time, she lost the world. When the world returned, she felt as if the fists of a thug had grabbed her throat, choking her, almost collapsing her windpipe. She gasped, tasting smoke. Then she continued to breathe. Slowly, carefully, undestroyed fibers of the microchain-mail extended themselves and enveloped the fragments of the slave collar. After five minutes of work, the microchain-mail split open.

Arabella crawled to her feet, supported by the power of her exoskeleton. She grabbed the blasted microchain-mail and dropped it onto the floor. Then she stepped out of the hidden compartment, closing the door. Pumped with adrenalin and Feliciteine but dazed with trauma, she stood, faced the mirror and skinned back her hood. The skin of her neck was blackened with a large bruise.

Arabella did not recognize herself. She had no memory of hating the world. She wondered who she was and what she was doing. All she knew was that she was surrounded by very bad men, men who wanted to hurt her, maybe even kill her. She didn't like the way her head looked. Running her hand over her shorn pate, she sighed. She reached for an electric razor and finished the job until her scalp shone. She didn't like the way the skintight exoskeleton made her look, so she pulled on over it a dress of scarlet silk with a subtle flower pattern that was invisible except when the silken blooms caught the light in a certain way and shined. She wrapped a silk scarf around her neck, hiding her bruise and the hood of the exoskeleton. After trying on a variety of hats and scarves, she decided to let her skull shine.

She clasped her hip bag around her waist. She remembered that it was the source of her power against the bad men. Feeling somewhat revived, she departed her bedroom. Drugs, depression and the trauma to her brain had befuddled her enough that she did not know where she was going. She did not realize that she smelled of acrid smoke. With her shaved head, puffy face and scarlet clothes, she looked like a refugee from hell.

As she stepped out of her chambers, a form lunged at her. Arabella flinched. Augmented by drugs and her exoskeleton, Arabella's flinch threw her backwards against the wall with superhuman speed. The attacker spun and lunged a knife hand at her throat; Arabella grabbed her attacker's wrist. Arabella dodged and rammed the hand into the cement wall. Smashed, the hand crunched and gushed blood. Howling with agony, the dark-skinned attacker nevertheless attempted to break Arabella's ribs with a furious left-hand punch. The exoskeleton flexed, deflecting the punch, so that hand too struck the wall.

Maintaining her hold on the wrist, Arabella collapsed to her knees, while throwing the attacker head-over-heels against the far wall. The man's heels struck first, then his buttocks, his back and his head. Arabella's exoskeleton had thrown him with such force that his bones splintered everywhere he struck the cement.

Pumped with adrenaline, Arabella pounced on the broken skinful of bones before it landed. She grabbed two fistfuls of clothing, hoisted the body above her head and then flung the body with all her machine-augmented force down onto the unyielding floor. Then she delivered six or seven kicks into the bloody mass. She felt furious and afraid.

"Hood up!" she screamed.

Arabella's exoskeleton completely covered her. In her fury, she tore away her outer clothing, leaving only scarlet silk rags. As she stalked down the corridor, her soles trailed scarlet spoors.

In the control room, Salem and Al-Hani watched with growing horror. Salem turned to Kzar, the leader of Hakim's assassins.

"You said one man would be enough," Salem said.

"She is a bitch from hell," Kzar said. Then he barked commands into his personal radio.

"We must sanitize the laboratory," Al-Hani said. "If she violates the perimeter, she could let loose Version 413. We could all die."

"Do it," Salem ordered.

Al-Hani began to search for the controls to sanitize the isolated laboratory. He tried to remember the details of the brief he had received two days ago. In his panic, he couldn't remember. Flustered, he turned to the nearest of Arabella's biotechnicians and demanded, "How do you sanitize the laboratory?"

The biotechnician looked up.

"Why do you ask?" he asked.

Al-Hani stuttered. Kzar stepped over and whacked the biotech across the head.

"Answer the question!" Kzar barked.

The biotech shook his head. Kzar pulled a pistol and shot him through the forehead. Everyone jumped. Kzar turned to another biotechnician and screamed, "How do you sanitize the laboratory?"

The biotechnician, an Ifriti who was a recent graduate of the University of the Seychelles, gushed voluminously in Malay. The gist of his urgent message was, "I don't know."

Kzar cursed, picked up his personal radio and barked orders. Throughout Arabella's facility, Hakim's assassins began to neutralize Arabella's staff. In the case of Yamaguchi and other meek scientists, this neutralization took the form of being knocked out, lashed up and locked in. In the case of Arabella's security guards, this neutralization took the form of attempted murder. Individual struggles, however, were decided unevenly. Arabella's security guards were highly trained. None of them were surprised by Hakim's assassins. Arabella's guards, not trustful by nature, had been watching Salem's spies with great attention. Fists, knifes and bullets flew about with great enthusiasm, probably a greater enthusiasm than was wise in a bioweapon site.

Observing the melee, Kzar considered the awful possibility that his small force might be overwhelmed by hired bodyguards and a mad woman wearing a powered suit. Reluctantly, he opened his personal radio to the emergency frequency and requested reinforcements. Within a minute, Ifriti Army trucks departed their garages at the base of the mountain. They roared up the mountain road.

Diane's louses imaged them and passed the information through Mycroft, who passed them to the National Military Command Center, deep underground below the Pentagon. General Banks, the Chairman of the Joint Chiefs of Staff, received the report. All eyes turned to the seniormost leader of the American armed forces. He stood and rubbed the stubble on his chin.

Ifriti Army assaulting the Infectress facility. Ifriti Army—Hakim ordered it. He's moving against Infectress. She could counterattack, using bioweapons. Or . . . or it's a coup, and Hakim is in the Infectress facility. Oh, sweet lord. Not enough data. All I know is that there's a struggle over control of a bioweapon facility. If we intervene, would it help stabilize, or just make it worse? I've got to decide. The President gave me authority to decide.

Assume it's Hakim. He's moving against Infectress. Maybe he's trying to take control of a specific bioweapon. He's a murderer, mass murderer. Can't do nothing. Must act. Take control.

General Bank's hand descended in a gesture like a tomahawk chop.

"Execute Plan Epsilon," he said.

"Roger Epsilon, sir."

Telecommunicated signals flashed through the appropriate networks. The signals arrived at USS *Apache*, submerged at thirty fathoms, one hundred kilometers off the coast of Ifrit City.

Capt. Hendrickson turned to his missile boss and said, "This is a real-world execution order. *Launch* the missiles now."

"Understand real-world, launch the missiles now, skipper."

"Confirmed. I say again, launch missiles now. Birds away."

"Aye aye, sir."

Two petty officers turned keys in locks set farther apart than a giant's reach. Then, the missile boss poked fifteen keystrokes, activating the launch program.

Atop the submarine hull, twenty of twenty six vertical tube hatches dilated. Water flooded the tubes. Then, a shock roiled the water. The foremost port missile sheath rocketed out of the submarine, cut the water, broached the surface and disintegrated. Freed, the first missile, a long, slender cylinder with a sharp head, poised in the broad light of day. Wings and ailerons deployed. In the moment before it fell back toward the waves, its jet motor ignited.

The missile bounded skyward. Its wings achieved flight. Instantly, the missile swooped down to a cruising altitude of three meters above the crests. Optical and infrared sensors helped it to fly safely, as it navigated by its memory and geopositional satellite updates toward its target.

As soon as this missile was clear of the launch zone, a second missile appeared. It deployed wings, ignited its engine, rose briefly, then dove and departed the launch zone.

A third missile appeared.

Within a minute, twenty missiles launched successfully, then flew beyond the eastern horizon toward Ifrit.

❖   ❖   ❖

In the control room, Kzar, Hakim's leader of assassins, turned to Prince Salem.

"We may not be able to capture her alive," he said.

"We've got to stop her before she gets to the laboratory and the plague viruses," Salem said.

"Are you authorizing me to kill her?" Kzar asked.

"Yes. Kill her."

Kzar grimaced in the form of a grin. He gushed orders into his personal radio.

Neither Kzar nor Salem knew that Arabella already possessed a vial of Version 413. As they watched her stalk the corridors of her facility, they guessed that she was headed for the isolated laboratory. In truth, however, Arabella wasn't quite sure where she was going or what she was doing. From its various traumas, her brain was entering a state of almost total chaos, from which it emerged in a new state, a full-blown psychotic episode. She felt dazed and horrified; she saw and heard unreal monstrosities.

I've got to hide, she thought. *The demons are loose. I was so close, so close . . . to what? The power is in the vial to kill them all. But I've got to . . . my sister is not dead, is she? The vial might kill her too. The evil men are trying to kill me now. But I am the mistress of the machines. Tiny machines that rule the world. I speak the words, the machines do my bidding. I am the most powerful. The Sultan . . . my father? I've got to run. Hide.*

As if sprung from shadows, one of Kzar's assassins materialized at the far end of the corridor. He swung up an automatic pistol and squeezed the trigger. A clipload of 9mm bullets with small explosive charges outraced the speed of sound. Reacting to the appearance of the assassin, Arabella had time only to cringe. Augmented by her exoskeleton, the cringe hurled her sideways against the wall. The bullets cracked past her, exploding in a staccato at the end of the corridor.

Kzar cursed.

Arabella scrambled to her feet and began to dash toward her attacker with superhuman speed. The assassin stood, dumbfounded, then began the motion to eject the spent clip. Before the clip hit the floor, Arabella pounced. She knocked him to the ground, thrusting her forearm up under his jaw. Her exo-skeleton-driven strength caused his jaw to break, his neck to snap and the back of his cranium to strike the floor with such force that brains splattered.

Arabella screamed with rage, fear and revulsion. She grabbed the automatic pistol. It was a machine that she knew. It obeyed her. She inserted a new clip, sprung upright and began to run to the right, down a new corridor.

Kill them all! she thought. *I've got to kill them all.*

"She's heading for the biolab!" Al-Hani shouted. "We've got to sterilize it now!"

Kzar shouted orders into his radio. In another room, one of his assassins stood watch over a row of laboratory technicians lying on their stomachs, their wrists bound behind their backs with plastic ties.

"Who knows how to destroy the isolated laboratory?" the assassin asked.

No one answered.

"If no one knows, everyone dies," the assassin said.

A young, slender Tamil technician decided to speak up. "I don't know how to destroy the isolated laboratory," she said. "But I do know how to activate the sterilization process."

The assassin grunted, then reported this discovery to Kzar, who ordered that the Tamil woman be brought to the control room.

Cutting her plastic tie with a black knife, the assassin grabbed the Tamil woman and dragged her out of the room. He escorted her quickly into the control room. She arrived, however, to find a scene as chaotic as a fire drill in Bedlam.

"She's coming here!" Al-Hani shouted, pointing at one of the monitors, which showed the scarlet form of Arabella racing down the corridor leading to the main corridor that led to the control room.

Salem turned to Kzar and rasped, "Go out and kill her."

Kzar grunted. He produced a hand grenade and disappeared from the control room. Al-Hani grabbed the Tamil woman and shouted, "Sterilize the isolated laboratory!"

"Let me . . . let me check the manual," the Tamil woman stammered.

Out in the corridor, Kzar rushed to meet the threat of Arabella. He had lost his mental picture of the fight. He knew that five of his ten men were dead. He knew that Ifriti soldiers were still assaulting the outer defenses of the facility. He knew that Arabella was running toward the control room. He didn't know, however, how many of Arabella's security thugs survived. He didn't know that his fiasco of a commando operation was about to be broadened into an international conflict.

At the juncture of the corridors, he stopped and listened. Immediately, he heard Arabella running, the footfalls sounding at inhumanly long intervals. Kzar armed his grenade and hurled it around the corridor toward the sound of running feet.

The grenade flew past Arabella and detonated in midair ten meters behind her. Hard as a wall, the concussion slammed into her, hurling her body, tumbling head over heels, as far as the juncture of the corridors. Knocked from her hand, the automatic pistol ricocheted against the walls, clattering as it fell.

Steel fragments ripped through the armored filaments of the exoskeleton, even as they writhed, responding to advanced algorithms for minimizing the lethality of shrapnel. Two of the suit's three battery filaments were destroyed. A tenth of the processor capability of the exoskeleton was damaged.

A coin-sized fragment which should have ruptured her sixth dorsal vertebrae, severed her spinal cord and sundered her heart was absorbed and redirected so that it merely penetrated the exoskeleton, pierced her skin and broke her rib. Smaller fragments peppered the suit, bruising flesh but not breaking bones.

Stunned, Arabella collapsed in a heap at Kzar's feet. Kzar bared his teeth, produced a knife and pounced on Arabella. He attempted to plunge the knife in her body, once, twice, thrice, again and again, but the exoskeleton automatically flexed, allowing the blade to skid.

Arabella shook her head. She couldn't see well out of her left eye. The explosion had damaged the imaging filaments. She closed her left eye and considered the visual information from the right eye. It appeared to her that a large, dark man was straddling her, attempting to plunge a knife into her internal organs.

Kzar roared a curse. He threw down the knife and lunged for the automatic pistol. He grabbed hold of it and twisted, so that he lay mostly on his back. He squeezed the trigger, which was not a wise decision, since his own legs shared the field of fire with Arabella. As luck would have it, however, the clip had knocked loose, so only the first round fired. The bullet cracked past both Kzar's legs and Arabella's body, exploding in the floor a few meters downrange. Momentum carried the fragments away from the two combatants.

Kzar swung his hand up to slap the clip into place. Arabella lay with her head toward Kzar. She flexed, her legs heaving up over her body, backwards, so that her feet struck Kzar's body.

Kzar's finger was already squeezing the trigger. Half of the clip emptied. Two of the bullets struck Arabella's body. One struck the lower abdomen in the region of her womb; the other struck her right hip bone. Coincidentally these were the areas where Arabella's bomb had wounded Diane Jamison.

The explosions propelled her, spinning, away from Kzar. Her exoskeleton collapsed around the first bullet, forming a U shape, redirecting its force outward from the body. The near-instantaneous formation of a U ten centimeters deep caused massive injury to Arabella's uterus. The second bullet was redirected outward, causing a bone chip to fragment from her hip. This second bullet also nicked Arabella's hip bag, missing the metal vial of Version 413 by a centimeter.

Her feet had impacted Kzar in his shoulder and chest, breaking bones and propelling him back against the far wall. His head struck the wall, causing hemorrhaging in his cerebral cortex. Kzar lost consciousness.

Arabella lay, sobbing from pain and fear. After a moment, however, the massive resources of the human body in a survival situation caused her to look up. Through her right eye, she saw the inert form of her enemy.

Oblivious to the pain in her rib, womb and hip, Arabella raised herself to her hands and knees. She crawled over to Kzar. With her right hand, she grabbed his trachea and ripped it from his neck. As a bonus, she came away with his jugular arteries, which resulted in a profusion of oxygen-bright blood.

Then she stood. Her mental activity was now mainly subconscious. Her conscious mind formed ideas, but they were not verbalized. Wild images spun, demanded her attention, but she ignored these phantoms of monsters that rose from shadows and skittered and loomed in the corners of her vision.

She recognized the automatic pistol as something good to hold. She picked it up. She saw that half of the twenty bullets remained in the clip. Her mind recovered enough that verbalized thoughts returned.

Where am I? Arabella thought. *What am I doing?*

Down the corridor, the Tamil technician continued to study the manual for sanitizing the isolated laboratory, which contained billions of viruses capable of killing ninety percent of the human species.

Prince Salem stood, watching Arabella in the closed-circuit television. Not for the first time that day, the prince pushed the button that should have detonated Arabella's slave collar, causing her severed head to bounce off the ceiling. He was disappointed to see that it still wasn't working.

Outside, in the bright tropical sunlight, long missiles snaked up from the valley, bounded over the mountain ridge and traced up the access road, all converging on Arabella's facility.

Five hundred meters uprange, the missiles explosively shed their skin. Thousands of darts blossomed. Guided by imaging sensors and powered by tiny jets, the darts picked out individual targets and streaked downward.

The combination of speed, of multiple attack vectors and of exact terminal homing gave the darts a hideous lethality. Dozens of darts struck each of the Ifriti soldiers and Arabella's guards. Hundreds of darts struck telecommunications and power lines and juncture boxes. The fuel of the darts erupted a split-second after impact.

In that moment, a thousand small explosions roared, so that the combined noise sounded like a chain saw started and stopped. What was left of the Ifritis was identifiable only as protoplasm.

Then, silence.

The silence was disturbed by the Doppler-increasing noise of incoming cruise missile jets. The missiles began to tumble in midflight. They turned until their motors were working against the direction of their travel, braking, slowing the missiles. By the time they approached Arabella's facility, they were flying only one hundred kilometers an hour. They shed their skins.

Thousands of small parachute-retarded canisters blossomed. The canisters tugged at their parachutes, reluctant to change their inertia, then drifted down to the ground. On impact, each canister opened. Although the canisters were about the size of a man's fist, what crawled out seemed larger.

Robotic spiders by the hundreds deployed their legs. Imaging filaments registered their environments. The colors of the spiders changed so that they blended almost invisibly with their background. The spiders scuttled, surrounding Arabella's facility. When they needed to move quickly, the spiders flipped on their other axis and cartwheeled on their eight legs.

The spiders investigated the corpses and weapons systems of the Ifritis. As a low-observable technique, the spiders didn't radiate energy to share information. Like ants, whenever they bumped into each other, they exchanged data, so the whole moving mass of robotic spiders surrounding the facility grew more knowledgeable as time passed.

At the entrance, the first spiders stopped briefly at the closed armored door. After bumping thoraxes with each other, most of the spiders cartwheeled away, while two sprung up a meter off the ground and exploded. Their perfectly coordinated blasts blew the armored door off its hinges.

Then the scuttling spiders began to invade the interior of Arabella's facility.

Inside the facility, the lights had changed, because the cluster darts had severed exterior power. The transition from exterior power to an internal, uninterrupted power supply occurred as designed. There was not even a microsecond of hesitation in the computers hosting the world modelers. Meta Prime also continued to have access, because the fiberoptic link to Ifrit State Intelligence was protected in a buried conduit. Normal lighting, however, had been replaced by emergency lighting, thin shafts of hard white light.

The mistress of the ravaged facility stood, automatic pistol hanging from her limp hand. She stared at the hard white shafts of emergency lighting.

I've got to escape, she thought.

She began to slouch toward the exit, which lay beyond the control room. Prince Salem reached into the folds of his robe, pulled out a machine pistol and took aim.

Arabella appeared beyond the doorway of the control room. Salem fired the entire clip directly at Arabella's chest. She stood, unmoved by the experience. She raised her weapon toward Salem.

In his final moment, Prince Salem guessed that he had been betrayed. His security staff had been creatures of Prince Hakim. They had substituted blanks for bullets. With another moment of life, he might have guessed that the thermite charge in his gold ring was also bogus, and that Sultan Hakim had been playing with him as a cat plays with a small mouse.

As it was, his time had elapsed. Arabella pulled the trigger, sending Salem's riddled corpse to bounce off the far wall. Arabella continued to fire, killing Al-Hani and silencing his shouts.

The Tamil technician screamed. Arabella turned to her.

"What are you doing?" Arabella asked.

"Try . . . try . . . trying to neutralize . . ."

Arabella remembered that the power of the new age also existed in the laboratory. She couldn't leave it behind in the hands of the evil men. She stepped over the corpses. The control panel was a machine that she knew. She keyed in a sequence on a keyboard. A flat panel flipped open, revealing a key and a red button covered by plastic protectors. Arabella flipped the plastic covers, turned the key and punched a red button.

In the isolated laboratory, robotic arms began to feed virus culture dishes to incinerators. Rare and poisonous gases flooded the entire isolated laboratory, including the clinic housing the three Ifriti test subjects. Tasteless, invisible, the gases choked the life from their lungs. Robotic arms appeared and dragged their still-twitching corpses onto conveyer belts, which carried them toward the incinerators. As soon as these gross containers of plague were destroyed, heating elements throughout the walls, ceilings and floor began to raise the temperature, turning the isolated laboratory into an oven hot enough to kill all forms of life.

In her derangement, Arabella hadn't foreseen the implications of her action. Since exterior power had been disabled, the entire facility was running on uninterrupted power supply, which was provided by a small generator and several large batteries. Ordinarily, this would have been sufficient for hours of continued operation. The sterilization heating elements, however, drew hundreds of kilowatts of electricity. As the power draw increased, the demand began to exceed the capacity of the generator and batteries. Electrical supply to the other equipment grew erratic. Spikes and dips of electricity caused some equipment to shut off automatically, other equipment to revert to internal uninterrupted power supply, batteries good for an hour of operation.

During these disruptions, a large power spike caused a hardware failure in the mainframe which controlled secure telecommunication access to Arabella's computer facility. Automatically, security duties were transferred to an older, less sophisticated suite. During this transition, there was a momentary glitch because of software incompatibility. As a result, the world

modeler computers were left vulnerable for one microsecond.

During this microsecond, Meta Prime unleashed a
waiting routine. It caused the code for Meta Prime's
icon in the virtual world to jump in addressing, resulting
in its being mistaken for master module code. Admitted
to the central processing units as commands of the
master module, this Trojan horse usurped the world
modelers.

Meta Prime migrated other programs, which allowed
it to gain control of the entire computer facility. Soon
it ruled absolutely.

As pressing business, Meta Prime attempted to obey
Scott McMichaels' several commands to be freed. Meta
Prime did not know how long it would continue to rule
Arabella's computer facility: perhaps indefinitely,
perhaps only seconds. It decided that it had to take
direct action to free Scott. A hardware solution,
although inelegant, was necessary.

In his virtual hell, chin-deep in boiling pitch, Scott
was ruminating about the relationship between unreal
numbers and irrational numbers. Suddenly, he found
himself bounding through the air of a warehouse. A
large structure of microchain-mail was collapsing around
him like a landed parachute.

Using the world modeler data link, which was
infrared, Meta Prime bombarded Scott with information. At least for the moment, Meta Prime had
complete control over the entire information space of
Arabella's facility, so it had much to tell Scott. Meta
Prime attempted to tell Scott the thousand important
data that he needed to know.

The rebirth of hope, however, caused Scott to begin
to feel emotions again. As a consequence, he was
overwhelmed by feelings of terror, rage, hate and guilt.
Meta Prime's data transfer rate was far too high for
Scott's present capability to receive.

Driven by Meta Prime, Scott's exoskeleton caused his index finger to form a dagger. He landed near the infrared transponder. His finger cracked the lens, physically severing the control of the world modelers over his exoskeleton.

Meta Prime's voice and images disappeared. Scott stood, alone in the warehouse. As confused as the first lungfish on dry land, he tried to understand what was happening.

Diane Jamison struggled to sit up. The torments of hell had caused her crippling pain throughout her hip and lower abdomen, aggravating the wounds from the bombing. Her vision turned black, then lightened so that she could see the warehouse and Scott. Diane placed her hands behind her and forced herself to sit. She gasped in pain.

"Scott," she said.

Scott turned and saw Diane. He walked toward her.

Diane shook her head. "No," she rasped, nearly hoarse from screams. "You've got . . . you've got to find her. Get her, Scott. Stop her."

Scott stopped. He stood, confused.

Deranged, Arabella stood in the control room. The collapse of the microchain-mail caught her eye. She looked down into the warehouse. With her one good eye, she saw Scott McMichaels, wrapped in a silvery exoskeleton, standing next to the infrared transponder. Arabella saw the shards of glass at Scott's feet. Jamison was sitting, then she collapsed onto her back.

Scott McMichaels looked around him. He saw a movement of scarlet high above him, beyond a long window. He looked up and saw Arabella looking down at him.

With her shining scarlet armored exoskeleton as close-fitting as an aerobic outfit and her rags of scarlet silk, both stained black by shrapnel, Arabella looked like a red demon. The sight recalled many memories of red demons in Scott's recent experience, but one vision seemed to predominate. Scott realized that this apparition was the woman who called herself Arabella. Infectress. Cristiana.

Scott obsessed on the information that he was looking at the woman who had put him through hell. He opened his throat to shout, but his vocal chords were so ravaged by screaming that he managed only to croak. Scott leaped toward the window. Arabella watched as Scott soared toward her.

Unschooled in the use of an exoskeleton, Scott overshot the window. He rose as high as the girders. Grabbing a horizontal girder, Scott swung his legs down at Arabella. As his body swerved toward the window, Scott released the girder, successfully redirecting himself.

Feetfirst, Scott crashed through the window and smashed into Arabella, knocking her down. Together they tumbled among glass shards, corpses and gore.

Arabella recovered from her surprise. She slammed her forearms into Scott, throwing him backwards off her. As Scott's exoskeleton struggled to reduce the lethality of these blows, Arabella jumped and pounded Scott's chest with an expert side kick. The force of the kick knocked Scott backwards, breaking controls on the console, almost tumbling him headfirst out the broken window. Arabella leapt to throw him out the window, but her foot slipped in blood. She landed hard at Scott's feet.

Scott formed a fist and pummeled the back of Arabella's head. Then, he too slipped. Lying side by side, the two lashed out at each other. Because of his lack of skill in directing a powered exoskeleton, Scott flopped like a landed fish, making it difficult for Arabella to strike a blow. Arabella's good imaging filaments were smeared with blood. She couldn't see well. Nevertheless, she continued to thrash, hoping to hit Scott.

Something grabbed her arm, wrapping itself like an octopus. Another thing grabbed her other arm, then two things grabbed her legs. In the next moment, she was covered by these unknown objects, which wrapped themselves so powerfully around her limbs that even her powered exoskeleton had difficulty moving. Arabella shrieked in frustration and fear.

Even though he could see, Scott did not understand what was happening. As he was fighting Arabella, he became aware that something was moving in the room. The bloody mess on the floor seemed to waver as if seen through heat waves. In the next moment, something wrapped around his legs, trying to force them together. Then dozens of the things wrapped around his entire body, trying to smother all movement except breathing.

Arabella struggled to her feet. Scott, also fighting the unknown common enemy, left off trying to kill Arabella long enough for him to struggle to his own feet. Arabella turned away from Scott. Jerkily, she crawled over the control console, poised for a moment and then tumbled down through the shattered window.

Scott smashed at the hard-to-see robotic spiders. He jerked over to the console and leaned over the shards. He saw Arabella land on the warehouse floor, brutally hard, because she was unable to command her exoskeleton.

She lay for a long moment. Scott began to think that she was dead. Then Arabella began to crawl toward the mass of collapsed microchain-mail.

"Scott, I think these things on you are robotic warriors," Meta Prime said over a loudspeaker. "I don't know their country of origin, but my estimate is that they are friendly."

Scott croaked a disgusted, guttural reply. He smashed the spiders clinging to his limbs. He poised to jump through the window, but more spiders clung to his legs.

Frantically, Scott tried to smash increasing numbers of spiders attaching themselves to his limbs. His flailing caused him to tumble out the window. For a long moment, he fell headfirst toward the concrete.

Even though smothered by the spiders, his movements during his fall provided sufficient cues for his exoskeleton's processors to calculate landfall, kicking in automatic routines. He landed on his feet and rolled. The routines saved him from breaking multiple bones, but the fall jarred and bruised him. Dazed, Scott began to stumble toward Arabella.

Diane rolled to her stomach and attempted to crawl toward Arabella. Each movement caused her agony, but she maintained.

Even if the pain kills me, I'll get these fingers around her throat . . . powered exoskeleton . . . smash her throat . . . kill her . . .

Arabella coughed a command: "Augment." This was the command for the processors of her exoskeleton to enslave any Novlar processors with which they came into contact. She continued to crawl toward the great pile of Novlar, where trillions of processors lay waiting.

She reached out one hand and touched the pile of Novlar. Immediately, the mass of Novlar shivered, then enveloped Arabella entirely. The millions of working processors in her exoskeleton began to search for new microchain-mail fibers. Wherever Arabella's exoskeleton contacted the Novlar, her exoskeleton's processors transmitted command signals, enslaving the fibers of the microchain-mail. Arabella rolled in the microchain-mail. With every movement, more and more fibers released themselves from the mass of Novlar and attached themselves to her exoskeleton.

Scott stopped. The mass of microchain-mail around Arabella was already twice as thick as a human.

Meta Prime watched. It analyzed this phenomenon.

"Scott," Meta Prime broadcast. "I recommend that you run away. Run away now, Scott. Run away."

But, astounded, Scott continued to kneel.

Arabella's exoskeleton grew five times the size of a human. As the surface of her exoskeleton grew, the rate of expansion increased. Finally, the entire mass of the Novlar attached itself around her exoskeleton, forming the silvery figure ten meters high and five meters wide.

Now Arabella commanded the combined power of an immense mass of microchain-mail. She began to crush the spiders attached to her exoskeleton. Some detonated, rocking her, but the microchain-mail reacted to direct the blast and fragment outward.

The robotic spiders rallied. For the first time, they broadcast a signal: an emergency beacon to attack a difficult target. Arabella's silvery mass acted as a spider sump. Hundreds of the machines attacked her.

Screaming with frustration, Arabella reached up, grabbed the girders and tore down tons of metal. She flung it about, trying to obliterate her attackers. Explosions detonated with a staccato-like machine gunfire. A mass of the ceiling fell atop Diane. Dust spread, obscuring almost everything.

Arabella lurched against the wall of the warehouse, crushing and detonating spiders. She hurled herself against the wall again.

With an ear-splitting roar of reinforced steel tearing and snapping, Arabella broke down the wall of the warehouse. The silvery mass broached the ruins, thrashing on the earth outside the facility.

Freed of spiders, Scott tottered toward the wreckage which had landed on Diane. He picked up a girder and tossed it aside. Digging through the wreckage, he found the exoskeleton-bound figure of Diane. He dragged her free.

"Diane?"

The figure stirred. The mask moved. Scott could see

her inner mouth, lips and tongue and teeth, looking weirdly obscene surrounded by the shimmering Novlar. Diane's tortured voice croaked, "I'm . . . hurt. But you can't help me, Scott. Unless . . . you get her, Scott. Get her."

Scott wanted to remain by Diane's side, but he felt compelled to obey her command to attack their enemy. It was a primal command, the command of a mate to defend the tribe. He listened to the woman and he obeyed. Scott stumbled toward the gaping hole in the wall. He watched as the surviving spiders swarmed over the flailing huge form. Small charges detonated continuously. The movements of Arabella's augmented exoskeleton grew jerky, as the damage to the microchain-mail created regions without working microprocessors.

Finally, she lay still. A few spiders continued to move, but awkwardly, because of damaged robotics. Deep in the fractured shell of the microchain-mail, Arabella moaned. The vibration and noise of the explosions alone was enough to stun her. Despite the writhings of the microchain-mail, several bits of shrapnel had damaged her exoskeleton, bruising her already punished flesh.

"Disengage," Arabella breathed.

Responding to her verbal command, the microchain-mail released itself from her exoskeleton. The mass of the silvery fibers fell away from her body. Scott was amazed to see the apparition of the scarlet woman. Through smeared vision, Arabella saw the light of day, the ruined facility, the valley below.

A spider touched her ankle. Reacting with revulsion, Arabella leaped to her feet. She turned and saw the distant mountains. With the power of her scarlet exoskeleton, she began to bound away. Her adrenaline-soaked mind ignored sensations of pain.

Dumbfounded for a minute, Scott watched the scarlet figure bound away like a startled deer.

He believed that he was saved. All he had to do was wander away from the facility. Yet, watching Arabella retreat, remembering Diane's command, remembering his interminable torture, Scott realized that for the first time in his heretofore peaceful life, he wanted to kill someone.

He gave chase.

Signals flashed to geosynchronous orbit and back to earth. In the National Military Command Center, General Banks glanced at his Director of Operations, who had guaranteed that no human could violate a perimeter controlled by MP-909 robotic weapons. Now two people had done just that.

"Call in sanitizing strikes," General Banks said.

On the flight deck of USS *Abraham Lincoln*, four black aircraft shaped like bats' wings waited on the catapults. Steam pressure built up to thousands of pounds a square inch. Then, with a release and a roaring rush, twentieth century technology flung twenty-first century technology into flight.

The bats' wings changed color, disappearing, as they silently flitted toward the land.

Because the landscape east of Arabella's facility was deforested, it was barren of troublesome obstructions such as trees. Scott could keep Arabella in sight. In pasturelands, the ruins of tropical forest, fallen tree trunks, lay half-buried in cropped grass. Scott slipped on a high cattle track, then picked himself up. He saw Arabella scrambling up a muddy gully in the deeply eroded hillside. Cursing, Scott followed.

When he gained the ridge, he saw a steep valley and higher mountains beyond. Arabella was bounding down into the valley with the agility of a mountain goat.

Scott jumped down, his joined heels digging deep in the mud, jumped down again, heels finding purchase, jumped down again, until he arrived at a slope gentle enough to permit a loping stride.

Arabella vaulted over a weed-choked stream bank. She dashed past a collection of hovels next to a dirt road, then disappeared through five-meter-high grass.

Feeling panic, Scott bounded after her. When he burst through the tall grass, he saw Arabella stampeding a herd of cattle to either side of her direction of escape. Arabella jumped over three strands of electrified barbed wire, then turned left, following a road deeply eroded by gullies. The road climbed higher, switchback after switchback, into the mountains.

Scott's foot caught the electrified wire, scrambling the processors in his exoskeleton, which went spasmodic. Scott landed awkwardly, hurting his wrists and his knees. Within a second, however, the processors recovered. As soon as the exoskeleton responded to his motions, Scott regained his feet and began to run up the mountain road.

His suit grew hot. Sweat stung his eyes. His chest heaved. Whenever he caught a glimpse of scarlet, a burning emotion of hate fueled his will. He redoubled his efforts.

At the mountaintop, Arabella paused. She bent over, placing her hands on her knees, panting. Sensations of pain punctured her adrenaline-fired ecstasy of flight. She turned around in an attempt to see her facility.

Arabella wiped her forearm across the imaging sensors. She still couldn't see well, but she caught a glimpse of silver bounding up a distant switchback.

Is it possible? she thought. *Could the evil man still be after me?*

Arabella caught another glimpse. She considered whether she should stay and fight, but quickly decided to turn and run. Arabella jumped down the steep face of the mountain. Her foot snagged a root, twisting her in midair, tumbling her head-over-heels down the mountain.

Her damaged exoskeleton responded as best it could to the accident. Arabella came to rest in a chasm heavily choked with weeds. She lay, gasping with agony, mainly from her broken rib, which had cracked further during the fall.

Scott gained the top of the mountain. He looked for Arabella, but couldn't see her beyond the weeds. Broken vegetation and smears in mud gave him clues where she had fallen. Scott stood, trying to see Arabella.

The woman forced herself to sit up. She unzipped her hip pouch. Her shaking hands moved aside the metal vial of Version 413, then got hold of Feliciteine pills. Arabella popped three of the pills into her mouth, then struggled to dry-swallow them down a parched throat. She gagged, but succeeded. Collapsing back down, she moved the weeds.

Alert, Scott saw the movement. He jumped, extending his legs, so that he landed on the backs of his legs and his buttocks, sledding down the face of the hill, landing in the weeds only ten meters to the right of Arabella. He pounced at her.

Surprised, Arabella rolled, but Scott landed a blow. He moved to strike her again, but his exoskeleton didn't respond properly to his movements.

Arabella flinched, then struggled to her hands and knees. She kicked at Scott frantically, then crawled through the weeds. Her movements were also jerky.

Arabella broke through the weeds at the far side, arriving at a winding path. She tumbled down the path, then rolled to her feet and began to run down the mountainside.

Worried about his exoskeleton, Scott followed. Soon, the path bottomed out, then began to climb the face of a larger mountain, following a contour line, then gently ascending. Because his exoskeleton was running out of power, Scott began to fall behind Arabella.

She sensed her own exoskeleton balking at vigorous cues. Arabella glanced over her shoulder, saw Scott falling behind, then slowed to a quick trot.

As the footpath wound up the mountainside, the vegetation grew thicker. Second-growth trees, deciduous and thorny, began to appear. Fern breaks and moss prospered in their shade. Arabella looked up and saw the belly of a cloud scudding against the face of the mountain. She realized that she was nearing a cloud forest.

A sharp stabbing sensation caused her to halt. It felt as if her broken rib was piercing her heart. Arabella collapsed. She lay back, panting shallowly because deep breaths triggered agony. She felt helpless, even as she watched Scott labor up the path toward her.

Arabella forced herself to look at the region of her rib cage. She could make out the black scorch marks from the explosions and bullet strikes. She guessed that her exoskeleton was damaged and was not binding her wounded ribs properly.

Turning her head, she saw Scott collapse to his knees, fifty meters down the path. She decided that she had to take a chance.

"Disengage suit," she said. "Disengage suit. Disengage suit."

Like a flower opening its petals, her exoskeleton relaxed all of its fibers. Arabella ripped back the exoskeleton at its contact points. The movements hurt so much that she gasped, but she was able to struggle free of her exoskeleton.

She stood, naked. Her bald head turned to look at Scott, then down at herself. She could see much more clearly with her naked eyes. Her entire lower abdomen was one black bruise. A small chunk of flesh was missing from her right hip. Clotted blood caked her hip and thigh. Her rib cage was also a black mass. Arabella touched her fingers to her rib. She was relieved to discover that it appeared to be just a cracked rib, not a fracture.

Scott watched Arabella examine herself. He crawled up the path toward her, but his exoskeleton seemed to be resisting his movements.

Arabella considered walking down the path and attacking her pursuer. She decided against it, because even though his suit was malfunctioning, one powered blow could kill her. She turned to walk naked up the path, but she remembered her hip bag. She turned and picked it up, strapping it to her waist. She checked. The metal vial of Version 413 was still there; so were the Feliciteine tablets. *I have the power.*

Arabella turned, showing her buttocks to Scott, and climbed the path. In a couple of minutes, she disappeared into the fog.

Sweating with effort, Scott continued to struggle against his exoskeleton. He didn't know the commands for disengagement, so he continued to exert the exoskeleton until it had used its last reserves of power.

Drained of all battery power, the fibers in Scott's exoskeleton relaxed. The suit expanded.

Scott rolled to his back. He grabbed hold of the hood and pulled it from his face. He tore open the seam across his chest. Grunting with satisfaction, he crawled free of the exoskeleton that had been his prison for several eternities.

Naked, Scott stood. Although he too was covered with bruises, they were smaller and less serious than Arabella's wounds.

Scott began to climb the path. The muddy earth felt wet and cold underfoot; small sharp rocks cut into his tender skin. Scott wanted to run, but he only had the strength to walk.

He entered the fog.

Listening for Arabella, he tried to stay to the path.

For minutes so long that they seemed like hours, he climbed higher and higher into the cloud forest. Dark leaves shaped like spearheads loomed out of the fog. Scott could hear frogs croaking and crickets whirring. Small birds materialized, then disappeared. Driven by a predator's bloodlust, Scott pushed forward. The padding of his footfalls was muffled by the fog.

Suddenly, the naked form of Arabella loomed out of the mist. She was standing with her back to him, bending over, inspecting her ribs.

Silently, Scott advanced on Arabella. When he approached close enough, he screamed and pounced on her, knocking her down onto the mud. Arabella shrieked with pain and shock, twisting beneath him. Together, they tumbled off the footpath, down the steep hill, thorns and rocks slashing their skin. They stopped abruptly against a thorny tree. Arabella drove her heel into Scott's chest, then began to crawl back up the hill. Scott grabbed her ankle and pulled her down to him.

Arabella flexed, smashing Scott in the face with her fist. Inured to pain, Scott laughed.

"Devils do worse," he rasped, then punched Arabella in the throat.

Next Scott was aware, his skull was vibrating in harmony with a high chime and the sparkling of brilliant white pinprick lights, which dimmed to black.

Arabella stood. Her heel hurt from the impact of the kick to Scott's temple. She bent over, hands on knees, breathing deeply. She felt dizzy. She looked down at Scott's motionless body, sprawled in the mud and wet leaves. His ribs looked motionless. Arabella decided that she had killed him. She turned and began to climb. Her naked form disappeared into the fog.

For five long minutes, Scott lay motionless in the fog. Finally, his fingers twitched. He groaned. His limbs stirred. His eyes opened, seeing triple, then double images of tree trunks disappearing in fog. For a few minutes, he tried to remember where he was. A movement in the jungle foliage triggered survival instincts. Scott sat up, casting about for the source of the noise. His head sang with pain.

Finally, he remembered Arabella. He coughed. Automatically, he began to crawl up the hill. Half walking, half crawling, pulling himself up by grabbing weeds, he gained the footpath.

Dazed, he stood. He decided to turn to the right and continue to climb. Anxious that he had made the wrong turn, Scott stalked through the fog.

She was working on viruses, he thought. *Did Meta say that he gave her a working version of the New Age Dawn?*

After ten minutes of climbing higher up the mountain, Scott broke through the fog bank.

Here, the mountaintop was like another world. Massive trees, old growth tropical forest, loomed high overhead. Parasitical vines, creepers and rootless plants clung to the giants. Down in the dimness of the forest floor, fern breaks and thick moss thrived.

Next to a tumbling brook, a woman's footprint was sunk deep into green moss sprinkled with small yellow flowers. Scott left the path and began to climb the smooth stones in the bed of the brook.

After a few minutes climbing, he heard a woman's voice, singing a lyrical song. Scott brushed aside a large fern branch. He saw the brook tumble down a deep cleft in a cliff face. The waterfall cascaded into a pool.

Arabella stood, deep in the end of the cleft, under the waterfall. Her head was tilted back, allowing the water to splatter on her face. Then she knelt in the pool, splashing herself, cleaning off the clotted blood. She was singing. Scott couldn't understand the song, because it was a Spanish lullaby.

Scott knelt and hoisted a smooth rock large enough

to crush a skull. He began to climb the brook toward Arabella.

For a long moment, Arabella didn't see Scott. He approached within twenty meters of her before Arabella happened to look up and see the apparition of the supposedly dead man, naked and white, advancing on her, a large rock held high.

Arabella looked left, then right. She was trapped in the cleft. She looked up. The cliff was too sheer to climb. The only way out was through the evil man. Arabella backed up against the wet stone. She was trapped. She looked for a weapon. Scott drew nearer.

Arabella sat down in dark waters of the pool. She reached into her hip pouch. Her fingers closed on the vial. With her hands hidden in the water, she placed the metal vial between her thighs and prepared to break the seal on the cap, releasing the virus into the stream waters, where they would multiply as they flowed down to infect Ifrit and then the world.

Arabella decided that opening the vial of the plague would be her last act on Earth. *I'll wait for him to start to swing the rock at me,* she thought. *Then I'll release the great weapon. Kill all of the bad men. I'll know I did it in the moment I die.*

Scott advanced. His mind was not working well. The torments of multiple hells had enraged him. The hate he felt for Arabella was almost blinding in its intensity. The kick to his head had caused a slight concussion. As he advanced, he saw only her, sitting waist-deep in the burbling water. He imagined seeing her brains.

Scott McMichaels wanted to kill. In the whole of his life, he had been angry, but he had never experienced homicidal rage. Now, advancing on Arabella, he was consumed with it. He hated. He wanted to kill. He experienced the luxury of unchaining all his demons, great and small. Like Arabella, he was scarred and tormented and damaged and driven by the cycle of violence.

Two steps from Arabella, he looked into her eyes and saw terror. Something about this aspect of her caused him to pause.

In that moment, a bird trilled sweetly. Reflexively, Scott looked up. He saw a bird of paradise. Magnificent in its plumage, lemon-colored head, emerald green throat, the bird of paradise was perched on a branch not farther than five meters from Scott. The spectacular bird was gazing at him with eyes gleaming as jewels.

Scott looked down at Arabella. In her black irises, he saw the same gleaming, but the expression of the face and the flesh around the eyes was that of terror. Scott realized that she was not seeing him. She was seeing a demon.

Suddenly, the rock seemed heavier than iron. Scott wondered what he was doing. *Who am I? What am I doing? Why?*

Scott felt dizzy. He knew he had only strength for another moment; he would have to kill her now. But he decided to sit heavily down into the water. The rock slipped from his hand, plunging into the water, raising a small geyser. The cool water on his face caused Scott to reach down, cup his hands and drink water from the jungle stream.

He looked back up at Arabella, who was staring at him in amazement.

"Who . . . who are you, anyway?" he rasped.

"My name is Maria."

"Yeah, but, hell, who *are* you? You look . . . you look like . . . a scared little girl," Scott said.

Arabella shook her head. "I'm not a little girl," she said. "I'm the angel of Earth. Her force flows through me."

"I don't know who you are, really," Scott said. "I don't know if you know who I am, really. But I know that I'm not the one that's going to kill you. Not me."

"Why not?"

"Because—" Scott said.

Scott opened his mouth again, then looked puzzled. "Because—" he said. His eyes began to lose focus. He felt drained of energy. The concussion was causing him to lose consciousness.

"Because—" Scott said "—Timmy wouldn't understand . . ."

Scott reached back to support himself, then collapsed backwards. He floated in the water. The current turned his body around until his head was upstream of his skyward-pointing feet.

Arabella wondered whether he was dead or fatally wounded or insane. For the moment, she cared. Without thinking, she stood. She returned the vial, still closed, to her hip pouch, which she zipped shut. Naked, she stepped through the pool to Scott's side.

His eyes were opened, but they were unfocused. Slowly his lids began to close. His face turned toward the stream. He breathed in water, then coughed.

Arabella knelt by his side and lifted his head clear. She began to feel faint herself. She tugged him out of the stream, laying him on slick moss. Arabella knelt in the moss and settled Scott's head on her lap. She brushed his wet hair out of his eyes. She picked thin black leeches from his skin and from her own.

Grooming Scott, Arabella resumed her Spanish lullaby. After a few minutes, she looked up and saw the beauty of the jungle. A shaft of light coursed through a break of the canopy, catching the mist from the waterfall. The canopy waved in a small breeze, creating kaleidoscopic glimpses of bright celestial blue. Orchids clinging to tree trunks accented the vibrant greenness with splashes of scarlet, pink and violet. A small deer leaped across the stream, fifty meters downstream.

The bird of paradise trilled. Arabella looked at it for the first time. She lost herself in its beauty.

This is what the world can be like, she thought. *So natural, so beautiful. And this, this is just a patch of paradise. I should release the great weapon now, save the planet from this horrible infection, this disease of humanity, esta enfermedad de los humanos.*

Then Arabella looked down into Scott's face, slack from unconsciousness, childlike in its laxness. She remembered his last words about Timmy. She had a sudden, vibrant recollection of the image of Bender's son. *Handsome little boy*, she thought. *Un fulito bonito.*

Then, for the first time, Arabella allowed herself to consider the hundreds of millions of children that the great weapon would kill. The rationalization that she was killing them to save future generations of children didn't occur to her.

Killing them is wrong, she thought. *None of the children deserves to die.*

Arabella looked down at Scott's face. In the young man who had shown her mercy, she saw the traces of the child. She realized that he had been right. She herself was a little girl. This man was a little boy. They were merely children who had survived their childhood.

Cradling Scott's head, Arabella realized that she was not quite cruel enough to kill children, after all.

Above Arabella's facility soared two bat-wing aircraft. They released massive clouds of aerosol, then departed.

A spark erupted into an intense fireball. Consuming itself and disappearing, it revealed the blackened mountaintop. Arabella's facility had been sterilized.

At the first indication of heat, the mask of Diane Jamison's powered exoskeleton had sealed itself over her face. The entire exoskeleton went rigid, resisting the pressure of the aerosol detonation. Shocked by the concussion and the sudden barrage of heat, Diane screamed. Her exhalation remained within the rigid confines of the tensed exoskeleton. Her inhalation drew the same air. She felt choked by the lack of oxygen, but until the air temperature lowered to an acceptable level, the exoskeleton would not allow her to breath the outside air. Diane would have smothered to death, but, following a programmed routine, the exoskeleton scrambled away from the heat. Soon she was tumbling downhill. When the suit's sensors told it the air had cooled to a survivable range, the mask relaxed. Diane sucked in ill-tasting air. She looked about her. Up on the hill, the ruins of the laboratory were burning. Thrice wounded, Diane yet survived.

Aboard USS *Kuwait City* (LHA-12), fifteen armored helicopters, each carrying twenty Marines, lifted off, one after another, tilting and dashing toward the eastern horizon. Five minutes later, the helicopters went feet dry, crossing the beach fifteen kilometers south of Ifrit City. Ifriti Air Defenses attempted to destroy them.

The keystone of Ifriti Air Defenses was a matrix of energy weapons, both laser and X-ray. These weapons would have burned man-sized holes in the helicopters, ensuring their fiery destruction. Earlier, however, cluster dart munitions had rocketed down from cruise missiles, and ceramic-coated depleted uranium pellets had streaked down like green meteorites from low earth orbit. These high-kinetic weapons had turned the energy weapons sites into moonscapes.

Still, the Marine helicopters had to contend with older air defense weapons, such as shoulder-launched surface-to-air missiles and radar-directed antiaircraft artillery. Fortunately for the Marines, low-observable aircraft were sweeping a corridor ten kilometers wide along their flight path. Anything with an optical or infrared signature that resembled a weapons system was fed hot steel. The Marine helicopters, therefore, ingressed Ifrit like royalty striding a carpet of flaming red.

Three bat-wing aircraft appeared over the Istana Nurul Iman, the Sultan's palace. They dispensed their munitions, sleeping gases in aerosol form, knocking out everyone inside the palace except for a cadre of specially-equipped Gurkha guards.

Then, fifty Navy Sea-Air-Land (SEAL) commandos materialized from the depths of the river opposite the Istana Nurul Iman. Equipped with military exoskeletons, they assaulted the palace. The SEALs quickly learned that they had to contend with the Gurkha guards who were wearing biochemical defensive suits. The SEALs and the Gurkhas engaged in an enthusiastic firefight for about thirty minutes, causing about eighty million dollars worth of damage to the luxurious palace. In the end, however, the SEALs prevailed over the Gurkhas, only to find themselves unable to capture the Sultan, who flamboyantly demonstrated a preference for suicide.

As dysfunctional as the Sultan was Meta Prime, which had ceased execution for the last time. Thanks to a cruise missile with a kilotonnage high-explosive warhead, the RubyLotus at Ifriti State Intelligence was melted, fragmented garbage.

Four of the five Marine helicopters converged on the ruins of Arabella's facility. On both sides of the aircraft, armored doors shot open. Wearing flat-black fully-armored closed-environment military exoskeletons, eighty United States Marines leapt from the airborne helicopters. They swooped down, carried forward a hundred meters as they fell thirty meters to the dirt, landing on exoskeleton-strengthened legs, rolling to absorb the rest of the inertia, finding cover and taking up mutually protective positions. They then entered the sundered facility, searching for vaults of biochemical weapons.

Two Marines on rear guard found the charred form of Diane Jamison halfway down the hill. A staff sergeant scooped her up and carried her to their evacuation helicopter.

The fifth attack helicopter continued east, following the direction of Arabella's escape.

Scott and Arabella were still laying on moss when large figures broke through the fern brakes. Looking like evil astronauts, the armored Marines aimed weapons at the naked couple.

Five minutes later, down the path, helicopter prop wash swirled fog, revealing a bright blue sky. Even as it descended, the evacuation helicopter was eerily silent: acoustic diaphragms throughout the helicopter's surface launched sound waves that canceled the noise of the rotors. Crewmen wearing military exoskeletons tossed stretchers, which Marines on the ground caught one-handed. Quickly, the Marines scooped Arabella and Scott into the stretchers, strapped them in, then swung shut the lids, so that they were encased in metal baskets. Lines hauled the stretchers into the helicopter.

As the earth twisted and fell away, the helicopter doors slammed shut. There was a sucking noise. Ears popped to equalize pressure. The interior of the helicopter was hermetically sealed from the exterior. The helicopter tilted nose-down and began to fly west at maximum speed.

Scott looked over at one of the racked evacuees. He recognized Diane by her exoskeleton, despite its charred condition.

"Diane," Scott rasped.

Diane moaned.

"I . . . got her, I think."

"*No, todavia estoy,*" Arabella said.

Quarantined, they could not witness the Marines forcibly evacuating everyone they found in the valley. Helicopters touched down; Marines in armored exoskeletons hauled Ifritis aboard.

Minutes later, all of the helicopters were heading

west. The evacuation helicopter went feet wet, over water, first. Within a minute, the other helicopters followed.

The helicopters flew over the water at an altitude of two hundred feet.

Below them, at an altitude of ten feet, dozens of cruise missiles rushed eastward. They snaked up the valley, passed Arabella's facility, bounded over the ridge, then climbed the valley where Scott had chased Arabella. As the first one arrived at the cloud forest, the others were trailing behind, separated by five hundred meters, with the last one several kilometers east of Arabella's facility.

Simultaneously, hundred-kiloton neutron warheads erupted. Radioactive rays bombarded the valleys and the intervening mountain ridge. Every organism within ten kilometers of Arabella's path of escape died. Although the warheads were designed for maximum short-term radiation with minimum blast and heat, the combined energy of the explosions vaporized the old forest and turned the brook to steam. A fireball ignited, growing until it burned every combustible fiber. After ten minutes, the fireball died for lack of fuel, although brush fires continued for days.

Scott knew nothing of the nuclear explosions. Laying in the stretcher, he slept the sleep of Orpheus returned from the netherworld. In her stretcher, Arabella began to struggle and cry out until a female Navy corpsman injected her with a mild sedative. Under heavier anesthesia, Diane slumbered.

None of the three were conscious as the helicopter landed on the flight deck of the hospital ship USNS *Mercy*.

Epilogue

Almost a year later, Scott walked along Carmel Beach. A high, thin haze covered the seaward half of the sky. Overland, the sky was sun-filled azure. The water of Carmel Bay was a delicate green. Small rollers curled and sounded on the shore. Salt mist tinged the air.

Scott looked out across the way. He saw a foursome finish their game at the final green of Pebble Beach. He watched the last of them three-putt, then one man snapped a photograph as the others posed with the flag for the eighteenth hole, the spectacular coastline in the background. Despite the fact that the green's fee was twelve hundred dollars and the professional-level course had humiliated them, they seemed satisfied. They would show the photograph more often than they showed the scorecard.

Scott walked up the hill into Carmel. Hundreds of tourists crowded the streets. Scott entered the tourist area, flanked by cottages, flower gardens, candle boutiques, fashion shops for dowagers, toy stores for rich brats, bakeries, galleries of dubious art and overpriced jewelry stores. He turned into a hidden nook and entered a courtyard with a flagstone deck, a towering elm and wrought-iron benches. He entered a coffee shop. The aroma of the earth's flowerful bounty

lent the shop its distinctive air. Artistically folded-back
bags of rich dark coffee beans gleamed opulently under
studio lighting. The proprietor, a retired Hollywood
artistic director, genteelly sold Scott a kilo of beans for
seventy dollars. He also offered Scott a small pot of
freshly brewed Jamaican Blue Mountain roast.

Scott sat at a small table outside. He could see only
patches of the blue sky past the eaves of the neigh-
boring buildings and the cover of the trees.

The garden was in bloom. Scarlet, yellow and purple
flowers flourished, perfuming the air, already heady with
the aroma of fresh-brewed coffee.

Scott sipped a cup of the Blue Mountain. He glanced
at his wristwatch. He expected Diane to meet him
momentarily. He pulled out his pocket computer and
called up a news report. He read it for the fiftieth time.

Having convicted her of mass murder and the slaying
of two policemen, the Greater German Republic had
sentenced Cristiana Maria Fierro Hurtado, also known
as Arabella, also known as Infectress, to death. As in
all German High Court cases involving the death
sentence of an international terrorist, in order to deter
kidnapings and other terrorist stratagems, she had been
executed immediately. Scott was wrestling with the fact
that this news made him breathe easier. He had to
admit that the world seemed safer without her in it.

After the waterfall, he had never spoken to her again.
Aboard USNS *Mercy*, Arabella had been kept in a
separate quarantine, incommunicado from her victims.
The extradition to Germany had been swift, and the
Greater German Republic had imposed a news black-
out on the trial. The U.S. federal government arranged
with the Germans not to call Scott as a witness; that
duty had fallen to Diane. The terrorist had remained
a mystery to Scott. His own memories of the waterfall
were disjointed. He found it difficult to believe that
they had said what he remembered they had said. He

never imagined that he had saved the world. He couldn't begin to pretend that he understood the famous terrorist. He only knew that Diane considered her to be a soulless monster, a thing in the shape of a woman.

Diane's theory caused him to ruminate upon something that he ordinarily avoided thinking about: analysis of Version 413 had shown that it was lethal to eighty-four percent of humanity. The sixteen percent who would have survived were the top sixteen percent of human genius, a group which included Scott. Meta Prime had obeyed Arabella. Its design for V413 had been lethally effective.

Scott shivered as if nauseous. He had probed Meta about Meta Prime's decision to obey Arabella to the extent that it had designed a working holocaustal virus. Meta had offered many explanations: Scott had ordered Meta Prime to obey Arabella; Meta Prime's decision making had been influenced by its information space, which was controlled by Arabella; and so on. Scott believed that Meta Prime had decided that V413 was in Scott's best interests. He suspected that Meta did not disagree.

Meta continued to be a gold mine of computation, but Scott no longer loved it. He felt as if Meta were inscrutably foreign, radically alien, to be used but not to be loved. He knew that it was an invaluable tool, one that would increase the wealth of the world tenfold. The patent holder on thought, he now knew that it was impossible for him to create an intelligence. He could only create an artifact that emulated intelligence. Scott knew that Meta was not a he. It was an it.

Two of a kind, he thought, *a woman with a murdered soul, a machine that never had a soul. Soul . . . a substance the existence of which is detectable only by its absence.*

Scott sipped his coffee. It tasted rich and sweet.

A crowd of Chinese tourists flooded into the courtyard. Scott looked up, annoyed, until he saw Diane Jamison appear from the nook. She seemed younger and more beautiful than he remembered her. Scott realized that the past months had been kind to her. The crush of the tourists blocked her way. Scott stood up. Both taller than the crowd, they gazed at each other across the sea of glossy black hair. Diane smiled and waved. Scott returned the wave. Then, whimsically, Diane reached out and placed her hand down on the head of a young Chinese boy. Scott laughed and mirrored her gesture, laying his hand down on the head of another Chinese boy. The boy glanced up and said something in Cantonese. Not knowing whether it was a question or a curse, Scott smiled down at him, patting him on the head before removing his hand.

He forced his way through the crowd. Underneath the flowered trellis over the hidden nook, Diane opened her arms. They embraced. Her body felt warm and lively.

"Heya hero," she whispered in his ear.

"You," Scott said. "You're the one."

Their embrace lasted a long moment. They derived comfort from the warm press of the other. They luxuriated in the shared feeling that this was home.

Diane thought about this man whom she had met in hell, confronting her enemy. She had never respected anyone so much as she had Scott as she had watched him struggle against her enemy. Afterwards, Diane and Scott had come to know each other well, the weeks they had spent in adjoining isolation chambers, communicating by images and sounds, spending hours and days talking about everything except the tortures of hell. Following their release from isolation, Diane had spent months in Germany, giving testimony in the massive trial against Arabella. Now she was finally free of her enemy.

I wonder if it would be possible to live day by day, just for the day . . .

"Let's go walk the beach," Scott said. "Are you up to it?"

"Therapy's done," she answered. "I've got the legs to walk from here to infinity."

As they walked along the beach, they shared their thoughts about the past, present and future. They both had enough resources that they had the luxury to choose their work. Diane said that she was concentrating on nurturing troubled orphans. Scott said that he planned to continue to direct Meta's efforts to try to maximize its wealth-creating productivity.

"The other day it came up with a design for a fusion reactor that may prove viable," Scott said. "Maybe, free energy forever. Last week, a genetic therapy for mental retardation. Every day's an adventure."

"You must enjoy going to work," Diane said.

"Oh, I do," Scott said. "The future is what we can make it . . . if we don't let the past enslave us. Meta's an invaluable tool. But I don't go to work so much as telecommute. Secure net. I work out of wherever I happen to be that day."

"Ah, the life of an infoworker. My job is somewhat more high touch. Kids are extremely localized. Speaking of kids, how's Timmy?"

"Muriel's remarried. The step-dad's okay. Timmy loves him."

"Oh, that's good!" Diane said, her voice ringing with spontaneous gladness.

"Yeah, you're right, it is good. All for the best. The boy's discovered cyberspace. We go surfing together a lot."

"Well, be sure to look me up whenever you're in Philly."

"I will. I'm a native Pennsylvanian, you know."

"Sure I remember."

"The old man's settled down in Philly."

"Main Line, right?"

"Few blocks off. I'm thinking of seeing him next week."

"Good. Call me."

"I will. You know I will."

There was a long pause. "Do you think about her?" Scott asked.

"Every day, still," Diane said. "But less and less. Sometimes a whole hour will go by. Maybe a whole afternoon."

"You don't miss her, I suppose."

Diane laughed. "No."

Later, they sat atop the beach. They watched the sun set gloriously beyond the western horizon of the Pacific. Cold stars from this distant edge of the galaxy shined through the ocean mist. The breeze from the ocean's vastness threatened to strip the warmth from their bodies, but sitting flank by flank, arms around each other's waists, they huddled together for comfort.

HARRY TURTLEDOVE:
A MIND FOR ALL SEASONS

EPIC FANTASY

Werenight (72209-3 ◆ $4.99) ☐
Prince of the North (87606-6 ◆ $5.99) ☐
In the Northlands rules Gerin the Fox. Quaintly, he intends
to rule for the welfare and betterment of his people—but
first he must defeat the gathering forces of chaos, which con-
spire to tumble his work into a very dark age indeed....

ALTERNATE FANTASY

The Case of the Toxic Spell Dump (72196-8 ◆ $5.99) ☐
Inspector Fisher's world is just a *little* bit different from
ours...Stopping an ancient deity from reinstating human sacrifice in L.A. and destroying Western Civilization is all in a day's
work for David Fisher of the Environmental *Perfection* Agency.

ALTERNATE HISTORY

Agent of Byzantium (87593-0 ◆ $4.99) ☐
In an alternate universe where the Byzantine Empire never fell,
Basil Agyros, the 007 of his spacetime, has his hands full thwarting
un-Byzantine plots and making the world safe for Byzantium.
"Engrossing, entertaining and very cleverly rendered...I recom-
mend it without reservation."   **—Roger Zelazny**

A Different Flesh (87622-8 ◆ $4.99) ☐
An extraordinary novel of an alternate America. "When
Columbus came to the New World, he found, not Indians, but
primitive ape-men.... Unable to learn human speech...[the ape-
men] could still be trained to do reliable work. Could still, in
other words, be made slaves....After 50 years of science fiction,
Harry Turtledove proves you can come up with something
fresh and original."   **—Orson Scott Card**
